I0818203

The Snow Fence

Rebekah Tyne McKamie

Settings Christian Publishing, LLC
Calhan, Colorado

Settings Christian Publishing, LLC, Calhan CO 80808

Published 2021
Printed in the United States of America

Hardback Print ISBN: 978-1-7348040-3-4
e-book Digital ISBN: 978-1-7348040-4-1

Library of Congress Control Number: 2021906384

For my husband R.J.

God knew what He was doing.

Preface

Renewed Edition

To my beloved reader:

The Snow Fence, my debut novel, was originally published in October 2015 but that edition is now out of print. Since then, it has only existed in libraries and digital formats. To remedy this situation for those of you that enjoy the gentle whisper of turning pages, I planned to republish the book in the fall of 2020 and call it the "2020 edition." However, for reasons I need not mention, a 2020 edition of *anything* did not seem prudent.

In June 2020, God led me to pursue a graduate degree. As a graduation gift to myself, I decided I would present *The Snow Fence* in the refined form this story deserved six years ago.

Except here's the thing:

I really didn't change much. Sure, I made thousands of little edits that I hope will earn the gratitude of my original editor. But the story itself is untouched. As Seth might say: *It already is.* So this edition, though refined in some ways, is the same story you loved, just renewed.

Thanks for reliving this story with me. I hope it blesses you anew.

Because of Grace,

Rebekah Tyne McKamie
September 2021

Acknowledgments

Renewed Edition

Disclaimer (Updated 2026): A traumatic moment or season can change a person, even causing them to be broken and remade. God is faithful to teach us a new song, but we cannot carry many of the old tunes with us. This book was written "before" one of those moments, and these acknowledgments reflect that version of me. However, in reverence for the way that God uses our *whole* journey to shape us, and because even reading them to modify them is simply too painful for me today, I left them intact.

I would like to thank:

My dog Sugar. You're nine years old now, but no one believes me when I tell them that. Thanks for "helping" me raise the kids, training all the other dogs, and remaining at my feet as I write. It would be weird to do all this without you. I try not to think about that day.

My professors, fellow students, and my coursework at Liberty University. Thanks for draining me of all life and reason for a year and consequently giving me the tools to improve this work and potentially many others.

My family at RMC Ellicott Campus. If I mentioned all your names here, it would take up too many pages, and I'd probably still leave someone off the list inadvertently. But you know who you are, and you are all precious to me. I tried not to let it leak that I lived a double life as a person who records the imaginary lives of imaginary people. But you found me out, and you built me up. Maybe you have nothing to do with this edition of this book, but I am indebted to you for much of how I have grown in the past four years. Thanks for being there, even when we couldn't meet.

Melanie. I hope you find this "renewed" edition to be what you wanted for the first edition. I have now submitted to your edits and relinquished much of my bullheadedness—in this case, at least. Unfortunately for all of us, I still have plenty of bullheadedness for the next project.

My parents, because it feels weird to not put you in this section, even though I can't even begin to mention all the reasons I'm grateful. Here is one more book for your display.

My babies. I know you hate it when I call you that now, since none of you look or act like babies anymore. It has been an honor to watch you grow in stature and spirit. I love who you are, and I am thankful for everything it took to get here.

R.J. You're still my favorite, and I know people are going to roll their eyes if they even bother to read this section. But this edition, this story, and this version of the girl you love would not exist without you. Anyone who reads this should know that.

The One true living God who sent His Son to die for my sins. Thank you for giving me these words through Your Spirit. I'm a mess with or without You. But thanks for taking this mess and using it for Your Glory. I don't deserve to know You or worship You. But I suppose that's why we call it grace.

Chapter One

AWAY

They say it in a laugh, like a joke, but I really was born in a barn. My mother has worked hard her whole life. She is obedient, graceful, and delights in everything she does. I love her, and I love my two brothers and my sister. They never say anything nice about my father. They say he visited once in the night and left just as quickly.

I'm glad they don't hate me as much as the reason I'm here. I'm just not sure why they don't blame my mother, as well. I think they are just disappointed that she won't be able to work as hard now. That maybe we've softened her, and she won't have such a stern heart to help her do her job.

I see both. I don't mind the soft, and I don't mind the stern. My mother keeps my belly always full, and she smiles when she watches us play. I love her. And I'm glad I'm hers.

My brothers, however, I could do without. They are bigger than me and push me around. When they play, they always want to play mean. I tell them to stop when they hurt me, but they never listen. They just come right back and hurt my ears again. They only stop when mother corrects them.

My sister is a little more spirited than me, I'll admit. But she has the gentleness of our mother and understands quickly when she's hurting me. I don't blame her for picking on me. I'm the smallest. I can't run as fast or jump as high. That's also the reason I'm the last to eat. But like I said, I am my mother's, and she always makes sure my belly gets full too.

I noticed after an exhausting morning today that I haven't seen my mother since last night. They started giving me food I have to chew and talking about which one of us will be the best worker. I'm a good listener. My siblings don't understand what the people do or say all the time, but because I don't run as fast, I sometimes sit and just look into one of their faces.

The one they call Pete has medium-colored hair and usually gives the others commands that they follow immediately. I assume he is their leader. They talk about how, when he was younger, he used to do a lot more of the working. My mother was a part of that, I think. My mother; Where is my mother?

Pete and his mate are considering something. It takes me a moment to understand what they are considering. But when I do, I am inspired. I suddenly muster all the strength in my tiny muscles and run and jump with the others, tackling them to the ground and calling out for them to go here or there. Because I understand that the three of us that will not be the best workers have to go "away."

I don't understand away. All I know is that when they say that word, the horses get upset. The donkey shivers, maybe because of the flies, but maybe because of away. And despite my exhaustion over showing them I can be the best worker, like our mother, their eyes go to my brother—the bigger, stronger, prouder-looking one. The mate of Pete takes him in her arms, and my brother pretends to be nice and gentle and good and kisses her face until she giggles, though usually only the smaller people do that.

"Let's go see if we can find Starla," she says. That is what they always call my mother.

The rest of us realize that away is a place where our mother isn't. And we all cry because we don't want to go away. I'm mostly crying because I couldn't be strong enough—or big enough or proud-looking enough—to stay with mother and work. My remaining brother and sister play and wrestle as they cry to try to impress them again. I find a corner of hay where it seems cozier and look to the ground as I cry because my fate is away. I perk up a little when Pete looks at me and puts his rough hand atop my head.

"Don't worry, little girl. I bet there's a better purpose for you." His gruff voice sounds mean, but his touch is so soft. And I suddenly like that word he says. "Better."

I want to see mother again. I love her. But better gives me hope, even if better means away. Every time the sun gets lower on the other side of the sky, water and rumbling and bright lights conquer the blue now. Then, when dark comes, after the sweet-smelling water retreats, the night is cool.

My brother and sister let me cuddle with them when it is cold or when the deafening cracking scares me right into my insides. If away is without what they call "thunderstorms," it seems less terrible now.

Pete also pokes us with little things that pinch from time to time. "Shots," we are told—shots for our away. A strange man comes and touches us all over and gives us pills that make us sick. Better sure takes a lot of worse.

I've grown fond of my sister in the five nights since we've seen our mother or brother. She is patient with my slow running. She keeps me warm in the cold. And when I cry, she helps me do it.

Our brother misses our other brother and mopes around unless he can coax one of us into wrestling—usually me. And he usually wins, though I don't give up the fight until he's pinned me against the ground.

This morning, Pete carries the three of us into the covered back of his "truck," he calls it. I'm scared because the big black thing growls like thunder whenever Pete gets in or just before he gets out. It moves and takes him places. I suspect that today is the day we go away. Pete's mate kisses us all and gives us a teasing last look at our mother and brother before I am left, heart pounding, as the dust kicks up under the truck and the barn where I was born gets smaller and smaller behind the fading image of my mother.

I know the truck has stopped when Pete opens the back again, and I wake up to the bright sun and the contradiction of his growly voice and smile. He builds a little pen for us to play in. We do so, and he moves something across a big piece of cardboard. He puts the cardboard out so that others can see the markings on it, and his fat legs dangle from the back of the truck and he crosses his arms as he looks out to the road.

The sun moves across the sky. I eat, drink, play, and sleep as always. But the sleeping is often interrupted by some of the smaller people that pick me up and touch me all over. In just a short time, I am irritated with the touching. It often hurts. If this is away, it is certainly not better.

There are so many persons of so many sizes and temperaments that they begin to blur. But there are a few I'm sure I won't easily forget. The first is a girl person. She is alone and bigger than the "child" persons that violate us. But she still looks young in her face.

"What kind are they?" Her voice is sweet as she crouches to our level.

"Their mother is my border collie Starla. She's a great workin' dog," says Pete. "The father, we aren't too sure of. Though from the looks of them, I'd say it was my neighbor's old boy—a retriever. Golden."

"They're beautiful. I've been thinking of getting a puppy. I live alone, and there have been some break-ins in my area. It'd be good to have a second set of ears, you know?"

"Ah. A guard dog." Pete puts his hand on my brother's head. I assume a guard dog is mean and mischievous. At least, that's what my brother is. "If you want someone to make you feel safe, he's your man. He plays rough, but I saw him scare a fox out of the barn the other night while his sisters were sleeping."

Either my ears deceive me, or I had failed to see the upside of my brother's meanness. I'd never seen a fox. But I guess that was my brother's intent. And just as I learn to appreciate him, I see the medium age girl person smile when my brother licks her hand.

"How much?" she asks as she picks him up.

Pete laughs a growly scary laugh. "A price? Just take good care of him, and he'll take care of you."

The girl thanks Pete and walks away. Away. I understand now. When I'd like to apologize to my unappreciated protector, to thank him, to kiss him goodbye; a single whimper must suffice. My sister is rejoicing at our brother's away. She plays with the ball Pete suddenly provides. But I find a cozy corner in which to mourn.

After many more "almosts" and roughhousing children, a person and his mate come along. They are a little older than the girl that took our brother. This girl has sad eyes and this man seems to be protecting her in some way. The girl kneels at the side of the pen and smiles at us. She says nothing. But my sister sees something in her sad eyes that I cannot. She is licking her over and over, wagging her tail. My sister is scooped up into her arms. The girl's sad eyes give way to a smile far beyond the opposite of the sadness. The man with her speaks.

"Sorry, she just wanted to hold a puppy. We saw your sign. We've been trying to have kids, and people get weird when she asks to hold a baby." The man person's eyes sadden too, even in the words that make him laugh big and loud.

"Kids?" Pete laughs again. "I had three. They were expensive, hated me when they got older and left as soon as they stopped hating me. But dogs are cheaper and stay loyal in a way that people will never understand. That one there is as sweet as they come, just like her mother. For some reason, she's a dimwit—but not where it counts."

The girl looks at her mate with a mixture of sad and hopeful eyes.

"Seriously, Babe?" says the man person. The girl person still doesn't say anything at all. Pete speaks for her.

"Sorry to tell you, sir. But that puppy is already hers." He smiles.

The man person smiles and laughs. And with another whimper of a goodbye, I am alone. I'm not my mother's—not anyone's—and too little and weak to ever work for Pete. Perhaps there is no away for me and nothing better. I retreat again to my cozy corner. The sun is going somewhere out of my sight. The rain is light today, but the darkness is starting to come in with the cold. I have no one to cuddle against—no sister to cover my chilling nose and no brother to stand guard.

"Well, you ready to go home, little girl?" Pete asks me. I know home. And reluctantly, I stand, waiting to go back into the truck all alone.

But in the approaching dark, I see something a little like Pete's truck or the big things that took my brother and sister away. But it sparkles like it is new, and it smells different.

The girl person that comes out reminds me of my mother for some reason and wears clothes that smell more like a place where clothes are made than like a person. Her coat is made of leather, and I drool at the thought. The man person comes out of the other side and walks like he is the master of Pete, his truck, and all the homes and aways I can imagine. They are much older than the other puppy-takers, but more determined than the multitude of non-puppy-takers.

Pete sighs when he sees them. "Hoity-toities. You'd be spoiled, that's for sure."

I cannot decide if he is happy or sad about these words. But I do know that there is something I like about these persons. So I creep forward to get a better smell of what it is. That's when "it" creates another opening in the back part of the car. It is something between a child and a man, though it moves much more like a man than a child. It wears boots, like Pete. Jeans too—the only clothes I really understand. And when it walks behind the other two, who are now linked by the paws, something inside me changes.

It kneels at my side, having breached even the walls of the pen. Part of me is scared of the boots because Pete's have caught my jaw before when I walked too closely beneath him in the barn. But then I see his face. He seems to be under the size allowed for hair on his face. But even what is scarce of its near blackness, he allows to grow.

His eyes are kind and dark. And when he smiles and places his hand on my head, I feel more wanted than Pete ever made me feel. I love him more than I loved my mother or my brothers or sister. And I push my nose up to ensure he never again makes me live more nights without the comfort of his hand.

Something in the way the young he-person looks at me makes the older she-person make an unsettling growly sound.

"It's a mutt, Seth. We take you to every breeder in the county, and you want to stop along the road for a mutt? It's getting cold, let's get home." I don't like her voice. I think it has mean in it. And I know now that the young he-person is her offspring. Maybe the mean is the way my mother's mean used to be. The soft mean.

"And she's the runt. No good for showing or breeding." Pete is insulting me. But somehow I think it might be to my better.

"I want this one." The boy Seth's voice is calm, sad, and quiet. Yes, I decide, much more like a man than a child. Pete likes this boy, I can see. But the father speaks instead.

"She's the last one. You don't even get to choose, Son. It's good to choose from a variety, not make rash decisions. Even if the animal comes from good stock." This meanness seems to be some encouragement to Pete to correct what the woman person had said.

Pete speaks up. And if a person can encourage a person, Pete will always grant the same to a dog.

"We had four. We kept the strongest for a working dog. The other two went to good homes, I think. And I was secretly hoping this one would be left behind so I could take her home for good. Everyone comes and sees the runt. The shy one. But she's my favorite. She's wise. Patient. Loyal. Sharp as a tack. I've never seen that in a dog this young, even from the best line."

With this, the two older ones look at one another. The man speaks. "But I think we've seen it in a teenager."

The woman nods and they both look to their son, probably the only one in his litter. The boy they'd called Seth scoops me up without another word and looks to his father. But the mother speaks.

"The standard poodle would have been twenty-five. I'm not paying any more than that for a mutt." The woman goes back into the big car thing, holding the leather against herself like the night is much colder than it is.

Pete laughs once she is out of sight. "I gave the others away. I'm no breeder. Just a small farmer whose cattle dog got herself knocked up. Just take good care of her." He pats my head within Seth's arms. "Be good, little girl."

The father opens another piece of leather from the back of his pants and hands Pete a stack of paper things with a curious smell. Pete tries not to take the paper things. But Seth's father insists.

"I was raised on a small farm." The man gets closer to Pete's ear.

"We didn't have no poodles. God bless you and yours."

Before Pete's smile as Seth takes me inside the soft part of the big car, I almost hear him whimper. But when he nods, I know he wants me to go away. To better. To home.

Chapter Two

A Home and a Name

The boy Seth puts me onto wood floors that slip and clatter beneath my claws and creak when I step wrong. The stairs ahead of me, beyond the first fireplace, go up until they land once on a floor of rooms. And then up again to another open floor they call the attic. But they tell me I'm too little to go up on my own. So Seth carries me.

I'm scared of new sounds and new moonlight—a new place. Seth puts me in a big wood room with a big square thing against a wall on one side. It has an underside where I hide as the boy sheds his clothes, then puts on another, softer set. Then, when I think he's forgotten about me, he scoops me up, climbing under something soft atop that big square thing, then sets me on top of that layer close to him.

I tremble and cry a little, missing Pete and the barn and home. But Seth pets me and shushes me until I don't remember my eyes closing, only opening to a room filled with sunlight. I am alone.

Then Seth returns and carries me down, and I cautiously explore the level I'm now trapped on. The house is big. The things they say make me think that it is bigger than many other houses. The room they first put me in is what they call the foyer. Seth follows my sniffing and tells me the next room is the formal living room. There is a hallway from there with a door at the end, but Seth does not take me there. He takes me down from a platform to the game room, and the fancy dining room finally brings us around to the kitchen. Then he calls the window room the family room. The windows look out at a big yard and woods and a creek. I like the window room.

There are other rooms they say are for baths, but they close the door to those so I can't enter them. Then the woman, "Mom," squeals when the floor beneath me gets wet. Seth takes me outside to the yard with grass and bugs to chase. It reminds me of my last home, and I like outside more than I like the window room. I see a smaller house outside, connected to a path that joins it to the big house. I stop to sniff at it.

"That's the guest house." Seth barely says it before I hear a voice come from that side of the house, and a female person, the size of Seth, appears, bounding over.

She is thin, scrawny, with dark skin and hair, darker even than Seth's, all waved and curled into two braids over her shoulders. She is something between a girl and a woman, and Seth swallows harder when he sees her. I don't know Seth very well, but I know he favors this person over even his parents.

"You got a puppy! I was hoping you'd finally cave. Your parents think it will be good therapy, right?"

"Right." Seth smiles at the girl.

The girl sits on the grass at my level and puts her hand out for me to smell. She smells like sweet and clean and something spicy. This is also how she tastes when she makes a silly noise in her throat as I lick her fingers. I like this girl.

"Did you buy her a ball or something?"

The girl talks very fast and very much. But I like that she throws a ball for me to go get. Before long, I realize that she will continue to throw it if I take the ball back to her. Seth and the girl walk, and she talks about how smart I am, and they take turns throwing me the ball.

"Have you picked a name for her yet?" she asks.

"No," he answers. Seth doesn't talk very much at all.

"Well, it'll be easier to teach her things if she has a name. Let's see. She's kind of gold-ish. What about Goldie?" The girl makes the sound in her throat again that girls tend to make a lot.

Seth smiles and shakes his head as they come to a tree. They have to move the long, stringy leaves aside to crawl beneath it. There are some tree stumps under the tree that makes me think they come here often to play. They sit on the stumps, and Seth pulls a box from a hole near the tree trunk. He opens it and unfolds a hinged piece of wood onto the stump between the two. There are squares on it, alternating light and dark. Then, one at a time, the girl watches Seth put taller, figure-shaped wooden pieces onto the squares. Dark on Seth's side, light on the girl's.

"What about Queenie? Like the chess queens? There are lots of chess pieces. I bet you could find her a cool chess name. We could even do something in Japanese! Wouldn't that be cute?"

"Maybe." Seth centers each piece on the squares just right. The girl still looks on and seems trained not to help him, even though the process is slow. But I notice that one of the pieces looks a little like the treats he'd given me in the car last night. I help myself, hoping it tastes the same. It seems a little more bitter and crunchy, but I like the feel against my teeth and continue to chew. After few minutes of Seth concentrating on the board and the girl watching, she looks at me and gasps.

"No, Doggy! Bad dog! Don't chew on this." And she taps my nose, tearing the wood piece from my mouth. "Oh no. You can still tell it's a queen, so it should be okay, right?"

Seth takes the piece from the girl and breathes funny in his throat, losing focus of the chessboard. He breathes several times, seeming to get markedly upset.

"No, Natalie. It has holes in it now. The other ones don't have holes. We can't play chess today." Seth begins putting the pieces back into the box, breathing hard and panicking. I'm suddenly regretting the choice to chew.

"Seth." The girl, Natalie, puts her hands on Seth's hands. Her voice gets gentle, not like the little girl voice she was using before. She must be a big part grown-up. "It's okay. It's just a chess piece. Your puppy doesn't know better. You have to teach her. Maybe she can teach you too. She might mess up little things. But she won't mess up big things. We can still play chess with a queen that has holes. God is still in charge, and I'm still your best friend, and we are still together under the willow tree, right?"

"Right, Natalie. Thank you." Seth smiles again, recovering from the odd fit. He begins resetting the pieces, and the patient Natalie looks out beyond the weeping leaves, listening to my panting and smiling at the creek. Suddenly, Seth speaks while still setting pieces.

"Willow. Her name is Willow."

"Perfect!" Natalie returns to a giddier voice. "See? You're so much smarter than me, Seth."

"My Intelligence Quotient is higher. But I think you're smarter, Natalie."

"Well," Natalie says. "Either way, I think Willow will be a blessing."

Chapter Three

The Guest House

Most of the days, most of the year, Seth will have cereal at six in the morning. His mother will drive him to a place called school, and I will nap and chew rawhide near Mom as she moves about the house or sits and reads a book. She is stern when she will be stern. And she is soft and wonderful for the rest of always. The soft, the stern, and the way Dad speaks of her teaches me what it means when a woman person is beautiful.

I'm now accustomed to the time when Mom picks up Seth from school and sometimes takes me along if Seth has requested it in the morning. I also learn that Natalie is Seth's very best friend and that she visits our house every day after Seth's school. Natalie has school at her home. Natalie's house is on the same street; Plaid Row, they call it. But since all the yards are big, her house is a bit of a walk until around the corner. When we pass Natalie's house on the way back home, she is always sitting outside, waiting for Mom to stop and pick her up on cold days or to walk on her own behind the car when the weather is nice.

On the days we merely wave as Natalie walks cheerily along the road, Mom will always say the same things. "I really love Natalie. She's so beautiful with all those curls. She seems to be a bit of a free spirit. Maybe a bit fickle. But I do love the way she treats you. No one else treats you like she does."

I think Seth thinks Natalie is beautiful, too, but the way Dad thinks Mom is beautiful—a way I can't explain quite yet. Natalie's parents don't prefer Seth to visit Natalie's house. They think he is odd. Different. Bad, even. I often see a dark woman or a lighter man looking out the window, worried, as Natalie comes with us. But knowing that Seth is Natalie's only friend in the world.

While Mom and I are at home, Dad goes to a place called work. Dad also works in his office after returning home, but only until Mom begins to look very sad. Then Dad will come from his office and talk and laugh, and they will eat. They call it a family: all these days over and over and all this laughter and maybe Natalie too. All the wisdom the two younger ones stay silent to acquire from a Book and Seth's dad. That's what a family is. I get a sense that it started with the way Mom and Dad seem to like each other very much. But like me, their favorite person is Seth.

He is honest and doesn't think mean things are funny like the others do. He is what they call authentic. He is who he is, no matter what anyone else says he should be. Seth likes using his hands and tools against wood in the big room at the end of the hall by the living room. He likes shaping it into things and nailing it together to build things. He spends a lot of time doing this and a lot of other time with Natalie under the willow tree. Some people change at this age in the teenage years. But Seth is the same, likes the same things, and has the same best friend. Seth is my favorite. Natalie is a very close second.

Seth has turned sixteen years old now. He has taught me to fetch and come and stay and all the things Dad says I should know. I am good and follow Seth wherever he goes. When I came home with Seth a year and a half ago, he would take medicine to make him feel calmer. To make him not have fits like when I chewed on the chess queen. But now, he stays calm without it. Mom and Dad and Natalie say that this is because of me. But I think it's a toss-up between the way Seth looks and acts almost like a grown man now—and the way Natalie looks almost like a woman.

But Seth says it is God. And that God made me and made everything come together to help fix Seth. On Sundays, Natalie will not come around the back to find Seth. She will come to the front door that dings when they push the button. And she will be wearing a dress and her hair will be fancier. Mom and Dad take the two teenagers to worship this "God." I don't know God, but they do. And they are nice because of Him, and He gives us the air we breathe and the food we eat. Therefore, I like God.

On Wednesday nights, Seth and Natalie drive together in the car he can now drive by himself. And they go in regular clothes to "youth group."

That is a gathering of other people their age that worship God. Normally, they come home smiling and laughing and go out back to play chess until Mom worries about the darkness and tells them to come in. When they play, sometimes they say many words together that are somehow different from what Mom or Dad say. Words I don't know, but they still understand as words. But even their mouths must move differently to say them. Mom says Natalie knows Japanese and taught Seth so the friends could have "secrets." I don't always understand. But I like to listen.

Chess is a game that makes no sense to me. But whatever it is, Seth always wins. Natalie is weaker in the game, and I don't understand why she plays with him when she knows she will lose. But they smile and play under the willow with the smooth pieces and the queen with the chewed holes until Natalie sighs and Seth smiles bigger. I think Natalie likes to lose. Or maybe she just likes Seth's smile.

There is another game, however, that Natalie always wins. It is something she must do in the formal living room at the big black shiny thing, where she presses her hands on things called keys and sounds come out. It is loud and complicated, this game. But even though Natalie says she isn't very good at it, Seth can watch Natalie play it for hours without ever joining in. This is rare. Because the chosen game is still chess, and the chosen piano player is usually Mom.

But sometimes it snows. And Seth has another chess game he built that he keeps in the guest house when the willow is too wet or cold for chess, and Natalie doesn't want to play the piano game. I like the guest house better than I like the big house. The upper level of the big house is filled with large bedrooms with fireplaces and fancy bathrooms, sometimes a part of the room. The guest house has a kitchen with a little eating nook, a living room, and a loft that is like a bedroom. It is simple, and I don't understand why the people need a house much bigger than this and leave this one empty except on snowy chess days.

Tonight is a Wednesday night, and I wait for Seth's car to crackle up the drive to the garage that holds six cars. I wait inside the window room where the back door is because it is snowing, and I know Seth and Natalie will play chess at the guest house. I whine until Mom and Dad let me out to be with Seth and Natalie. But when I see them come out of the garage, Seth seems like he is having one of his fits but without the words. Natalie is following him, and they are both covered in the big wet kind of snow by the time they reach the guest house and turn on the light.

"Are they here, Willow? I was getting concerned about the storm." This is Dad. Then Mom says something she always says.

"Seth is fine, Randall." As if she is never worried. Odd for a mother, I'm told.

"You want out, Willow? Go keep an eye on those kids." I bolt out the door to the door of the guest house before Dad finishes talking.

But I'm left out in the cold wetness because Seth will not calm down enough to notice me at the glass door to the guest house. They are yelling. This is not a pleasant chess night like I hoped. I hear their muffles through the door.

"Why do they let them make fun of you like that? You'd think the youth leaders would say something," Natalie asks of Seth, who is pacing the living room, rubbing his hands on his pants.

"I don't know." Seth is worried that he doesn't have an answer.

"I wasn't asking. It was rhetorical," Natalie clarifies.

"Thank you for standing up for me." Seth doesn't meet Natalie's eyes like other people do when they talk. But Natalie doesn't seem to mind.

"Well, they were being mean to you. I don't know why having an abstinence speaker come in suddenly turns into making fun of *you*. Saying you shouldn't be there because you'll never find someone to make love to anyway. And I don't like that word they said: 'Retard.' You're not a retard. Don't they know how smart you are? I dare any of them to play chess with you just once." I can't decide if Natalie is talking to Seth or Natalie. Either way, she is very angry.

"I'm different. I know that," Seth says, beginning to slow his pacing.

Natalie goes to the kitchen sink to wring out her hair. Her hair is different, like Seth's thinking is different. Natalie has slanted eyes because half of her is from a place they call Japan. But her hair is long, tiny curls because of her other half. They are flatter wet than they are dry. She doesn't braid them much anymore. I guess women don't do that sort of thing, and she's sort of a woman. Natalie returns to Seth, who had stopped his pacing to watch her wring out her hair.

Now Natalie seems upset but without the pacing.

"Well…is it true?" She demands.

"You said a lot, Natalie. I'm not a retard, though. That was true." Seth is trying to sort out what she's asking.

"No..." She looks at the floor, just like he does. "Do people—like you—have they done that? Made love, I mean?"

"God wants all people to wait until marriage for sex. They said that tonight, Natalie. They said it wasn't in the Bible, but it is. They made fun because I told them Hebrews 13:4. 'Marriage is honorable among all, and the bed undefiled; but fornicators and adulterers God will judge.'" Seth corrects his female friend, saying more words than I think he is supposed to. "Fornicate means—"

Natalie laughs a little, interrupting him. Seth does not like to be interrupted but makes an exception for Natalie sometimes. "I know what fornicate means, Seth. But can you fall in love? Get married? Have kids? Stuff like that."

"Mom read people like me tend to make loyal friends and faithful husbands," Seth states facts, as always.

"I'm not talking about on paper. I'm asking, is romantic love something *you* understand enough to want someday?" Natalie shrugs nervously. Having something specific she needs to know. But because she's a woman, she doesn't always come out and say it.

"Yes. Of course, Natalie." Seth is annoyed that Natalie would have to ask.

"Well, how do you know that?"

"Because I'm in love with *you* already." Seth smiles. He scrunches his eyes in confusion like the whole world should already be aware.

Natalie startles. "Just because we're best friends of opposite genders, that doesn't mean you're in love with me."

"You're pretty—" Seth starts but is frustratingly interrupted.

"No. See, you don't understand. Being attracted to someone is not the same as love."

"Of course, I'm attracted to you. You're beautiful; everybody's attracted to you. My mom says even all the girls are jealous. And that's why none of them will be friends with you. And the boys say things when you aren't around—things about how you look. But that's just outside. You're beautiful inside. They miss that part." Facts. Logic. Who needs charm?

"Seth—" Natalie is beginning to melt like that big wet snow. But she's fighting it enough that Seth breathes in quickly and continues atop her words.

"When we were ten, and you couldn't find your bathing suit in your room, so you wore all your clothes into the middle of the creek and said you like to wear more anyway, that's the day I first loved you. I love you when you're all dressed up on Sundays and when you're nice to me when no one else is. But I still love you when you are all wet out of the creek, and your hair is messy. Even when you yell at me because of my fits. You're beautiful. But that's not why I love you." Seth says most of this to the ground, then accidentally catches a glimpse of Natalie's Asian eyes before he meets the ground again.

"How come you've never told me that?" She seems shocked but not angry.

"Because you are my only friend, and if it scared you away, I wouldn't have anyone to play chess with."

Natalie laughs. "I'll still play chess with you, Seth."

"That's good." Seth laughs too, in relief.

Natalie takes a step closer to Seth. "I was eight when you made the chess set. You'd get mad if I made a sound. That's how I learned to be *still*, Seth. I saw all the heart and fits and time you put into it. Everyone else sees the fits. But I've always seen your heart. I was only eight. But I knew that if someday you gave me just a tiny piece of that heart, I'd be set for life."

Seth clears his throat, loving her, but having no idea the impact of his next words. "You have *all* of it, Natalie. *Subete*. All," Seth clarifies in Japanese.

Natalie smiles, trying not to let on to what is happening in her soul, with a term she often uses with Seth. "*Kekko*." Very well.

But it is so cold and wet. So, I give the glass door a modest little scratch to let them know I'd like to be let in. Natalie flies to the door, worried for me in a sweet high-pitched voice. Seth catches my collar as I bolt inside, and Natalie moves to the linen closet in the wall under the loft for a towel, then returns to pat and rub my fur to dryness. As Seth holds me from jumping onto the couch, Natalie dries and asks Seth a question.

"So does that mean you're my *Koibito*?"

Seth smiles. "Doesn't that mean like 'lover'?"

"Yeah. Or sweetheart." Natalie giggles.

"We can't be 'sweethearts.'"

"Why not?" Natalie is hurt.

"Because they would make fun of you too. I'm used to it, but you aren't. I want to protect you from that." Seth pats my head once and releases me to seek the comfort of the sofa. Then he sits on the floor cross-legged, and Natalie sits on her knees in front of him.

I can quite nearly smell Natalie thinking. Or maybe she is feeling. Feeling everything at once. This is just a moment before she rises up on her knees and leans forward, connecting her mouth with Seth's. She reclaims her lips after just a few seconds with a squeaking or smacking sound. Then something remarkable happens to Seth. He smiles and looks Natalie directly in the eyes, not even straying his eyes from hers. Natalie talks somewhere low inside her throat as she sits back down on her folded legs.

"Officially sweethearts." She smiles even through her pounding heart. "*Koibito*."

"How do you say 'I love you' in Japanese?" Seth is filled with wonder, repeating what he's been practicing while sanding wood for years in his woodshop.

Natalie giggles, taking Seth's hand and weaving hers into it like teenagers do to test waters. "You don't. It's not really a common thing to say in Japan. Words that strong, said as much as we say them in America, become meaningless after a while. It sort of waters things down, I guess."

"Well, in case they tease, I'll want to remind you. So what can I say?" Seth unknowingly calls to the surface in his young companion things intended for a wiser age.

Her heart pounds. "How about *Subete.*" Natalie smiles at the word that won "all" of her moments ago. "I'll know what you mean."

"I like that." Seth stands and helps Natalie to her feet. "We better get you home. It's snowing. I bet your parents are worried."

"My parents are gonna flip." Natalie sighs. "I'm not sure how okay they'll be with us dating."

These are the last words I hear as they shut the lights off, and we all exit back into the snow to take Natalie home.

Seth is still silent until we breach the house's back door to see that his parents are snuggling in the window room. Seth is soaked in wet snow all over but doesn't seem to even notice, though usually he'd be throwing a fit over even a slight variation in his clothing. Mom stands and gasps immediately—not because of the dripping hair or shaking fur that splatters the wet all over the window room. But something on Seth's face makes Mom say something odd.

"Sweetheart, are you alright? You look like you've seen a ghost." She takes him by the shoulders and tries unsuccessfully to meet his eyes.

"Natalie and I are in love." He says without expression. "I'm wet."

Then before either of his parents can respond, he heads up to his room to become dry. Since I'm big enough now, I follow him up the two turns of steps to the bedroom we share. As usual, I am forsaking a fancy "pet" bed for a curve of Seth's leg. Tonight he forsakes sleep to contentedly examine moonbeams on rafters.

Love. That means something, I think. Strong enough that they won't say it much for how strong it is. Maybe it's the thing that binds together the pages of that Book Dad reads. Or maybe it's the thing that binds together a family. Whatever it is, it is strong enough to bring life to the mundane and warmth to the snow. Peace to chaos. And chaos to peace.

Chapter Four

Control

"Patience goes a long way, Seth." Dad seems to fidget more than normal as he converses with his son in his office. I lie at Seth's feet against the massive ornate oak desk, chewing the wonder of the world that is rawhide. I like the way his shoes feel beneath me. Not comfortable at all. But Seth. And love. And that is what matters.

Seth nods. Dad is not satisfied.

"Do you understand my meaning? This is in regard to Natalie."

"I know." Seth's response seems clear to me, but Dad still doesn't believe his answer.

"What I mean is..." Dad clears his throat. "Mom and I will be away for two months. I trust you quite a bit. I know you'll keep up with the house and the lawn and any questions the company might have. You're all but a man now, Seth. You'll do fine on your own, especially with Willow around. But it'll also provide plenty of opportunities for you and Natalie to be alone together. You've been dating several months now, and you've honored God. But without accountability, things we don't intend to do can happen if we're not careful. Now I know how you feel about this girl and—I guess what I'm getting at is—"

"You do not want me to fornicate with Natalie." Seth often says all at once what others are scared to say at all. I like this better than back when he used to say nothing. And better than when others don't say what they mean to. Perhaps others keep their mouths closed for the same reason Mom quiets me when I bark hysterically, trying to get to Seth when he's mowing the lawn, and they won't let me out. But I can't help but cry when my favorite person is outside without me. I cannot hide what is in my heart. Seth's speech is the same way. Dad finds it amusing in this case.

He laughs a little and uses his teaching voice like a father does. Seth listens to his father, which is why he is all but a man at sixteen.

"That's right, Seth. Your mother is worried sick about it, actually. We adore Natalie, and we know she adores you. God put in women an ability to trust the man she loves with all of her. And in men, he gave us this weak spot for a woman who trusts us to do right by her. It's easy to lose control over that delicate balance, especially when you're sixteen. And son, there's nothing like losing control with the woman you love. But only in the right situation will it do you any good in the long run." For some reason, Dad is nervous to talk about this.

"Now, marriage is like a fenced pasture. With a fence, you can let the cattle graze and the horses run, and you don't have to worry if they'll come back where they belong. They've got nowhere to go, really. Losing control physically makes everything else go haywire, too. Your emotions and fears and everything will run wild. But without marriage, you don't have anything to rein them back in. Best bet is to build that fence before you let the cattle graze. You understand?" Dad puts a humorous growl into the last words, and Seth smiles a little.

"Sex is for marriage." Seth puts forth his raw understanding with a nod. "I will ask God to help me stay in control."

"Good man. Your mother will be happy to hear that. I've been begging Mom to go on this trip for years, so I trust you won't give her a reason to worry. Staying in a cabin for two months with a backpacking excursion or two isn't exactly her idea of a twentieth wedding anniversary spectacular. But I intend to change her thinking about that. It may put us out of cell range some of the time, but we will try to call every day. The board knows to trust you, and Mom insisted I leave notes about how things work in the company in case you need reminders. We'll be back before you start your junior year. In the meantime, you have a great summer, son." Dad is shuffling through papers on his desk, readying the office and house for the departure.

"Dad?" Seth inquires quietly.

"Yes, Son?"

"We have 20 acres behind the house. Why don't we have a fence?"

"Nobody has fences around here, son. With the woods and creek and all, it might as well be wild. The fence thing was an analogy, Seth. I didn't mean—"

Because of Dad's way of saying it, Seth and Natalie have always argued whether the glistening string of water running through the land is a "crEEk" or a "crick." Seth smiles a little, knowing Natalie would likely say, "Seth, there are two 'e''s. How does that spell 'crick'?"

But instead of mentioning it, Seth carries on with his mission. "I saw a fence in one of Mom's paintings with carved posts and pickets on barbed wire. A snow fence. They are usually just in short sections, but can I build a snow fence all the way around?"

"This is your land too, Son. You needn't ask. Just be careful. Barbed wire can bite."

I can tell that Seth is happy to undertake the ridiculous new obsession and that Dad is happy to know that Seth will have a task on which to focus control.

Seth and Natalie are hand in hand as they wave goodbye to Mom and Dad. But only after Mom acts all sappy and kisses and hugs Seth in tears a dozen times, deciding half a dozen times that she simply can't leave her "baby boy" alone. Each new concession comes with some motherly advice. "You make sure you go to church and that you get plenty to eat." or "No girls in your room besides Willow, I mean it." or "Don't forget to say your prayers and read your Bible. That's so important." Each time, Seth and Natalie and Dad all assure Mom that God will watch over him. And Willow too, they say. But I know Natalie will do most of the watching.

As soon as the packed vehicle is out of sight, Natalie kisses Seth's cheek. "I bet I can beat you to the willow!" And she takes off at a full sprint, leaving Seth and me in the dust.

"S'go, Willow!" He grunts before running after Natalie. I beat them both to their beloved tree.

Just as when they were children, the two have a unique relationship. Their battles are fought over a chessboard. Their bonding occurs in rolled pants dips in a creek. And any touch is in a peck of a kiss before a giggle and a run. It is different from the touches and kisses of Mom and Dad.

There is something deep and mysterious about those—love that needs a fence.

And then there are Wednesdays when they enter the big house after dark, and Natalie will cry. She will sob and fret over the way the youth group treats her now that she has chosen Seth over the acceptance her looks apparently owe her. Seth doesn't know what to do when Natalie cries. She just tells him to hold her. And she places a pillow on his lap and curls up, trembling from the sobs of rejection. He merely strokes her upper arm.

"*Subete*." Seth will remind her that he loves her with everything in him. One might think that Seth's human vessel lacks the ability to convey that kind of love.

"*Kekko*." But it seems to be more than enough for Natalie. After a couple weeks of this, something begins to change. They are children, they say. Caught between too young and something infinite. Seth and Natalie love one another with an understanding no one sees but me. What they have together is not driven by lust like in my species. But I think Dad tried to warn Seth that even if something is not driven *by* passion, it can be driven *to* passion quite quickly. Like the way rain warns with only clouds sometimes.

Distant thunder in midafternoon finds Natalie strolling across the front yard to the edge of the property that meets the road on the opposite side of the house as the guest house. She is as confused as I, due to a new behavior of Seth's. For weeks after Natalie has left for something called a "curfew," Seth ventures to his woodshop, making what looks like big thick table legs. He is crafting them beautifully and uniquely with his many saws and tools. Today, two weeks after his parents have left, he has constructed five of these. He has also ordered bundles and bundles of barbed wire and cut out simple wooden planks.

Today, he stands staring at all the supplies, very still, barely blinking or breathing, even after Natalie arrives on the scene. But she knows better than to interrupt his thoughts with even valid questions. Suddenly, he departs, seeking some mumbled tool from the shed this side of the house. He returns with something that digs round holes in the earth, and he places one of those posts in a deep hole, surrounding it with some gray slush. He takes some tools and drills a hole in the post, then carefully slides barbed wire through and twists the end to secure it. Then, he digs another hole three feet from the first, setting another post, and cuts the barbed wire to attach the two. He connects them again with another length of barbed wire near the bottom of the post. This is when Natalie's scrunched eyebrows change into a smile.

Seth continues by using massive staples to connect wooden planks to barbed wire.

"A fence," Natalie says with a nod. "What are you fencing in? The part of the yard you mow? For Willow?"

"The land," Seth answers, finishing the section and moving his operation to the other side of the house.

"All of it? You have 20 acres. Most of it is hilly or through the woods."

"I know," he says. Then they arrive where Seth sets a post on the other side, marking the endpoint of the fence.

"But...seriously? Seth, you carved those posts yourself. They're gorgeous, but it would take you half a lifetime to build a fence this size with pretty posts like that."

Seth tilts his head. "Twelve years if I do two sections a week."

"Your parents are millionaires. You could probably hire someone to build a much simpler fence in a lot less time if you really—"

"Fences keep bad things out and good things in. I want to build a fence." Seth finishes his section and packs up his tools, moving them back to the shed.

Natalie follows. "Will you need help?"

"Nope."

The distant thunder, by this time, has become a less distant thunder. And the moment Seth shuts the shed, the sky opens in a torrential downpour, soaking us all without further warning. The young couple runs hand in hand across the back yard to the guest house, where they immediately fetch towels for the three of us.

"That was crazy! We look like we jumped into the creek!" Natalie exclaims, drying her hair gently. But Seth doesn't respond to even that word they don't agree on because he is too busy feeding his eyesight with the way her wet clothes cling to her female frame.

After being dried, I find a comfy spot on the couch. Natalie catches Seth staring and smiles.

"Does your mom still keep robes in here for people that come to visit? I don't want to sit around in wet clothes." Natalie searches the linen closet and finds her prize. "Yes! Your mom is a great lady. Think you can start a fire?"

Natalie heads for the bathroom, the door next to the linen closet, and Seth uncovers the woodpile next to the hearth at the far end of the little house. He builds and lights a fire in time for Natalie to emerge from the bathroom in a purple robe, clothes in arms ready to lay on the hearth for drying. It is something the childhood friends have done many times after a swim or Colorado rainstorm. When Seth is searching for the green counterpart to the robe, he is finally honest.

"You trust me too much, Natalie."

"What do you mean?" She giggles, approaching Seth's button-up collared shirt, undoing buttons nonchalantly like his mother would. Seth likes the way t-shirts feel, but he likes the way button-up shirts look. So today, like most days, he wears both.

"I mean stop." Seth uses his grip on her wrists and an extension of his arms as a warning, which makes Natalie's face distort with hurt.

"I was trying to help. Those buttons make you so mad when they are wet like that." Natalie retreats to a sit in front of the fireplace. I join her, loving when they sit on the floor. But the two don't interact as Seth gets frustrated over wet buttons before going into the bathroom to change into the robe. He eventually joins us by the fire, sensing something is wrong with Natalie but never understanding just what.

Seth does not always understand feelings anyway. But Mom has a word she uses for Natalie that makes it even harder. Fickle. She follows her heart—a good quality in an adult that understands what is good for the heart. But not in an adolescent. One moment she can be dancing in the rain, and the next she will be sulking by the fire. She is good—a better person than most. But for certain, she is fickle. Mom knows because Mom is the same—the silent treatment a common expression. Seth sighs.

"I did something wrong. You have to tell me, Natalie. I can't guess, you know that." She takes her eyes and moves them all sad and passionate to meet up with Seth's through the space between them.

"You said I shouldn't trust you. If I can't trust you, who am I supposed to trust? No one else cares whether I'm happy. I hate my parents."

Disheartened Natalie, Seth has mentioned to me in his woodshop or in his room at night, is just as beautiful as smiling Natalie.

"You don't hate them. You can trust them. They love you."

"But they don't trust *me*. Seth, I love you, and every time I mention you, they practically leave the room. I told you I should never have told them we were dating. I didn't like the lie either, but just let me trust you, okay? What's wrong with that? It makes me feel like you don't love me when you say that."

"*Subete*. Of course, I love you." Seth says with wide-eyed desperation. "That's my point, Natalie. You should never trust me to stop loving you. Do you understand?"

Then Natalie curls up with Seth, which does something to his breathing and his smell. Maybe the exact thing he'd been avoiding. It happens quickly and imperceptibly to the eye, with something that in another situation might be innocent—just a graze of his hand against a russet knee barely outside the security of a fluffy robe.

"*Kekko*. I understand." She whispers. Then something dark and eerie overcomes the room. Something I can almost see, though nothing in the way she'd spoken indicates darkness. Nevertheless, I whine, trying to warn them.

But then they kiss. And I try to stop the kiss because I somehow know Seth will be angry over it. Instead, Seth takes the kiss. And the next. And he pushes me away between kisses until I cower under an end table. Then Seth watches Natalie stand and is unsure of what she's doing. Then she brings him to a stand, leading him someplace I've never seen them go.

The guest house loft is simple, they tell me. Just a bed and a closet and some nightstands. I've never been up there because the stairs are too steep and shallow for my paws. They know that and climb them, leaving me helplessly below listening for danger and darkness, though it sounds so merry from where I sit. There are moments when Seth objects. But it is as though Natalie has given him drugs, like the medicine that once calmed him. Today, he calms completely. He stops objecting past when I fear Natalie might object to that same medicine. And then after a trembled breath, silence occurs—a loaded, shocked silence.

And in a moment, fickle Natalie shifts into full sobs and tears of anguish, blubbering words that Seth must shush with severe remorse.

"*Nakanai de kudasai*. Don't cry. Please don't cry, Natalie." Seth sniffles. "*Subete*."

Seth turns to apologies in two languages. Over and over and over for hours, it seems. Then things are quiet, and they whisper even longer, as the fire turns to embers and the rain outside decrescendos to a halt. I'm asleep when I hear footsteps. When they both have drier clothes back on them. They hug profoundly, kissing once in goodbye when their goodbye has never been so solemn or short.

Natalie walks home alone, and Seth paces the guest house, rubbing hands on pants and mumbling to himself. Actually, to God, I think. Yes. To God. Because he finally finds himself on his knees asking for something I don't understand. Forgiveness. That's something Seth tells me he's giving me when he doesn't give me anything but a smile and a release of punishment for the scrap I stole from the trash. Maybe that nothing means something more to a person. Because Seth begs for it until wetness escapes his eyes. I know that the wetness is the only part I can remedy when I knock him to the ground in kisses. But I think it's God that brings him to a smile, to embrace me, and to whisper,

"Thanks, Willow. Let's go build something."

Chapter Five

What Natalie Wants

The kind of clouds worthy of names are the same clouds that gather and turn to rain. Storms. It is innocent now, watching them drift—calling them turtles and pie slices and boots. Lying on their backs as the wind carries their laughter away. Now, with the way they laugh, it almost seems impossible that those clouds could become something, anything else.

They have forecast rain. But they don't ever heed the warnings of a storm when there are just a few drifting clouds in sunlight. Even the setting of the sun seems so far into that away. Yet they know if they laugh too long or take advantage of wonder, they will be duped into the wonder of rain at dusk.

I tried to warn him not to come. He thought I was being loyal to Dad and the promise he had made me promise: to take care of Seth while they were away. To not let him drive too far away. Only to the place he goes that they call church. But loyalty was not my goal. I could smell the rain coming; why couldn't they?

He obeys. He is loyal to whatever they tell him or ask of him. So why, when she came to the door and only asked the once, did he go without question? And she didn't even try.

She simply said, "I'm going to the park. Want to go?"

The park is a truck ride away. She doesn't own a car. How did she plan to get there? Well, I wasn't going to let him get hurt and then take the fall for letting him go. So I got my leash. Alright, so the thought of that word "park" was not so bothersome either. And I don't really mind Natalie, even though she's never needed anything but Seth's twenty acres until her parents told her she couldn't explore them anymore.

For the past month, they have not explored or played chess or piano. They divide the time between the guest house loft and somewhere else, barking at each other about the guest house loft. Natalie does most of the barking. Seth builds two sections of his snow fence a week. Natalie tells him he'll never finish. She has never told him "never" before. Never makes Seth wince. So does the barking, and even when Natalie comes to the door or around the back of the house like she has his whole life. Fear and feelings like wild horses, he tells me. Like Dad warned.

Seth throws fits like when I met him. He breaks things he builds in his shop. Tells lies on the phone to his parents, when Seth has never told lies. Loving her is easy, he says, even though she barks. Stopping, he says, is something he's lost control over. And his irresponsibility will be noticed soon if he doesn't stop.

All I know is I like the park part of outside. They let me run and chase the ball until their silly little arms grow weary. They hold hands and laugh at the way I run—a rarity in recent times. And now we lie together in the grass.

They think they see shapes of things. But I see clouds that will bring rain before they expect it. Otherwise, they would not be lying there, head beside head, bodies out on opposite sides. The laughter, to the others at the park, which is smaller than those twenty acres, is usual for lovers their age. But the laughter, to me, sounds like a desperate attempt to forget a goodbye. Like they never came in from the rain that day they forgot they were only children.

"I'm never having kids," says Natalie suddenly.

Seth, like Seth used to be, doesn't say anything at all. And even though Natalie had paused for a response, she continues even when she doesn't receive one.

"My little brother was a pain even before he was born. And now he's six and it has gotten progressively worse. But it's not even just him. My mom was studying to be a rocket scientist—literally, Seth! But she just gave up all that because she wanted to homeschool us. And my dad was so brave. He ran away from home and everything to be free. Then he met my mom, and we came along, and we ruined them. I'm never letting that happen to me. I'd never want to lose who I am just to have annoying little brats running around and breaking my heart." She sighs like Seth had been arguing with her. But he had been silent. Maybe she wanted him to argue because now she is annoyed.

"Just take me back. I think it might rain." And she rises. So does Seth. Seth whistles, and I follow him. Not understanding, as I often don't, why Natalie, who talks so very much, is silent all the way home. Or why, when they've both forsaken parents and God's rules for a month, she chooses her home over a loft and chess and barking.

Her home is cluttered outside today. Boxes. Couches. Beds in the lawn all strange, but no one seems to comment on the strange. Natalie hops out of the truck like always, walking away almost too fast for Seth to catch up. But he catches her anger and her sobs into a hug that I see is closely observed by a tall man with Natalie's same eyes loading lawn clutter onto an enormous truck.

"*Subete*," Seth promises, to Natalie's surprise.

"*Kekko*." Natalie nods, then turns, using all her strength not to look back as Seth gets back in the truck and Natalie's father comments on Seth's confused Japanese. As she enters the nearly empty house, Natalie passes a quietly compassionate dark woman and a riotous six-year-old, all having finally found their excuse to rid their lives of Seth Gowan.

Away. I hate away. It is where Seth's parents stay even after they promised to be back. Seth had talked, or rather listened, to the voice of his father through the phone up until that promised time. The very last time he had held the little piece of plastic to his ear, he had said some strange words to his father person. They were words Seth told me would make his mother cry, and his father be disappointed. He had said,

"Dad?" And his father had listened. Something about the way he'd said it had demanded sincere attention.

Through the phone, Dad had announced his listening. So quiet with him in the phone, but I perked my ears. "Son?"

I heard Seth say what he had to say to the listener. Blunt, or so he thought. "Natalie is having a baby."

I had heard the response from the other end. Not the response Seth had meant to find. "I don't follow. Her parents again? That's to be expected. They are still pretty young. How old is her brother Neil?" I heard Mom in the background, *"He's six now, isn't he?"* Then Dad again, "Six. That's right. The little tyrant."

Seth had ruffled his hair in frustration over his parents' cheeriness—their undying belief in their only son's character. Then he'd sighed, repeating himself, as he hates to do. "No, Dad. *Natalie* is pregnant."

A silence of calculation had fallen over the connection between the phones. Then I'd heard a clear gasp from Mom like when I've peed too close to her rose bushes. Dad had not been so quick to understand, but not for lack of intellect or wisdom. I think his mind could just not twist to help him understand.

"Natalie is sixteen. How could she be pregnant?"

Seth didn't know whether this question was one he should answer. So he asked, mixing the question with nerves. "Is that rhetorical? Natalie does that a lot. I know how she got pregnant, Dad. I just thought you would know too."

"Rhetorical, son. Sorry. Is the baby yours? That wasn't rhetorical."

"Yes, Dad. Natalie is pregnant because of me."

"Oh, son…" Dad had whispered and sighed, destroying Seth a little. He winced, awaiting the reprimand Dad never delivered. He continued in calm. "When did this happen?"

"We think it happened our first time together, which was about a month ago, even though the doctors count her as being six weeks along." Seth had sighed heavily from nerves and from relief that the secrets were out.

"The first time?" Dad had chuckled. Bringing further relief to his distraught son. "Tough break."

I heard Mom scold Dad with a stern "*Randall*," which had made Seth smile. Then he'd felt safe to open up, just a little.

"Natalie cried that time."

"That's normal for women to do the first time, Son." Dad, torn between father and friend, had realized the alikeness of the two. "How are things now?"

"Well," Seth had started. "She trusted me, just like you said. And I lost control like I promised I wouldn't. Things are bad. At first, it scared us because it wasn't what we intended. It wasn't like us. Then it started to be the only time we *were* like us because the rest of the time we were mad at each other. I think we were mostly scared God would punish us, which He did."

"Things get tough without that fence, don't they?" Dad had used a tone that soothed. But no matter the circumstances, a baby is a blessing, not a punishment."

"No, Dad. God is punishing me." Seth had paused, fighting tears. "We wanted to get married and keep the baby, but Mr. Nakano said we can't. They found a couple in South Carolina to adopt the baby. So that's where they are moving. Natalie is gone, Dad."

After Seth had broken the news, the silence that occurred on both ends of the phone was almost something I could taste.

"Does Ken take you for an idiot?" Dad's rare temper had sizzled. "Seth, giving up that baby requires your consent."

"I know, Dad. I want what Natalie wants. Natalie wants to honor her parents, and she doesn't want children. And Ken—Mr. Nakano—asked me not to contact her."

"I'm sorry this is happening, son. Mom is packing up now. We will be there by tonight to help you sort this out. "

"No, Dad. Your vacation was important to you and Mom. I knew you'd want to come home if I told you. That's why I waited. God is helping me through this, Dad. I just called to ask for your forgiveness. What I did was inexcusable, and I'm so sorry. Is Mom crying? I didn't mean to make her cry." Seth's words were broken by heavy breaths and a fitful outflow of remorse. We heard his mother break down in the background.

"Hush, Son. Mom is crying because you are the *most* important thing to us. If we had been there, this may not have happened. We are certainly not going to let you go through all this alone. Mom is going for a walk, and I'm going to get a hold of Mr. Billings, alright? Then we'll be heading home. I love you, son. Of course, I forgive you. Christ died for all this a long time ago."

And then they had said goodbye. But the parents had stayed away. And Natalie went away. Seth and I are learning now what alone means.

Chapter Six

What Alone Means

"Forty-eight hours," Seth says, after looking in the computer on the second office's desk.

I assume this is a measure of time. Seth looks up into the air to count another measure. Then he nods his head and says something I understand fully.

"S'go, Willow."

Seth does not like to talk to other people. But he talks freely to me and even practices what he'll say to other people, and I will listen. So this is what he is doing on the way to wherever it is the little screen is telling us to go.

"They've been missing fifty-five hours. I called them twenty-seven times. Dad always answers."

I wish Seth had told me I'd be alone in the car for more measures of time. But Seth always cracks the window, and I enjoy the way the people smile at me when they pass the car. Even the ones that dress alike with shiny things on their alike shirts. When Seth returns, he tells me what happened inside.

"They are starting their search tomorrow. If the weekend comes before they find them, we will go help them, Willow. They might not know where to look."

Later today, the man that usually just joins Dad in his office comes to the house. They call Mr. Billings a lawyer, but Seth says he is more like an uncle, whatever that is. Today Mr. Billings does not go into the office with Dad. Dad is away. Mr. Billings follows Seth to where the next section of fence is being completed.

"Is this like them, Seth? Not calling? It doesn't seem like your dad at all."

"They always call. Mom gets concerned."

"I figured as much. I don't mean to upset you, but I went ahead and pulled a copy of your dad's will just in case this doesn't turn out well. I want us to be as ready as possible. Would you like to hear what I found out thus far?"

"Yes, please, Mr. Billings." Seth pours cement.

"First of all, are you sixteen?" Mr. Billings bends and shuffles papers against his legs in a file, making sure the summer breeze does not carry the papers away.

"Yes, sir."

"Good. Your father requested that you be considered an emancipated minor should anything happen. I guess there aren't any suitable relatives to take you in. It looks like he asked me to look in on you as well. Does that seem alright? Betty and I would be fine taking you. He may have written this before they diagnosed the, uh—what is it?"

"Depends on the doctor you ask. But Asperger's Syndrome used to be the consensus."

"Right. You seem to be doing fine on your own. I just thought I'd ask."

"I have Jesus. I have Willow. I'm not alone."

"Right. Right. I understand." More paper shuffling. "Your dad also left you the entire estate, should something happen. You'd also have charge over all his accounts and the entire company. He seems to have a lot of faith in you, Seth. I'm just wondering what a sixteen-year-old would do with a multi-million-dollar construction company and a 14,000 square foot house. With a guest house, six-car garage, and a chapel, might I add. It looks like your parents live debt-free. So, we'd just need to transfer the deed."

"The 14,000 includes the guest house and the chapel. Dad said to trust the board but verify where necessary. You and the rest of the board will call for hard questions. I will answer. I will do more when high school is done."

"Understood." But no one really understands Seth, so I know he's lying. Mr. Billings makes a noise in his throat before he closes the folder of papers. "Seth, your dad let me know about the situation with your girlfriend. Your dad wants you to have a say. I'm willing to do whatever it takes to—"

"I want what Natalie wants. Natalie doesn't want the baby or any others or me. Please don't ask about that again." Now Seth is rubbing his hands on his pants.

"I'm sorry to hear that," says Mr. Billings, with sadness in his voice. "What I will do is look into this couple that's adopting the kid. I'll make sure all the paperwork is in order so that we don't find ourselves in the gray legally. Is that alright?"

"Yes, sir." Seth does not like to live in the gray, especially now.

"It's possible, Seth, that you've been dealt quite a tough hand all at once. Do you think you can handle it?"

"No." Seth is honest. "But God handles my life for me now completely."

Seth packed tents and a big plastic container of food and water for the trip to the mountains in the car. The air up in the mountains smells sweeter. Wilder. Seth smells it, too, because he opens the windows so we can both smell it when we drive.

But on the breezy mountain drive, I'm nearly startled out one of the windows. Seth's eyes are on the road. He doesn't even squint at the glowing Man suddenly sitting on the seat between us. I nearly cry out a warning until the Man speaks.

"Peace, Willow." The words are not just for my ears. They move through me, leading me to a peace greater than even the wild mountain air had been providing—almost to sleepiness if I weren't so eagerly wondering about this Man. But he doesn't leave me to wonder long.

"Remarkable boy, isn't he? They only see the broken vessel. I knew it'd take a dog to see deeper. He is important. They are all important. Therefore, your life will be healthy and long, Willow. All you need to do is what they ask. There will be times they will ask things greater than even your keen senses and obedience can overcome. But I have already overcome those things. Step lightly, Willow, when the rocks are loose."

The Man goes again—not in a flash—but simply out of my sight, as if He always was and still is there, just hidden. His words enter into my memory, into my very will, placing health in my bones. I do not understand much of what He says. Who are "they"? When are rocks loose? What is "remarkable"? But I am also assured that I will understand later. I am leaving questions to the free will of the people.

If I could imagine someone bright enough and good enough to be their God, I'd have imagined this Man. Only I guess I thought He'd be bigger. But who is to say that Someone big enough to make the mountains isn't also good enough to fit inside Seth's truck?

Seth makes sure to stay in a place where he has "bars" on his phone. But we are far enough away so that we must pitch a tent to be safe at night. Now, after the tent is up and we share a sandwich, Seth wants to use the rest of the daylight. He had done something strange before we left. He had gone into the laundry room and picked out the smelliest shirts he could find for each of his parents. I didn't understand why until just now.

He retrieves the two shirts and a long leash, puts the leash on me, then makes a clear instruction as he shoves the shirts into my nose.

"Go find 'em, girl."

I didn't need to be reminded of what Mom and Dad smell like, but the last sniff keeps me focused enough to catch a phantom whiff on the wind. I stand a moment, trying to trace the source. The breeze gets still, and before it can start again and take the scent away, I'm pulling Seth's strength behind me, forcing him to run what he says is a mile to an empty campsite.

The site is covered in their things—shoes with chew marks from less obedient days and a scarf Mom wears when there is a chill in the breeze. Seth mentions that it looks like they had packed the truck and left just a few things out at the campsite. The fire is cold and dry. But just when Seth wonders, I catch a trace on the ground that reminds me of Dad. We follow this along a path for half the distance it took to get from our campsite to theirs.

I whimper when the path slides my paw aside, nearly causing me a tumble. *Step lightly when the rocks are loose.* Seth makes a similar sound when he must stabilize himself after running into my tail at a complete halt. He is questioning my tread, which in a person would be a tiptoe. But in a few feet, we both see that if we had not stepped lightly, we'd be tumbling, not peering, fifty feet down a recent rockslide into a ravine.

His eyes are trained to know them. My nose is the same. All senses tell us both that the man holding the woman in the ravine is Dad with Mom.

Once when I was a puppy, a tiny mouse made the mistake of stepping in the path of a horse. At least, that is what Pete had said. It had gotten caked inside dirt against the foot of the horse until we had all smelled it. Even the people smelled it. The breeze aside, that ravine smells a little like Mom and like Dad. But a lot like that dead mouse on that hoof. I look up to see that Seth is looking at his phone.

"Thank you, Lord. Two bars should be plenty." Then he dials a number. "Mr. Billings? We found them... No, I don't think they are alive. We are going down to check."

Seth is cautious and walks down the long way, leaving his phone on the path with some invisible beacon Mr. Billings says he will tell them to find. We assume the rockslide occurred just as Mom had walked by. Dad had likely not received a warning about loose rocks when seeking her later. Mom is crushed beneath a boulder at her waist. Dad's legs seem out of sorts. Neither one could have gotten out for help. So they held one another until they likely succumbed to these wounds and the chill of night.

Some persons hear the word they say about Seth and think he doesn't feel or love. Perhaps the only two people that really understood how wrong that is are clinging to one another in death as they did in life. And Seth is crying. I am holding him because I know we're alone now. Well, besides the Man holding us both. I don't see Him. But my eyes are not all I trust.

By the time the people with the vehicles and bags and uniforms arrive, Seth is all out of tears, leaving them to assume that he never cried them at all. But since we are alone together now, I suppose I'm the only one that needs to know.

He has them turned to ash and placed deep in the ground at the last section of fence he built before we found them. A carved stone became a memorial in our own yard. Seth had not wanted them in some far away cemetery.

Seth rises each morning at six without an alarm—only some driving force in him to greet the morning. He sits at the breakfast bar alone and eats a bowl of some light-colored cereal with milk and a spoon, like always. Then, at first, he returns to his bed.

He will cry and punch things, break things, always alone—no one to comfort or heal him except me. He clutches my fur at night alone in this massive house that smells of them. I don't do the things he does, but I feel the way he feels. I hate and despair. There is nothing but this forever without Mom or Dad or Natalie. No stitch for a wound like this. Not even the six-a.m. cereal or the persistent building of a snow fence.

Mr. Billings says the board is taking care of things for a while until Seth feels like he can fill big shoes. Seth tells Mr. Billings that word Natalie would say. "Never." But Mr. Billings waits. He doesn't come by. I think he just stays away with his body, though. I think he talks to God about Seth. Because slowly, something changes.

One morning, Seth has an idea. It is after the night I groggily see that Man again, touching his chest and his head. Seth rises at six, bitter and alone and hating. He finds a Book on a shelf in his father's office. Over his cereal today, he cries, gritted teeth, reading aloud as if forced to by threat of death this day in July.

"Psalm one. 'Blessed is the man who walks not in the counsel of the ungodly, nor stands in the path of sinners, nor sits in the seat of the scornful;'" Then he stops. Sniffles. "Scornful…scornful."

Seth rises, walking back to his father's office and retrieving another book from the walls lined with them. He returns and speaks aloud again after looking in a few places. "That means hateful, Willow. Hate. Hate is a sin. 'But his delight is in the law of the Lord, and in His law he meditates day and night.'"

Seth is taken aback. Convicted. But loved. But how so when alone? He reads aloud again. Almost as though he's lulling himself like a child. "'He shall be like a tree planted by the rivers of water, that brings forth its fruit in its season, whose leaf also shall not wither; and whatever he does shall prosper.'" Then Seth cries again. And if I didn't know he'd lost everything in life worth having, I'd think he's smiling a little as he closes first his nonsensical Book, then his wet eyes.

"God, I don't know why I have to be alive now. But since I am, help me. Help me *live*." And then I'm sure that even though he's crying, Seth smiles.

He doesn't go back to bed today. He spends the morning looking through every inch of every drawer and shelf and wall of his father's office. Learning it. He is overwhelmed today. Discouraged. But day by day, he has cereal and a psalm at six. And day by day, I think Seth starts to breathe a little easier. Get angry less. He even begins school on schedule and comes home and works in his father's office. Knowing it, feeling it, accepting phone calls, and working and prospering through the grief.

It is December. Early December, because Seth told me so. When he opens his eyes this morning and looks different. He sees the sun streaming in and the snow falling outside. And instead of forcing the smiles, the work, and the knowing, he awakens with it. Aside from
cereal and fence construction. Despite a broken heart. Grief. Stress. Burdens. He opens his eyes today and smiles—breathes like breath is new, then whispers.

"'Let everything that has breath praise the Lord.'" That means us, Willow. Us too."

Chapter Seven

A New Family

I didn't mean to run off. I've no desire to go anywhere or leave Seth more alone than he is. I just saw the truck is all—the same kind of truck at Natalie's house that had taken her and her family away. Maybe it had taken six months, but it had brought her back. Except when I'd arrived, Natalie was nowhere to be seen. Instead of darker skin like her parents and her, I see skin that is almost transparent, blue eyes on two parents and four children, and hair that shines against the winter sun like the snow.

Three of the children are girls and relatively young, moving colorful miniature versions of appliances and assorted baby dolls into the excited giggliness of the house. The oldest child is a boy Seth's age. The girls spot me, dropping everything to coo in my direction. I am fulfilled, like with Natalie, when they pet and pat me. I'm wondering what they mean when they ask if they can "keep" me.

The boy comes over, dropping to a squat and checking my collar. "Let's see where you belong. Willow? Looks like you live up the road there. Let's get you home."

As soon as the boy with sunny hair takes hold of my collar, I see that Seth is jogging and whistling down the road and stops in front of the boy and me. I greet him, and the mother and father join the boy when they see a neighbor has arrived.

"Hey, I'm Nathan. Is this your dog?" The boy extends his hand, and I watch Seth remind himself that he is supposed to shake it, and then he does.

"I'm Seth. Yes, this is my dog. Her name is Willow." Seth is never at ease with new souls. The boy, Nathan, seems to be a bit amused by this. The mom, with slightly darker hair than the rest of the family, speaks up.

"Hi, Seth. I'm Karen, and this is my husband Bill. This is Laura and the twins Shelley and Kelli. We just moved here from Oregon. Bill is the new Chief Financial Officer of Gowan Construction. Nathan wasn't too happy about the move, but—"

Seth lights up a bit, rattling off facts. "Dr. William Holm. Age 48. Twenty years of experience in major construction companies. Degrees in finance, accounting, and management. Books on those subjects. The board liked that. But I liked the commendations for strong ethics."

"You're Seth Gowan. Pleasure. Kids, meet my boss." The air of pride changes in the man, and he stretches his hand out to Seth, who shakes it.

"Boss? You can't be a day over—" Karen seems surprised.

"I'm seventeen. I'm a junior at Allen Prep."

"Allen," Nate replies. "Me too."

"I don't know why I agreed to pay for that school. Prep for what? Culinary school? What a joke," Bill grumbles.

"Bill…" Karen tames him, and I see that the remark had hurt Nathan's feelings.

"He only complains until I make him a grilled cheese sandwich that makes him incontinent." Nathan rises from hurt with rebellion. Feisty, I decide.

"So, where are your parents, Seth? Surely you don't live in that estate alone." Karen is certainly a mother.

"My parents died six months ago in a hiking accident. I'm an emancipated minor. My friend used to live in the house you are moving into. I think that's why Willow came down. Sorry if she bothered you. She doesn't usually run like that. I'm building a fence, so—" The Holm family's faces fill with remorse. Even the two small twins. Karen speaks again.

"No bother at all. You and Willow just gained six new friends. Do you have food in that house up there? You cook and shop and clean and —"

"Yes, ma'am," Seth replies. "My parents taught me well."

"Even still," Karen adds. "If you and Willow help us unload this truck, you'll need to stay for pizza. I'd like for you to come here as often as you want. Anytime. You may be well-raised and brilliant, but you still need a family. Understood?"

"Yes, ma'am." Seth understands full well.

We both enjoy the Holm family this evening. After unloading and some unpacking, we stay about an hour to talk with the family. Nathan goes by "Nate," we learn. Laura, who is eleven, likes to look at Seth, but he doesn't notice. Shelley and Kelli take turns brushing my coat in their room, which is across the hall from Nate's.

"Which room was your friend's room? I bet he didn't have to fight three little sisters for the best one. I do have a name carved in my door frame, though. Natalie? So maybe one sister?" I can see the teenagers through the two open doors, though I'm falling asleep under the wonderful touch of the girls.

"Natalie was my friend. She had a little brother. Neil. I never went in her room and only came to the house once. Her parents didn't like me and my Asperger's." Seth has more trouble speaking of Natalie than he does his parents.

"Well, that doesn't matter to me; assuming it won't keep us from having epic parties in the mansion you have to yourself. Did your parents leave behind a wine cellar? A house like that's bound to have one."

"Well, they didn't take it with them." Seth's literal answer causes Nate to laugh. "But God doesn't like drunkenness. My parents would only have a glass before bed. My Mom collected wine. She had a room specially built—thousands of bottles."

"Seth, I'm a future chef. You won't catch me wasting fine wine on 'drunkenness.' But you might have to back off on that God thing. My whole family thumps me with Bibles whenever they can. Including my idiot dad, who has no business talking about righteousness. When God shows up and tells me to worship Him, then I might give it a second thought. Maybe." Nate's true colors shine. Seth keeps his head.

"He doesn't need your worship to still be God. I will see you at school and make sure you don't get lost." Seth walks into the hall.

"S'go, Willow."

It is in February that Mr. Billings comes to the house with papers for Seth to sign—papers to give up Natalie's baby as his so that a couple can adopt it. Mr. Billings says Seth has a chance to fight, but mentions that this paperwork is only necessary because Natalie refuses to leave him off the birth certificate when the baby comes.

Seth replies with a slight smile. "So, you've spoken to her? This is what she wants?"

"Considering her father wouldn't even hand her the phone, I get the impression that this is what *he* wants. But she's bullheaded, from what I hear. If she didn't really want this, I think you'd already know." I like that Mr. Billings at least understands Seth's need for direct information.

"Well, I want what she wants. No matter what that is."

"You do understand you are literally signing away your firstborn child?"

"God has another plan for him." Seth bites his lip to fight tears as he signs the papers.

"Him? Did she tell you it's a boy? Mr. Nakano mentioned she didn't want to find out."

"Him." Seth nods, smiles, and slides the papers back to Mr. Billings across the desk.

It is in March that Seth falls in love with a piece of photo paper after he reads aloud a letter from the mailbox.

"'Seth,

If my dad knew about this letter, he'd kill me. He's found ways to ban me from all contact with you or anyone else. But I'm in the hospital, so I will hopefully get a nurse to send this for me before he gets back.

I wanted to send my condolences, finally. I heard about your parents, and I've been a mess knowing you're alone now. I wanted to come back to you, but my parents and morning sickness prevented that. I hope Willow was strong for you and that you took this straight to Jesus like your dad would have wanted. I'm not there, but I have faith that God has a wonderful plan for you. My parents can't ban faith.

I'm risking life and limb because you deserve to have this picture at least. He looks like you, I think. He's healthy and perfect and he has good people to raise him. I think they named him Cameron. You didn't have to sign those papers. But thank you.

Tell Willow I said hello. Lord willing, we'll meet again someday. Don't you dare forget me.

Love,

Natalie'"

Attached is a photo of a tiny person, all wrinkled and puffy all at once. I don't see the appeal or the resemblance to my master. But Seth is brought to his knees in tears.

Chapter Eight

Moving Forward

Sometimes I really hate Nate. Sometimes I love him better than most. Tonight, as always, I experience a fair amount of both—but mostly the hate.

Nate quickly drinks liquid from a tiny glass, then climbs the ladder he'd set up to connect the back yard to a section of roof beneath the second story. A group of three dozen teenagers cheers him on. Nate's current fling pretends to be concerned for his safety. One of the prettiest of the girls, of course. A trophy, aware of how disposable she is.

Nate wobbles in full laughter twelve feet up, walking along the roof. If Karen were here, she'd have had a heart attack by now. So, I bark at him myself.

"Hush, Willow. He'll be fine tonight. Barking won't fix him." Seth is shaking his head, likely thinking about his liability in all this. He's watching as some of the other big strong boys hoist a couch over that Nate dramatically jumps onto from the roof.

They call it a party. But it smells much more like a battleground to me. They see laughter and fun and maybe a bit of danger. But what I see in flashes just before each blink terrifies me. I can't see them in full form, nor do I understand exactly what they are. But I see them in blurs of light all over. Battling. Not of flesh and blood, Seth might say. Principalities. Powers. Wickedness. Maybe that's what they are. The children who party don't see it, I'm sure. If they could see, they would obey Who Seth obeys. They might know that what they do is not a matter of danger or rebellion, or fun. It is a matter of life and death.

Nate is greeted in kisses when he reaches land again by his arm candy of scarce apparel. Then that group of three couch-carrying boys approaches Seth after huddling to prepare some cruelty. They wear matching patches on matching jackets. Some symbol of their social status, I think.

"Hey! Nice party, Retard," says the smallest of the three, slapping hands with another his size and a quite large boy for their age. Then they all start making some barking noises and flailing their arms around.

Just as I begin to growl, I decide it would have been more strategic if the big one had said the mean thing. That way, perhaps the push Nate delivers to his chest with one arm may not have knocked the sayer onto his back. But when it does, the crowd silences.

There is some hierarchy here, like wolves. I've heard that the boys go to one school and the girls to another. But they all know one another from gatherings like this. The boys all seem to answer to Nate, who in my knowing might be considered the most foolish. He always has the prettiest girl wrapped around him until he finds a prettier one. Seth says he fornicates with them. Nate always drinks and swears and acts silly the most. Yet he is somehow at the top of the hierarchy. Perhaps there is something in that foolish leadership that fools them all into thinking they can be cruel. That is, until Nate continues to prove that they are lesser for it.

"Hey Dirk, you know Gallahan's Calc test? The one 'nobody' passed?" Nate says this in the silence he's created while drinking a beer. Like he didn't just force another human to the ground. The human on the ground answers, rising with hurt pride.

"Yeah? So what?"

"Seth aced it," Nate reveals. "If he's the 'retard,' what does that make the rest of us?"

"Man, come on. I was just—"

"Just what? Shutting that ugly hole in your face? I hope so. Because if you wouldn't say it to me, you probably shouldn't say it to Seth." After Nate steps on a can to crush it, the chaos begins again. And no one bothers Seth.

An hour after Seth begins cleaning an empty main level, that arm candy walks in the window room from the upstairs, shoes in her hands, swarming with principalities, to retrieve her purse.

"Night, Seth. Great party." Then she walks across the inside of the house, exiting through the front door. Seth's phone rings. I hear Nate's tinny phone voice.

"I climbed out a second story window in back. Come check out this view, Man." Seth sighs and exits into the back yard again, and sees that Nate is sitting atop that section of roof, now sobered from drink but drunk from something else. Seth shakes his head.

"Willow, stay." Seth climbs the ladder, joining his friend on the roof.

I don't see what they see, but Nate thinks whatever it is is beautiful. I know Seth's house is up a mountain a little and overlooks the city. Maybe that's what they see. I wonder why Nate allows all those fragments of spiritual wickedness to rule him when no one but him would have climbed so high to see such innocent beauty.

"Did you fornicate with your girlfriend in my house?" Seth sees the funny mixed look of guilt and ease on Nate's face.

"Definite possibility." Nate smiles a half smile with his sparkling blue eyes.

"You shouldn't do that, Nate," Seth says it like he sees. Like he knows about the life or death.

"What, you've never 'fornicated'?" Nate mocks with quoting fingers.

"That's irrelevant, Nate. God is forgiving, but it makes Him mad when you don't even try to obey Him. It's an insult to Christ's sacrifice. Sex is intended for marriage." Seth tries like life and death again.

"Well, considering my parents are secretly miserable, I am never getting married. So, abstinence until marriage doesn't apply to me. Women are beautifully crafted by 'God,' Seth. Just because I'm not getting married, it isn't fair that I miss out on His exquisite creation, right?" Nate and Seth don't always see eye to eye.

"I really do think that is fair, actually." But Seth sees clearly, even standing alone.

Nate laughs endearingly. "Seth, you amaze me. You have the ultimate dream life for a guy. No parents. A mansion. More money than your great-grandkids would spend in their lifetime. You're smart, good-looking—but you don't waste a bit of it on crap like I do. These idiots act like there's something wrong with you. But I'd give anything to have it all together like you."

"'Anything' like letting God in your life?" He'd received a worthy, truthful few compliments. But Seth knows that anything worthy should be sent straight back to God where it belongs.

"Figure of speech." Nate rejects the mere idea. Looking back out at that view a moment. "I'm pretty wired. Let's get your place clean."

Then sometimes, I find myself only loving Nate, without the hate. Sometimes because he has charm and knows what to say and how to say it. But mostly because he is Seth's friend without pretense, walking up and down the street, no matter the company. Nate confiding and protecting. Seth listening and encouraging. I also love the Holm family and that we spend so much time with them, like if they were our family too. Mrs. Holm is sweet. Dr. Holm keeps quiet because Seth is in charge of all his work, even though Seth never mentions it.

This all continues for summers and Christmases for the rest of high school for Seth and Nate. A family. And friends. Nate sinning at every chance. Seth walking with Jesus, as he says. He says Nate hasn't sinned the right way to stop him yet. Like Seth had with Natalie. But he hopes it won't be long.

Over those hot summers and snowy winters, budding aspens and falling leaves, Seth builds a snow fence—two sections a week without fail. He carves the posts by hand by my night watch in the woodshop. And he fastens them outside by day, no matter the weather, working his way down the lawn as graduation approaches. We miss Mom and Dad and Natalie but carry on by the grace of Seth's God and with help from the Holm family.

"So, my dad won't pay for me to go to culinary school in Boston. He says I can either study something 'of consequence' anywhere in the country, or I can stay my butt here to learn how to be a 'pansy cook.' Jerk." Nate likes words that make Seth cringe. Nate is slouching heavily, bouncing one of my tennis balls off the opposite wall in the window room, narrowly missing one of Mom's old paintings hanging there.

"There are culinary schools here in town." Seth encourages.

"I know, Man. That's not the point. The point is, I don't want to live at home. I'm 18. I want freedom. Is that a lot to ask?" Nate keeps bouncing and slouching.

"I guess not." Seth does not understand the draw toward freedom. He's had far too much for far too long. "I know it's only up the street. But you can live here if you want."

"Yeah…" Nate says like he hadn't really been listening at all. Then he stops bouncing the ball. "You're a genius, Seth! How many bedrooms do you have, again?"

"Six total. And then two offices."

"Dude!" Nate lights up. "You could make a killing renting out rooms in an old house like this. I know you like being alone, but come on, this house is being wasted right now."

"I don't need money," Seth says this with a tone like a preface. So Nate listens. "I have an attic, too."

"Yeah, I know. I took Maddie Walker up there during a party one night, remember? You were so mad!" Nate doesn't seem to care about Seth's feelings on the matter. He is laughing.

Seth rises and recites some deeply rooted thought process, "I will move to my parents' old room. My current room is a secondary master with a five-piece bath. I won't charge you to live there if you find other tenants. The other rooms are worth $500 a month because they are fully furnished, and there are enough bathrooms for everyone to have their own. Mom always said the room behind the stairs on the second level was haunted, so I can't rent that one."

"You've considered this before." Nate was caught off guard by the details.

"I had a feeling you'd suggest it. I had Mr. Billings draw up leases so that everything is legally sound. I have some rules you have to follow, but other than that, I think it will be a good use of the house."

"Okay, wait…what about the guest house? You could get $1,500 for that. Easy. Maybe more with the land you have. It has a loft or something, right?"

"I'm not renting out the guest house." Seth's final words before heading up to his room to pack his things. Nate and I follow.

"So, what are your 'rules'?" Nate asks this from the doorway as I retreat to my own bed in the room.

"I can only rent to males. No girls are allowed in bedrooms. I set the alarm at midnight on weekdays. No one goes in the guest house, just like always. You have to clean up your own messes in the kitchen and play chess with me once a week." Seth rattles off.

Nate laughs. "Chess? I've known you a year and a half, and we've never once played chess."

"I miss it," Seth confesses.

"Okay…" Nate has learned to accept even strange insistences of Seth's. He steps into the room and looks around. "You'd really want me to have your awesome room? For free?"

"Not free. You have to follow the rules and interview tenants for me. They have to be trustworthy."

"Seth, I mean money."

"'The wicked borrows and does not pay back, but the righteous is gracious and gives.' You are my friend. I don't want to know if you are wicked."

"Alright, I'll—" Nate's vibrating and ringing phone interrupts his talking. "Hello?...Hey Maddie, what's up?...Tonight? Sure, Peaches. I have some packing to do, but I'll pick you up at six for dinner…wherever you want to go. My treat….Alright. See you then." Nate hangs up the phone. Seth shakes his head.

"What? I'm taking her out to dinner! I'm 'gracious.' See? I'm not wicked." Nate cannot fool Seth.

"You should marry Madison Walker. She is your favorite." Seth takes a box and sets it down by the stairs to take it down to his parents' old room.

"Never getting married. Especially not to Madison Walker." Nate checks the time on his phone.

"Why not?"

"Because Madison Walker is a sinner. Fornication." Nate winks, somehow being alright with this word that makes Seth start. Nate leaves to pack his things so that he can take our room for himself. For free. Sometimes I think he really is wicked.

Seth has not even opened the door to his parents' room for two years. Seth does not like change and tells me his crib used to be in the room upstairs where we sleep now. Seth does not make sense of the way most people think. But he makes sense of life anyway. Because Someone talks to Seth that I can't always hear.

I know he's terrified, just like the night two coyotes almost got a hold of me when I was a puppy. His mother had held both of us then. But now the terror is inside, and Mom is the reason he's so scared but isn't here to hold either of us. So, I nudge Seth's leg, which makes him smile. He reaches for the door handle over the piles of boxes and loose clothing he'd stacked in the hall before opening the door.

The age of the double doors and solid brass handle and hinges make for a hefty creak when he sets them ajar. We both wait in the dark hall as Seth swings them open. He exhales once before switching on the light. The light reveals something eerie, even to me. The French doors from the sitting area to the bedroom are open. We see a perfectly made bed with an enormous pair of slacks spread across them, likely by Dad, who was the only culprit for such a mess.

Everything else is in order. Mom's jewelry and scarves are in boxes and on hooks. Seth steps inside, inspecting the massive bedroom with vaulted ceilings and two-story windows and wood paneling that Mom had white-washed to make it not feel so "old and dark." The clawfoot tub and ornate twin of vanities for sinks are still in the wide-open bathroom with the shower of mosaic stone tile that extends beyond it to envelop the walls and floor. The walk-in closet, the size of Seth's upstairs room, is filled with neglected designer clothes.

Seth is silent as he looks it all over. He goes to his mother's vanity in the closet and runs a finger along it, collecting some of the layer of dust that covers every surface. It reminds him that they are not about to arrive home from that anniversary trip of a lifetime. He goes to a wine bottle with a bow on the table in the sitting area. Reads me the tag tied to it.

" 'Stacy,

This was bottled the year we did the same with our love in marriage. You'll likely want to hold onto it for your collection. But I'd rather we share it when we return, and celebrate twenty years of holding onto each other. Lord willing, I'll have the honor of loving and protecting you for decades to come. Happy Anniversary.

Randall' "

With a knot in his throat, Seth takes the bottle to a slotted place in the corner of the bedroom where Stacy always kept her most favorite wines—the ones they had shared in the evenings for twenty years. Then Seth redirects his attention.

"It's dirty in here. We have to clean it before we go to sleep, or we'll get sick."

To some, what Seth says may seem insensitive or unsentimental. But if you know Seth, which I do, I know that all those tears he cried at the base of that rockslide are still happening somewhere inside him. And that while he's talking about cleaning a room and even trotting down to the basement for cleaning supplies, he's really missing them. He's making a monumental choice to move on. If I knew how to be proud, I would be today. Because Seth listens, even when the Voice is inaudible.

Chapter Nine

HOUSEMATES

At first, I have trouble sleeping in a new room, but only until Mom and Dad's life room starts to smell like Seth, and his crib room starts to smell like Nate—like hate and love all at once. Just like him. I prefer the peace of Seth.

Seth is always doing. Other people sit and watch the glowing box, laughing and cheering at whatever is on it. But Seth only sits when he is doing. He sits behind his father's desk doing. Dusts, cleans, and fixes, mows, and maintains. Builds furniture and fence posts in his woodshop. Builds a fence to surround the yard. He only stops doing to eat, and only sometimes. But I think he really does the most over cereal at six in the morning. Or when he retreats to the sitting room in his new bedroom—to his father's old chair. That's when he opens a leather Book and lays it open on one hand, a glass of red wine on his side table after his age allows.

I know Seth does all he does to keep his heart from slowing down long enough to remember. To stay at peace. But it is when he sits with that Bible that he slows down enough to remember that God is in all he does. And because Seth does so much, he has no trouble at all sleeping in that enormous bed his parents used to share. But just in case, I share it with him.

Nate, I think, does a lot less. Therefore, he sleeps a lot less. He goes to a place called "culinary school" for most of the day. It didn't take me long to realize he is learning how to use a kitchen. Seth's kitchen has dozens of feet of counters and cabinets that no one person could ever fill. But Nate manages to dirty the entire kitchen much of the time.

Nate runs a quite effective con with the other men that have come to live in the house. Whatever his food assignment or experiment for school, he will share it with the others, as long as they clean that big kitchen after everyone has eaten—even though the piece of paper Mr. Billings wrote says they are to clean up after themselves. And even though many housemates might avoid one another, this house on Plaid Row is a much different thing entirely.

Derek Vargas was Nate's first find. A young warrior of sorts, stationed at a nearby military base, he was astonished at the opportunity to live in a mansion for just $500 a month. He lives for the rules of that military and respects fully the rules of Seth. He has no trouble signing the five-year lease Nate had told Seth was "ridiculous." Derek is stuck here on orders for those same years.

He takes the room across from Nate's upstairs, and Seth lets him put exercise equipment in a section of the attic. Derek is small for a warrior, they say. His skin is much browner than Seth's, and he buzzes his black hair short like the military asks. He wears glasses when he arrives home and removes other glass shards from his eyes. Derek's strength is far greater than his stature. The decorative cross he hangs on the wall in his room still has a Man left dying on it. But I still think he gets his strength from that Man, just like Seth.

Due to military precision combined with Latin warmth and zeal, Nate saw "Vargas" as a more fitting designation than "Derek." After only knowing him a short time, so did everyone else. Vargas begins to tease Nate for gaining weight from all his "studying." So, Vargas and Nate go for runs together, up and down the street and farther away, early in the morning. Nate is wild, and I think Vargas is helping tame him. Vargas works long days and exercises long nights. He doesn't go out at night like Nate does or see women. He goes to a different church from Seth, but sometimes when I follow Nate upstairs, I see Vargas reading a leather-bound Book as well. You may have guessed; I like Derek Vargas very much.

The second tenant had to fit a "tour" of the house into his schedule. When Nate made the appointment, he had made fun of the man behind his back. But when he'd arrived, the man had commanded all in the house to respect. Ezekiel, or "Zeke" Young is a businessman. His skin is deep, dark brown, and he wears expensive clothes and puffs out his chest when he walks. The five-year lease was appropriate for him because he needed cheap rent in a "suitable" environment to save for his own house as he climbs some invisible ladder at his job. Zeke does a lot, too. He spends much of the time at work, and Seth gives him the secondary office for when he is no longer allowed at work at night. He has no time for church, but Nate often convinces him to "blow off steam" on weekends somewhere I assume there is drunkenness and women.

Zeke lives in the room next to Vargas. He thrives on precision and doesn't sleep well at night. Maybe it is the abundance of mirrors in his room. But maybe it is something else. I wonder because there are flashes of battles near him sometimes. Battles with darkness. Battles with Light. Each day the battles get more intense. I wonder if Someone considers him worth the fight.

The lease demands it for them all, and instead of making it a chore, the guys decide that Thursday night is chess night. After they all become the allowed age, Seth allows them to choose a bottle of wine from his mother's wine cellar on Thursdays. Provided, of course, Nate has prepared a gourmet meal with which to properly pair it. Nate never disappoints.

Zeke was a chess champion at his high school and holds an undergraduate finance degree and an MBA. Nate had graduated near the top of the boys' class at their prep school. Vargas has the mind of a warrior—a strategist. But none of them, not even combined, can beat Seth at chess. Though he'll admit that they do prove to be a greater challenge than "previous opponents." I think he means Natalie. But he wouldn't dare mention Natalie.

They all look different. Sound different. Come from different places. But it had only taken a short time together, and a click of God's will for the four men to nonverbally consider themselves a family. Now, years later, the bond is set in something deeper than stone.

Tonight is the first Thursday of the month, three years into the leases of them all. It is summer, and Nate has just graduated from his culinary school but still dirties the kitchen daily.

Tonight, I get dry kibble, as always. But everyone else is dining on some type of fish with citrus salsa and something called "Sauvignon Blanc." None of them see the irony of dining so well on TV tables in the game room or in taking bites between moves and having to change chairs every time someone else must play chess. Seth is currently beating Vargas, and the four men are connecting, which I don't think requires the chess table.

"I hate my parents," Nate grumbles. "I had to spend the weekend helping Dad in the yard like some underling. Dad kept telling me what a failure I am, of course. Even though I somehow landed a job as a sous chef at an award-winning restaurant. Chef is even considering using the dish I prepared during the interview. Pretty sure 'failure' isn't the word for me. They should just adopt *you*, Zeke. They'd be the proudest parents ever."

Zeke laughs his gritty laugh. "I'm twenty-six. Not in the market for new parents, Nate."

"Twenty-six? Gees, Man. Shouldn't you be looking for a wife by now?" I like the way Vargas talks. A little whiney. A little like his tongue wants him to say different words than will be understood by this company. Sometimes it does when he's praying or angry that someone reset the weights on his bench in the attic.

Zeke laughs again. "I don't even have time to sleep. What would I do with a wife?"

Nate lends his "expertise," "Zeke, women don't require a whole lot. Buy her a house, knock her up a few times and bring home flowers sometimes. My dad is an evil crap maggot and my mom sticks around for that other stuff. But that's just marriage. I tend to go for the women that don't even require the flowers. Marriage is never happening to me."

"Language, Nate! I swear, an evening with *mi mama* and you wouldn't have lips to talk with no more." Vargas says what Seth is thinking as he moves the queen with the holes in it.

"You '*swear*' that?" Nate teases. All the men erupt in laughter. Then Vargas sighs as he loses his bishop.

"I agree, Nate. Marriage is a joke. Have you looked at the divorce rate? Truth is, don't nobody know how to make a woman happy." Zeke is shaking his head. Seth winces. A mistake. Because Nate sees.

"Did your parents have a joke marriage too, Seth?" Nate would have crossed a line if he was able to see them. But he usually knows better than to ask Seth personal questions.

"My parents were very much in love." Seth mumbles. "Checkmate."

Vargas grumbles, and Nate cracks his knuckles as he trades him places. Seth is already perfectly centering each piece in its square, and Nate realizes he has a few moments to spare.

"So are mine. But my dad treats me like shiii—dirt—and Mom just defends everything he says. She practically worships the ground he walks on. But I know she hates it, even though she'd never say it because she's a saint. Marriage just seems like a dysfunctional relationship to me. How can you ever really be who you are if you have to walk around losing yourself in the process of pleasing someone else? That's why marriage fails." Nate is adamant.

"I don't know about that, but I prefer to focus on the Lord. I only joined the Army to see the world so I could know how God wants me to serve when I'm a priest. Celibacy can be a blessing." Vargas often talks of his aspirations to be a Catholic priest someday. But this part of things just rang in Nate and Zeke's ears until their jaws dropped with wonder.

"Celibacy? Like, no sex, ever? Are you okay with that?!" Nate pretends to choke.

"I'm *called* to that, Man. There's more to life than sex. But even from my perspective, marriage is a lot less dysfunctional than jumping from one honey to the next, telling everyone you're never settling down. Everybody settles down." Vargas takes offense and attacks Nate's perpetual way of life. Nate is unmoved, and in fact, gasps in Seth's direction.

"Guess who called me, Seth? Maddie. Madison Walker is in town for the weekend to see her parents. We have a date Saturday night." Nate is overjoyed.

"Madison Walker is a sinner and fornicates. That's what you said three years ago. And you were dating that waitress, I thought." Seth will never fully understand Nate's ways.

"That waitress said the 'M' word on the second date. We didn't have a third. Maddie knows better. We have an understanding." Nate and Zeke laugh together about this. Seth sighs, aching somewhere deep for the flippant transgressions of his dearest friend. Nate catches the sigh. "Oh please, Seth. As if you have any room to talk about relationship issues. Your perfect parents are dead, and you haven't been on one date the entire time I've known you. Aren't you a celibate like Vargas over here?"

Seth clears his throat. Hurt. But draws strength from that unseen place yet again. "I don't know how to answer that. Checkmate."

Seth rises and heads to his room, but I do not follow. I'm as dumbfounded as they, though I may be the only one aware. Seth is thinking of Natalie and knowing far more about women than the men in this room even think possible for him. But he says nothing. Nothing about the purity or wild of love. Nothing about the child he has in the world somewhere. Nothing to humble them or educate them at all. No. Because that would dishonor her. If I know Seth—and I know Seth—it would take far more than a tipsy Casanova to make him do that.

"You really think that was necessary?" Vargas defends.

"I'll go apologize as soon as he cools down. I just get so sad thinking he might never get to be with a woman, you know? And it's not by choice like with you, Vargas. How can he be so obsessed with a God that made him just different enough to be miserable? I respect the guy. I guess I just don't get it." Nate clears plates, and the three men move to the kitchen to begin cleanup.

I sit pretty enough for Nate's heart to bend and give me a morsel of fish off a plate. A treat. But I decide I prefer my kibble after a night of a grumbly belly, knowing Nate's apology is as over-seasoned as his snapper fish.

Chapter Ten

From Yesterday

"I don't know why it bothered me so much. It's always been that way with her. But I felt sick almost." Nate is tying the special slip-proof kitchen shoes and seeking his chef coat in the "mudroom/laundry room" behind the garage. He is shaken to his core.

Nate had thought himself lucky that his date with Maddie had coincided with one of Seth's business trips—a job site in Phoenix, this time. With "Mr. Rules" gone and only a functionally mute dog to look after, he'd thought he was free enough to bring her home after dinner. And, tragically caught underneath my stand-in master's bed with unquenchable darkness, I'd felt free to distract myself with rawhide. The rawhide had been some "red" spike of a shoe that Maddie had paired with a sparse black dress. The kind of rawhide with consequences, though at the time I'd been deprived by my caretaker and had no other choice.

"You have a conscience." Seth is standing near him, having heard a confession of broken rules the moment he walked in the door from the airport. But Seth had expected it and forgiven freely.

Broken rules like eating a shoe, though I hadn't been punished too severely. I'd only been subjected to the screeching of a cute strawberry blonde with gray eyes when they'd halted their midnight whispers to hear me chewing beneath the bed. Apparently, the shoe had been expensive. A gift from a boyfriend. A married boyfriend, who also happens to be Maddie's boss in Los Angeles. Nate had been spooked enough for a nearly naked shouting match to occur in the upstairs hallway, in view of the other housemates.

"I didn't think I had a line, you know?" Nate is tormented. "But I felt like an accessory to adultery. Is adultery somehow worse than garden variety sexual immorality?"

"Adultery generally hurts more people. Maybe that's why it feels worse. But they are both sin and always hurt at least two people." Seth teaches gently, without judgment.

The shouting match had ended with Madison's far-too-late exit. And though the housemates ordinarily tease about girls and stature and profession, and everything in-between, Nate had been victim only to an inquiry of his well-being, followed by peace as he retreated to his room. And that, only after thanking me for the rawhide I chose.

Vargas had taken the moment Nate's door closed to mention the vow of chastity he'd eventually take. Zeke had laughed, considering the same.

Nate nods, mulling over Seth's teaching. "I'm finally done with shallow Madison Walker. You happy?"

Seth smiles. Nate disappears into the garage.

"S'go, Willow." Words I'd missed for the 36-hour business trip. Seth leads me into his woodshop, where he begins inspecting large pieces of wood to decide on the best one for a fence post. He finds one, then locates his safety glasses just as his phone rings.

"This is Seth." He answers after the sigh, expecting to be faced with some difficult corporate decision. What he receives is something far more daunting. I sit up and perk my ears to listen to the caller.

The caller gives a sigh of relief. Nothing more.

"H'lo?" Seth asks.

The caller speaks one word that makes Seth have to find a chair immediately. Odd. It is only his name.

"Seth."

He doesn't answer for a moment, in shock. I've only heard that the caller is female and dislike how the phone changes the timbre of voices.

"Seth? You there?"

"I'm here. Natalie?" At the sound of the name, I rise to my feet, beginning to search for her long-lost scent.

"Yeah." Another sigh of relief. "It's me. Is this a bad time?"

"Not at all," Seth says too quickly. "I just wasn't expecting you to call."

"I know." Natalie sounds nervous. "You sound different, Seth. More—"

"Normal?" Seth chuckles. "I have tenants. They've helped me to be more social. They play chess with me."

"Really? That's great! I'm glad you didn't give it up. You were so good when we were kids."

A silence falls. Seth breathes in to speak. So does Natalie. But I see that Seth still regards even Natalie's breath above his own.

"Listen, Seth. I'm in a bind. I hadn't even worked up the courage to call you at all, let alone after five years, to ask a favor I certainly don't deserve. But I'm out of options." Natalie sighs nervously.

"How can I help, Natalie?" Seth offers with compassion.

"Well…" Natalie talks, and Seth listens. Just like in the old days. I learn through her strange timbre through the phone that Natalie had finished her home high school early and attended college the following year. She graduated a month ago with a bachelor's. After being allowed nothing but books, newspapers, and magazines while she'd been pregnant, she'd fallen in love with journalism and food—the other thing she'd been allowed to her heart's content. She says she's become quite a foodie and decided she wanted to be a food writer, though the demand was not high in the profession.

Natalie still plays the piano. She had minored in music in college. But more than journalism and food and music, Natalie missed home. She landed a part-time job as a high school choir accompanist and another job as a part-time food writer for a local online review website. They are two jobs she knows she will adore, but her parents forbade her to come back to the place of her greatest sin.

She had packed up her car in the night and stolen away at two in the morning. She called her parents from the road—two states away—only so they didn't file a missing person report. But when she'd arrived in town, she realized that her two dream jobs would only earn her an apartment in an atrocious part of town. So, she had stopped into the church, thinking they'd all shun her for her previous transgressions. Thinking every door was closing and she'd have to return to her parents' house. But she'd found that the church had no idea why she had really left. Seth had been telling them her father had found a better job in South

Carolina. Which he did, as it turned out. But Natalie had been able to come home and find a fresh start. All glory to God, she'd said. But thanks to Seth.

The people at church told her that Seth was renting rooms in his house, and it was time to reconnect with an old friend. Natalie had rattled off all this information, complete with a promise of pure intentions but a desperate hope that he has a room available temporarily. Then she'd sighed. And Seth had spoken.

"I do have one room available, besides the haunted one, but it would be inappropriate for you to be on the floor with all the men."

Seth has a sadness in his tone. Natalie's is deeper.

"Oh. That's fine, I understand. You're right. I certainly don't want to be inappropriate. Can you tell me how you found housemates? The lady at the church said none of them go to church with you, but that you seem to get along great with them. I could afford a place if I had a roommate."

"My best friend Nate found them. It was part of his agreement with me. He doesn't pay rent," Seth says, standing, beginning to pace.

"Oh. Okay. Well, I thought I'd ask. It was good to hear your voice—" Natalie is exceptionally sad. Probably worse, knowing Seth has claimed himself a new best friend. Five years, Natalie now realizes, is a very long time.

But Seth interrupts her. "The guest house is vacant if you're interested."

"What? No way could I afford to rent your guest house. A room I could afford. But not a private guest house on your twenty acres. If I could afford that, I wouldn't have risked calling you. But hey, if our willow is still standing, I could probably afford to live under that." Natalie is hurt.

"Why would I charge you rent, Natalie?" Even the notion is foreign to Seth.

Natalie almost seems upset. "Seth, I know this is sudden. And yeah, I'm one step from heading back to South Carolina. But I'm not burdening you for *free*."

Seth first chuckles, then sighs, the past flooding in with necessity when they'd both been avoiding the subject. "It isn't free, Natalie. I have a debt that I can never repay you. But take the guest house as long as you want, and we'll consider it a start."

"Seth…" Natalie starts weakly.

"I still have Mom's baby grand, but you'd have to come into the main house if you wanted to practice for your job."

Natalie laughs at his gentle form of insistence. All business and logistics to protect his generous, remorseful heart. And not a malicious cell in his body. "You're saving my skin right now, you know that? You don't have to do this. I wasn't sure you'd even want to speak to me. Let alone—"

"I have some cleaning to do in there, and I have to make sure everything is in working order. When do you need to move in?"

"This motel room is paid up through Wednesday night, and I have an article to write sometime that evening. So, could I come by on Thursday morning? I know you're probably busy, owning a company and all—"

"I'll have it ready by Thursday."

"Are you *sure*, Seth?" She hushes her tone.

"I have a lot of work to do, but I'll make it a priority."

Natalie giggles. She had been thanking him, not doubting him. "Okay. See you then." The two say goodbye and hang up the phone. Seth seems to be trembling.

"Fence is only half done." He is deeply troubled by this. But I'm not sure it has anything to do with the fence.

When Nate arrives home tonight and shares Sunday's rejected entrées with the roommates, there is a heavy air, like everyone has something to say. I soon find out it's true. Nate, of course, starts first.

"Guess who found a final tenant to finally occupy the last room?" The room is still heavy, even more now, as unknowns hang over the prospect of a new housemate. "Come on, guys. At least hear me out."

"Alright. Go ahead. Seth has the final say anyway." Zeke is skeptical.

"Okay." Nate muffles, then swallows his bit of food and leans forward at the fancy dining room table where they now eat dinner after a mishap with a TV table, wine, and a chessboard. "This eighteen-year-old kid somehow conned Chef into letting him play guitar in the dining room tonight. Yikes, right? Except he was amazing! Sure, he sang all kinda Jesus freak stuff, but the kid has a voice like an angel and plays the guitar like a demon. He said he's about to go to college and can barely afford tuition with his scholarships, let alone a place to live and eat and practice for the $700 a month he has for everything. Said he was trusting God to figure things out. I told him no way. He could live here. His name is Christian. Literally. Good kid. I told him to stop by chess night to meet Seth."

"So we've inherited a minstrel?" Vargas's opinion comes with a snort.

"What do you think, Seth? I'm sure he'd sign at least a five-year lease. He's a college freshman." Nate seems overly hopeful.

"I found a tenant as well." Seth's news always flows in suddenly like a broken dam.

"Wait, Seth, we only have one room left unless you put him in the haunted one. What are the odds?" Zeke is amazed.

"Well, he can have my room in two months. I'm being deployed." Vargas must take his cues from Seth on news giving. Jaws drop in shock. Fear. Sadness. And questions abound for the young soldier. He answers them all in a string. "I can't tell you where. Classified. But there is a desert and a war. Fifteen months or more. And no, my lease isn't up. I was actually hoping you could save my room, but if you need it, I'll figure something out when I get back."

"We can save it. And I won't charge you since you'll be fighting for our country," Seth says with a remorseful nod. Already missing his friend. "My new tenant will be staying in the guest house."

The room erupts yet again. Zeke speaks up. "Seth, every one of us asked if we could rent the guest house. But you said we couldn't even set foot in it. What changed the rules? Nate having a girl over last night?"

"Hey! I confessed! He forgave," Nate defends.

"The rules didn't change. This is an old friend of mine with special accommodations. I still prefer you not set foot in the guest house, but that will be up to the tenant. It seems we'll have a lot of changes come Thursday night." Seth demands all ears with the details. The way he speaks makes none of them resent whatever Seth has decided.

Though Seth usually sleeps soundly, I have to depart to my own bed for his tossing and turning on Wednesday night. Thursday proves to be a drizzly day. But Seth completes a fence section on Thursdays and finds himself digging post holes in the rain in the woods. He had spent much of the week cleaning the guest house for Natalie. He had not so much as made the bed since she'd left. In fact, the last person to turn down the sheets had been Natalie herself. Seth dare not tell her that. He'd cleaned and laundered the place from lintel to loft, forsaking much else in his life until today, when I'm shivering under the trees.

Even through the drizzle and beyond the scent of Seth's small barbed wire cut and the swish of his raincoat and the clatter of the post hole digger, I still catch her on the wind. I remember her like the day they'd named me. And my heart leads me to bolt at a full sprint in her direction. I run past the willow by the creek and up to the dark hooded figure sitting on wet grass across from Mom and Dad's memorial stone. Something about her stillness makes me stop my spirited bound and sit by her side.

"Hey, Willow." I remember and love her gentle but determined voice. Which is much clearer than through the phone half a woodshop away. She pats my damp fur, and I lick her hand. "I should have been here, Willow. I know you took care of him. But I should have found a way to be here with him when they died. I'm so sorry."

Natalie rises. She is taller than I remember her. She begins to walk the fence, touching each uniquely crafted post as she goes. She stops when she feels the same presence I feel. I know this from the way her speech is meant for a person.

"Did you ever get my letter?" She inquires without looking up.

"I did." Seth is simple with his words. Never the depth of them. Natalie nods.

"I see your parents are by your fence. I think they would have liked that." Natalie says after an awkward silence.

"My parents are in Heaven." Seth nods. Then realizes it was too abrupt. "But my dad did think my fence was a good idea."

"I see." Natalie exhales weightily.

"Do you have a lot to move?" Seth moves on so his heart does not fall behind.

"No. Just a carful. I was in a hurry. I had to leave a lot behind."

"I'll make sure you have what you need."

The two unload the car into the guest house, picking up not from where they left off, but from before they went astray. It is like they are fourteen again. This all occurs in hooded raincoats, laughing as they remember each other's laughs. But once the car is unloaded, they both know better than to stick around in the guest house. Seth takes Natalie to the main house and makes her a cup of tea. They both remove raincoats and receive variants of shock as they do.

"I thought I was seeing a shadow. But I'm loving the beard!" She compliments.

"Where are your curls?" Seth moves on, yet again, asking of Natalie's jet-black bone-straight, shoulder-length hair.

"Good question. After the, um—you know the pregnancy and everything. It just grew in straight. Hormones, I guess. My mom is convinced I've been straightening it. But my dad is happy that I look more Japanese now. You like it?"

"I do. I guess we both grew up." What Seth means is that Natalie has always been beautiful. Even when a child. But she'd gradually picked up beauty along the way. Since the two have not met eyes in a handful of years, Seth sees that she is stunning. She's not something between a woman and a girl. She's a woman completely. And if I'd been removed from Seth the same number of years, I'd be commenting on the reasons Natalie doesn't know whether to look at him or avert her eyes.

But Seth moves on, showing Natalie the lease agreement and telling her about all the tenants. She stops him at the explanation of Nate.

"No way! Like literally my old house? Down the road?"

"Yeah. I've seen your name carved in the door frame in his old room."

"That blows my mind! And you two are close?"

"Like brothers. The Holms sort of took me in when Karen found out about my parents. Bill is my CFO. The girls are sweet, too. You'd like Laura, she plays piano."

"Wow. That's great, Seth! But you say Nate is kind of a womanizer?"

Seth nods. "He likes girls. Girls like him. I think he respects women. He just doesn't really have boundaries. And he's charming, be careful."

Natalie chuckles. "Oh, please. You know how much charm annoys me! Even with a good, honest guy, I managed to get myself into a pickle the last time I dated."

"What happened? Did someone hurt you?" Seth protects, not catching her tone.

"Besides eighteen hours of labor and a nasty parent-forced breakup at sixteen, no, he never hurt me." She smiles. Clears her throat when Seth looks down nervously. Then she gives an amusing run-down of the things she's just learned. "So. Derek. You guys call him Vargas. Nice, but as spicy as his heritage when he wants to be. Zeke. Tall, dark, and handsome. Workaholic, which coming from you, means he needs therapy. And Nate with a tough reputation to unsell. I get them all?"

"Well, and Nate also found some eighteen-year-old kid I haven't met yet. He should be here tonight," Seth adds.

"So which ones know about *us*?"

"None of them."

"Not even Nate? I thought he was like your brother. He lived in my old room. Don't most guys talk about that kind of stuff?" Natalie tries to call a bluff.

"I'm not most guys." He shrugs. "Even Nate knows only that we were childhood friends."

"So, I gather we are pretending we were never in love?" Natalie asks boldly.

"I'm not pretending. But God may have other plans for us than to be in love again. The last time things made sense was when we were best friends. Maybe we should pick up from there?" This logic confuses me. Because I know that Seth still loves Natalie just like he did the day she left. Why is he just letting her believe he doesn't?

"I was hoping you'd say exactly that. Clean slate." Natalie sighs, a lot of pressure relieved. "Now tell me about chess night."

When Vargas huffs and puffs through the door at the end of his twelve-hour day, Seth and Natalie are still sitting at the breakfast bar talking. Catching up, mostly, I assume. I napped through most of it.

Vargas is in full uniform when he arrives in the kitchen. And stops in his tracks. A celibate, but not blind.

"You must be Vargas." Natalie says, rising and offering a handshake.

"Yes, ma'am. Seth..." Vargas speaks as he shakes Natalie's hand. "Tell me this is not your new tenant."

"Vargas, this is Natalie. An old friend of mine. She will be staying in the guest house." Seth introduces.

"Pardon, Natalie. You're just a little more female than Seth led us to believe." Vargas clears his throat.

"I said my new tenant has special accommodations requiring her to occupy the guest house. Being female counts." Seth smiles as Vargas shakes his head.

"Alright. Just be prepared for Nate to try to bed her and Zeke to hire a lawyer to review the lease. Who knows what the other new kid will do." Vargas grabs a water bottle from the fridge.

"Bed me?" Natalie is offended. Unleashing that part of her that makes her nature free. "I live for the Lord. 'Bedding' is something I launder, not something anyone does to me."

"I said try, and you'll be glad of your worthy foundation. Jesus has not quite tamed Nate yet." Vargas chuckles. Natalie does as well. One positive relationship formed.

Zeke rushes in the door, checking his watch, hoping he isn't late for his likely two hours of work addiction before chess night. He nearly misses the beauty standing in the kitchen. But only nearly.

"Uh, friend of yours, Seth?" Zeke asks, gently shaking Natalie's hand. Vargas answers somewhat condescendingly.

"This is Natalie. New guest house occupant." He takes a sip of water. Zeke meets Seth's eyes violently.

"Seth, the lease says you will only rent to men. Don't know if your condition allows you to know the difference. But this sista ain't no man. You just upset the balance of the entire house. Nate is gonna—well—no offense to you, Natalie. But you'll see." Zeke falls just short of hiring that lawyer.

"None taken. Zeke, right? I'll try to stay out of your way. I have my own kitchen and everything. And once the school year starts, I'll be pretty busy. I have to be at a high school four hours a day and find time to write at night." Natalie finds Zeke's soft spot as well. All work, no play.

"Write?"

"I'm a food writer. Not a fun job, I'm finding. And I'm pretty sure I can handle whatever the notorious Nate can throw at me. A handsome but sleazy sous chef accidentally found his way into the dining room at a place I reviewed last night. That and some excessive salting made for a tough break on that restaurant when the review published this morning." Natalie has gained much more suave the past few years. Fitting easily into the company of anyone, it seems.

"Sous chef, you say? What restaurant?" A light goes on in Zeke's reasoning.

"*Le Cloture*. A French inspired place downtown."

Silence and hidden chuckles overtake when the final and already notorious current housemate enters the kitchen just in time. He's removing his chef coat for his home version on the workday he's allowed to shorten for the standing gathering, already planning out what vegetable to mince.

That is until he catches sight of Natalie. Nate's first reaction to a beautiful woman usually involves some flattery. A deliberately corny pickup line, and often a kiss on the hand. But today, Nate stands, jaw on the floor, posed a few seconds mid-coat swap. Oddly, Natalie sees him, and her hand goes to her mouth. Eyes lock in an awkwardness no one wants to understand.

And then the humming. The constant, angelic humming I should have prepared my life for. It comes from a person with funny-shaped luggage strapped to his back. He's a young man with wild dark hair that grazes his collar and blue eyes like Nate's, looking around in wonder at the house. But stopping in the kitchen with a few strangers. Me being the most aggressive stranger currently, I growl immediately. Nate finally comes to and reacts.

"No, Willow. This is Christian. The guy I told you all about on Sunday." Nate continues to glance periodically at Natalie, extremely uncomfortable.

"Oh, this is totally happening." Christian loves the house. Who wouldn't? Seth shakes his hand and retrieves a lease for him to sign. Seth is often a quick judge of character, almost like he knows someone already. Watching them, I almost miss the heaping tension in the kitchen. But really, such would be impossible. All at once, it begins to unfold in the stark silence.

"Let's order pizza tonight, guys." Nate's eyes are stuck on Natalie's.

"Good plan." Natalie agrees sassily with her unintroduced acquaintance, crossing her arms.

"Have we ever ordered pizza, Chef?" Zeke cuts in, not understanding the exchange. No one does. Another silence. And then the collapse of all things good and holy. Because Nate fears no confrontation.

"Do you have any idea what the word 'salty' does to a restaurant? Or what it almost did to my job?" Nate is accosting Natalie as if she's a lifelong mortal enemy. Everyone stirs.

"I'd say your job found itself on the chopping block somewhere around 'inappropriately flirtatious kitchen staff.'" Natalie's eyebrow flicks. Like it used to when Seth would say the wrong thing or her little brother Neil would cross her.

Nate chuckles with sarcasm. "Oh, cute. 'Chopping block.' Chef wanted me to deliver my *perfectly* seasoned dish to the 'VIP' myself. Until now, it's received rave reviews. No flirting necessary, but you believe whatever you want if you're that desperate, honeybun."

"Desperate? Pretty sure: 'Go on and finish that bottle of wine, sexy. I'll give you a ride home.' Does not require desperation to translate." Natalie's voice raises, and internal laughter occurs throughout the room.

"I was trying to butter you up, tightwad!"

"Obviously. I left feeling like I'd taken a bath in butter."

Nate now points at the suddenly lively and opinionated Natalie. A woman, indeed. But Nate doesn't speak more than a grumble through his teeth before addressing Seth.

"Why did you let her in, Seth? Do you know who this is?"

"This is Natalie." Seth is calm, despite heated tempers.

"Natalie Nakano, I'm aware. Food writer for the most read and trusted restaurant review column in the region. But does she have to stand in our kitchen?!"

"She has her own kitchen in the guest house. But Natalie is welcome anywhere in my house, Nate. Just like you." Seth's words are still calm.

Nate's hand goes to his forehead. "Natalie. Your friend who my parents bought the house from. Wait, you rented the guest house to a girl?! *This* one? Do you realize your friend is a food critic? Like, the enemy of a chef."

"She mentioned something like that. She also plays piano." Seth is still unrealistically calm like he has uncommon knowledge in his heart.

The surprisingly un-rattled newcomer interjects, intrigued. "Piano?"

"I'm Natalie, in case you didn't hear." Natalie turns to Christian, then lights up. "Is that an acoustic?"

"Of course. Classical. Fits my voice. She and I make beautiful music together." Christian removes the guitar case from his back, balancing it between fine tile and calloused hands.

"I'd love to hear you play sometime." Natalie deliberately ignores the still fuming Nate.

"You too. I'm Christian, by the way. Name, profession, and life." The two shake hands in a smile.

I suppose it is only natural. A family isn't complete without a little music—and more than a little rivalry.

Chapter Eleven

THE CHAPEL

"It's that time again! Mother and father dearest have once again complained that their chef son hasn't made them a meal in eons. Is it alright if I have my family over this coming Thursday? I know it's chess night, but it's my only night off next week." Nate is consulting Seth in a Saturday morning laziness about the house. Seth is going over site inspection reports as he's talking to Nate, drawn from his office by the presence of Natalie.

"The girls, too? I bet Natalie will be relieved to have some female company."

"Laura is sixteen and the twins are twelve. They hardly count as female company. But my mom is coming. As long as Nat can keep her mouth shut for one evening about my cooking, I don't mind her being around." Nate looks the way of the piano.

Natalie and Christian are playing through some old hymn books on piano and guitar. Natalie, finding the task nearly robotic, has been listening to the conversation without difficulty.

"It's Natalie. A 'gnat' is a bug. I'm not."

"That's debatable," Nate says in a yawn.

"Children. Let's try to get along." This is from Christian, the youngest person in the house. "You know anything else, Natalie? I'm a fan of the old hymns, myself, but you look a little bored."

Christian Kessler. I know him now. He is the product of Jesus, a past veiled in mystery, and what happens to a soul when music flows through the veins. After high school, he was thrown into the world with a guitar to make something of himself—bright-eyed and perpetually smiling, with a voice like an angel. He is who he is, even when who he is irritates and plays guitar until three o'clock on a Monday morning. A streak or two of wild, and a few wilds yet unexplored, Christian is under the wings and in the hearts of all—like a little brother who has yet to find his way. Therefore, when he suggests a change from hymns, Natalie knows just what to do.

"Good call. Try to keep up, Sweetie." Natalie closes the hymnal and gives a half smile before lighting up the tone of the house and the piano with a proud and loud rock and roll complication at the keys.

Christian laughs and promptly does improvisations on his guitar, throwing some vocal licks in that bring the entire household into the formal living room for a listen. After the last chord, applause erupts.

Seth smiles and speaks.

"I've never heard you play like that, Natalie."

"I know!" Natalie is out of breath but laughing. "Gosh, my father would kill me if he heard that. I joined a jazz combo in college and never told my parents," she whispers, "The devil's music."

"That's crazy good, guys. This house has been too quiet without you two." Vargas is sitting on the arm of a couch nodding. "I'm sad I have to leave in six weeks."

"Awwww, Vargas!" Natalie whines and rises to embrace her recently forged bond. "I hate that you have to go!"

"I'll be back, Lord willing. I'm more worried about the state of Nate's abs once I leave him to himself." Vargas ends the embrace in time to punch Nate in the arm.

"I will keep it up and not disappoint my personal military trainer," Nate promises. "Otherwise, I'll pay for it when you get back."

"Hey, I didn't get a hug!" Christian has a well-known puppy crush on Natalie, who is obviously too much woman for him. So the embrace is like a sister's.

"Ain't never happening, Man," Zeke teases the teenager as always.

"Don't crush the kid's dreams, Zeke!" Teasing continues from Vargas, who then gasps, remembering to mention something. "Oh! *Mi mama* is coming into town when I ship out. Should I tell her to get a hotel, or you think we can find a place for her?"

"Don't be silly, Vargas. Seth's mom spared no luxury in furnishing the guest house. The pullout couch has a great mattress in it. *Tu mama* can stay with me." Even with Natalie's generous offer, it is not the subject that brings curiosity to the eyes of every man in the room. She notices. "What?"

"You knew Seth's parents?" This is from Nate, who normally has nothing nice or even neutral to say in Natalie's direction.

"Of course, I did." Natalie glances uncomfortably at Seth, smoothing that now straight hair over one shoulder. "They were like a second family to me since mine hates me."

Everyone takes a seat, all eyes and ears on Natalie, because Seth is a steel trap when it comes to his past, particularly his parents.

"I hear Randall Gowan was a genius businessman." Zeke begins, but Nate interrupts.

"No, I want to hear about Stacy's haunted room."

Natalie laughs and looks to Seth. "You told them it was haunted? That's what your mom used to tell us, even after we found out what was actually in there. What were we, nine?"

"What's in there?" Nate's eyes are filled with wonder. They all are. As if she's speaking to a room of kindergarteners.

"I've actually never set foot in there to this day. She sort of freaked out when we tried. But Stacy was an artist. It was her art room. All these beautiful paintings you see around the house are hers. One time Seth and Randall were hunting or something, so she took me into his woodshop and helped me do a painting for Seth's thirteenth birthday. It was atrocious, but he left it in his woodshop anyway so that every time I went in there—" The eruption of disbelieving exclamations overtakes Natalie's sentiments.

"You never let us in your woodshop!" Vargas accuses. "That's the room I always took for being haunted."

"I'm sorry, Seth. I guess didn't know I was breaching such taboo subjects."

"Everything is a taboo with Seth! You kidding?" Nate is the most interested and farthest into years of unknowns. "We mention women, his childhood, that fence, anything. And he shuts down. No one ever goes in his woodshop. He could be a flaming homosexual and has his parents' brains in jars in there for all we know. I'm his best friend, Nat. How do you know so much?"

“It’s Natalie.” She slides the correction edgewise among the marveling.

“I just thought we weren’t allowed in the woodshop. Like the guest house and the room upstairs.” Zeke admits.

Natalie’s eyes alight a moment when the guest house is mentioned, but she returns quickly to the present. “Well, did you ask? His woodshop is my favorite room in the house.”

“They’ve never asked,” Seth admits for his companions.

Natalie giggles. “Don’t they know all they have to be is persistent with you?” Then she rises and leads the flock of people to the hall that no one ever enters. It turns out to have a door at the end and then a hall of windows opposite a wall. Natalie backs up against the ornate double doors with her introduction.

“Seth’s parents bought this house from an older couple who had restored it to use for their wedding business. That’s why there’s a nice size lawn out back before the trees and why the kitchen is huge and why there are so many guest rooms. The bedroom Seth uses now, which was his parents’ room, used to be the bridal suite, for both a bride’s dressing room, and for the wedding night for the couple. The old owners lived in the guest house. They had the lawn for ceremonies and receptions, but since the weather is so unpredictable in Colorado, the couple knew that they would have an advantage over other venues if they built a chapel. None of you ever wondered why there are stained glass windows along this wing on the second story?” Natalie, a museum docent in another life, is amused at the attentively shaking heads of the men who surround her. “Well…it’s gorgeous in the morning.”

Natalie opens the door to my favorite place. Immediately, I go to the pillow designated for me and seek the toy I shouldn’t have left in here yesterday. It is ordinary to me—admittedly flowing with more Light than darkness, but I always attributed that to Seth. It’s a rustic little chapel, ceilings vaulting above the two open stories, with colorful windows that let the light stream through. They are praying hands, doves, floral vines. And at the front of the room, there is a large, rustic wooden cross with a rather dusty purple sash laying across it. Only half the chapel is filled with pews. The other half is, of course, overtaken by power tools, tables, and things made of wood and shelves filled with little wooden shapes of things. The atrocious painting is still on the wall since Seth's thirteenth birthday with a chair beneath it—Natalie's chair Seth built for her, where she would sit for hours as a child, watching Seth work. Natalie now touches it with a nostalgic smile.

"Randall and Stacy were the last couple to get married here before they were going to sell the place. Stacy fell in love with it on their wedding day. Randall wrote a check. That's how things went with them. But they were so in love and so down to Earth. They'd have been just as happy with nothing. They were when they were kids on neighboring farms." Seth and Natalie lock eyes a moment with memories of their own childhood together in this house—maybe with a spark of something that was, which only Vargas sees, but chooses not to mention.

Everyone is in awe at the brand-new but already ancient story. Vargas appreciates the house of God. Christian wonders at the acoustics, humming a little to invite them.

"Seth, you built all this?" Zeke admires the mastery of furniture, likely seeing dollar signs.

"And all your beds and dressers and mirrors. The desks in the offices. Everything wood in the house stopped here first as an ugly piece of nothing." Natalie shares, moving her bare feet across swept wooden floors.

On her. That's where Nate's eyes are.

"And they used to call him a retard." Nate tries to connect two pasts.

"Yeah, they did." Natalie looks up to see Nate has been staring.

"That's why you should always ask to see someone's woodshop before judging them." It's obvious she's not talking about Seth at all.

"Good advice." Nate deflates defensively.

Natalie rolls her eyes, leaving the room and concluding her history lesson, wounded by her adversary. The housemates depart to work in offices, write in guest houses, work out in attics, head to work in a restaurant, or play guitar upstairs. Seth hears a knock just before his office door opens an hour or two later.

Vargas obstructs the doorway, sweaty from working out and with some epiphany. "I narrowed it down to three options. You're either gay, celibate, or you and Natalie had a serious romantic relationship."

Seth narrows his eyes. "What makes you—?"

"All the pigs in this house are trying to calculate how far out of their league she is." Seth smiles at Vargas's accurate measure of Natalie's superiority to most. Then Vargas tilts his head. "Except you."

Seth smiles a little, then sighs frantically. "We were kids, and we agreed to keep it in the past. You can't—"

"So, she doesn't know you're still in love with her?"

Seth shuffles some paperwork. "It's irrelevant."

Vargas laughs his high-pitched laugh then comforts with a smile. "Secrets will go to the desert with me."

Seth nods. "Come in. Close the door."

Chapter Twelve

Sister's Keeper

"The baby grand!" Exclaims Laura Holm, her bright blue eyes lighting up over the wooden masterpiece of an instrument. "I'm so glad you still have it!"

"It was my mother's," Seth reminds her. "I will never get rid of it."

The Holm family files in the door. The twins remember the years of grooming and long hours of fetch and have brought a brush and ball for the purpose. Even as preteens, they giggle the same, and I enjoy them the same.

But Laura is different. She has breached that place I watched Natalie breach so long ago. Laura had always been serious and reserved. She always played the piano twice as beautifully as Natalie. It had been all that mattered to her. Now she does the same but with a woman's spark in her eye.

Nate had always shrugged off his younger twin sisters as annoyances. But Nate has been ruthlessly mean to Laura our entire acquaintance—snapping at her for breaking a rule or saying anything out of line and forbidding her to join Seth and Nate in whatever activity they undertook. For a time, I'd attributed this to the way Laura looked at Seth. Sort of the way Christian looks at Natalie. But Nate had voiced his indifference toward the crush early on, still treating Laura with fervent impatience.

As they arrive today, greetings seem to happen all at once and atop one another.

"Zeke, it's been far too long," Karen says with an outstretched hand after warmly hugging Seth.

"Yes ma'am. It's good to see you again."

"Ah, Derek. I want to thank you for your service to our country." This is from Nate's dad with a handshake. Nate rolls his eyes in jealousy.

Natalie arrives in the foyer, and Bill and Karen's eyebrows perk in unison for the stunning elegance she wears with even denim. Nate reluctantly supplies the introduction. "Mom, Dad, this is Natalie. She is the food critic that tried to ruin my life a couple weeks ago, and also the Natalie that lived in my room before me. She just moved into the guest house." Nate can put so much love and hate into a short amount of words.

"Ah. The guest house. I always thought it was a shame Seth wasn't using the place. He is such a good boy, that Seth. Making sure there is a separation between boys and girls." Karen means this as an endearment to Seth, a loving insult to her son, and small talk all at once. Vargas bites a smile and shakes his head at the information she obviously lacks.

"Where is the troubadour you spoke of, Nate? Is he around for us to meet?" Bill is looking about the entryway when an angelic humming trots down the stairs directly into it.

"The late Christian Kessler." Zeke laughs at his reference to Christian's deceased sense of time.

Warm meetings and greetings last only a moment longer before the hungry humans adjourn to the dining room. But I don't know how they miss the last introduction. The smell of it overtakes me, especially since they are teenagers. But there is also some nearly visible birth of a boundlessly pure light that no one else sees. The handshake is met with two awestruck faces. And a few words that fall well short of that boundlessness. I often wonder why people bother with speech at all.

"I'm Christian."

"Laura."

"Nice to meet you, Laura."

"Likewise, Christian."

I'm the only being to notice when Christian asks to borrow Nate's phone as he's plating appetizers, sending a number from it into his own, and when both teenagers mysteriously receive and send text messages throughout four courses. I even notice this amid various conversations at the long table, and despite Natalie's attempt at respectfully concealing sour faces while consuming the meal. It is even stronger than Nate silently savoring when Natalie instead conceals a smile over dessert, heavier than

Vargas's increasingly melancholy air, and louder than Zeke's financial nonsense with Bill. There are giggles and forks against plates and chaos. But I notice the smell of Christian much more.

The group finally adjourns to the formal living room with that bitter drink coffee. And though it is obvious to me, no one understands why or how Christian comes to the knowledge of the question he asks.

"Can I hear you play, Laura?"

"I better not. I haven't practiced today." She crinkles her nose. All who know her well know that the three hours yesterday make up for the lack of today.

"I just had it tuned," Seth encourages. Natalie smiles at Seth over this information. He'd had it tuned for her to practice on.

"Go on, sweetheart. It's the first thing you noticed when you walked in," Karen emboldens her daughter.

"You ever accompanied anyone?" Christian says this with some loving ease like family.

"I've done a lot of that. But I don't prefer to. Are you the Natalie they told me they hired to finally relieve me?" Laura looks to Natalie sweetly as she sits at the piano bench.

Natalie giggles. "Yes, ma'am. Small world."

"Why don't you like it?" Christian inquires of the soft-spoken young lady as he leans against the piano's curve.

"Well, I have to play quieter than I'm used to, and I don't always agree with the singer or conductor's musical interpretation, but I still have to follow them," Laura explains.

"She means she's too good for it." Shelley, half of the Holm twins, interprets. Humble Laura takes it as an insult.

"No, it's not about good. I'm just a pianist. Not an accompanist. It's hard to follow sometimes. What's on the page isn't the music, you know?"

"Ah, so accompanying holds you back as a musician. I see." Christian is eager to hear Laura play. Clears his throat. "*Ave Maria*? The Shubert. I'll follow *you*."

"That's a demanding piece," Laura warns and doesn't seem to understand what Christian is so obviously doing.

"I'm a demanding singer. Ready?" Christian flirts.

Laura is not amused or convinced. She just smiles and sets her fingertips on the keys. She begins, with ease, some elaborate introduction with waves and sweeping emotion. Then she stops and waits.

Christian is frozen, heart pounding. “I’ve never heard the intro like *that.*”

“I got bored one summer and modified an orchestral version. I can play the simple one if you want. I just thought you were following *me*.” Laura bats her eyes, challenging him in her gentle way.

Christian smiles at her final remark. “Here’s hoping.”

Dr. and Mrs. Holm assume their daughter is successfully warding off the advances of the smitten young man. But in a reality understood by those present who’ve heard Christian sing, she is an inch away from the hook. She plays the introduction again. And when Christian opens his mouth, she is snagged. A word and a half in, when he sweeps up to a tender note in “*Maria*,” Laura’s stable and skilled fingers fumble over themselves, and she stops playing.

The whole room is concealing laughter with red-faced effort. She clears her throat. “Sorry.”

“I thought you were a pianist. Can you handle this?” Christian teases.

Laura nods coyly.

“You sure?” Christian flirts.

“Yes! Last chance. We’re annoying the audience.” Laura giggles.

“I am extremely entertained.” Vargas allows. Everyone but the furious Nate is just as amused.

“Okay, Laura,” Christian determines. “Let’s make music.”

When the Holms leave after a few more impromptu performances, Christian is left waving on the porch with Nate and me. And when earshot is breached halfway to their house, Nate silences a mere squeak of Christian’s.

“Save it. Not happening.”

“What?” Christian pretends.

“Dude, stuff like that doesn’t get past me. I invented that stuff. She’s sixteen. And my sister. No.”

By now, the two have walked inside. “Almost seventeen. And I’m only eighteen. Completely legal and decent.”

"Well, maybe it's 'decent' for me to drop that piano on your head." I lead the two into the kitchen, where the others are already cleaning up.

"Beautiful *Ave Maria*, Christian. Did my heart good." Vargas compliments the singer.

"Thank you, Vargas. Glad someone appreciates my art." Christian glares at Nate.

Natalie chortles. "Art? Christian, you need to go take a cold shower. That was the most desperate peacock dance I've ever seen."

The others laugh appreciatively. Until Christian's phone chimes. And he checks a text with a smile. Clears his throat obnoxiously. "'I had a great time making music with you tonight, Christian. When can I see you again?' Ha! Laura must have a thing for feathers." He is

sending another text.

"You're dead if you touch my little sister. I'm not kidding." Nate's temper is rising.

"Relax, Nate. I don't even do what you think I want to do. Jesus freak, remember? Your sister is r*efined.* I'd be an idiot to go after her for immoral purposes. But she's amazing. Beautiful, too. Did you think no one would ever notice?" Relief floods the kitchen when Nate simmers a little, only resorting to a playful slap on the back of Christian's head, sending his wild hair flying until he smooths it.

Nate leans against the counter next to where Natalie is drying the pots Seth is handing her.

"Can I help you, Nathan?" She doesn't even look at him. She knows he's asking what he always asks.

"You liked my tiramisu." He's caught her.

"Mussels were overcooked. Calamari was salty. Fried zucchini was greasy. Well-plated, though. Never seen it done that way." She still need not look at him.

Nate laughs in mild offense. Natalie continues as she hands Vargas a dry pot to put away.

"The salad dressing was the bottle you brought home from *Le Cloture.* I saw it in your fridge. You cheated."

"I made that batch myself at work." Nate is telling the truth.

"Still doesn't justify the overly spicy marinara. Chicken parmesan usually demands a bit more acid. The chicken was dry, too." Natalie is smiling at Nate's shaking head.

"You are impossible! I was the greatest thing around until you came and ruined my meals for everyone. My mother loved my chicken parm. Even my dad, who is impossible to please. At least admit that you *flipped* for my tiramisu. I watched you." Nate has turned to Natalie, who turns and looks up at him.

The awkward silence is only avoided by running water and the simulated tap of Christian texting. The dinner critique is earning the listening ears of even me. Because something smells funny. Natalie finally speaks.

"Tiramisu was perfect. But you're still a conceited pig." Natalie takes the next pot from Seth.

Nate laughs. "Yes! I pleased the unpleasable!"

"Just my tired palate, Nate," Natalie says harshly, getting under Nate's skin yet again, enough for him to leave the room.

Vargas clears his throat in Seth's direction. But everyone looks at him to inquire. It is while they are both looking away that Seth nonchalantly soaks Natalie's shirt with the sink sprayer. She screams, then giggles as she reciprocates with a flick of her hands. My attention shifts to Vargas whispering to Zeke, who is wiping counters meticulously.

"I'd get a bid in while you still can." A half-joke from the soldier.

"I already have the upper hand," Zeke says under his breath.

Just as an exhausting evening is wearing down, I feel something go dim. The doorbell rings and everyone looks around. Nate reenters the kitchen, accosting Christian.

"That better not be my sister."

"No, she just told me she's about to go practice piano before bed." Christian reveals from his text conversation.

All the housemates suddenly place their index fingers on their noses to decide who will get the door. Seth was washing pots and missed the exchange. He sighs, and dries his hands before I follow him through the dining room and game room and living room to the foyer. He opens the door, lighting up the dusked porch. Seth startles.

"See Dad? I just heard Natalie laugh. I told you we'd find her here." It's a young voice from a boy of Natalie's complexion. And a man, fully Japanese.

"Mr. Nakano. Neil. Hello." Seth is terrified of these faces from his past.

"Where is she?" The man responds, entering the house. I'm growling as much as Seth will allow. Seth does not allow a lot of growling from me. He instead steps in front of Mr. Nakano and speaks firmly with his own sort of growl.

"Natalie came here for a fresh start. She'd like to keep the past in the past. Please give her that respect."

"For your sake or hers?" The Japanese accent rings clearly.

"Both, sir. But you can only see her if you don't tell the others. This is my house, after all." Seth's heart is pounding.

"Very well." Seth is relieved at the man's concession.

When Mr. Nakano enters the kitchen, it is clear his presence is more commanding than even Zeke's, and sets Natalie's lovely smile to a gasp.

"Papa. What—how did you find me?" At her panicked words, all the housemates are at the ready. She is now dabbing her slightly wet shirt with a towel.

Her dad had been surveying the room in disgust. "You ran off in the middle of the night to come live in a frat house?"

"No! It's not like that at all. I don't even live in the main house. I was invited to dinner." Natalie is trying to explain everything all at once.

"You expect me to believe you didn't run straight back to—" Mr. Nakano heeds the throat clear of Seth and does a right angle. "There were plenty of job opportunities back home with better pay, yet you ran off. Your mother is devastated. I'll help you get your things. Let's go."

"How old are you, Natalie?" Zeke is the first to speak up.

"Twenty-one." Natalie mumbles, drying her hands in shame.

"Twenty-one, and you come pick her up like she's some schoolgirl?" Vargas puffs his meager chest valiantly.

"Guys, stop it. God called me here, Papa. I had to listen." Natalie tries, her tone terrified.

"When will you stop using God as an excuse?" Natalie's father asks.

"When you stop using Him as a weapon." Natalie finds some strength.

"Last warning. Get your things."

"The lady said she wants to be here," Zeke reiterates.

"She belongs at home with us," Neil demands with conviction.

"What are you, like four?" Nate asks the boy, using his flippant sort of charm to pipe in unexpectedly. He's approaching the tussle with thumbs hooked in pockets like the tension doesn't exist at all.

"Eleven," Neil mumbles.

"I can't stand kids," Nate confesses. "They think they know everything when all they really know is what their parents tell them. What confuses me, 'Papa,' is why you'd raise Natalie with class and then automatically assume she forgot all that just because she's in a room full of guys. This girl drives me crazy. I can't stand her half the time. But she is absolutely classy. Impeccable taste in food too. So, she's not leaving."

"Uh, yeah, she is." Neil tries to stand up to Nate. "She's not living in a guest house next to a bunch of dudes. She's not a party girl."

"You don't know your sister, little kid. I mean look at her now, a glass of white zin and she's doing dishes like some wild woman. You should have given her more warning so you didn't catch the lady in such a crude state."

Reluctantly, Natalie joins in the laughter at Nate's sarcasm.

"What Nate is trying to say is that you know your sister is a good Christian girl. Trust her heart." Christian finally addresses Neil, but reasons with Nate, tying in exactly what he'd hoped to. Nate shakes his head at the texting teen in a smile.

"She'll be safe here, Mr. Nakano. We'll take care of her and honor her God's way." Seth's words. Apparently, the words that matter. Mr. Nakano and Neil retreat to the entryway. Natalie follows. I'm the only one permitted to go and keep her safe.

"This is what you want? Not just rebellion?" Mr. Nakano confirms.

"I want this. I love this. I love you too, but God closed every door but this one." Natalie nods.

Her father takes out his wallet. "Let me at least pay a couple months' rent."

Natalie lowers her voice significantly. "Seth doesn't charge me rent, Papa. He says he has a debt to repay. He insisted."

"No rent? Are you sure you two aren't—" Neil asks in shock.

"Neil! No! That was a long time ago. These guys—I trust them. They really are gentlemen."

"Nonsense," says wise Mr. Nakano, cradling his daughter's cheek. "They are men, but none of them are gentle. Seth is still in love with you. The blond one likes you. The black one wants to win you, and the boy with the phone likes looking at you. Other than the brown one cheering them all on, you have yourself in a cozy little scrape, my dear one. Just make it God's choice."

"And if that's Seth?" Natalie challenges.

"Then don't bother coming home for Christmas." Her father's last words before a slammed door. Natalie is stunned a few seconds, mindlessly scratching the head I offer beneath her hand. Then she passes through the kitchen to bid the boys goodnight.

"I meant to tell you, Nate. I'd have paired a chianti with chicken parm." She's really telling him *thank you*.

Nate chuckles. "Well, for your preferred acidic sauce, yeah. But not for my spicier one." In other words, *you're welcome*.

"I thought I had 'impeccable taste.'" Natalie hips her hands.

"Well, let's just say a recent poll after *Le Cloture's* review revealed that my salmon is a little salty. Who knew, huh? We modified the recipe," Nate says, but breathes in time to allow too much flattery for his arch-rival. "But your wine pairings—you just haven't been drinking long enough, Pollyanna. You could use training."

"I take that as a compliment. Seems you're content with being a drunken bonehead." A crooked smile.

"Awe, was that a pet name?" Nate humorously puts his hand to his heart.

"No offense to Willow, but I suppose every dog needs a name."

Nate tilts his head in some sort of appreciative smile and chuckles once. Natalie beats him at his own game, as usual.

She smirks in triumph. "Night, guys."

"Night!" Even Christian looks up from his phone for the sake of Natalie.

"Dude! Stop giving my sister texting thumbs so she can still play piano by morning." Nate scolds. Natalie giggles at the boys as the door shuts behind her. And I watch her walk solemnly to her home through the darkness, contemplating her father's words in her heart. Nate watches too, to the amusement of the rest of them.

"She says dog. I say peacock. Nate has a crush." Christian singsongs, finally pocketing his phone.

Nate snickers at the door, still watching her walk. "Christian, women are like roses. I'm not sure exactly how experienced you are with 'roses,' but let me educate you. The more beautiful the rose, the more thorns it has, as a means of torturing the male of our species. So, considering Natalie looks like *that* and the fact that she's already proven her ability to make me want to shoot myself by being impossible and turning around everything I say, I'm not about to purchase that particular floral delicacy. Some poor idiot, who she'd probably trick into marrying her before he actually got his hands on her, would end up doomed to a life of sore, bleeding hands. While Nat, excuse me, 'Natalie' provides quite the view, what you see is *not* what you get."

Nate returns to the kitchen once Natalie reaches her door.

"I see. So too sophisticated for a 'drunken bonehead.'" Vargas speculates with cruel mockery.

"What?" Nate takes offense, and whines like a resentful child. "I'm sophisticated…"

Zeke chuckles. "All I know is I like her. She's easy on the eyes, and she gets to you. I've never seen you give a rat's behind what anyone thinks."

Nate rolls his eyes. "Zeke, she's a food critic. I'm a chef. Half my job is to care what she thinks."

The other men immediately laugh and shake their heads at the shoddy reasoning.

"Despite potential thorns," Christian sighs, changing the subject, "I'm totally marrying your sister and having five kids with her."

"Do you have a death wish?" Nate growls at the boldness.

"You're right. Six kids. We'll name them all 'Nate.'" Christian laughs.

"You met her four hours ago." Zeke whines.

"I *died* four hours ago." Christian, the romantic minstrel of a young man, lies on the bench in the back of the booth in the breakfast nook, taking on a Shakespearean accent. "Ah, Laura. Such a lovely murderess."

"Where did you come from?" Vargas and the others dote on his dramatic flair.

But Christian's next words are oddly said with complete sincerity in a stare at the ceiling. "You could ask me that desperately a thousand times, but you'd never *really* want to know."

"That's about all I can take. Goodnight, guys." Zeke retires.

"Ditto." Vargas follows suit.

"Don't touch my sister." This is Nate's goodnight, already headed to the back staircase.

"Chill your face. I'm not a dog like you." Christian grunts, rising from his spot and meeting Seth eye to eye for the first time ever.

Seth's eyes narrow, and then break the gaze for the floor with a sort of remorse. Then he breathes a couple times. Then he meets Christian's mysterious eyes again with a proud smile and a chest deep chuckle like his father used to make when filling another room with Seth's furniture. All these reactions seem like the introduction, the devastating climax, and then beautiful conclusion to a story no one was telling aloud.

It is something he's done before when coming to understand someone. Something that has caused others to retreat, feeling uneasy, saying something offensive. But it's something that Christian seems to appreciate with the innocence of his smile.

"Thanks for letting me live here, Seth. It's been God's greatest move in my life so far."

"Glad to have you, Christian. But God has barely started." Seth chuckles. "Goodnight. Lock up, please. S'go Willow."

Chapter Thirteen

Step One

I'd been specifically and honorably requested, with much effort. So, I stand on a leash on something called a tarmac. Christian and Laura are hand in hand. Natalie is sniffling. And a short, fat woman with Vargas's features is weeping. And all the other men are pretending they are not already missing Derek Vargas.

The pleasant September evening on the deck is emptier without the spirited truths of Vargas. Still, things become entertaining when Nate emerges from the back door with snacks to find Laura upon Christian's lap "learning guitar." His arms are wrapped around both her and the instrument until Nate threatens to remove those arms. This is just one such recent incident, as Laura now accompanies Seth, Natalie, and Christian to church on Sundays. In fact, Laura is here whenever Christian is—all to the utter disgust of Nate.

Natalie and Laura bond, discussing piano this evening. Laura compliments Natalie's ability to surrender her talent to the interpretation of another as an accompanist. Natalie compliments Laura's ability to play "Liszt" on a whim, whatever that means. The men listen to the bonding but are far more amused when Zeke chooses the first evening without the prying eyes of Vargas to request a date with Natalie.

Zeke is kind, honest, and wise—strong and handsome, too. So maybe Natalie lacks the perception of these things. Or maybe she is offended that Zeke throws around ideas about his fortune or the color of skin they sort of share. Either way, though flattered, she politely declines that date. Once Christian walks Laura home, and Natalie heads to her house, Nate and Seth take on Vargas's job of loving ridicule.

"Amateur." Nate scolds Zeke, shaking his head. "The race card? That's the best you could do?"

"You win some, you lose some." Zeke seems unoffended at the rejection.

"Natalie seems like a tough sell, for sure. But you could have done better than that," Nate teaches.

"I wouldn't be talking, Nate," Zeke says with high-pitched attitude. "This is Natalie. You'd be lucky to get her to put down that ten-foot pole she has when she's in the room with you. At least she's *nice* to me."

"Zeke, we've been over this. If I wanted her, I'd have her." Nate mumbles as he fiddles with his wine glass. Seth accidentally chuckles. Nate crosses his arms in annoyance. "Something funny?"

"Not at all." Seth smiles knowingly, refraining from participating in calculating his chances with Natalie. Missing Derek Vargas indeed.

Christian returns to the back deck after walking Laura home and sits back with some content sigh, taking in the breeze like lifeblood. Nate's blood reaches boiling point immediately.

"What's *your* deal?" He asks harshly.

Christian clears his throat. "I love her." He sighs. "I feel crazy and at peace all at the same time. It's completely wild. There's no way I'm not marrying her."

"You serious, Man?" Zeke had been smiling until he sees the sincerity in Christian's face and the anger in Nate's.

"She's sixteen," Nate says gruffly.

"Actually, she just turned seventeen. I took her out for her birthday, and you almost gutted me, remember?" Christian retorts. "Nate, I love her. Love is looking out for the best interests of someone else and laying down your life, in any way possible, for the good of another person. I don't know why you think I'm doing anything but that."

"Because you're an eighteen-year-old kid. Eighteen-year-old guys think about the best interests of their girlfriends only when their girlfriend decides that could involve sex at some point," Nate reasons. "If you haven't already, you will. And then things won't work out, and she will be heartbroken. That's 'love' to someone your age."

"In other words," Christian finds interest in Nate's reasoning. "You've never actually been in love."

"Love is pain. Why would I want pain? That's generally something I avoid." Nate rolls his eyes and walks inside, leaving the other men to think about what none of them are willing to mention.

Nate prepares a traditional Thanksgiving meal—the kind that begins as some sort of naked bird, taunts the senses all day long, and draws in all family and friends to the same table. They even spend some time with Vargas on a big screen, watching him someplace far away. The Holm family is present for the feast but heads home after the sun goes down, minus Laura, of course. The house is quiet when Natalie goes to her house to pack for a month-long trip to see her parents, and Zeke works in his office. It is only Seth and Nate in the window room, Seth removing bows from my fur that were placed by the Holm twins.

"Do you think Nat liked the meal?"

"She told you the parts she liked and didn't like. But she doesn't like to be called Nat. She tells you that, too." Seth yawns.

"Yeah. She's pretty honest, huh? She always been that way?" Nate's line of questioning is a loopy one, but not born of wine or fatigue.

"Yes." Seth removes the last bow and sits up in his favorite chair.

"She's pretty picky. You think she's ever dated anyone?" Nate seems like his mind is someplace far away.

"Yes." I think Nate likes asking questions more than he likes hearing answers, to Seth's relief in this case.

"I know she's your friend, and none of us want to upset the balance of things around her. So is she off-limits or what?"

"Natalie sets her own limits." Seth seems to be allowing the conversation to take a terrible turn.

"She turned down Zeke, meaning she doesn't care about everything he can offer. So I have no idea what she's looking for."

"You like her." Seth smiles, teasing his friend.

Nate chuckles. "Definite possibility."

"But you said love is pain."

"Yeah, but some roses are worth their thorns. You know?"

"She's a virtuous woman, Nate. No, she doesn't want kids, but she does believe in marriage. And abstinence, too, just like me. She's soft on the inside, even if you just see 'thorns.'" Seth speaks openly.

"Stuff to consider, I guess. You know I haven't been with anyone since that Maddie incident? It rocked me, you know? I'm just not sure what I want anymore. I'm actually terrified. Because I think I might want Natalie." Nate chuckles. Seth dies a little. And then Nate's ears perk like mine, and he sits up straight. Like he's heard something—or hasn't.

"Something wrong?" Seth notices.

"Have you seen Christian or my sister recently?"

After a short canvas of the main level does not turn up the two young people, the three of us sneak up the stairs. We cross from Nate's room to Zeke's. Empty. Vargas is absent. But there are muffled voices and laughter emitting from Christian's room. I can smell Nate's breath change when his heart enters his mouth.

"What do I do?" Nate whispers to Seth, who shrugs. "That's my sister. I will *kill* him. Does he know that?"

All at once, Nate lunges and opens the door. The scene infuriates him with ease. Two teenagers are seated on the edge of Christian's twin bed, lips locked far too hopelessly to have completely separated for the sudden breach of the door. Laura gasps, and Christian begins making some feeble attempt at using his hoodie sleeve to rid his mouth of Laura's lipstick.

Nate explodes. "What the heck are you doing with my sister in your room?! Laura, come on. You know better."

"Nate, I'm sorry. You're right. We were just—" Laura tries to explain, her heart in full rhythm.

"Just what? Becoming a statistic?" Nate grabs Laura's wrist and pulls her to a stand from the bed. "He can ruin your life in ten minutes you could have been just as happy playing piano."

"Nathan, calm down," Laura tries again.

"Calm down? Tell me why I shouldn't kill him!" Nate fans his fury.

"Nate. Come on, Dude. This is not at all what you think, okay? You just have extremely crappy timing." Christian finally defends, laughing at some irony.

"Who cares about timing? You know Seth doesn't allow this. Heck, I haven't broken this rule in eons." Nate demands.

Christian explains with defensively raised hands. "I got Seth's permission. And your parents' permission. Privacy is hard to come by on Plaid Row. This was the only place I could take her since it's so cold out."

"Privacy for what?" Nate desperately seeks answers, even in the hateful tone.

"So he could propose to me," says Laura timidly. She brings one of her tiny but strong hands into view with a dainty little diamond that reminds me of her. "You walked in on my answer."

The two exchange a loving smile. Seth smiles too, from our corner of the hall.

"Propose *marriage*? You're seventeen, Laura. Are you pregnant?" Nate is reddening.

"Why would it be more acceptable for us to atone for sin than it is for us to just honor God in the first place?" Laura is hurt. Probably by more than her brother.

Nate sighs. "You two have a lot of life to live before you should think about getting married. You barely know who you are as people. How can you give all that up for another person?" Nate pleads.

"Maybe I need her in order to know who I am. And maybe she needs me. God knows what He's doing." Christian stands, hands on hips, and becomes much more than just a wandering minstrel. "Self-discovery is kind of boring alone."

"So you're using my sister for 'self-discovery'?" Nate asks with cruelty.

"No, I'm *marrying* her. Right after she graduates. We didn't expect you to understand. But not biting my head off the next time I kiss her is a valid request, I think." Christian stands his ground, taking the hand of his bride-to-be.

Nate chuckles bitterly, as he always does when the two teens dream together of marriage and a family someday. "Did he con you into this?"

"With love and honesty?" Laura says in offended sarcasm. "Sure, Nate. Yeah. You know how reckless I tend to be when it comes to crafty men like *you*."

"Just don't bring her in here again." Nate is disarmed, and his concession feeble.

"Nate, I respect you. And Seth. And your parents. And especially Laura. This was a onetime thing—I mean until—well, Seth said Laura could move in after—" Christian winces.

"You're gonna sleep with my little sister across the hall from me." Nate turns his back, shaking his head at the ceiling. "Unbelievable."

Christian pleads. "When she's my wife, yes. Not until then, and only until we figure things out and get on our feet. The alternative would be little sisters with boundary issues and your dad staring me down constantly."

Nate sighs, thinking them ignorant. "Usually, step one is getting on your feet, and step two is the other stuff like the joke that is marriage."

"No…" Christian looks to the beaming Laura again, squeezing her hand. "I want to take step one *with* Laura."

We spend Christmas with the same pair of 'children' at the Holm household. Zeke travels to Michigan to be with his mother. Natalie is in South Carolina. And Christmas night, when the three housemates arrive home, without Laura this time, Nate lies on the couch in a contemplative quiet he's taken on over the past few weeks, even after voicing his reluctant acceptance of the impending nuptials.

Christian finally seeks the translation. "What is with you recently?"

"If you must know: I can't get her out of my head," Nate admits, comfortable enough in present company to allow some vulnerability. "That's what's 'with me.'"

Christian laughs. "Who, Natalie? You're grasping at the wind, Dude. That's never happening."

"Let me remind you that I'm allowing you to marry my teenage sister." Nate blinks slowly. "'Never' shouldn't be something you accept. But since I'm aware of how Natalie feels about me, I'm kind of a disaster. So, some understanding would be appreciated."

"I totally understand." Christian smiles at Seth about Nate. "You feel insane and at peace at the same time." Nate sits up and snaps, pointing at Christian, then realizes what he just said as he lies back again.

"This sucks. Bad." Nate's heart, all out of rhythm and reason, is the loudest thing in the room until Christian speaks.

Christian is always willing to encourage and reconcile. "You know, Laura has been texting with Natalie the whole time she's been gone. Today Laura told me that Natalie hated her Christmas dinner and wished she could have been here."

"Whatever. She hates my cooking." Nate smiles a little.

"Just like you hate Laura." Seth speaks some wisdom that Christian considers in his heart.

Nate knows exactly what Seth means, but changes the subject instead of mentioning the obvious.

"Hey, I've been thinking. Since it has been decided that marriage trumps the 'no girls' rule, you and Laura can have my room after the wedding. It's way bigger and has a big bathroom attached. She'll be the only girl in the main house, and I think she'd appreciate a little more privacy. That sound okay, Seth?"

"That's fine." Seth concedes easily.

"Wow, Nate." Christian laughs. "Privacy? I recall you going ape crazy about the arrangement a few weeks ago. Now you want to give her *more* privacy with me?"

"She's my sister. Contrary to what she believes, I do *not* hate her, and I want her to be comfortable. Well, as much as she can be having to share a room with you and your midnight guitar playing." Nate chuckles.

"I want you to be my best man, Nate." Christian blurts.

"Why?" Nate snickers.

"Among other things? I was sleeping in my car, and you took me in and treated me like a brother. I already asked Seth and Zeke to be groomsmen. But I want you to stand next to me when I marry Laura." Christian sighs.

Nate laughs. "Is the maid of honor that friend of Laura's? Erica or whatever? The one that had the crush on me? That might be a bit awkward to escort her. I don't know if I can—"

"Erica and all Laura's other friends from her 'Christian' school conspired and ousted her when we got engaged. They used to say how great we were together and how cute our kids would be. But now, suddenly, she's 'ruining her life.' Oh, or being 'immature,' as if Laura is capable of that. Laura is fresh out of besties." Christian reveals with a frustrated sigh. "Anyway. Seth and Zeke get to escort the twins. And you'll be escorting Natalie."

"In that case? I'm in."

Chapter Fourteen

FICKLE

The falling snow makes for brutal fence building weather, but it has never stopped Seth in years before. He sniffles his nose to red when everyone is still sleeping on New Year's Day. He wears a heavy coat and gloves, building his ridiculous fence in the woods. He's had to clear trees these past few years, making the process he thought he might shorten remain at "twelve years total." But he's using the trees to make the posts and other furniture—not wasting a thing except time, in my opinion. The only thing he needs to keep in wouldn't leave him for a million rawhide mansions.

He's concentrating, but I know he still hears the crunch of snow beneath her boots. She sits on a stump. "Happy New Year, Seth."

"How was your Christmas, Natalie?"

"I hate my parents, and my bratty brother is doing the puberty thing. But the birth of our Savior never gets old, so I had a good time." She laughs once. "Still working on this thing, huh? You know, I bet if you worked all day, it'd be done in a weekend or two. Instead of an hour at a time for how much longer?"

"Six years, five months." Seth answers. "Patience goes a long way. Dad always used to say that."

"I remember. Seth?" Natalie begins to say what she came to say. "Is it over between us?"

Seth scrunches his eyebrows; a life without Natalie not an option anymore. "I'm not sure what you're asking."

"I'm asking if you think that God wants us together, like a couple. You and me." Natalie explains. "Because when I was in South Carolina for five years, I grew in ways I probably couldn't have if I'd been here. It's weird, but even though it took a lot of pain to get there, I felt like I was right where God wanted me. Just like when I had to run away to come back. I wasn't being rebellious. I was following a path God paved. When you aren't where God wants you, you can feel it, you know? There's chaos that disobedience causes, even if something seems righteous logically. But when you're within His will, there's this peace…" Natalie has to stop and think a moment.

"You feel at peace now that you're here. But when you think about being with me—" Seth starts.

"It's chaos," Natalie finishes. "Maybe I just have some emotional link to the way it felt when we sinned or the way we treated each other afterward. Or to giving up—" Natalie's eyes wrinkle in severe pain. and she chooses not to continue that line of reasoning. "Maybe that's it."

Seth nods, concealing the severity of his pain somewhere deep I haven't found yet. "Maybe." He staples a picket.

"But doesn't that sound crazy? I love you, Seth. I need you in my life. I had a gaping hole in my heart without you that filled in the second I heard your voice on the phone. But for some reason after coming all this way, dead set on rekindling what we had before—" Natalie sighs. Whispers. "Why is there chaos?"

There is a silence Natalie knows better than to interrupt as Seth's wisdom gathers—a wisdom she now recognizes grew exponentially with time and pain and life. Something she can trust to have come from a worthy Source. Finally, he speaks.

"My mom used to say you were fickle. She loved you, but she didn't know how trustworthy you were because of how easily you'd change your mind." Seth says, not even pausing in his fence efforts as he looks up to smile at Natalie.

"Considering I went from being obsessed with abstinence to getting pregnant at sixteen, I kind of was fickle." She laughs bitterly at the way she was before time and pain and life overtook her too.

"You still are. Except now since you've learned to trust God for your decisions and the direction of your life, 'fickle' just means you'll move with God when He moves. But since you're somehow also stubborn, you'll be steadfast in God's direction until He moves again. Natalie, that's admirable." Seth looks up with his deep-set, sad eyes at Natalie and the way she takes in all he says.

"So, you understand then, why I don't think we can be together?" Natalie says into those eyes.

"I do." Seth nods. "My fence isn't done."

"What?" Natalie laughs a little in confusion, still not understanding Seth completely.

Seth says it in English, "Despite how I might feel, Natalie, God's plan is unavoidable." Seth staples another picket. "I have chaos, too."

Natalie sighs in relief. "So, tell me what you think God's will is."

Seth doesn't miss a beat or prepare Natalie for what is about to be spoken into her life.

"This time next year, you will have kissed your brand-new husband at midnight for the New Year. I won't even be there when you get married. But God will bless that marriage. He'll use it for some wonderful works." Seth smiles in the distance like he does when he sees a doe on our property. But today, there is no such scent on the wind.

"Seth." Natalie chuckles. "That is extremely specific."

"I know." Seth staples his last picket and carefully piles the materials into the cart he's built to store them on site. He covers it with the tarp he modified for the purpose. And then he begins to walk back up to the house through the woods.

"A year? That seems pretty close to, you know, now. I'm not even involved with anyone." Natalie follows, dumbfounded. "Who would I marry if not you?"

Seth chuckles, like Natalie's desperation had been a joke. "Stop fighting the way you feel when you already know what you're supposed to do."

"But what I feel makes no logical sense in this case. It's not even—it's impossible, okay? Even if it was somehow attainable, it certainly wouldn't bring peace." Natalie sighs, convicted. "And since when are you a prophet of God?"

"God's peace doesn't always come through the easiest or most predictable path, and neither does wisdom." Seth has never mentioned this to me, but he is delighted to share it with Natalie and her blank stare.

"So, you're saying you know things? Impossible things." Natalie is fascinated.

"'For with God, nothing shall be impossible.'" Seth quotes Scripture, and Natalie believes him completely.

Seth stops walking a moment at the edge of the woods, leans forward, and kisses Natalie. It's something sweet and beautiful—with a history, but with an innocence.

"What was that for?" Natalie is enchanted.

"That is the last time I can do that with a clear conscience. I prefer a clear conscience. Happy New Year." Seth replies, then lets Natalie take his arm as a guide to the house.

"Ah! The prodigal food critic returns!" Nate lights up when we all enter the back door. "Want some coffee?"

"I'm not sure you've learned how to make a proper cup of coffee yet, Nate." Natalie sits at the breakfast bar.

"You're impossible, Nat." Nate chuckles.

"Not a bug." She singsongs, receiving a "satisfactory" cup of coffee and an "ordinary" plate of French toast from Nate.

A gasp comes from somewhere in the window room. I growl until I realize that Laura is rising from under a blanket on the couch.

"Oh my gosh! It's light outside. Mom and Dad are—"

"Completely aware that you fell asleep on the couch at four in the morning with all of us present. The New Year's chess tournament got wild last night." Nate calms his sister.

"Oh, who won?" Natalie asks, smiling at Seth. Laughter is the only response.

"Where's Christian?" Laura asks, stretching and joining her already plated meal at the counter. Nate winks at his sister just before she is startled by a kiss on her cheek from Christian.

"Morning, Sunshine. Didn't think you'd still be here." He coos, then steals another proper kiss hello.

"Me neither," Laura responds. Nate walks back down the counter to avoid disgust.

"What's your day look like, Nat—alie?" He asks with a sly smile.

"Why?" Natalie wonders, always catching the hint of charm in the act.

"Just wondering. I'm off today, and I just need to know how many mouths I'm feeding if I feel like cooking." Not a hint of truth.

Natalie, and all the others, hear it in Nate's tone. But she obliges anyway.

"I have reservations at Donato's at six and a review due at nine in the morning tomorrow. I thought it was unreasonable to go on a holiday, but some readers wanted to know how the current number one restaurant does under pressure. Before that, I need to practice the show choir music for this quarter, so I'll sort of be around, but not for dinner." This causes Natalie a yawn and Nate a glance at the clock. Nate slips out of the kitchen as Laura lights up.

"Is Miss Berry finally doing that Gershwin medley? I'd be so mad if she waited until after I graduated."

"It's in my packet. Not sure I'm too fond of the arrangement, though." Natalie is wondering where Nate ran off to in the middle of a conversation. Zeke enters where Nate left and greets everyone.

Then Nate reenters, setting his cell phone on the counter with a sigh. He serves Christian and Zeke, then stands in front of Natalie again with a smile that makes everyone wonder if he's up to something.

"What?" Natalie wonders only at the flutter of her heart when misty blue eyes search her coffee-colored ones.

"The Nakano reservation at Donato's just mysteriously changed to a table for two. Weird."

Natalie gasps. "Nate! That's my *job*! You can't just sabotage it like that! I know you think that was my goal with that first review, but I didn't even know you then. Maybe you hate me, but be decent enough not to—"

"Relax, no sabotage. Food critics bring dates all the time. What would really be unprofessional is calling and changing it *again*." Nate smiles.

"Who says I want to go on a date with you?" Natalie puts up her transparent guard around what I know is sweet and tender.

"I just want to listen to you criticize someone *else's* craft for once. I'm actually very much looking forward to it." Nate, oddly, lets his guard down, which softens Natalie a little.

"Okay, you can come, but you have to behave while you satisfy your morbid curiosity with my job. Did chef ask you to spy, or—?" Natalie rolls her eyes.

"What? No! Who said I was curious about your job? I said I wanted to listen to *you*. The rest is a clever ruse to go out with you. This is a wooing situation, not a spy tactic." Nate is honest, seasoned with charm. The others are holding in laughter, and Natalie isn't fooled.

"In that case, I'm wearing an ill-fitting pants suit, and I'm driving. And so that you don't get the wrong idea and try anything more akin to your nature, we won't put that pesky 'date' label on it." She concedes only with adamant terms to the snickers of all.

Then they prepare for the fact that Nate hasn't agreed to anything or backed down. Nor has Natalie had to ward off Nate's form of skilled battle tactics, though she'd been warned.

Nate clicks his tongue and leans onto his elbows, his face twelve inches from hers. "No, it's a date. Which means *I'm* driving. You're wearing something you'd describe as pretty and modest, but I will likely find unbearably sexy. And when we get home, I'm gonna give you a kiss—on the cheek. Because you're too classy for anything else on a first date." The immense and wildly unexpected flattery catches every one of us off guard.

"Are you sufficiently wooed? Do we have a date?" Nate coos into that same space, smiling at the way it feels to have finally bested Natalie into speechlessness.

"Um…" Natalie clears her throat. "Sure, Nate."

Seth asks a question only his condition would allow in just the right place to break the tension. "What size do you wear? Shoes too."

"Seth!" Natalie whispers. Used to correcting his awkwardness. "You can't ask a girl that."

"I'd say six, maybe eight if she wants a roomier fit. Eight for shoes, definitely." Nate knows the female anatomy all too well and winks as he turns with finesse to wipe the counters.

"Perfect. Come with me. Laura, you too." Seth rises and leads Natalie to his room. Laura and I follow enthusiastically. He leads them to the closet and clicks on the light. Both women gasp. Seth, I can tell, is happy that his mother's expensive and lovely taste in evening wear will not be forgotten tonight. "Help yourselves. Take as much as you want. You're smaller, Laura. Mom was smaller before she had me."

Natalie whispers, grabbing Seth's wrist as he tries to leave. "You knew about this, didn't you?"

"Nate likes dark blue," Seth smirks, gently loosing his wrist.

"Then I'm wearing red." Natalie hips her hands defiantly.

"I don't think that would help." Seth finally escapes when Laura gasps at a pair of shoes she tries on.

The giggles and shopping begin. I'm female but prefer not to indulge in this. I follow Seth back to the kitchen, where Nate is laughing in a release of nerves.

"See, Zeke? That's how it's done." Nate says quietly in case the girls emerge. "You appeal to *her*. Not her race, dipstick. Stuff she likes about herself. Not stuff she can't control."

Zeke chuckles. "Only a man that's already in love would think it through that far."

Nate shushes Zeke violently and makes sure the girls aren't coming back.

"They'll be in there a while. Mom had lots of clothes." Seth reassures, not even blinking at Nate's panic.

"Is that true, Nate? I was under the impression that you hated her." Christian teases.

"Hate. Love. You can't really have one without the other if you think about it." Nate shakes his head, thinking himself hopelessly foolish as he slumps his weight onto the counter with a sigh. "My heart is pounding right now."

Laura bursts forth with hopping and screaming, startling Nate.

"Seth!? Did your mom go through a phase of white dresses when she was a teen?"

"Yes." Seth clears his throat. "Dad said she'd wear white on dates to send him a message, whatever that means."

Laura giggles. "I just found my reception dress in your closet! Are you sure I can have whatever I want?"

"Yep." Seth reiterates.

"I love you!" She giggles back to Seth's bedroom.

"Hey! Can I see it?" Christian hollers after her.

In the distance from two women, "No!"

It is a full hour into the New Year's Day afternoon before the women emerge to the typing of keys, shuffling of papers and the laziness of channel clicking. Natalie walks straight through with an armful of clothes and shoes to take to her house. Nate shakes his head at her secrecy.

Laura drapes her treasures over a chair and sits against the waiting curve of Christian's arm.

"You're pretty much gonna die tonight, Nate. She hides it, but that girl has a great body under all those clothes she wears." Laura giggles, adjusting her modest sweater above modest jeans. When Christian considers the concept, I think he dies a little too.

"I won't be exploring under any clothes tonight, Laura. It's not like that with her." Nate makes this clear to his pure sister.

She yawns. "You won't need to."

Rarely outside of a chef's coat or t-shirt, Nate impresses in a cream blazer and sky blue tie with a black shirt, dark wash jeans, and leather tennis shoes that trot down the stairs. His hair is gathered and hardened into his usual short peak in the front—a haircut Zeke had insisted on years ago that suits his masculine features well. He smells different, too. A trick, I think, for the human female olfactory senses as if Nate wasn't already attractive enough.

"Looking pretty sharp for a sub-first-base date, big brother." Laura accuses from the piano bench.

"Do you ever go home?" Nate is nervous, trying to locate his keys on surfaces and in drawers throughout the formal living room. The squeak of the back door stops him.

"Couldn't miss this." Laura smiles as long, dark legs approach, attached to black heels on one end and a navy silk work of art on the other.

It isn't even tight. Only Natalie's collarbone and calves are showing. She's arranged chopsticks in the top half of her hair, claiming—with finesse—that corner of her heritage. Barely a stroke of eyeliner. Barely a dab of lipstick. But it does not take much of anything at all to take Natalie from stunning in denim to ravishing in evening.

"Ready? I like to be early to see if they'll seat me." Natalie offers to the frozen Nate.

"Can I have a minute to catch my breath?" Nate admits.

Laura giggles. Nate locates his keys—in his pocket—just in time to follow chortling Natalie into the garage.

When they return after a couple of hours, I hear them laughing in the garage. But I'm already entranced by Laura at the piano and the transcendent beauty of Christian's voice. They are choosing wedding music and pay no heed to the applause of Zeke and Seth as they run through options for the different parts of the ceremony. Because they'd "only been sight-reading."

Laura sighs, stopping in the middle of a song. "I still like *Ave Maria* for the processional. It's the first thing we performed together. I think we fell in love during that song."

"But we're Protestant." Christian smiles warily.

Laura shrugs. "We'll call it a tribute to Vargas since he can't be here for the wedding."

"Alright, I'm convinced."

"That was easy," Zeke comments.

"I'm practicing the husband thing. We'll be yoked, so sometimes it's easier to just do what she wants than to stubbornly lead us in my undetermined direction." Christian smiles brightly. "And who doesn't want to make Vargas proud? *So Ave Maria* it is, m'Love."

The young couple giggles along with the head shaking, as Nate and Natalie burst through the door in their laughter.

"You didn't have to tell him right there that '*Le Cloture*'s tiramisu is a thousand times more satisfying.' We don't even have it on the menu." Nate is full smiles.

"Well, you should. If you can make something like that, you should serve it. I know it has roots in Italy, but you guys pride yourselves on diverging from traditional French, right?" Natalie had him convinced before she spoke.

"I'll ask chef about it." Nate glances into the living room at the others, realizing he's being watched. He clears his throat. "So, good review or bad?"

"Excellent. I enjoyed every minute." Natalie nods with a smile. "But *Donato*'s will suffer in print, I'm afraid."

Nate laughs, flattered.

"But I have to get home to write that. Maybe I'll pop in tomorrow sometime." Natalie walks toward the back door.

"Wait," Nate calls her to turn. Then he approaches her and kisses her gently on the cheek as agreed. A strand of her hair is drawn out by his and falls gently to her cheek against her expression of quiet wonder. Nate whispers, "Goodnight, Natalie."

"Night." She walks away but stops at the door knowing his eyes haven't left her. "But call me Nat."

As soon as the door closes, Nate exhales, sits on the floor in the midst of all his onlookers, and lowers himself to his back, his hands on his hair. His sister is giggling. I lick his face for its proximity to me. Nate speaks, not caring about the slobber.

"What did I just get myself into?" He is asking no one in particular. Maybe just him.

"I know what he's thinking," Christian says to Laura, who catches the cue to play the piano and illustrate the pivotal moment similar to this one that they shared not too long ago. "*Ave Maria...*"

Everyone laughs but Nate, who is too caught up in this moment to have view of any other.

Chapter Fifteen

The Solution

"What are we doing?" Natalie hums dreamily. Her breath is visible, but it is still a warm night for February. Nate's hands encase her shoulders over her coat. Hers rest on the wool layers over his chest inside her gloves. Reddened noses are inches from one another.

"I don't know what *you're* doing. But I'm trying to think of a way to get you to kiss me," Nate croons, not having caught the sincerity in Natalie's question.

"You know that's not what I mean. I mean where is this going?"

He sighs. "Yeah, I know."

Nate has sworn for many weeks to the others that they are "just dating," without commitments or confessions. This is what he's always said about anyone, even when it involves much more than food critiquing and holding hands and cheek kisses. I've found a spot to rest just feet from them, having already been outside when they'd skirted along the side of the house to reach Natalie's front porch. But even in clear view, I can't be sure why Nate hesitates with his answer when his truth is so simple for the others.

She's vulnerable in his secure embrace. Looking frightened but safe. She tries to un-ask what he's already mulling over, knowing she probably crossed some sacred line with him by doing so.

Natalie searches his eyes. "The sushi was good. Reminded me of my grandma. Glad you recommended it."

"Nat…" Nate is trying to get her attention but has nothing to say just yet.

She remains just above a whisper. "I'm sorry. I didn't mean to sound like I was pressuring you. I'm okay with just sushi, Nate, if that's what this is."

Nate laughs low and charming. "No, you're not."

Natalie exhales frustration through the cloud of steam they share. "This can't work. Think about it. It's widely known that you don't believe in marriage, and you don't like labels and commitments. That means that whatever this is could never be fulfilling for me. And I'm not willing to do things like kiss you without a serious commitment. So, this could never be fulfilling for *you*. We're polar opposites, Nate. I'm starting to think that as much as I enjoy spending time with you, we might be fooling ourselves."

"You're right. It's completely illogical that we keep this up." Nate sighs. "But before we figure things out, we should talk about an element you're missing. It could either be a problem or a solution."

Natalie scrunches her eyebrows together in confusion, then all but hiccups before she relaxes them with a sigh. "Oh no. Please don't tell me you're in love with me."

Nate laughs, somewhat offended. "Okay, I won't."

"Oh my gosh, you are!" Natalie exclaims, stepping back from his embrace.

"Apparently, that's a problem." Nate, never in the position of even slight rejection, is putting hands on hips and puffing breath up to the stars as Natalie turns and paces a couple of times.

"Yeah!" Natalie says with attitude. "You're extremely charming. Seth warned me. But I don't fall for charm."

"Seth warned me you were impossible in many ways. I don't like difficult women," Nate admits. "It's completely ridiculous how I feel. And it's probably wrong. Can we make an agreement to just forget about this, please? At least give me that."

"You're not getting out of this that easy!" Natalie raises the pitch of her voice.

"Come on, Nat. I—" Nate's voice trembles a little.

"No, you don't understand. I didn't agree to go out with you because you so cleverly rigged everything against me the first time. Trust me, I'm not that easy. I didn't fall for your charm, Nate. I fell for *you*." Natalie sighs, not realizing that her heart escaped through her mouth with so much passion.

The two stand five feet from one another, stunned speechless, only the reddened noses and clouds of cold animating them until Natalie's nerves get the best of her.

"Say something. Please?" She crosses her arms.

"Uh…" Nate has to search for that something. Laughs at the fact. "I want to make this work."

"There are lines I won't cross," Natalie reminds. Then demands, "So don't pressure me."

Nate chuckles. Tilts his head. "Me too, and likewise."

"Will this be exclusive and not just casual dating? I'm not wired that way. I'd like a relationship."

"Of course. I love you, Nat. Can't believe I just said that. But I do. I love you. You're it for me. Whether or not it's official, and no matter what lines I can or can't cross, I'm committed to you. I want you happy, whatever that takes." From Nathan Holm? It came from his mouth, and it was honest. Almost tearful. Something in him must be changing.

Natalie steps back into his embrace. Looks up at his vulnerable eyes and smiles. "I don't know how I ever hated you."

Nate laughs, putting something finally into words. "I don't know *if* I ever hated you."

Then Nate, never calling from a woman something he didn't orchestrate, is pleasantly startled when he receives and savors an indulgent kiss from Natalie. Nate exhales, heart pounding.

"You okay?" Natalie bests him yet again, biting her lip. "That's what you were after, right?"

"But I didn't think you'd actually…" He whispers with a laugh then tries to regain his bearings. "You gonna invite me in next?"

"Don't even joke about it, Pig." Natalie pushes his chest away playfully and backs toward her door with a flirtatiously stern, "Goodnight, Nathan."

"Goodnight, Nat. Wow, that really does sound like a bug sometimes." Nate jokes.

"See?" Natalie hips her hands and smiles.

He chuckles. "Well, goodnight, Bug."

She giggles and disappears into her house.

I follow the dreamy Nate back into the main house, where he finds a window room full of people. One of them is his little sister, whose only companions besides family now reside in this house. We enter to forced silence. Then Nate has some heartpounding, narrow-eyed thought as he boldly stands in their midst and checks the angle of their vision out the windows toward the guest house. What he discovers causes an embarrassed sigh. Laura is the first to give in to the silence and giggle. Christian shushes her. Zeke chuckles. Even Seth is amused. Zeke finally allows an opinion.

"Just be glad Vargas isn't around."

Christian indulges, accent and all, at the invitation. "Yeah, he'd be like, 'If you're gonna be kissing her like that, you need to put a ring on her finger.'"

Nate laughs once, then clarifies with a smile, "She kissed *me*."

"You seem devastated." Laura smiles with sarcasm as she kisses the hand hers is weaved into.

"I *should* be," Nate says with sincerity over a commitment he hardly believes he just made. "But for some reason…"

"Love catches you off guard, doesn't it?" Christian chuckles.

"Yeah." Nate scratches his head. Beaming like a little boy.

Laura gasps. "You did not just admit the 'L' word. Do you even believe in that?"

"I'm not sure it *matters* what I believe." Nate comes to a greater truth than he realizes, but in a laugh. "Goodnight, guys." He sniffles once, then smiles, pocketing his hands. His mind is somewhere else as he climbs the stairs.

"Who else totally saw this coming?" Laura asks the room in a raspy whisper.

All hands raise.

Seth smiles. "They hated each other far too much."

Chapter Sixteen

Like Cancer

"It's growing on me—slowly—like cancer," Nate says to Natalie as they dance on the handmade dance floor at dusk after most guests have left.

Natalie gives an offended laugh. "I'm not proposing. I asked how you felt about the idea. Your sister took the plunge. Thought your perspective might change."

"About cancer?" He weasels out with a joke. "Sorry, Bug, I can't think of a positive perspective of cancer."

Natalie laughs at Nate's rebuttal. The two of them dancing, carefree—no pressure at all, or so it would seem.

Christian had paused upon entry into Nate's cleaned and packed room last week to switch belongings from one room to the other. Goosebumps had overtaken his arms, even with the late spring upon them moments before. Most people have never seen in that room the things that are almost always tangible to my senses—the darkness and whispers that steer me away. Christian, however, seemed almost in fear, searching for what his eyes failed to see—what his Light keeps far from him always. Nate has no such Light. Seth had seen Christian's pause, his rub at goosebumps, and the way he'd flown to the window to try to let in more light.

"It won't feel like this after you and Laura move in." Then Seth had grabbed a box of Nate's. And Christian had nodded like his heart had understood Seth's words as bad news, not good.

Nate and Zeke had ascended the stairs to help after Seth and Christian had moved boxes and bags and other material things for a time. Then, when it came time to move Christian's things, it had taken only one trip back across the hall.

"This is all the stuff you have?" Nate remarked.

"A good thing," Zeke had laughed. "He's gotta fit a woman in this room too."

Christian had chortled like a child en route to a carnival. "Yeah."

They'd teased Christian for a time, then Natalie and Laura had arrived with the Holm family and Laura's things to add to Christian's new room. Seth had donated a beautiful handmade dresser he had 'lying around.' And even though there had been an hour-long stream of belongings come up the stairs from vehicles outside, the room had seemed to grow with the belongings and was brought to comfort around them. In the end, Laura had looked around and sighed in hopefulness with her family looking on in terror for Laura's next move in life. The young couple had laughed and embraced, overjoyed for the impending change.

It's a change that Nate compares to cancer while dancing with his love and wonders why, when dipping her at song's conclusion, he receives a coy giggle—not a kiss.

I'd enjoyed the wedding and the choice to have it on the lawn of our house so I could run and play with the identically dressed Holm twins. Many guests had arrived solemn and skeptical. Then they saw the way Christian and Laura love each other with constant cheer. They saw the way they had chased one another, laughing and shrieking into the creek in full wedding attire with handfuls of cake. Then, happy she'd acquired a shorter, drier dress, Laura had sat in front of her guests, husband by her side, on the piano bench where they accompanied one another with music, bringing skeptics to tears.

It was after dancing and gazes that matured and deepened between them as the day went on that no one even thought to argue about their age. Not with the way he'd pursued her and twirled her and kissed her all day in flowing white with flowers and veil, unapologetically young and vibrant. Guests were changed even without seeing the way the Light and that Man I know had not allowed anything of sin to enter the property. Now, the two newlyweds are no longer present, and I gathered they won't be for a few days. But they'd left behind some kind of redemption that had permeated into every guest.

Natalie had played the piano today for the ceremony, and the men are tasked with moving it back indoors, but without able bodied Christian's help this time. Nate is exhausted from preparing ninety plates of salmon with only Zeke to assist him.

"That piano *cannot* move again." Nate huffs and puffs, sitting at the chessboard after the piano is reassembled.

"It probably wouldn't play if you tried. I was worried the first time." Natalie tests the keys with skill, making sure they all work.

"Well, apparently, Seth offered to let Bill use one of the accounts he oversees to buy a more portable one, but your dad refused, Nate. Said he was already being too generous with the wedding." Zeke reveals as Seth sets up pieces on the other side of the board from Nate.

Nate nods. "Well, if no one puts the brakes on Seth, he goes a little crazy with his 'generosity.'"

"Christian's parents didn't even show. What's the story there?" Natalie is looking like a bridal magazine with the way she now drapes herself over a couch in her maid of honor gown.

"I guess he doesn't have contact with them." Nate yawns, already losing a chess match.

"Shame," Zeke says. "Nineteen-year-old kid on his own."

"He's got us, Laura, and Jesus. So he's set, in my mind. And what a great wedding. They have so much fun together." Natalie reminisces.

Seth and Zeke agree, though exhausted from said wedding. Nate, of course, scoffs. "They *did* have fun together. Now they're married. Instead of sending them off with bubbles, we should have done a funeral dirge." Nate finds this hilarious. Natalie does not.

"They love each other, Nate," Natalie says sheepishly. "They'll have a good marriage. You'll see."

"Nat, there is exactly one reason an abstinent seventeen- and nineteen-year-old get married." Nate chuckles. "Yeah, they'll have a *great* marriage until the novelty wears off. Then things might get ugly around here when they actually have to deal with real life together. My sister is a rich little princess. This will be a culture shock, especially when she completely forgets who she is since she quit out on her college scholarships to play happy housewife. Great wedding. Good job helping to plan it, Bug. But they are headed for doom."

"And you'd know since you've been married before." Natalie sarcasms viciously.

"It's just the way things are." Nate is never willing to lose a battle, and few are willing to fight him. Likely one of the reasons they found themselves in love, Natalie is one of those few.

"It's only the way things are if you don't understand the way God designed marriage."

"Well, maybe God's design was flawed. Ever think that?" Still fighting.

Natalie sighs in frustration. "It's like….a recipe! There we go. You have two dishes on the menu at *Le Cloture*. And the way you make them, they are flawless. Right?"

"Heck yeah," Nate whines proudly.

"See? But sometimes, even though all the ingredients are right, some buffoon at the meat station overcooks the filet mignon, and the sauce guy thinks he knows better and adds a little too much pepper. And if everyone starts to stray from the recipe, eventually you don't even want your *name* on the dish. Because it isn't your recipe anymore. See? A marriage fails because people think they know better and stray from the way God designed it. But your sister and Christian, Nate? They didn't care what everyone else said because everyone else besides God tends to fail miserably. They are so young and so aware that God's recipe is perfection, so they'll follow it because they *know* it'll work. And they want Him to *want* to put His name on it." Natalie's analogy is accepted by all with nods. Even Nate is thinking.

"But how do you know the recipe is perfect? Not mine—mine just are. But for marriage. How do you know it is people that do it wrong and not God?" Nate, the blasphemer, just pushed the most delicate button of an exhausted woman.

"We are *made* for marriage, Nate. Men are stubborn. Women are manipulative. Men are pigs and have strong arms. Women are trusting and like to be held. We know each other's strengths and weaknesses. Heck, sometimes we *are* each other's strength and weakness. But in some crazy, *perfect* way, it makes us compatible for greatness. Yeah, we disagree. We're practically different species, we should! That was part of God's plan too so that we learn to love and commit to another person unconditionally. Because that's what He does for us. The right way to make it work—to cook it, if you will? Is marriage. A perfect recipe. If it gets screwed up along the way, don't blame the chef." Natalie is on her feet by now. Passionate.

Nate nods. Loving her. But still in button-pushing mode. "You're cute."

"You're a conceited pig," Natalie yells, offended at the cast-off of her passion.

"You're a brainwashed Jesus freak." I nearly hear the whispering—feel the darkness now.

"Brainwashed? I have free will to choose my own values, just like you. Just because I choose to live for Christ, that doesn't mean I'm brainwashed." The battles begin that no one sees. Natalie untouched.

"But why do *I* have to be dragged into it?" Nate whines.

"You *don't*." Natalie is tearing up a little with the cold remark and gathering her shoes.

Nate must practically chase Natalie out the door before she walks down that path without him forever. I follow for the opportunity to go out on this warm night.

"Are you breaking up with me?" Nate's heart is pounding as he catches up to her in the darkness.

"That was quite a conclusion jump." Natalie laughs bitterly. "I will if you want me to. Wouldn't want to brainwash you."

Natalie turns, but Nate gently grabs her wrist.

"That's ridiculous, Bug. I *love* you. That doesn't just stop." Nate nearly whispers, even outside.

"*Do* you? Prove it." She questions him in the same volume, eyes glistening.

"Fine!" Then Nate pulls Natalie closer by her wrist and kisses her with charm. Something I've seen him do with a dozen others.

When Natalie regains her lips for speaking, she includes pain and fire in her scorn. "Oh, since you put it *that* way."

Then with a forceful snatch of her wrist, she is across a path to a place she calls home. Nate watches her, then goes back inside, where I follow him. Nate sits back in a chair, staring at a wall. Not silent, except for what our ears can hear. Everyone seems to sense this.

"She's somethin,' isn't she?" Nate smiles, still contemplating Natalie's words.

"*Livid* would be my guess," mumbles Zeke.

"She'll forgive me," Nate hopes in his pride.

Seth's steel trap opens with discretion. "That may be true, but it should not be your primary concern with her. You shouldn't try to change that she lives for Christ. Without Him, she wouldn't be who she is."

"And yet it's okay when she tries to change me?" Nate argues.

"She's not trying to change you. She's trying to *find* you, Nate! You can't expect everyone to believe that you are actually a conceited pig. We've seen the way you look at her," Zeke butts in.

"Then you know I'd give my life for that woman. Would it hurt her to respect my feelings on the marriage thing?" Nate shows some of his pain from the argument.

"In my opinion Nate, she's already given up her life for you. Seth is right. She lives and breathes God's will for her. So even if you give up on your idiotic opinion of marriage, she'll still lose. She'd be yoked with a man that doesn't even understand the majority of who she is." Zeke defends with a passion I haven't seen from him until this very moment. "It's not a sin, per se. But it's not something *I'd* ever do."

"Since when are *you* a Jesus freak? Does God know all the stuff we used to do?" Nate asks in confusion of a man that once supported his sin.

Seth asks the same with his eyes, only with a smile.

"It's called forgiveness. *Real* forgiveness, not just what you expect from Natalie." Zeke sighs. "I've been emailing with Vargas a lot. Christ is the only worthy pursuit, Man. I'm sick of all that vanity."

"Whatever. I'm going to bed. This is just like my childhood." Nate storms up the stairs to his room, complete with a door slam. Just like childhood, indeed.

Seth clears his throat. "Did Vargas tell you—?"

"You bet." Zeke laughs. "What is the matter with you, Seth? Natalie would have everything she needs if you married her. Actually, all that woman *does* need is a man of God to love her. You've gotta be in *misery,* Seth."

Seth nods. "Nate needs her more than I do."

The following Thursday night brings all the tenants together for the first legitimate chess night in a while. Laura and Christian share stories about some honey and a moon where there was a cabin and a guitar involved. It must have been a place where a few wilds were explored because they smell different. But I like them just the same. Maybe even better.

Nate and Natalie aren't speaking, so it is good that this uplifting conversation occurs over dinner. The house has smelled like more hate than love for almost a week. Finally, dessert is served, and Natalie's sour expression changes. All of them are wondering if it will morph into a smile. It does. Tiramisu.

Nate smiles. "Forgive me yet?"

Natalie holds up a finger until after she takes a bite. She lets her eyes close, her mouth in a smile around that bite. And then she opens her eyes and nods. She stands and pulls Nate into the kitchen to avoid the coos. Unable to coo, I follow. The two embrace and Nate whispers in Natalie's ear.

"Don't give up on me, okay? I love you, and I'm really trying to figure things out."

"I know you are." Natalie then kisses the lips of the chef. Zeke enters with incomprehensible words that he stops abruptly in his exit. When the kisses continue, I exit as well, nudging the hand of Seth, who'd need it if he'd seen.

When the two return a moment later, Seth begins setup of the chessboard. Natalie and then Nate fall. Zeke and then Laura.

Christian is last, always having the strategy that he just knows will trick Seth. He's determined in this, and then Laura kisses his cheek. I hear the whisper in the ear.

"Goodnight."

Christian is still focused on the chessboard but pulls Laura onto his lap. "Wait a minute, I'll come with you."

She speaks just above a whisper this time, rising from his lap uncomfortably. "No, it's okay. You hang out with everyone. I don't want to be a party pooper."

Christian turns to read something in her eyes. "You alright, m'Love?"

"Yes!" Laura says in jumpy awkwardness. Then she softens to a loving smile. "Other than being exhausted, I'm fine. Love you like crazy."

Christian nods and reaches out to squeeze her hand. "Love you like crazy, too."

When the door closes upstairs, Zeke and Nate take to laughter of ridicule. Christian looks to Seth's smile and then inquires.

"What is so terribly funny?" He is smiling.

"You just got turned down flat." Zeke lets him in. God's still working, I guess.

"What are you talking about? We were on the road all afternoon after hiking five miles this morning. She's tired." Christian chuckles, supplying little information.

"Classic excuse. Cliché, even. You need to read up on women." Nate laughs.

"What? You mean the female half of our species does not require *sleep*? Amazing! I recall watching an angel sleep a few times this week. That's a weird anomaly." Christian is smiling to himself in the wisdom of sarcasm and secrecy.

"You're such a gentleman, Christian," Natalie coos from the couch.

"A gentleman—or a doormat who is falling for the same dangling carrot routine in every marriage ever." Nate still hasn't grown weary of his opinion of marriage. Natalie is very weary indeed.

"You guys are so oblivious. Christian was not 'turned down.' He was actually just released from discussing whatever issue they left at the door when they got home." Christian smiles appreciatively at Natalie's female perspective.

"Like a fight? That was the wimpiest fight I've ever seen. Christian, women are crazy. You're gonna need bigger guns." Nate is amused with himself. Natalie is not.

"It was nothing big, I promise. But we prefer to discuss things in private. Airing dirty laundry is not very loving, Nate." As Christian speaks, he checks a text he'd received on his phone. Then bites his lip with a smile. "We're fine. Just getting settled in is all."

"Checkmate." Seth's chosen word of the night. And every chess night.

"Aw, come on! I was distracted. Rematch?" Seth nods at Christian's request, resetting the pieces.

"So, you are suggesting that an easy, happy marriage is actually a myth, even in the first five days?" Nate teases mercilessly.

"Of course, that's a myth. This morning, my wife got me up before sunrise and didn't even let me eat more than a granola bar before we went for a hike, which is not my thing, with a guitar on my back. The top of the mountain was frigid before the sunrise, but Laura made me play and sing old hymns with her anyway. And then, when I wanted to take a nap, she instead made me drive like a bat out of hell to make sure we weren't late for chess night. And she kept talking incessantly about our issues so that I wouldn't fall asleep driving. I got here tired and irritated and sore, all because of her. It's been my hardest day in a long time." Christian is ranting, and everyone is confused at his sudden shift in position.

"Ha! Told you!" Nate thinks he's won. "You are stuck in misery forever."

"I just told you what you wanted to hear," Christian admits the lie. He returns with a radiant smile. "The version I'll tell our grandkids is: There are probably mountaintops in Heaven with Laura and a guitar. Best morning of my life thus far."

"But then you had a fight." Nate tries to tear a hole in Christian's optimism. A futile goal.

"No. *Then* God gave us a car ride to talk about things we hadn't talked about yet. Some hard stuff. She's never opened up to me like that. She's never opened up to *anyone* like that. You're right, Nate. An easy, happy-go-lucky marriage is a myth. It should be. I hiked up a mountain before my muscles were even awake. You were all comfy and sleeping in your beds. But when I was sitting on a mountain singing? You were asleep then, too." Christian, young and wild and supposedly immature, has won us all over again. Even Nate shuts his mouth for the evening.

I love this version of family. The house is full, and schedules, meals, and activities are constantly buzzing. I follow Seth in all his doing and greet home comers and stayers and see them off whenever they take a leave of any kind. I watch heart-to-hearts and head-to-heads. I enjoy cuddling with girls who giggle about boys and smelling newlyweds steal kisses all day until they find moments to steal away upstairs undetected. I listen to tapping keys and work boots and chaos. I love them all scattered in daily life. But I always look forward to chess night when it all slows down and buzzes as one.

Thursday night comes around again and again, and a month after the wedding Laura lies on the leather bench in the game room, Christian's lap her pillow.

“You should play something,” Laura requests of her husband and no one objects, since even midnight music has been forsaken for weeks.

“No, you. My guitar is all the way upstairs,” Christian reasons.

“I’ll get it,” Laura says sweetly with a smile, sitting up and giggling when her likely two-minute exit requires some goodbye kisses to her lips and hands.

“You two are adorable,” Natalie comments. Nate pretends to vomit onto the chessboard. Christian slides into Laura’s previous spot, dreamily awaiting her return.

“Hey!” She says gently after bouncing back down the stairs with a guitar case on one shoulder. “You stole my spot.”

Christian smiles and sits up, reaching out for his other love and receiving the guitar with suspicion as Laura sits next to him.

“This was out, leaning in that corner upstairs. You got the case out of the back of the closet and put it away to bring it down.”

Laura nods. Shrugs. “Wanted to keep it safe.”

Christian wears a smile of distrust as he opens the case. Seth is checkmating Nate, and the transition of players distracts from what Christian discovers after the unzipping and some residual string sounding. But everyone is settled enough to clearly hear that they should turn to meet his pleased laughter.

“Are you serious, m’Love?” Christian asks, now holding something plastic, long like a pen that smells a little like one of the people’s bathrooms. The color drains from his face.

“I told you it was a possibility.” Laura whimpers, now looking nervous, tucking her hair, near tears. “You’re upset.”

Christian’s eyes widen as he tries to remedy Laura’s coming flow from her eyes. “Upset? I didn’t see it coming so soon, but I am the farthest thing from upset. Why are you crying?”

“You *know* why.” She sniffles and begins moving that dainty left hand with the diamond under her eyes to keep the tears from streaming.

“Shhh, stop that.” Christian stands, the guitar forgotten, dropping to the ground with a deep drum-like clatter. He leads his weeping wife out of the influence of the others to a loving lean against a piano in the next room. The others hear nothing but their own concerned and confused thoughts. I hear tender whispers. Professions of love and optimism.

"Guys…" This is from Natalie, who is rescuing the poor guitar from the floor, which reveals the stick of truth beneath it.

"What?" Nate is trying to stop the big brother in him from glancing and wondering at the goings on at the piano in the next room.

"You need to promise not to flip out." Natalie says, holding that stick behind her back.

"Is she…." Seth asks, not intending to finish the sentence but having recognized Christian's chillingly familiar reaction. Natalie winces and nods, allowing Zeke to stand and take the stick from her hand. When he sees it and chuckles, she smiles at him.

"The 'Hi Daddy!' is cute, huh?" But Natalie's affection is cut short when Nate jumps up and snatches the proof from Zeke.

"Laura Renee Holm!" He yells so she can hear.

"Kessler!" She corrects from the other room. Christian laughs.

"Already?!" Nate is in severe distress. But even Seth joins in with the rest, applauding and congratulating to encourage them.

Nate mocks them with waving arms. "Yay! Teen pregnancy!"

"Nate, this is not the same thing as teen pregnancy." Natalie scolds in frustration, knowing the difference.

"She's seventeen. And pregnant." Nate shrugs viciously at his girlfriend. "The only difference is I'm supposed to pretend to be happy about it."

The parents-to-be contain themselves and rejoin the others in the room, Laura catching the end of Nate's opinion. She slides past, headed out back.

"Where you going, m'Love?"

"Just need some air. Feeling queasy." Laura lies, tears welling again.

"I'll grab you some water." Then, Natalie and Laura leave the main house, likely not for the purpose they stated.

Christian conceals anger in his pursed lips that does not release until he hears the back door close.

"Why do you have to do that, Nate?" The release is controlled. Gentle, even.

Nate begins with quiet, then turns to anger as his scolding progresses. "Because here on Earth, that little 'Hi Daddy' on that plastic stick requires *money*—which you don't have an abundance of—and a decent place to live—you have a bedroom. Babies are disgusting, expensive parasites that ruin lives. You guys are still kids yourselves. Do you actually expect to be decent parents? I can't believe you let this happen."

Christian is wrestling the anger, shaking his head, formulating thoughts.

"Be careful, Christian," Seth warns in his friend's ear, finding his way out of the room with Zeke.

Christian, several inches shorter than Nate and far skinnier, approaches him, looking him dead in the eyes. "Yes, Nate. We expect to be decent parents. Just because you aren't expecting a blessing, that doesn't mean you shouldn't treat it like one."

"Doesn't mean you can magically be ready, either." Nate steps forth. Ready for battle.

Christian begins to lose his cool. "You are a thorn in my side, Nate. But that's nothing compared to how you're hurting your little sister."

"Oh, so now *I'm* hurting her? Chris, if she had the sense to listen to me, she wouldn't be feeling so queasy right now. That's *you*, my friend," Nate goads.

"That's the thing, Nate," Christian enunciates his brother-in-law's name with anger. "You're the only person she *does* listen to. She worships the ground you walk on. So, you can imagine how great she feels when you tell her best friend and your girlfriend that marriage is like cancer. Or her husband that children are like parasites. Or my personal favorite: That I've brainwashed her into thinking she's following her heart when in reality, I'm suppressing her talents and dreams so I can be warmer at night while I pursue mine. I guess my master plan of selfishness is ruined now that I have to quit school to get a job to support my family."

"Well, if it's so obvious that I'm wrong, maybe she shouldn't listen to me." Nate gets defensive.

"Oh, I agree. Believe me. Nothing suppresses talents and dreams like being on God's path and your hero hating you for it." Christian's jaw clenches.

"I don't hate her, Chris," Nate mumbles. Finally convicted.

"She says you've spent her entire life convincing her otherwise," Christian reveals.

"Yeah, I've been hard on her, okay? She's at the greatest risk of being like me. Every time she gets close, I try to stop her. So yeah, the fact that she decided to risk everything she's worked for to follow her heart is going to infuriate me. Save the whole marriage thing, that's exactly what *I* did and the reason our *dad* hates me." Nate causes a smile to form across Christian's face.

"You're funny," Christian says. "Laura's always told me that you're Bill's favorite child. And that the three girls' achievements combined don't hold a candle to how proud he is of *you*."

"Well, he has an interesting way of showing it. All he ever does is tell me how worthless my career is and how much more potential I had. As if 'common sense' will make me change my entire life." Nate stops himself mid-mockery. Because even though he'd been imitating his father's gruff voice, he still hears his own in it for the first time.

"If what looks like *hate* translates into how much you love her and want what's best for her, I'd say Laura has an amazing brother." Christian nods. "But since I'm her husband and the method is breaking my wife's heart? I'm gonna have to ask you to change your tactics."

"Any suggestions?" Nate concedes, still defensive.

"Well, you could *tell* her she's leading an honorable life, but actions speak louder than words. Maybe consider leading one yourself." Christian pleads. "Be what you want *her* to be proud to be."

Nate has been beaten and stands stunned at the young man in front of him. I hear that the girls are sharing the kind of laughter that follows tearful encouragement as they approach the house from Natalie's. When they emerge into the game room, I hear Christian's heart skip a beat like it always does when Laura comes into his field of vision. Natalie raises an eyebrow at Nate, proving all of Christian's words. Laura makes her way to Christian's arms, but Nate intercepts the embrace with a hefty one of his own.

"I love you." His words are sincere in her shoulder. Years overdue. "You're gonna be a great mom."

"Did my husband yell at you?" She is crying again. Laughing a little too.

"Yeah. He'll be a good dad." Nate sniffles as he looses the embrace and addresses Christian. "We just fired a station cook for having no motivation to work or succeed. Since you have nothing but motivation and my word is law at *Le Cloture*, the job is yours if you want it."

"Station cook? Nate, I've probably eaten at a handful of restaurants in my life. I'm not your guy." Christian laughs.

"You'd be doing what you do when you help me out with dinner here," Nate encourages.

Christian snorts. "What, get yelled at for doing it wrong?"

"Pretty much," Nate confesses. "But it's a place to start. And you can probably break out your guitar every now and then. I'll call Chef tonight."

Laura looks to Christian. "Chris, you have school."

"Obviously, God has other plans, m'Love." Christian puts a hand on Laura's belly with a loving smirk.

"We haven't discussed this yet," She whispers, taking his hand.

"The only thing we're discussing tonight is baby names." Christian gives Laura the stern look of a loving husband, tucking youthful hair behind his ears.

"What?!" Nate recalls something one might think he wouldn't. "Chris, the night you met, you said you were having five kids and naming them all 'Nate.' What happened to that?"

Laura is flattered. "The night we met?"

"He's wrong, love. Don't listen to him." Christian backs up, heading toward the stairs with Laura but bowing his head at Nate a little. "I said *six*. Six kids."

"Good call," Laura coos. "Six is a better number." The parents-to-be head upstairs, terrified but trusting God.

Zeke has already retreated to his office and Seth to the window room after putting a forsaken chess set away. I watch Nate put a hand at the small of Natalie's back and pull her close.

"What?" She wonders at the deep gaze she's receiving.

"Three of my grandparents died of cancer," he reveals, then smiles. "Marriage is like cancer."

"You're morbid." Natalie tries to pull away, hating the lot of her heart these days. Nate effortlessly uses his strength to keep her close. "It's impossible to prepare for. It can suck the life out of you while you give up everything to fight for it. And more often than not, it seems like that fight is all in vain. My fourth grandparent—Mom's dad—he got cancer too. But he *survived* it. He'll tell you that it was worth the fight and that he was a stronger, better person because of it. He says you learn a lot about yourself and a lot about other people and the good in the world. But no matter how things turn out, even the thought of cancer is terrifying if you've seen all the bad it can do."

"What are you saying?" Natalie's question is abrupt. Such is their way.

"I'm saying I love you, Bug. Be patient with me?" Nate kisses his girlfriend goodnight and makes a phone call on his way up the stairs. Seth sits with me on his designated chair for this room. Natalie waits until she hears Nate's conversation fade behind his bedroom door to join us in the room with haste.

"Marrying him is a terrible idea." She whispers to Seth.

"I know."

"He doesn't know the Lord. He's conceited, and he still over-salts food on occasion. We fight all the time. Marriage would complicate things even more." Natalie is only using Seth as a sounding board.

"I know." Is the response amid the smoothing of fur at my side.

"I love him. He acts so macho and callous sometimes. But inside he's just *goo*. That heart of his—it's crazy that people don't see it." The sounding continues.

"I know," Seth agrees.

"Seth! An opinion would help! You know him better than I do." Natalie had never asked. Seth smiles.

"He loves you. But is confused about how to show you." Seth offers—not good enough. Natalie already knows this. "He doesn't want kids. You don't want kids. That's rare to find."

This helps Natalie somewhat. She nods. But Seth then delivers a blow. "It won't be anything like Christian and Laura. You'll cry a lot. He'll yell a lot. You will tear each other's hearts out. But you will love each other in a way people miss when they are too nice. It will be that way from the very beginning and not let up for a long time. A lot of pain…"

Natalie catches the certainty in Seth's voice. "You *know* that, don't you?"

Seth nods.

Natalie sighs with remorse. "I'm going to ask you to do something for me."

"I won't tell him," Seth assures her. "I know you think it will be bad for your relationship with him. I wasn't planning on it. It isn't my place."

"But you told Vargas. Now Zeke knows too," Natalie murmurs.

"It is *my* secret to keep or tell, too. I assume it was probably exactly what Laura needed to hear a minute ago," Seth reasons.

"It was," Natalie smirks, amused at Seth's perception. "But I swore them *all* to secrecy with Nate. I'm asking the same of you. I love him, Seth. I don't want to destroy what we have because of something I can't undo. From what you're saying, there will already be enough pain as it is."

"Yes, but honesty is—" Seth tries.

"*Please,* Seth. Please."

Seth softens. "If that's what you want, Natalie."

"Thank you." Natalie begins to leave the house, then turns back to Seth. "Just tell me…will the pain be worth it?"

Seth nods. "Pain points us to Christ. You know that. Christ is always worth running to."

We retreat to the bedroom, where Seth follows the pointing arrow of pain right into a leather-bound Book.

Chapter Seventeen

Suspicious

"I just discovered why God didn't make me a sympathetic puker," Christian says with a chill as he replaces the yogurt he'd just taken upstairs two minutes ago.

"I take it she's not making it to church again this week?" asks the dolled up Natalie from the pajamaed arms of Nate in the kitchen.

"No, but she's making *me* go. She says she's starving, but she literally heaved at the *sight* of the yogurt. I feel terrible for her. I don't know what to do!" The exasperated Christian bangs his head on the fridge door as Zeke enters the kitchen in his expensive modern plaid shirt, giving Christian strange looks.

Natalie giggles. She crosses the kitchen, walking into the pantry, and emerging with an unopened package of saltines and a bottle of water. "Tell her not to even *try* to get out of bed in the morning without eating two of these and having a few tiny sips of water." She hands the treasures to Christian. Seth, long-finished with his Sunday morning cereal but still sitting at the breakfast bar, is amused at Natalie's assured information.

"Thank you," Christian says with deep gratitude, departing the kitchen again. "Don't leave without me, guys. She'll kill me if I don't go this week."

Natalie returns to the doting arms of Nate, looking up into his eyes. "Are you sure you don't want to come? I think you'd like it."

"Sorry, Bug. I'm not quite ready to drink the Kool-Aid yet. I'll let you know." Nate kisses her at these words, and Natalie leaves his arms in sadness. Nate leans back, physically moving Zeke out of the way, to watch the heels take her away. When she turns the corner and leaves his sight, he makes some sort of carnal grunt in his throat that calls the men to laughter.

"Still won't let you touch her, huh?" Zeke mumbles.

"Uh, no. You kidding? That woman and her boundaries are going to be the death of me. But until she gouges out my eyes, I'm still *looking*." Nate defends his actions. Smiling a little to himself like Natalie's beauty is still in front of him. I don't think he even needs her there to admire her. Because he loves more than her beauty.

Christian enters again in a sigh. "Okay. Now we can go. Nate, will you please take care of Laura while I'm gone? Just make sure she doesn't pass out like she did last week? I told her to come down when she can so you don't have to go up and check on her."

"Yes. Go! Nat's waiting in the garage already." The three men heed Nate's instructions, and I am left with Nate, who promptly grabs the yogurt inserted into the fridge by his brother-in-law, taking a seat with his favorite news channel in Seth's forbidden La-Z-Boy. But he's not paying much attention to the TV since he is looking at pictures of something on a lap computer.

Laura comes down in pajamas, carefully lowering herself onto a loveseat with moaning, grasping her head as if it would spin out of control if she didn't. Nate, of course, laughs affectionately.

"You okay, Sis?"

"Who would have thought that two one-cell halves of DNA could combine and multiply into so many ills?" Is Laura's reply. Starting to sound a little more like her husband.

"Actually, a lot of people have thought that. Probably not at the time, though." Nate chuckles, taking a bite of yogurt that nearly gags him. "Gah! This stuff is terrible. No wonder the sight of it made you sick."

"I'm sure in an hour or so, I'll eat three of them and then half of whatever else is in there. I don't understand my digestive system in the least right now." Laura shakes her head. "I sent poor Christian to the store to get me raw tomatoes last night. It's all I could think about for hours. I feel like I've gone insane."

"So would you rather be doing this or going to school to study piano as per the original plan?" Nate is still seeking her best, but in better tones these days.

But even in her sick dizziness of a form, Laura smiles. "This. Hands down. I actually never wanted to go to music school. I've been studying piano my whole life, and I love it. But it's not who I am. I know you think Christian was the reason I didn't go. But he was just an extremely willing scapegoat."

Nate snorts at her explanation. "So being the color of my sheets for weeks on end and puking at the sight of yogurt is—"

"Par for the course, Nathan. I can't even describe the peace I have about this. When I think about this baby coming and how my husband has such a servant's heart, I realize that I'm living my dream, even though I didn't know what my dream was." Laura smiles.

"You sure it's just one kid? I remember Mom was pretty sick when she was having the twins." Nate yawns, ignoring Laura's smile.

"Yeah, just one this time. But considering Chris was a twin and then Kelli and Shelley, twins will likely happen if we keep this up."

"Wait, Chris is a twin?"

"Yeah. But Jonathan died when they were seven." Laura sighs. "Can you imagine? The girls were joined at the hip at that age."

"Wow. That's unreal. I guess I understand why he doesn't talk about his family." Nate winces the remorse.

"Trust me, you don't." Laura chuckles a terrible chuckle. "But since thinking about it doesn't help my morning sickness, let's not go there."

"Fair enough. Hey, when does the mall open on Sundays?" Nate shifts to get more comfortable.

"Ten, I think. Since when do you go to the mall?"

"And they get back at around eleven-thirty, right?"

"Right. Why are you asking me this?"

"Well, I'm looking at these rings online, and I was gonna order one, but I just feel like I need to touch it first, you know? I already have some ideas, but I could use help deciding; if you feel up to it." Nate says nonchalantly.

Laura gasps. "A ring for *Natalie's* finger?"

"That depends. If you can keep a secret, then yes. If not, then no, definitely not."

"Whoa! Since when are you okay with engagement? You know that leads to marriage, right?" Laura giggles.

"Well, that's the idea. But if you help me, you have to keep this from as many ears as possible."

Laura drops to a whisper. "Shhh, Willow might hear you."

Nate laughs and heads off to his shower. Pretty soon, Laura stands, beginning to feel better, and consumes more food than I've seen even Nate, who is easily twice the weight of Laura, eat in one sitting. She dresses and meets Nate downstairs in time for them to sneak out for an hour. The house is silent until Nate and Laura come scurrying in the house in laughter like children. I follow them up the stairs, and they frantically search Nate's always slightly disheveled room for a hiding spot for a little box.

"In your socks. That's where you always used to hide bottles of liquor. Of course, Mom used to find them and water them down." Laura winces.

"That explains a lot," Nate chuckles, quickly hiding the box, and suddenly finds a friend where he'd once seen only a sister.

They panic when they hear a garage door open. Nate shoos his sister and quickly musses his hair, and returns to his pajamas, thundering down the stairs to his news show just in time for the entrance of all. He's glad for his tri-weekly five-mile run to cover the rush in his breathing. Laura simply sits in her room a moment and pretends to calmly walk down the stairs to greet the others as if she'd just gotten dressed.

Nate smiles at Natalie when she enters, seeking him after greeting Laura.

"Really, Nate? The sick preggy gets dressed before you?" She sighs in the disgust of her clueless reprimand.

"I had a late night at work." Nate defends nothing at all, then catches her before she makes it out the back door. "Wait. Come here."

Natalie's eyes widen in his warm hug. "Nate, your heart is *pounding*. Are you okay?"

"Just wild about my Bug is all," Nate lies, kissing Natalie's forehead.

Natalie's eyes narrow suspiciously, but she has other business to attend to. "So, my dad just called me on the way home to talk about Christmas."

"It's September." Nate is still adjusting to thinking past the weekend's plans.

"I know. He pays for my airfare, so he wanted to book my flights today. I said I wanted to talk to you first," Natalie reasons.

"Why do you need to talk to me?" Nate is more flattered than confused.

"You're my boyfriend, and I love you, and it made my dad furious that I value your opinion." Natalie seems far too pleased with herself. Nate chuckles. Natalie continues. "Anyway, the plan is to leave the fifteenth and be back after the New Year. Is that—?"

"What?! No. I won't get to do the mistletoe thing. At least don't leave my lips lonely on New Year's Eve, come on! And our first date was on New Year's Day. So technically, it's like an anniversary type thing."

Nate defends, pretending to be the pig she knows he isn't. Natalie gasps and smiles. "Look who's getting sentimental. What have I done to you?"

"Not sure, but I can't say I mind," he admits.

"Fine, I'll come back on the thirty-first in the name of sentimentality." Nate pouts. She giggles. "Okay, the thirtieth. Early morning. Any earlier, and Papa will think I just came for the presents."

"Thanks. I'll be your car service—in three months when this actually occurs." Nate kisses Natalie's hand. "Email me your flight info once you have it so I can put it on the calendar for work."

"Yes, sir," Natalie flirts. "I have a menu to research before tonight's review. Are you sure you can't come?"

"No, I have to get to work soon." Nate checks a clock on the wall. "Happy critiquing."

During the sick sweetness before Natalie departs out the back, near-silent whispers have circulated through the kitchen. When the door closes, and Nate turns with his dreamy smile, all mouths are about to burst with excitement. Nate rolls his eyes.

"Laura! That was like three minutes. You couldn't keep a secret for *three minutes*?"

"I only told Christian."

"Shhh." Nate says, putting up a hand until he sees Natalie enter her front door. "Okay, who did Christian tell?"

"I just thought Seth might like to know." Christian shrugs. "You know, but Zeke was standing there, so…."

"Not a hinted mention of any part of this to my family. I'm serious. It'll ruin everything." Nate is concerned for nothing, as none of these present would jeopardize this love story.

"How are you gonna ask her?" Laura wonders then smiles herself straight into nostalgia. "Christian wrote me a song on guitar. He had the ring hanging on his capo the whole time, and I didn't notice until he sang something about the ring on his capo." She giggles.

"We could help you, you know. Make it awesome." Christian is smiling from his wife's admiration.

"No. Actually, if you guys knew my plan, you'd do everything you could to stop me. But keeping quiet would be so helpful. And don't act funny. She'll notice."

Nate charms his way in and out of many things without speaking a word of reason to anyone over the next few months—an afternoon with Natalie's driver's license, a few days' vacation conned from a boss, another trip to the mall with Laura, and even a talk with Laura about personal female issues. I wonder if in a different life, Nate may have been a con man. But if so, Natalie never would have been a good mark.

"Why do you need two suitcases to *pick up* someone from the airport?" Christian accuses, causing Nate a near heart attack in the mudroom as he's headed back in from the garage and a secret venture.

"I just…give me a minute to come up with that one." Nate chuckles, beaming. Probably excited to see Natalie since she's been in South Carolina for two weeks to celebrate Christmas. He lies, "Thrift store! I went through my clothes, and I'm headed to the thrift store to make a donation before I go get Natalie from the airport."

"Pity you giving away that brand-new purple suitcase filled with brand-new women's clothes," Christian says, tying his shoes, headed to work.

"How did you—I mean, what makes you think—?" Nate growls in frustration.

"So, does Natalie know you're flying her somewhere for three days to propose to her? And do you think she'll actually be okay with it?" Christian accuses.

"She has no idea," Nate supplies far too easily. "I timed it so that I can talk someone into grabbing her other bag off the carousel and holding it, then I'll get through security and meet her at her gate to tell her we're getting on another plane."

"Yeah, she might kill you." Christian chuckles at the brilliance. "Especially when you tell her that you packed her entire bag for her. I hope Laura's research into her shampoo and such was accurate. And I especially hope that you respect the boundaries Natalie set for you. Because if not, *we* will kill you."

"Don't worry, Christian. I'll be a gentleman. Scouts honor."

"Where are you taking her?" Christian admires the romantic in Nate, who makes a lip zipping motion and winks.

"Happy New Year, Chris. We'll be back on January 2nd." Then Nate drives away, leaving Christian to deliver the news to everyone else.

New Year's Eve is an odd tradition. They don't celebrate anything at all except the hope of more passage of time. They drink, and kiss, and stay up until tomorrow, having gained nothing. Any celebration is a little duller without Nate and Natalie, who have been gone a day and a half. But the other Holms join us nonetheless. Minus the twins, who spent the night at a friend's. Laura is getting so round she can hardly move, the poor thing. I try not to step near her feet, so she doesn't fall when she walks. Zeke stays in town this year and plays chess. Seth has lit a fire in the game room. It is peaceful enough that everyone's thoughts can meet in the air. But some of them are forbidden. So the silence nearly wins out. Nearly.

"I didn't think Nate was this crazy," Zeke says aloud for God and everyone.

"I can't believe Natalie agreed to it." Christian laughs, rubbing the swollen feet on his lap.

"I just hope he doesn't try anything stupid, that pig," Laura says.

"Be realistic, Laura. Why else would a young man take a young woman on a private getaway? Look what happened to *you* the last time." This is from the slurred speech of last year's wine in Karen.

"Mom!" Laura cowers, embarrassed. Christian snorts, then chuckles shamelessly.

"Your mom's right, sweetheart. Nathan has been dating this girl for a year. *Our* Nate. You honestly think they haven't been down that road?" Bill is well acquainted with Nate's surface self.

"Natalie is my best friend, Dad. They haven't," Laura promises. "She'd have told me. And I doubt she'll change her mind just because he's proposing."

"Proposing?!" Karen's eyes widen. "I thought Nathan didn't believe in marriage!"

Laura covers her reddening face. Terrible at secrets. Bill chuckles, appreciating his son.

"He bought a ring months ago." Seth smiles at the stunned Karen.

"I caught him leaving for the trip," Christian confirms. "And he's definitely proposing."

Suddenly, Laura's phone chimes across the room. She moans, unable to rise and get to it. Christian fetches it without being asked, and Laura only has it a few seconds before gasping.

"Awww!" Laura reads aloud a text. "Natalie says, 'Hey, Sis! Guess what? Nate proposed to me in the airport yesterday! Sorry for the delay. We've had a crazy couple of days. But I wanted to show the ring to my best girlfriend first. After you reply, we'll send out the mass text.' Aw, I wonder if she knows I picked it out." Laura's hormones bring her to tears as she passes the phone around to show off the gold and jewels against Natalie's mocha skin. Everyone reacts their own way, with comments about Nathan's concession and impending wedding planning. The room is alive as Laura replies to the text. Everyone removes phones from pockets to await the mass text with a conspiracy to overload Natalie's phone all at once.

"Wow. Engaged after a year together. This is gonna take a while to get used to." Karen says, catching Bill's eyes.

Then all phones vibrate and chime one after the other. Everyone opens their messages with smiles, but a stunned silence falls as the message is read.

I catch a glimpse of Seth's phone. I see a photo with a massive waterfall as a backdrop, a perfect rainbow caught in the lens. In the forefront is Natalie, in a classy white dress with a red belt. Nate is in a white jacket and jeans with a red tie. Natalie is across Nate's arms with a red rose in her outstretched arm. Both have dramatically silly looks of surprise on their faces. And I gather from the chaos after the silence that the caption says,

"'Surprise! We eloped! Happy New Year! –Love, Nathan and Natalie Holm (as of a few hours ago).'"

Before the shock can seep in, let alone subside, Seth receives the next text. He chuckles. All inquire. "Nate asked if he could move to the guest house."

Karen receives the next. She laughs, a hand over her heart with a sigh. "Nate says, 'Don't worry Mom, I hired a photographer.'"

Laura cuts the tension by tapping her phone and setting it against a shocked mouth.

"Hey!" Natalie's distorted timbre whispers into my perked ears. She's the most excited I've heard her. Since she was a child.

"Oh eM Gee, Natalie! Are you kidding?"

"No! I left South Carolina yesterday thinking he'd never propose to me. But he *married* me, Laura. He planned this whole thing without me knowing. You guys aren't mad, right? Is everyone still there?"

"We'd have to get over the shock to be mad!" Laura giggles and whispers to the listening room, "She didn't know about it!" Then back into the phone cheerily. "And you agreed to this willingly? You know he's a pig, right?"

Everyone hears Natalie's laughter. But no one but Laura and sensitive ears hear Natalie's next words. A fervent but lighthearted whisper between girlfriends. "Yep. Theory proven."

Laura cackles. I hear Nate rumble a weary laugh somewhere close to Natalie before a phone rings in the background. Then I notice that Christian has activated his own phone.

Nate answers like Nate. A mocking, tired growl of a tone. "And you wrote a song."

The same tone. "And let her pack her own honeymoon bag."

"Touché." Nate laughs.

"I'll let you go. I'm sure you have a lot more people to explain this to." Laura's conversation again.

"We'll probably be on the phone all night. I'm glad it's New Year's, so most people are up." Nathan grumbles groggily from his end.

"I'm excited to come home and tell everyone the story!" Natalie says with joy.

"We look forward to it. Love you." Laura now.

"Niagara Falls?" Christian inquires. "Somewhat corny and cliché."

"Love you too, Sis! Bye!" The girls hang up.

"Well, my *wife* thinks it was *exceedingly* romantic." Nate rumbles the implication.

I hear Natalie snicker lovingly in the background. Nate chuckles, then yawns, which covers a voice that is suddenly far enough from him that I can't make out the words. "What'd you say, Lovebug?"

Laura jumps a little from a child's kick to her inner ribs, I assume. She and Christian meet eyes and smile, even though he's still on the phone, waiting to be spoken to again. Christian rests one hand on his wife's stomach, then chuckles a little before putting the phone on speaker. A fight worth hearing.

Nathan, trying to lower his voice. "Bug, I'm not video calling your dad at this hour. That guy can probably reach through my tablet and karate chop me to death in his sleep!"

"That is so racist!" Natalie whisper-yells.

"Can a white dude be racist after marrying a black-anese girl? Really?"

"No, but he definitely could have warned that girl's parents." Natalie seems worried, even in the distorted timbre. "Let's hope Dad is feeling benevolent when you do decide to call him."

Nate chuckles. Then pauses. "Am I on speaker, jerk?"

"You forgot to ask her parents?" Christian accuses.

"I didn't forget. It was deliberate. I didn't see a way to surprise Nat with her dad showing up and killing me midflight. And now my bride is giving me a death stare." Nate sighs. "I better go, guys. Hey, we'll be back in the afternoon on the second, so everyone should come over, and I'll make dinner. That sound okay, Seth?"

"Yes." Seth billows across the room.

"Have a nice honeymoon!" Zeke pipes in.

"Thanks, Zeke. I'm working on it."

"Love you guys!" Natalie yells from the background. Everyone answers the same back.

"Hey, cut him some slack, Natalie. He doesn't think things through." Bill adds on. Probably thinking he's being funny.

"Nope. Never." Nate is bitter with sarcasm.

"He means congratulations, Son." Karen interprets.

"Thanks, Mom. See you guys in a couple days." Nate, disheartened, hangs up.

Chapter Eighteen

Learning to Fall

I watch them unload Nate's car of luggage into the guest house when they return. And then they head toward the back door with bags of groceries, smiling at each other along the way. I greet them with the full joy of my heart when they breach the door and enter the kitchen. The others nearly scare the groceries out of their hands in the roar of applause.

The women coo over Natalie's ring, and the men tease Nate over the one Natalie insisted on buying him. Nate is eager to start in the kitchen, so everyone remains seated at the bar or in the breakfast nook to speak to him.

"We have to hear this story, you two," Laura urges Natalie. Nate grunts, unwrapping butcher paper after washing his hands. Chicken. In a perfect French accent, "There is nothing more irritating than an incompetent butcher. *Boucher Stupide*." He bends and begins the precision of removing bits of ribs from chicken breasts, knowing all eyes are on him.

"You're so cute," Natalie comments.

"Aw, my wifey thinks I'm cute." Nate says, not breaking his concentration. Laura giggles.

"So he asked you in the airport?" Laura asks, masking her eagerness. "Just, 'Hey, by the way, we're eloping'?"

"No, that would have earned him a swift knee in the nads." Natalie chuckles.

Then even Kelli and Shelley listen as Nate and Natalie take turns telling the story of the elopement. Of how Nate had surprised Natalie as she stepped off a plane when tasked with picking her up at the airport. He'd pulled her aside with a tablet at another gate, showing her pictures of Niagara Falls. He'd mentioned to Natalie that if a person were foolish enough to jump into the water, it would only be a matter of time before the current would carry them over the falls. He'd said that love is the same. It has a natural and powerful current that carries it to unexpected places in its own unpredictable timeline.

"Places like—?" Natalie had accused, thinking he was asking her to go places she knew it was wrong to go.

Then Nate had laughed at the raise in her eyebrow he so often earns, taken a knee in the terminal, and asked her to get on a plane with him. He asked her to marry him in Niagara Falls the following day. Because finally, he was ready to 'fall.'

Niagara Falls. Of course. An old-fashioned sort of romance, just as Nate knew Natalie would appreciate. Then after learning that Nate had made extensive arrangements for a tiny little ceremony complete with pictures, a preacher, brand-new clothes, flowers, and dinner reservations, Natalie only had to think for a moment before her tearful reply, "This is crazy. Let's do it."

Because of a waiting period for the legal end of things, they'd enjoyed a twenty-nine-hour engagement, during which Natalie bought her wedding dress and Nate his wedding ring. And because of love and becoming an example, they'd spent eight of those hours asleep in separate hotel rooms.

"Because girls," Nate addresses his twin sisters with drama in the teachable moment he's thrilled to own, "You should never share a room with a boy you aren't married to. Be like Laura and Natalie. Good examples."

"You're sweet, Nate." Laura is proud. Christian approves. Natalie giggles.

Shelley rolls her eyes, "We know you're talking about sex. We're not stupid."

Everyone snickers at her sassy innocence. Nate takes it further. "Yes, that. Especially wait for that. Like Laura did." And in the laughter, I'm the only one besides Seth and Natalie to notice that Nate left Natalie's name off the list this time. Natalie fades in her mind for a time, pondering this in her heart.

The pondering is likely the reason for what would be a full-blown fight between the newlyweds, were they not in moods that simply float above the room. But there is some benevolent argument when Nate asks Natalie to go find a good Chardonnay or White Burgundy after Seth offers wine as celebration. Natalie insists that while chicken pairs well with both, Pinot Grigio pairs well with his white sauce, regardless of protein.

It is only wine selection, but the disagreement runs much deeper than whatever the subject is for Nate and Natalie. Seth and I accompany the internally fuming Natalie to the wine room. She begins scouring the shelves for the Pinot Grigio least like White Burgundy, until Seth places a hand on her back.

"It's not a competition. You're on the same team." He offers gently, making the selection for her. "Chardonnay will stop a fight."

"But—" Natalie begins, wanting to win.

"Congratulations, by the way. I never got a chance to tell you." Seth interrupts with what he knows will shake Natalie deeply.

"Are you okay with this, Seth?" Natalie frets over the heart of her friend, accepting his congratulatory hug. "If I'd seen this coming so soon, I'd have talked to you about it."

"But I *told* you it was coming." Seth scrunches his eyebrows.

Natalie's eyes widen as she gasps. "You *did!* You said I'd kiss my new husband at midnight. Seth, that's creepy."

"Why? It already is." He smiles. "It was then, too."

"Whatever. But just because you knew about it, that doesn't mean you're okay with it," she reiterates.

"If you're happy, I'm happy." Seth chuckles at her worry when the hug ends.

"Is there anything else I need to know that 'already is'?" Natalie wonders.

Seth hands Natalie the bottle of wine in his hand with a smile. "Chardonnay."

Over Chardonnay and chicken with white sauce, the Holms welcome a daughter-in-law, and the housemates dwindle. Nate and Natalie sneak out during further celebration after dessert, having sent messages to each other's phones in the same room like teenagers. It's as if there is some happy fire waiting at the guest house. Seth notices, deeply saddened, but not because of that newfound fire. In fact, that fire is the coolest and least of his worries.

The next morning, Laura sighs in frustration, seated at Mom's piano. "I officially cannot make my hands cross my body. Maria keeps stopping me."

"*The Minute Waltz* can wait until after she's born, m'Love." Christian is leaning against the piano for his carpool sharer, listening to his wife's imperceptibly diminished piano abilities.

"I can't even play scales." Laura pouts.

Christian takes a seat on the bench, giving her a brush, a rubber band, and a chance to succeed.

"But you can put my hair up, right? It falls out all day if I do it. Chef sees one loose hair and comes at me with a cleaver."

Laura begins gently brushing and putting Christian's hair in a ponytail with a smirk. "You could take my dad's advice and cut it."

"You think so?" Christian glances back, wanting to please Laura at all costs.

"Don't you dare," She whispers, kissing his cheek and cuddling against his arm when the ponytail is complete.

Christian takes to rubbing his unborn daughter through Laura's belly. Already wrapped around "Maria's" finger, sight unseen, he leans his head on Laura's and sings his daughter an enchanting lullaby about fourteen angels to protect her. The others say the name they've chosen is odd for someone who could be born blonde. All except Seth, who mumbled to me in confidence that Maria may someday be cited as having a "normal" name. I don't understand. But I trust Seth.

"I don't know if I can wait five weeks for her," he offers lovingly after the song.

"You're tellin' me!" Laura giggles, wanting nothing more than to be un-pregnant and a mommy.

Christian rises and kisses Laura goodbye when we hear the back door open ten minutes later than expected. The footsteps sound odd until we see that Nate is embracing Natalie as she walks backward between playful and passionate kisses.

Nate groans amorously. "How am I supposed to go fourteen hours without kissing you?"

Natalie sees Christian and Laura, then giggles when Nate's next few kisses meet her neck. "I think you'll manage. But you better get to work before you get fired, or Christian here kills you for getting *him* fired."

"That restaurant wouldn't survive without us." Nate winks at Christian and almost releases Natalie, but at the last minute embraces and kisses her a few more times. "If you're okay waiting, I can bring home dinner for the two of us."

"Yeah, I'll wait for you," Natalie says sweetly. "And I don't have much to do today, so I'll start moving some of your things out to the house. Since you so conveniently packed your room, knowing you'd be moving."

"You are amazing," Nate thanks her. "And making it even harder for me to leave."

"Hate to break up the vomit fest, but we need to jet," Christian insists.

"Alright," Nate groans, releasing his wife finally. "Love you."

"Love you too." Natalie laughs at Nate's enchantment. "Go!"

Christian blows his wife a kiss. She "catches" it and pretends to put it in a shirt pocket she doesn't have for "later." Finally, the men depart, and Natalie sits in an armchair and sighs in some type of relief, burying her head in her hands, near tears.

"Are you okay, Natalie?" Laura startles.

"He noticed my stretch marks this morning." Natalie sighs again, heavily.

"Can't be as bad as mine." Laura mumbles, then lifts her shirt up atop her belly, revealing blue veins and red streaks across her fair skin. She is self-conscious and wouldn't show most people her bulging, uncomfortable plight. But Natalie is her dear friend and a girl and knows Natalie will say exactly what is truth.

"Oh, hush. You are so stinkin' cute." Natalie's near-tears turn to a near-smile as she warms her hands then touches her new sister-in-law's belly with joy. "A trip to Niagara Falls, and suddenly I'm this little girl's aunt."

"How do you know he noticed?" Laura knows where Natalie's heart is.

"You know Nate," Natalie smirks with sarcasm and sits back in her chair. "*So* subtle. I was getting dressed and he asked, 'Hey, what are those lines on your stomach?'"

Laura gasps, covering her stomach again. "Did you tell him?"

Natalie points to where she and Nate had entered the room. And lowers her voice. "Did it look like I told the guy I created a child with his best friend? No. I told him that when I started getting into the foodie thing, I gained a lot of weight really fast, then started exercising, and it came right off."

"You told him you had a *fat* phase?" Laura smiles in disbelief.

"Well, technically it isn't a lie, right?" Natalie winces.

"You need to *tell* him, Natalie. Truth always comes out, and he won't be happy if it doesn't come from you."

"I know, but—" Natalie sighs.

"But what?" Laura urges her friend lovingly.

"I was already thinking of a way to tell him because we were obviously getting really serious. I knew he was considering marriage as a possibility, I just thought I had more time. You marry a person as is. By then, you should know enough about them to know if you should flee or fall. The second he hit his knee in that terminal, it was too late to tell him." Natalie's heart is heavier than it appears.

"You're right. As is. And as *was*. And as will be. You can still tell him. Marriage is about unconditional love and forgiveness, Natalie. Like Jesus is." The eighteen-year-old wife declares, turning and calling quietly from the piano some song that makes her smile. The best she can, anyway.

"We don't talk about it, but faithfulness and forgiveness of our histories is implied. If he knew I'd had a baby, I bet he'd even forgive that." Natalie drops to a whisper. "But the fact that *Seth* is the father—that I *loved* him and Nate is the only person on this property who doesn't know—I'm worried that would be annulment territory in his mind. I can't let that happen. Not after everything he gave up for me. But at the same time, this secret is eating away at me."

Natalie gathers her hair over one shoulder, loathing pieces of herself.

"Secrets are deadly." Laura nods. "Truth is more freeing than damaging in the long run; powerful even. That's how it worked with Chris and me when it came to secrets."

"What secrets could two virgin teenagers bring into a marriage?" Natalie laughs, mistakenly thinking Laura's situation not near as dire as her own. She then immediately sees the flaw when Laura doesn't laugh with her and stops playing the piano. Natalie's eyes widen. "I'm sorry, I didn't mean—"

"No, it's fine. You have a point, Natalie. He and I have never even kissed anyone else, and we *love* that about our marriage." Laura shrugs. "But there's more to marriage than the physical stuff. When Chris and I met, I was a kid with no plans to date anyone, let alone get married eleven months after meeting a guy. But I'm telling you. Christian had secrets disturbing enough to change me. God used those secrets to help me grow into someone that could be his wife. If he'd chosen to keep the truth about his past from me, I'd still be a clueless little rich girl." Laura smiles a little.

"As intriguing as it is that Christian didn't just drop out of the sky like we've all speculated, it doesn't explain why you needed to *marry* him so crazy young. Couldn't you have been a great support for whatever this is as his girlfriend?" Natalie is hoping to solve a famous enigma in this house.

"I was for a while." Laura nods. "Until he mentioned that he has nightmares. He gets the vivid kind where you wake up in a panic and forget where you are and can't get back to sleep because you just don't feel safe. Now that we're married, he only forgets where he is for as long as it takes me to reach over and touch him. Seems simple. But he's sleeping more, and I get to watch his soul heal." Laura sighs, rubbing her belly with a silly smile. "Totally worth the collateral damage."

Natalie smirks, then gets concerned. "Nightmares?"

Laura nods. "Please don't mention it to Nate. But it's a part of his PTSD. When I made him go see someone, that was the diagnosis."

"Post-Traumatic Stress Disorder, are you sure? By name and definition, that takes extreme trauma."

"Yeah, I'd rather not—" Laura sighs, trying not to think about whatever it is that enters her mind.

"I understand. But will he be okay once the baby comes?" Natalie worries. "Christian is very sweet and very reliable, but if he has PTSD, don't you worry that he might—"

"Christian would never hurt a child, especially his own." Laura pulls herself from passion, changing the subject. "Is my brother still dead set on never ever having kids?"

"That's the consensus." Natalie sticks to her guns. "We'll just love on yours and make you and Christian do all the hard stuff."

"Alright." Laura nods. "So, when you gonna tell him about—"

"It'll be years before he finds out. And it'll be bad when he does." The girls look up at my always quiet master, who answers Laura's question with certainty. "Natalie won't be the one that tells him."

"So, are you saying you're gonna tell him so that doesn't come true? Why would you betray me like that?" Natalie takes up arms against Seth.

"It's not a matter of 'coming true,' Natalie. It already is." Seth explains. "You should know none of us would betray you."

Natalie sighs. Seth smiles and sits in view of the piano, waiting for Laura to play something. Seth will often listen to recordings of the piano as he works. Apparently, his mother began piano music as a calming mechanism even in his infancy. Seth had tried to learn when he was old enough but became far too frustrated. After that, he was content with listening to his mother or Natalie play. He knows that Laura is the very best calming mechanism. Laura smiles and looks to Natalie, having sensed Seth's request.

"I'm a little deficient at the moment, but I still think I could teach you that Grieg you refused to play at the wedding. Come sit with me."

Natalie rises and complies. "I could also teach you to be half-Japanese with the same amount of success."

Laura giggles and pulls a sheet of music, which she rarely requires, from behind a book or two atop the piano. She smooths it out, then with extreme patience, teaches a lesser pianist to play it beautifully. Laura is either meant to be a piano teacher or something much more important. That's what I think Seth sees as he listens instead of working like he's waiting for something.

After about an hour, we hear the familiar unlocking and creaking of the massive front door, all confused at who would be home so early until we hear the exotic balm of a voice and the boom of combat boots echo in the entryway.

"I live here for three years, and nothing ever happens. Then I go to the desert for seventeen months, and all I hear is that I'm missing things." He keeps talking, even though the gasp of the room is powerful enough truth to bring tears. "I hope whatever you all caught isn't contagious."

Natalie is the first to unleash an attack of a running hug when Derek Vargas comes home. Even a kiss on his cheek.

"Hey, you're a married woman!" Vargas returns her squeeze. "Which is the thing in my life I least saw coming. Tell me I'm not alone in that."

All humans in the room begin to laugh and affirm their own surprise.

"Not even you?" Vargas asks as he releases Natalie. She shakes her head, biting her lip.

"A surprise elopement. Only Nate." Laura giggles and begins to slide off the bench, starting the effort it takes to rise from it and greet a returning warrior. "Hey, Vargas."

"No, no, *Chiquita*. I will come to *you*," Vargas says, approaching Laura gently with a hug. "You are just glowing, little one. I bet the angels are jealous. Maria, right? Good choice."

"Yeah. Maria." Laura smiles the flattery with a head tilt and a tummy rub.

"Is your husband still living, or did Nate murder him? You were what, sixteen when I left? Now you're pregnant and married? Wow." Vargas confirms but also teases a little.

Laura giggles. "Not in that order! Nate is over himself a little. He actually got Chris a job at *Le Cloture* once this happened."

"To keep an eye on him, I bet!" Vargas cackles, then turns his attention and embrace to Seth. "Do I still have a place to live?"

"You'll always have a place here, Vargas." Seth tells the knowing.

"Well, since I haven't paid rent for quite some time, I'm feeling generous. Why don't you ladies get even more beautiful, and then we'll drop by newly saved workaholic's place of business and see if he'll come with us to *Le Cloture* for lunch." Vargas suggests.

"Zeke, take a day off?" Natalie scoffs. Then smiles. "That'd take his best buddy coming home from deployment."

"I don't have anything to wear." Laura sighs. "I'm the size of Titanic."

"My Mom's fashion sense didn't suffer just because she was pregnant with me, Laura." Seth smiles. "Go help yourself."

Meanwhile, as the girls head to Seth's closet, having been taught manners, I'm doing all in my power not to jump up on Derek Vargas. He sees, and crouches to my level, patting my head lovingly.

"Hey, old girl. Don't worry. I didn't forget about you."

Vargas is finally home. Christian and Laura are about to be parents, and Nate and Natalie are married. It all either seems like the arrival of all things hoped for, or like the groan of the earth before it begins to quake.

Chapter Nineteen

Labor Pains

It's early February, and Seth leaves his woodshop midday to make himself a sandwich, but gets caught in the formal living room just at the end of the hall. The others are at work. Laura is upstairs asleep. The kitchen is echoing malice.

"You'd think they'd fight at their own house," Seth says to me, allowing his tummy to grumble until the kitchen stops doing so. "Wonder what this one is about."

"Yeah. *I* talked to them. I talk to them all the time. I wanted *you* to talk to them." Natalie is in full attitude of voice.

"Oh my God, Nat. You hate your parents. Why does this matter?"

"I don't *actually* hate them. I just don't get along with them. You claim to hate your parents and yet we *both* talked to them on the phone, and you made them a nice little meal when we got home."

A laugh. "Your parents live in South Carolina! How am I supposed to cook for them?"

"I didn't ask you to. I asked you to *call* my dad. How hard is that?"

"He's scary."

"Yeah. What if Christian had eloped with your sister? You'd be 'scary' too. My parents are devastated about this. They haven't even met you or spoken to you. So to them, their only daughter lives with a complete stranger."

"I met your dad. Thus the knowledge of 'scary.' Remember? I got him to let you stay here when he came to get you that one time?"

"What does my mom look like? What is my little brother's name? You don't even know, do you?"

"Bug, that's not fair. I gave you the option to wait until we got home to have a big wedding. It was a serious option. I assumed you'd make a choice you could live with."

"My choice is not the problem, Nate. I just had this crazy idea in my head that you'd want to have a telephone conversation with my father at some point. We've been married a *month*, Nathan! I'm not even upset that you didn't ask him beforehand, okay? I get why you didn't. But you're making it harder for them to accept my 'choice.' What are you so scared of?"

"I'm not scared. I'm just—there's something about me he won't like."

Natalie sighs. "Is it the chef thing? Because I'm pretty sure *your* dad is the only crazy in the world who doesn't love that about you."

"It's the Jesus thing," Nate admits, bending after the flattery.

"You're on your own there. He used to think I was a heathen because I went to a more contemporary church than the rest of the family. He'll be irrationally angry when he finds out you hate God." Natalie's attitude returns.

"This is America, Bug. People with different beliefs are allowed to be together." Nate sighs, softening to a temporary resolution. "It's my day off. Can we not spend it in Seth's kitchen fighting?"

"Please?" Seth adds from three rooms away.

"Sorry!" They yell in unison.

Natalie asks for a true resolution, too quiet now for Seth to make out. "Okay but Nate, if you don't call him, I put absolutely nothing past him. He's not always rational."

"Okay, enough with the nagging," Nate whines abrasively. "Conversation over."

Natalie sighs, hurt.

The two walk the open connection of rooms to where Seth is, and Nate is seeking car keys in his pocket. "I need to go grab some sourdough. I'll cook for everyone when I get back. Okay?"

"Be safe." Natalie's goodbye after the kiss.

"Yes, mother. Laura sleeping still?"

"She's growing a person. Takes sleep." Natalie snaps.

"Be back." Nate exits into the garage then opens the door again, running into the room. "Neil! Your brother's name is Neil."

When he leaves again, Natalie sighs, lying back onto a couch near tears. "I dreamed about hell last night." Natalie trembles a little.

"You're not going to hell, Natalie." Seth sighs, knowing he is the go-to voice of reason for her.

"There was fire everywhere. It was just blistering hot, and my lungs were in agony. But I got out. Nate had to stay forever. I couldn't go back to get him. I could hear him calling for me. I knew if he just called out for Christ, he could come Home with me, but he wouldn't do it."

"Natalie, you knew that was a part of being unequally yoked." Seth convicts in his encouragement after a hard swallow.

"Worst part is I woke up screaming. Scared him half to death. But I couldn't even tell him my dream. He'd have made fun." Natalie sniffles, refusing tears. "I love him so much it's actually physically painful. But he's so caught up in this life, I don't know how to tell him that my love is nothing compared to Christ's. Oh, Seth. I've never done anything harder than this."

Laura yawns, coming down the stairs. "I was about to say the same thing." She winces uncomfortably as she takes a seat. "Natalie, we just have to keep praying that Nate sees it on his own. My whole family has been doing it forever. Mom even cries."

"She's not the only one." Natalie sighs. "Seth, tell me this works out."

"Everything works to God's glory all the time." Seth supplies.

Natalie sighs. "Thank you." That was all she needed.

Laura moans, putting her head in her hands.

"You okay, Preggers?" Natalie sits up.

"I haven't felt well all day. I even puked this morning. I haven't done that since the beginning." Laura's voice is weak and tired. Slurred, even.

"Contractions?"

"Some. No real pattern though." Laura rubs her belly.

"I bet you're in early labor." Natalie smiles. "You're due in a week, right?"

"Yeah, but, you think? How long does early labor last?"

"Depends on the pregnancy and the woman. I felt terrible for days when I did this. But my obstetrician out there told me that when you're young, you have to make sure you're on alert. Things can progress pretty quickly."

"Yeah, that's what mine said, too. I don't want to call Christian too soon. He'd leave work the minute I called. And they just started lunch service on Nate's day off, so they need him." Laura smiles, loving her husband.

"You want me to call your mom?"

"Um…" Laura seems to be having trouble sorting her thoughts. "Yeah? Yeah. She can come up here and keep an eye on me so you guys don't have to."

"We don't mind, Laura. Nate will be back any minute too. But I'll call Mom, okay?"

"Thank you."

Karen breaches the front door just before Nate does, and both family members fly to Laura's side.

"Hey, sweetie. You think today is it?" Karen asks.

"What, like baby day?" Nate pretends not to be excited. "What do I need to do?"

"Make some food, please?" Natalie asks gently.

"Yes, good idea. We could all have a long night. You feel like eating, sweetie?" Karen is sitting next to Laura, stroking her hair.

Laura falls asleep again, head on her mother's lap, and everyone converses casually in whispers around her for the next couple of hours.

I nap on the floor by Laura's couch, and the others comment on how I am protecting her. Well, of course. Christian is away. Then I hear an eerie shush that wakes me with a start. The others startle when I sit up. And I wonder a moment, Who the extra Man is in the room is until I recognize Him. He sits with Laura and looks at me once. He smiles as something seems to set to glowing beneath His hand in a touch to Laura's belly. I draw near, sniffing at the glow, though all I smell is Laura. The others are intrigued. Then the Man touches Laura's shoulder and drifts away like He did the day in the truck. I whimper. Whine. And begin to scratch at Laura's arm and lick her face.

"What is it, Willow?" Natalie is concerned.

Karen feels Laura's shoulder and gasps. "My God, she's burning up!"

Laura succumbs to my licking and sits up in a start with a kind of yelp. She clutches her belly and breathes. Then in a moment, she sets the room to excitement with her words, “Ow.” A squeak. “Will someone call Christian, please?”

Nate takes the job but becomes frustrated in the next few moments when only the same recorded words keep occurring in Christian’s voice. Nate tries another number, which never picks up at all. Then there is an obnoxious repeating beep.

“Why is no one picking up?” Nate tries to keep to himself, but Laura begins to panic with a new pain she’s having.

“But I need Christian,” she whimpers.

Nathan jumps up, checking for his keys. “I’ll speed very safely,” he tells his wife, running out the door.

“Aaaooowww.” Laura tenses.

“You have to breathe. Just breathe normal and relax as much as you can. Think about how limp you can make your arms and legs. Don’t fight the contractions, okay?” Natalie says gently.

Karen squints at Natalie. “Are you trained in childbirth?”

“You could say that,” Natalie says, breathing with Laura.

“You’ve done this before,” Karen concludes. “You’ve had a baby.”

Natalie glances at her mother-in-law after the contraction. “I’m amazed you didn’t know that from the way word travels around here.”

“With Seth, right?” Karen is kind, therefore these words are not accusatory.

“Natalie, I never—" Seth explains to Natalie in shock.

“We were sixteen. Nate doesn’t know.” Natalie sweeps Laura’s hair aside, removing blame from Seth.

“Of course, he doesn’t. Nate knows what Nate wants to know.” Karen smiles. “But all it takes is a little logic and some insider information to figure it out. We bought a house from your parents, Natalie. Bill and I sat at a table with a sad-looking Japanese man several years ago. He said they loved the house but had to move away because their daughter had gotten herself into the kind of trouble that involves an adoption process. When I met the sweet, handsome boy up the street, the puzzle was complete in my mind.”

“So, you’ve always known?” Seth asks, glancing at the uncomfortable Natalie.

"You're like another son to me, Seth. A mom always knows a lot more than you think she does." Karen rubs her daughter's back. "She's also good at keeping secrets."

Twelve tense minutes later, Christian runs through the door, ranting, "Love, I am so sorry! The stupid new apprentice set off the fire alarms because he put a towel on a burner. We had to clear out the whole place until the fire chief let us back in. I dropped my phone on the way out. I was stressed the whole time that you were trying to call me. I just *knew* it." By now, he's on his knees in front of her. "But I'm here, m'love. Tell me what's going on."

Then Laura, who had been far too even-keeled for hours of well-tended illness and even while in pain, bursts into a multitude of tears and blubbering no one catches much of. "Sick…hurts…call… I'm cold…fever…needed you…" But Christian, Laura's perfect match, just listens intently, rubbing her forearm. Perfectly at peace. When she's done, he smiles.

"So, what you're saying is we're gonna be parents today?"

Laura's tears break at Christian's words. She sniffles, then laughs a little. "Yes."

"That's what I thought I heard. You excited?" He remains at peace.

"I'm scared." Laura sniffles. "It hurts. It's gonna get worse. I really don't think I'm strong enough for this. I'm only eighteen. They're gonna think terrible things about us, just like they have since we got engaged. What if they don't even listen to me?"

"People suck, m'Love. But why are you worried about what they think? You are *so* much stronger than you know. You and God can do this."

Laura laughs. "That's easy for *you* to say."

"If I could do the pain, I would. But since I can't, Laura Renee Kessler, would you please do me the honor of being God's instrument and bringing my daughter into this world?" Christian remains ever romantic, kissing her hand, then whispering. "I'll be with you every second."

"I love you like crazy." Laura says in a laughed sob.

"I love you like crazy, too. Let's go have a baby."

From them flows joy. Love. Always. It is something God put them here to do, I think, against more odds than I think I know about. And Karen is focused on them. But I see the fear of Nate and the way he paces and stresses over even things he can't control. I see the tension. The way Natalie remembers but has to hide it. The way Seth wants to have the memory but must be at peace without it. Because peace is Seth's job. And though the depth of his knowing might be reason for destruction, Seth always does his job.

Chapter Twenty

HYPOTHETICAL

Seth was wise, I think, to have found some way to be at some job site somewhere else in the country on a cold day in February when lovers find new excuses to love. Nate had used something called seniority at work to not have to be there tonight, or so I learn in Christian's frantic mumbling, through puffs of breath as I follow him on the path to the guest house.

"Nate is gonna murder me for this," Christian tells me, which is precisely why I'd followed.

Christian hesitates, especially when a mere peek through the glass door speaks candlelight and wine to his eyes, and he groans, praying a prayer before considering a knock. He does not want to disturb the figures standing in the kitchen. I listen to the dimness as Christian hesitates.

I've always liked the way Natalie dresses. They call her classy, which only has a little to do with her natural beauty. The class is what she does with it. Tonight, she's in a gray dress with too much fabric that is missing a shoulder, and she isn't even wearing the red boots I'd seen her pair it with earlier. But Nate, in some great state of honesty, notes what is always evident of Natalie.

"You're exquisite." And he savors kisses at Natalie's neck and bare shoulder and ear as if he's sampling wine.

"*Aishiteru,"* She tells him in breathy enslavement. Her voice softening and forming as natural around the foreign word.

"You speak Japanese beautifully. I wish I knew what you were saying." Nate smiles in the dim light of the kitchen, ceasing his kisses a moment to look down into her eyes.

"Sorry. It just means I love you." She translates, some deep dreaminess occurring in her eyes that I've never seen.

"'Just' I love you?" Then Nate resumes his tender task, and Natalie speaks again quietly.

"Well, people in Japan often think words are a weak way to express love." Something I've heard her explain before.

"Tonight, I'll have to agree. Shhh…" Nate sighs and relaxes his forehead against his wife's. Natalie giggles as he playfully unbuttons his shirt then slides it to the floor. This is the moment when Christian turns from praying and realizes he should get to knocking on the door immediately.

The knock causes their combined heart to jump. Then they ignore it.

"Come on, guys," Christian says to himself.

Another knock. Longer, louder, more determined. Nate grunts, frustrated and cursing, and is unstable as he makes his way to the door. He opens it and leans on the doorframe with a threatening look that makes me cower behind Christian.

"I'm really sorry, but you need to come to the house like right now." Christian stands, whispering to the shirtless man on the lighted doorstep.

"Unless it's on fire, no thanks. And if it's on fire, no thanks." Nate has every intention of slamming the door in Christian's face. "I'm unbelievably busy."

"Oh, *that's* unfortunate." Christian comments on the way Nate's speech both smells and sounds compromised. "But may I recommend a shirt? I know you're not thrilled to see me, but it was better than the alternative."

"I disagree." Then Nate steps out of his way, gesturing to his wife in all her exquisiteness.

Christian winces with a friendly wave to Nate's preoccupation.

"Hey Chris, is the baby okay?" Natalie is leaning against the counter for support and uses the same compromised speech. I hear it well next to the clarity of Christian's.

"Baby's fine. But I need to borrow your husband for an urgent matter." Christian tells Natalie, then whispers to Nate. "Dude, your night is about to do a one-eighty. The alternative to me retrieving you would have been *Ken* doing it. But he still wants to see you."

"Ken…" Nate searches his wine-scrambled brain for the memory.

"Ken Nakano? Your father-in-law?!" Christian reveals. "He's here. And like, fuming, smoking-at-the-ears mad. That little kid with him punched me when I walked in the door from work. Neil, right?" Christian is still speaking low for the sake of Natalie.

Nate says some unholy word as he turns white. "I can't even see straight. Why *tonight*? We never drink like this. Why Valentine's Day?" Nate widens his eyes and stretches his face several times, slapping a palm to his forehead.

"Pretty low, I admit. But seriously, hurry. Zeke and Vargas are barely holding the guy." Christian urges, with nervous glances back at the main house.

Nate quickly grabs his shirt off the kitchen floor. He puts it on, reluctantly parting from Natalie's final gentle kiss and look of admiration. Then out in the cold, he's trying to remember how to button buttons as they walk. "What do I say, Chris?"

"How would I know? I didn't marry someone's daughter without so much as a phone call. You're in deep, Dude." Christian reminds Nate.

"Guuuhhhhhh." Nate stops, bending over, spitting, trying not to vomit.

"How much did you have to drink?" Christian sighs.

"Well, it took me a few glasses to admit it, but my wife is great at pairing wine with food. We weren't really expecting company." He stands back up slowly. "Maybe you should say a prayer to your God for me."

"Already done. Maybe you should start doing it for yourself. I love you, Bro. It was nice knowing you." Christian says before we all breach the back door.

Nate is frozen. So is the red-faced Mr. Nakano. Neil is breathing heavily. Nate loses verbal filters the more wine he puts inside himself, so what he says now is complete truth.

"I'm an idiot." A good preface, it turns out. Everyone in the room nods in agreement with the open shirt and flipped collar and the aroma of fermented grapes.

"Where is my daughter?" Ken Nakano intimidates with mere presence. His accented speech terrifies.

"Uh…" Nate searches his mind for a proper answer. "She's at home. We live in the guest house." Nate is compelled to lean against the door. Unable to hide the state of his mind.

"You said she was classy last time, and then suddenly she lives with you?" Neil, of course.

"Yeah, I moved in with her after I *married* her. I didn't touch the woman until then, I swear to you." Nate pleads with the boy.

"But you touch her *now* and didn't even call us," Neil argues, his voice now changing with age.

"Little dude, that is not even close to your business. Natalie is my wife. And I stand by the thing I said before. The classy thing." Nate looks to be fighting off nausea again.

"You're drunk." Ken proclaims.

Nate blinks his eyes widely, trying to see properly. "Definite possibility."

"Is *she* drunk?" Neil asks.

"Very," Nate answers with a sensual smile.

Zeke and even Vargas are relishing the misstep, snickering. Christian is shaking his head.

"A drunk man is an honest man," Ken comments, almost with a smile.

Nate speaks that honesty. "Mr. Nakano, we never drink like this. Especially her. We were settling a wine pairing argument, and we got carried away. You caught us on a bad night."

"Good." Ken smiles.

"Uhh…" Nate tries to sober, rubbing palm to forehead again. Calling up everything in him that could help him escape with his life. "I could really use some coffee. Can I make you some coffee? Nat says I can actually make a decent cup now."

"'Nat'?" Neil speaks up. "She's not a bug."

"She used to say that to me all the time." Nate snickers at the memory and his nickname for her. "Now I just call her 'Bug' to save her the trouble."

"Coffee would be fine." Ken concedes, seeing Nate's eyes sparkle when he mentions Natalie. "Neil, why don't you go find a way to entertain all these young men?"

Which, in real words, means they should all go away. Not wanting to watch the destruction of my hated and beloved Nate, I retreat with them to the living room. And here they sit in silence for far too great a time. Low mumbles emit from the kitchen no one is brave enough to hear.

Then the twelve-year-old boy clears his throat. "Is she happy? My sister. Is she happy with him?"

Zeke sighs when the other two will not answer. "Yeah. She's happy."

"And he loves her?" Neil asks. "Is he good to her and stuff?"

Christian fields this one. "Nate is a little rough around the edges, Neil. But he's all heart. There's no question that he loves her."

"Sorry for punching you. I was just mad that no one would tell us where they were." Neil rights the wrong.

"It's alright, Dude." Christian had already forgiven and glances up in the direction of the stairs. "My two-week-old daughter is upstairs sleeping with my very tired wife. I was just trying to keep things to a dull roar."

"Oh. I thought you were a teenager. I didn't realize you were married." Neil winces.

"I just turned twenty. My wife is Nate's eighteen-year-old sister. He's my brother-in-law."

Neil tries to tease. "And you already have a baby? Whoops?"

"We honored God, Dude." Christian says with pride. "No 'whoops' here."

"Admit it, Christian. There's no way you intentionally impregnated a seventeen-year-old on your honeymoon. An honorable 'whoops' is still a 'whoops.'" Vargas teases successfully. "Which is something that doesn't happen with a—"

"Vow of chastity." The chorus that Vargas conducts with silly arms, rolls their eyes then laughs.

Christian barely ecks out the rebuttal through the laughter, counting on his fingers. "A man's three greatest regrets in life: One: Falling in love with a beautiful, godly woman, two: Sex, and three: His firstborn child."

"Touché. Although I bet Nate is regretting a couple of those things at the moment." Derek Vargas nods, laughing again at his wise young friend.

Neil is still processing behind his glasses, starting to enjoy this group of near-strangers—likely having misjudged them completely after the brief meeting when Natalie had first arrived. "My dad is pretty crazy. I told him not to come, at least not tonight. But he's not really reasonable."

"Impeccable description, *Otouto*." Natalie startles everyone when she stumbles in from the kitchen with a bottle of water, having been booted out after the surprise of seeing her father speaking with Nate. My head is beneath her hand in an instant once she clamors her way to the couch and begins having trouble opening—or seeing—her water bottle. She barely manages, "Hey, Willow."

"Ay! *Hermosa, Senora Holm*!" Vargas whistles, admiring as art the wife of his friend, now with those high-heeled red boots on again.

"In other words, wow," Zeke says with a nod, admiring her regardless of marital status.

"Thanks." Natalie crosses her arms at the flattery of the men. "That was the idea. I was sort of on a date with my husband." She raises an eyebrow at Christian.

"I just drew the short straw, don't blame me." Christian sighs, then takes Natalie's bottle of water, opens it, and returns it to her with a smile.

"Thanks. Papa could have given Nate some warning." Natalie now accuses her little brother.

"I agree, *Ane*." Neil seems embarrassed. "But Dad was so mad that Nate didn't call to explain himself that he wanted to catch him at his worst when he had a lot more to explain."

"Well, he succeeded. My poor husband is inebriated in the kitchen with our psychotic father. And I'm pretty sure his shirt is on inside out." Natalie giggles wildly.

"Nate said you were drunk, too." Neil tests. "He doesn't seem like a good influence."

"We were tasting wine, *Otouto*. And we thought we were in for the night." Natalie starts, then sighs, speaking bitterly. "But you're right. There's no excuse. If you want to make Mom and Dad happy, you should not be anything like me. Follow the rules. Let Dad choose your wife, and let Mom plan your wedding. Understood?"

"Mom actually liked your wedding photos. She cried. Don't tell Dad, but she thought it was brave what you did. Then it broke her heart when the idiot wouldn't even have a phone conversation with them." Neil gives full honesty.

"Mine, too." Natalie sighs. "But he's not an idiot."

Vargas coughs. "Bull."

"Vargas!" Natalie is offended. "Since when do you not adore Nate?"

"I love the guy." Vargas half smiles. "But he's a fool."

"Guys, don't be jerks. Of all the flaws in Nate, his intellect is certainly not one of them." Natalie reasons.

"So you'd think he'd have figured it out by now." Zeke chuckles. "I did."

"Figured what out?" Neil is now worried.

"The only thing worth figuring out." Christian finally reveals the juice. "Nate isn't a believer. And he'll fight you to the death if you try to convince him."

"Guys! Don't you remember he used to do the same thing with marriage?" Natalie, still blinking away her fog, holds up the hand Nate used to change his mind.

"Natalie, you are so caught up with his hunky muscles and big blue eyes that you are oblivious to the fact that Nathan Holm may *never* turn to Christ. That one has a heart of stone, chica." Derek Vargas condemns a man.

Natalie's face is nearly condemned to tears. "Even if that's true, I love him. I can't just give up doing that, especially if that's the one chance he has to see God's love. Some support would be nice. Yeah, maybe I took it to the extreme, but you're called to love him too. Right? Seth would tell you guys the same thing. You'd listen to him."

"Seth? The guy that got you in trouble?" Neil clarifies with brutality and a memory not quite good enough. "Why should anyone care what *he* thinks?"

"Keep your voice down, Neil. Nate doesn't know about that. But Seth is wiser than all of us combined and you all know it. Even Nate knows it. Apparently, I'm the only person around here that remembers just how powerful God is."

And then, whether all convicted or all feeling sorry for the misguided woman, or some combination thereof, all men take to silence. But the boy sends the dagger to his sister's heart.

"You are such a screw-up."

"Leave it to me," Natalie mumbles in intoxicated and sarcastic frustration.

The kitchen trembles. Quakes. Then erupts from its gentle mumbles.

"No, you don't get to decide what I do or don't ask my wife, Ken!" Nate, apparently, has been shaken even from his reverence for his new father-in-law.

"Are you scared of her?" Ken intimidates.

"It's a ridiculous question. Fear has absolutely nothing to do with it."

"Oh no." Natalie's hand goes to her mouth as she's thinking the worst—or at least the worst she knows thus far.

"If you are not scared, ask her. You are too sure of yourself. You need perspective," Ken insists.

"Perspective? Seriously? You barge in on me and my wife on Valentine's Day to give me *perspective?* I can't wait to see your plans for our anniversary! You could use some perspective of your own." Nate storms into the midst of everyone, eyes on Natalie, whose heart is racing.

"Your husband has something to ask you," Ken prefaces as he approaches.

"Look at her. She's upset. You upset your daughter. Are you happy? Can we end this, please?" Nate turns back to Ken. Sobering due to coffee and adrenaline.

Natalie stands, facing whatever it is she must face. Speaking sheepishly. "What is it, Nate? I'll tell you whatever you want to know."

"I don't want to know," he reiterates, using his hands to both animate speech and bring some relief to Natalie. "Your dad thinks I need to know this crazy hypothetical thing."

"Hypothetical?" she clarifies.

"Yeah, about your Jesus thing." Nate relieves her completely, staying her dark secret in every heart but his. That's right, she remembers. Seth had said it would be years.

"Okay? Just ask. My mind isn't right. I hope I can answer." Natalie has not had quite as much adrenaline.

"Alright. If you had to choose. Between your Jesus thing. Your religion. And me. Your husband. What would you choose?" Nate's simple words take Natalie to a lean on the back of a couch and her heart to a place of devastation. The rest of the room gasps.

Natalie stalls. “Choose?”

Nate sighs. “If you could only have one. Either me or your religion.”

“It’s not really a religion, Nate. I’ve explained this to you. We all have. It’s a personal relationship with Christ, my Savior. A relationship with God,” Natalie explains.

“Well, that makes it easier. Would you rather have a ‘personal relationship’ with a guy you can’t see that lives in the clouds somewhere? Or do you prefer the flesh and blood kind of personal relationship?” Nate, I decide, does need perspective. But not like this. I growl at Ken.

“Baby, I love you.” Natalie squeaks. “Way more than just flesh and blood. You know that. That’s why I risked everything to marry you.”

“Yeah, me too. I hated marriage. But I’d die for you, Love Bug. Name the day. You’re my everything. I don’t know who I am without you.” Nate shrugs.

“Nate.” Natalie sighs. “That’s the thing. You’re the most important *person* in my life. But you’re *not* my everything. And I *do* know who I am without you. You say you’d die for me. But He already did. My everything, my identity. They’re all wrapped up in Christ.”

Nate nods. Taking the blow valiantly under the circumstances and with all the eyes. “So, you choose an idea over your husband?”

“I’m not making the choice, Baby. You said it was hypothetical.”

“Does it really matter? I gave up a heck of a lot for you, Natalie. My life changed when we met. What do I get? I get told that something you believe is more important than me. You say you’d choose God. But Nat, didn’t you tell me earlier that words are a weak way of expressing love? You’re a hypocrite. You got drunk with me tonight. Your God doesn’t like that, right? And you weren’t exactly face first in that Bible of yours when Christian came to the door, were you? Yet you’ll tell the world that I’m just second place. Sickens me, Natalie. Well, guess what? How about I ‘choose’ to stay on Seth’s couch tonight. You and God can have our house to yourselves on Valentine’s Day. I won’t interfere. This cold night just got colder, Natalie.” Nate is vicious. Animated. Hurtful.

“Nate,” Natalie squeaks through tears.

“It was nice to meet you, Ken. Neil. Thanks for the perspective.” And then he shuts himself in Seth’s room with a door slam.

Natalie breathes a few times in the monumental awkwardness. Then she looks at the father with a smirk on his face. She turns to him, eyes like fire. And gathers all the finesse and power within her to say with quiet truth what she's never told him.

"*Daikirai.*"

No one fully understands. But Neil begins to object, especially when Ken Nakano's face twists in shock. Devastation. And he simply walks out of the house the opposite direction of Natalie. Nothing solved, nothing gained. But so much lost.

Chapter Twenty-One

SUBMISSION

Typical Nate, they are all verbalizing in disgust about the barely breathing log of a man on the sofa. A hot temper and bull's head under pressure—ruin in its wake. And, of course, a fast-approaching hangover.

They are along the bar, sans Seth, in the next room when an alarm goes off on Nate's phone. He doesn't hear it, of course, so I lick his face to awaken him. He does so with a pained moan. He quiets his phone and then rubs his eyes between thumb and middle finger to convince himself he exists. Then, when his mind is alert, he stares at the ceiling with a sigh. Remembering. And shaking his head in self-hatred for doing so.

"Did you guys make coffee? Tylenol might be appropriate, too." Nate is grunting and squinting when he enters the kitchen.

"Make it yourself, jerk." His morning greeting first comes from his sister who is nursing the infant under the blanket, sitting in an armchair in the breakfast nook. Nate sits in another, finding standing a nauseating task.

"I wasn't wrong." Nate stays his pride.

"Congrats." Zeke scours the news on his phone as he sips coffee at the bar.

"You'll be lucky if you still have a wife when you go home." Vargas shakes his head, getting ready to head to work for the day. He dusts off the camouflage cover as he stands.

"She wouldn't leave me," Nate speaks the known truth.

"Ooo, teachable moment," Christian says with bitter enthusiasm from the bar. Something Nate always says. "Natalie won't leave you because she loves you regardless of the fact that you're an idiot, yelled at her in front of all her friends and her father, and probably made her cry herself to sleep. She's also most likely going to look inward and blame herself, thinking about how right you are. She's going to be better after this. Even classier than ever. Don't count on any more wine tastings. She'll likely apologize to you by the time you leave for work. Why? Because you were right? No. Because she likes to honor God above anything. Including submitting to an idiot husband. If you think about it, God is responsible for 90 percent of who she is. Bravo, though, on pointing out the other 10 percent. Now, what were you saying about not being wrong?"

Nate sighs. Always conceding to good reasoning in moments of weakness. "Okay so you're not wrong, either. I'm sorry. Okay? Is that what you want? I was so drunk and so mad at Nat's dad. I can't believe I took it out on her."

"Don't apologize to *us*," Vargas says, having set down a cup of coffee and two Tylenol on the table next to Nate. Nate nods, thanking Vargas just before the soldier exits the house for the day.

"With Nat, I think I can figure out how to fix this. But her dad will be a tougher sell. Ideas on how to get on his good side?"

"Give your life to Christ." Zeke knows the words are futile. Chuckles.

Nate laughs once. "Other than Kool-Aid."

"Call him and apologize for being a heathen. Pretty sure last night was a worst-case scenario." Laura suggests. "I was at the top of the stairs."

"He and Natalie aren't on great terms either." Zeke reminds. "Calling him may not bode well."

Seth emerges from his room, seeking coffee after a late-night arrival and early morning cereal. Everyone greets him.

"Call Neil," The master of the house suggests.

"Neil is twelve." Nate reminds Seth.

"If you convince Neil you are worthy of Natalie, you'll have Ken and Eden's approval too," Seth reasons. Probably some source of regret for him.

Nate, desperate for some resolve, takes out his phone. "Does he have his own phone? Ah! There he is. Neil Nakano. So glad I copied all Nat's contacts while I was tricking her into marrying me." He chuckles. Then breathes as he hesitates a moment, talking to himself. "He's twelve. Why is this hard?"

"*Otouto*. That's what she calls him. I've heard her say it before. Means little brother. Might help." Laura provides him just the confidence he needs. With a smile, he puts the phone to his ear, standing and starting the journey to the living room.

"S'go Willow," Seth is heading outside to build a fence section. When we arrive at the spot, I hear sniffles and smell Natalie. Seth sighs.

"Hey, Seth. Hey, Willow." She's curled up at the base of a tree, crying. "I saw your truck in the garage. I was hoping you'd come out here this morning."

"What's the matter, Natalie?"

"I shouldn't have married him." She smiles, trying to stop the flow of tears.

"Why not?" Seth asks, setting to work on his fence.

"I can't trust myself around him. I don't feel in control anymore." She trembles.

"You've never been in control." Seth gives her truth.

"I know, Seth. But he made me out to be a terrible Christian." Natalie chuckles. "He basically said I'm lying if I say I don't put him above God."

"I know what he said. He was selecting wine from my private reserve when I got home. I stopped him before he opened a bottle, don't worry." In reality, Seth had been glad to have more strength than inebriated and emotional Nate when fighting him for the bottle last night.

Natalie sighs. "Thank you. He'd have gotten alcohol poisoning with anymore. Is he okay? I bet he's still crashed. I should go wake him up so he isn't late for work—"

"He's fine." Seth smiles at Natalie's devotion. "He has a hangover, but he is awake."

"Fine is relative, I guess. I don't know how we'll get past this. How did I marry someone who has no trouble with blasphemy and is fine with me compromising my morals? I thought he was close to coming to Christ, but now I just don't see how he'll ever—" Natalie halts speech, sanctioning tears.

"'Wives, likewise, be submissive to your own husbands, that even if some do not obey the word, they, without a word, may be won by the conduct of their wives.'" Seth quotes.

"*Conduct*?! My conduct is terrible, Seth. I'm not going to win him by sinning with him. I drank with him. A lot. Like it was totally okay." Natalie is highly distressed.

"So drink less next time." Seth encourages with simplicity.

"I told my father I hated him! I've never said that to him. Neil is right, Nate is a terrible influence. Maybe even poison."

"Your dad was out of line." Seth falters, a rarity, a barbed wire thorn consequently invading his thumb with a drip of red. He covers it quickly with a shake of his head and the strip of old sock he'd so randomly tucked in his pocket this morning over cereal.

"Nate was right. How many times have I skipped reading my Bible to watch a movie with him or skipped church to let him make omelets on Sunday morning? I *do* put him before God." Natalie closes her eyes and leans her head against the tree. "What is wrong with me? I didn't think a man would ever lead my heart astray."

Seth chuckles through closed lips as he looks back at her from digging a hole.

"What?" Natalie says, wondering at his out of place amusement.

"The only man that ever led your heart astray was a man of God." Seth speaks of himself.

"Why do you always act like sleeping together was your idea? I still can't believe I talked you into it that easily. You're so strong." Natalie ruminates.

"It doesn't take a lot of strength to be sinful. Submission takes strength. Women think that submitting shows weakness. But I think God gave women that job because they are stronger. So, since men are accountable to make godly choices despite distractions, we both failed. Doesn't matter whose idea it was." Seth smiles back at a woman confused by her strength.

"Seth, I couldn't even submit to your godly decisions. How am I supposed to submit to an ungodly man?" Natalie is downtrodden. Worried she can't be strong enough.

"It's like Jesus on the cross, dying for ungodly people. It would have hurt a lot less if He'd just gotten off the cross like he certainly could have. But His submission saved the world. It wasn't easy, Natalie. But nothing remarkable ever is." Just information. No expression.

Both Natalie and I watch Seth build a section of fence in silence. And I remember that word 'remarkable.' Seth had been indisputably described that way. I'm beginning to see why.

I smell and Seth sees Nate coming. But Natalie is pleasantly surprised when he slides his back down, leaning against another side of her chosen tree. Without looking at her, he grabs her hand, weaving his into it on the pine needle and frozen mud ground beneath them.

"You weren't at home. I was worried." Nate smells freshly showered.

"That I left you?" Natalie includes thick eyelashes he turns to see and a kiss of Nate's hand in the question.

"I wouldn't have blamed you." Nate looks away again.

"Well, I wouldn't have left you." She concludes.

"I'm sorry," Nate whispers.

"Me too," Natalie whispers back. Seth smiles out of their vision when he hears a connection of their lips. A sad sort of smile. He knows the fight has barely begun.

"So." Nate smiles at Seth. "Two of these a week?"

"Yep," Seth replies, rejecting a warped picket into his bin.

"What, you've never been out here?" Natalie asks Nate.

"No. Well, just to where um…his parents are." Nate tries to be sensitive.

"Yeah…" Natalie remembers with a much greater burden than Nate.

"Your brother is hilarious. He says if your dad drives him across the country one more time for a half-hour-long visit, he'll call child services." Nate cackles.

Natalie looks at him, confused. "When did you talk to Neil?"

"A few minutes ago. Seth's suggestion." Nate winks. Natalie melts. "I heard that you told your dad you hated him in Japanese. Good job, Bug. I'm rubbing off on you. Neil says you're dead to your father. But he said that's always temporary."

"Amazing grace," Natalie says under her breath.

"What?" Nate hadn't heard.

"Nothing. When do you work?"

"Have to leave in an hour. Let me make you a peace omelet in the meantime." Nate stands and reaches down to help his wife to her feet.

"Sounds wonderful." Natalie takes the hand and keeps it, bidding me goodbye with a pat to my head. "Thanks, Seth. Fence is looking great."

Natalie and Seth exchange a smile. Once again, Nate misses what is right before his eyes.

Chapter Twenty-Two

Expectation

"It's good. I like it." Natalie nods with a smile on a Thursday evening in November, all eyes on her for the first bite of the first course.

"'It's good, I like it'? Who are you and what did you do with my wife?" Nate laughs.

"Okay. It is pleasing to my palate? Is that better? Good flavor balance." Natalie is already sorry she changed her tune.

"Why are you lying to me?" Nate accuses.

"Nate. I like it. What do you want me to say?" She smiles.

"I want you to be honest, like always. Why are you being so nice? This is a new dish. I need your help perfecting it," Nate explains.

"But you don't like it when I'm critical." Natalie sighs in frustration. She's trying to submit after the two had a loud knock-down-drag-out last week over her harsh criticism.

"I do. I just don't like to act like I do."

"So, who is dishonest now?" Natalie raises her voice.

"Us kids don't like it when Mommy and Daddy fight. And we are very hungry." Vargas butts in.

Natalie sighs. Nate tilts his head for a response.

"Too much salt," Natalie says timidly. Then Nate smiles and kisses her forehead, then moves to the kitchen for the other plates. Christian is already emerging with some.

Natalie turns to Seth with a familiar whisper. "I can't do submissive. He hates it."

Seth replies. "Yes, you can. But you still have to be *you*. He likes you."

The rest of the table is exchanging looks over the not-so-mysterious yet undefinable friendship between Natalie and Seth. Nate returns, taking his seat after serving plates as always.

"Chef is retiring. Me and the two other sous chefs are up for chef de cuisine. He's making his decision next month. I'd own a restaurant." Nate raises his eyebrows.

"That's great, baby! Would I still get to see you in the mornings and on Thursday nights?" Natalie missteps again.

"Yeah, I told Chef: 'I can only take over if my wife gets to see me in the morning and on Thursday nights.' He was like, 'Yeah that's cool. *Le Cloture* exists to please your woman.'" Nate missteps further.

"Nate!" Natalie is hurt.

"Thought maybe you'd be proud of me for once. Thought wrong. No harm done."

"Nathan." This time through her teeth. "Of *course*, I'm proud of you. I never *stop* being proud of you."

"Thanks." Nate smiles, then rises to get the next course ready. "Your haircut is sexy, by the way."

Natalie reaches up to make sure he isn't joking about her chin-length change before thanking him timidly. Everyone at the table is in constant amusement at the volatile marriage. Nate disappears a moment and returns as Christian is clearing the first course.

"My parents are coming for Christmas," Natalie blurts. Nate drops a plate, which is unprecedented in every way. The others laugh. She tucks her lips before the next comment. "My reaction exactly."

"Uh, why? We'll start with that." Nate's heart is pounding as he passes out soup, and Seth cleans up the mess on the floor.

"Because their son seems to have some cosmic attachment to his brother-in-law, and they don't think that'd be possible if he is the buffoon they mistook him for." Natalie flashes daring eyes.

I've been witness to heartfelt discussions over the phone between the now thirteen-year-old Neil and Nate, the brother he'd always needed. I assume that with an unreasonable father like Ken, many things had gone undiscussed. But, of course, Natalie had first sworn Neil to secrecy about Seth.

"So, our parents—our families are gonna like, meet?" Nate says with sheer pubescent voiced terror.

"Theoretically," Natalie says, also with terror, sipping some wine. "Mom and Dad are staying at a hotel, but they're letting Neil stay at our house."

"*Our* house?" Nate clarifies with a whine.

Natalie giggles. "They'll be here for our anniversary, too. Sorry, Baby."

Nate lights up, and the others laugh. "I called it! Didn't I call it? Ha! I'm okay. Warning. We have that. I can do this." Nate breathes.

Laura clears her throat, glancing at the nine-month-old in the nearby portable crib. "In other news, Christian and I are expecting twins." As nonchalant as can be.

Christian chuckles at the blank stares of the room and his wife's tone. "You're awesome, m'love."

"Wait, are you serious? You're expecting again?" Vargas is as confused as the rest of us.

"Twins." Christian reiterates with a sigh. "I was a twin. Laura has twin sisters and aunts. We were sort of doomed. This soup is *amazing*, Nate."

"Was that you buttering him up?" Laura giggles, tilting her head lovingly at her husband of a year and a half.

"Alright, Chris," Nate starts. Trying to be gentle. "So, you and Laura and three kids are gonna live upstairs with Zeke and Vargas?"

The latter two look at one another with eye rolls. From below, I've been privy to Maria's current phase of babbling half the night instead of sleeping. They are probably much more aware.

"No, Nate. Thanks for bringing it up. How about, 'Congrats on your persistent fruitfulness, guys!'" Christian sighs. For once not as cheery as usual. Nate takes the opportunity to tease.

"So where is my cuisinier going to store his family safely in this town? Buying is cheaper than renting these days. Is that your plan?" He chuckles at his own French accent.

Natalie rolls her eyes.

"A chef de partie would certainly do better." Christian has been asking for the deserved promotion and raise from his supervisor for several months now. This time in an even lovelier French accent. All learned from their boss, they've said.

"A chef de partie requires his own knives to move between stations. Also, the ability to taste wine. When you turn 21, your work ethic and palate with proper knives may earn sous chef should I become the owner of *Le Cloture*." Still-French Nate only makes Christian more distressed, though that wasn't his intention.

Christian returns to his native continent. He laughs, bitterly. "Knives cost about what I'd need for a normal down payment on a house or a vehicle with room for three car seats. My little two-door beater doesn't count. Oh, and since banks don't like zero credit history in a nineteen- and twenty-year-old with only high school diplomas, we'd need a stupid, insane, crazy down payment that I don't make in a year and a half. And since Laura's a cute little time bomb, that's not all gonna work out in time since I still pay rent and buy diapers and food, etc. That's even if you did promote me."

"You know my dad is loaded, right? I bet he'd give you every penny scot-free." Nate is now dropping his humor and actually trying to help.

"No, no. Your dad and money and me have a lot of issues." Christian conceals something in his wince.

"Come on, guys. We're family here. We could get together and help you out. You could even pay it back. It's not even a question. You two deserve it." Natalie speaks up. Everyone begins to agree, already talking logistics. But Laura shushes them frantically, looking to her husband for a reaction as if someone has just poured acid on his head.

"I'm trusting God on this one." Christian rises and heads upstairs, even when Laura quietly begs him not to. When the door shuts, and the others look to Laura with confusion, she explains.

"Guys, don't ever, ever, ever offer him money—especially a loan. Okay? Please. Just trust me. Never do that again." Laura is still frantic. "God will provide, okay? We'll be fine."

"Laura, what's the matter?" Natalie feels guilt immediately.

"Christian just," Laura stops her tongue and rethinks. "He doesn't like to owe anyone anything. Even a mortgage would be a stretch for him. It's extremely important to him. I can't stress that enough."

"Then why did he knock you up again if he knew you were genetically prone to twins and he was broke?" Nate wonders with spite, forgetting he's trampling a tender heart. Everyone knew it was coming.

"Are you serious?" Laura accuses her brother. "Don't you get it, Nathan? Nothing happens unless God wants it to. He's sovereign. We may have trials, but we live to honor Him. He'll take care of us."

"Laura, how am I supposed to sit here and watch you guys drown? You think some cosmic force is coming to your rescue because you 'honor' Him by giving it up to a guy that can't afford the repercussions?"

"I'm sick of you treating Christian like he did something wrong. You say 'giving it up' like I'm not *married* to him! 'It' is rightfully his."

"This is the twenty-first century. Women actually have a say these days." Nate mocks.

"In that case, it's rightfully *mine*." Laura tilts her head, showing a measure of her hidden strength. "Regardless, God is blessing us with more children. Therefore, God will give us the provision for the blessings."

Laura's faith makes Vargas light up a little. Her fight makes even Zeke admire her.

"They have doctors for that kind of thinking, Sis." Nate seems genuinely concerned, I think. Just blind.

"Wow," Laura says, shaking her head. "It must be exhausting to try to control everything in your life. I bet you think I'm a brainwashed, naïve little girl, don't you? But you have no idea what I've seen God do while walking in faith. Thing is, nothing is ever in your control, Nathan. You only *think* it is."

"Well, I'd rather not trust reality to some unseen narcissistic tyrant." Nate blasphemes cruelly, cackling. Natalie submits even her fervent desire to give him a nasty look.

"Whatever, Nate. Keep laughing like a child. But while you watch God work this all out, you should also pay more attention to what a great man my husband is. Your soup sucks. But *he'd* never tell you that." Laura concludes, whisking her daughter upstairs with bouncing and singing.

Chapter Twenty-Three

Accidental Hero

I begin to be irritated and bark at the noise they can't hear that comes with the vibrating phone. On top of that, it rings some silly ring and moves itself across the table.

"I know, Willow. But you gotta shush. Maria is sleeping. The phone is Nate's. He's out on his run. He'll get it when he gets back." Christian is enjoying the early morning in the kitchen, responding to recent insomnia. A rarity. Seth had let me out of his room even before cereal time when I'd begged to go see Christian.

"It's some Japanese character thing. So either Neil or Natalie. They've called six times. Should I answer it?" I look around. He's talking to me. And when it glows funny suddenly, I whimper. "Yeah, I thought so, too. Why else would I be down here?"

"Nathan Holm's phone. This is Christian. Can I ask who's calling?" I hear distressed breathing and sniffles. A boy's. The distress is coming from the other end when I perk my ears.

"Neil. Is this Neil?"

"Yeah." The same breathing and sniffles. "Is Nate there?"

"No, he left for his run right when you called the first time. Vargas said they are only doing five today. Can I take a message?"

"Yeah. Tell him thank you. But I'll be dead by the time he gets back." This is more than just a child's sarcasm. It is desperation. Christian knows this well for some reason.

"Whoa. What's the matter, Little Dude? I'm real close to Nate—he's my brother-in-law. You can talk to me. Remember me? You punched me the night you guys came to kill Nate?" Christian brings his usual cheer, with an addition since the house is covered in Christmas decorations.

"Yeah. I remember you, Christian. That's weird. Nate's my brother-in-law, too." More sniffles. More sadness.

"Yeah, so that kind of makes us brothers. Tell me what's goin' on."

"It's nothing."

"Don't lie. 'Nothing' is not a good reason to want to be dead."

"It's just this guy at church. I'm homeschooled, and so is he. So I guess I'm the only person he ever gets to treat like crap."

"A bully. Bullies suck, Dude. But one idiot's opinion is not a reason to die. God thinks much more highly of you than whatever this kid says." Christian finally sits in the breakfast nook, his feet up.

"Yeah, except he pulled down my pants in front of the whole middle school group. Girls, too. And I told my dad and he just said I was making it up so that I could miss church. He's gonna make me go back. I can't go back there. And I can't stay home. My dad is so crazy. So, I'm just gonna go home to Jesus. It can't be like this in Heaven." The thirteen-year-old's voice is changing. Squeaking and sobbing and destroying Christian deeply. He sighs.

"You're right, this isn't our home, Neil. People are mean and they suck and it only gets worse as you get older. I really hate to tell you that. I don't blame you for wanting to die. There are lots of times as a kid I thought about ending it all. I'd even measured a rope."

"My dad has guns. I have a twenty-two in my hand." Neil says.

"You shouldn't handle guns when you're upset, Dude. Go on and put that down while we talk."

"Okay." I hear a clack of metal against wood, and the concession of a thirteen-year-old that Christian silently mouths a "thank you" to God for. Then he continues in some cheer and some hesitation.

"Can I tell you a secret? You can't tell anyone. I'm serious. I've only ever told my wife." Christian begins where others may have said, *Silly child.* But today, I learn that Christian is different. And that this phone call was somehow meant for him.

"Yeah. I won't tell. I'm good at secrets." Neil is. Very much so.

"My dad used to have a torch for plumbing and stuff. You seen those?"

"Yeah." A sniffle. I see Christian keeps him talking as much as he can.

"Well, one time I ran away from home. Sort of. It was like down the street. I was nine. But I wanted to go Home. With Jesus. I guess I thought He'd just come rescue me off the street corner. Instead, my dad brought me home again and took that torch. And he just held that blue fire on the callouses of my heels. He just burned the crap out of them, no matter how much I screamed and begged. I still have trouble walking on my heels. I knew that wasn't okay, so I told my teacher at school what my dad did. And then my dad came to the school and told her I'd stepped on the oven door. There's not a worse feeling in the world than being trapped in hell with no one to believe you, is there? Sometimes you just want to go Home. But your feet are just too damaged to take you." Christian is a boy again knowing that pain. Even now, he rotates the feet atop the table that tell a truth I'd never known.

"Your dad did that to you? Why didn't they believe you? That's child abuse. Seriously." Neil is coming to a place of compassion.

"He was very rich and very charming. It worked every time. There were lots of times like that. You're thirteen?" Christian asks.

"Yeah. I wish I was eighteen."

"Eighteen was a good year," Christian attests, laughing at a memory. "At thirteen, all I could think about was kissing a girl. Finally happened when I was eighteen."

"The whole youth group has seen all they need to see of me. I'm pretty much never getting kissed." Neil returns to his pain.

"Neil, 'never' kind of puts limits on God. See, my parents screwed me up so bad that I still carry a lot of it with me, you know? As much as I wanted to get married someday, I didn't think God thought to make a woman amazing enough to deal with my baggage. Which I thought was for the best, because I probably wasn't fit to be a father, either. My only goal was to get away from home, which took earning a full-tuition college scholarship and living in my car, but I did it. Luckily, God had much better plans."

"Aren't you married and a father now?"

"Sure am. But love wasn't something I had a concept of a few years ago. My parents hated each other and resented me and I was teased my whole life. God used my angel Laura to teach me about His unconditional love and to show me that through Him, I'm fit for anything—even raising my perfect little Maria and two more babies on their way. Never say never. You just have to listen to His voice, not some dumb bully."

"It's hard to hear sometimes, but you're right." Neil sighs. "I kind of feel like an idiot now for thinking my dad was abusing me with some of the stuff he does. He's got all these rules I can't follow and I'm never good enough. He's insane, I swear. But I should feel blessed that he never like hurts me, hurts me."

"Sometimes dads are the bully, Neil. My dad told me I was a mistake every day of my life. That did more of a number on me than any torch. Not all pain is physical. But in Christ, all pain is temporary. One day, we won't even have scars on our feet. But Jesus will. Be patient for Heaven. Let Him be the only one that died for some idiot's sin, Dude."

"Yeah." Neil is sniffling less. "Thanks, Man."

"Call me anytime." He smiles. "I'll text you my number here in a minute."

"Thank you, Christian. I better go. My dad is awake."

"I'll be praying for you."

"Thanks."

Then the line dies. Christian removes his own phone from a pocket and types something from Nate's onto his. All while he smiles at the popping ligament from around the corner.

"Why are you up so early, m'Love?"

Laura emerges. "I came to ask you the same thing. Reached over, and you were gone." She puffs out her lower lip dramatically.

"Apparently, I was needed." Christian is still astonished.

"So I heard," Laura says, removing the phone from his hand. Then she bends down to still propped feet on the table and kisses a few various scars on them. Something she's obviously done before but would never speak of publicly. "You make me proud every day."

Christian melts, then smiles. "It's good to see you're not sick today."

"I'm actually okay a lot of days now unless I get emotional or try to do too much." Laura smooths her pajama shirt over her little bump with a smile.

Christian's hands join hers on her belly, and his feet join the floor. "I can't believe you're showing already. I bet it's boys." He sighs. Christian shakes his head. He looks to the floor, feeling for a moment the weight of all the burdens he's placed on God. Remembering many more.

"I know what you need." Laura pulls him to standing.

"Oh, *do* you?" Christian says sensually as he's led and directed to sit on a piano bench next to Laura. She laughs and rolls her eyes.

So many have sat on this piano bench in front of the same keys. Many can make them clamor with dissonance. Some can play "a little." Natalie plays a lot. But somehow, Laura, a tiny little doll of a woman sits down, and I think bits of Heaven trickle through her spirit onto the keys. No one who hears it can resist a flutter in their heart. Even though Christian has seen the farthest reaches of her humanity, he is still taken by the way, with a focused, straight face, she makes a hunk of manmade furniture sing as if to God.

Today, she plays something Christian recognizes and joins immediately with his voice. Again, they all have voices. Even I have a voice. But Christian's is special and is the only thing on Earth that can begin to compliment the way this piano sings. The song seems to float above the room and drift inside us like a mystery.

"O come, O come Emmanuel
And ransom captive Israel
That mourns in lonely exile here
Until the son of God appear
Rejoice! Rejoice!
Emmanuel shall come to thee,
O Israel."

"One of my favorites," Christian says while Laura continues to play something else to occupy her hands.

Then Laura sighs heavily and stops playing altogether. "There's a terrible void in the world of Christmas carols that I didn't notice until this year."

"And what's that?" Christian asks, running his fingers as a gentle claw through her shoulder-blade-length golden locks.

"Well, most songs are about Jesus, obviously. The birth of our Savior. That makes perfect sense. And Mary is mentioned a lot. When we were expecting Maria last year, I used to think about how hard it must've been to be her. Perspective, you know? But this year, with everything we have coming our way, I got to thinking, why aren't there any songs about Joseph?" Laura wonders.

"Because he's not even Jesus's father. Didn't make the cut, apparently." Christian smirks.

"Yeah, but God could have created or chosen anyone to raise Him. He didn't even have to be concerned about the guy's DNA ruining Him." Laura begins to play again. Some kind of lullaby. "But He knew Joseph had to be special. He had a big job from the beginning. Can you imagine having to help deliver Maria by yourself in a stable? And Joseph was a righteous man, probably a virgin himself. Yet he delivered a son that wasn't his after probably a lot of ridicule when people thought he'd defiled Mary. Then he raised Jesus. He had to provide for God in human flesh—teach him a trade and how to be a man. Yeah, Mary had a tough job. But can you imagine the stress of being His Dad? You'd think someone would have written a carol about Joseph." Laura stops playing again.

"Well, Joseph had the assurance that no matter how bad he screwed up raising Him, Jesus would still be the Messiah. He knew God wouldn't let His Son starve, so teaching and toiling and providing, it was all just obedience." Christian places his wife's hands back on the keys. She plays again with a giggle.

Laura plays the introduction to another song she knows Christian will sing. He complies only after he moves her hands to the right, dissatisfied with the first key of the introduction. But the higher key he chooses invites all those in the enormous house to join the couple in the room. And serendipity welcomes two runners and Natalie in just in time to be blessed by the hymn of a broken-winged angel before six in the morning.

"Why should I feel discouraged?
Why should the shadows come?
Why should my heart be lonely,
And long for Heaven and home,
When Jesus is my portion?
My constant Friend is He:
His eye is on the sparrow, and I know He watches me
His eye is on the sparrow, and I know He watches me;

I sing because I'm happy,
I sing because I'm free!
For His eye is on the sparrow, and I know He watches me."

Laura looks over and sees that Christian's eyes are glistening in the applause. Then, as she plays her conclusion, she whispers in his ear. "You're no different from Joseph."

His response is a kiss that contains as much heartache as it does passion. And an appreciation of the kind of wife women two or three times her age can merely strive to be. Before Christian even recovers from the kiss, Laura's eyes widen, and she bolts to the nearest bathroom, hand over mouth, which brings everyone else to laughter.

"If only she had that reaction to your kissing *before* she got pregnant." Nate supplies, breathing deeply with a fist bump to the also-sweaty Vargas.

"Ha." Christian shakes his head, only concerned with one Voice today.

"Maria's calling for 'Didi.'" Zeke reports, having come from upstairs to applaud the gorgeous hymn with "amen."

"Sorry." Christian jumps up, wincing over his disruptive daughter. "I bet minivan shopping will cheer her up!"

"Minivan?" Nate protests. "You need knives. For a huge promotion and raise, remember? Laura will tell you the same thing."

"I'm sure she will." Christian shrugs. "But if I can't get the important things home from the hospital, what good is something like a raise?" He disappears up the stairs to take care of something important.

Before I join Seth's whistle for his customary cereal, I notice Nate staring with some remorse at the now-empty piano bench, forsaken for morning sickness and childcare and minivan shopping. He'd somehow been present but missed the music—and only seen the emptiness.

Chapter Twenty-Four

Never Enough

Ken is tall, broad-shouldered, and proud of the way his eyes slant and his voice booms, nearly rejecting the language it must speak. Eden is shorter than Natalie, dark-skinned and eyed and curvy, lovely of form and face. Their splendor combined to make Natalie something heads must turn twice to confirm. It is like she split in two and grew older, walking up the drive with another combined male version behind them.

Natalie sighs, smoothing her hair repeatedly as she stares nervously out the front window. "She's gonna hate my hair. I should have left it longer. Why didn't I wear the purple sweater? I thought the red was Christmassy, but what if it just seems risqué? Red means so many things. Maybe I could change really fast."

"Yeah. I'll just press pause, and they can stand there in the cold while you run out back and grow your hair and change." Nate laughs, then tries to encourage on this Christmas Eve. "It's your parents. They came to see *you*, not your purple sweater, right?"

"No, Baby. They came to interrogate me for a week about why in the world I married *you*. Therefore, a haircut, a red sweater, *everything* I do is under scrutiny. But you're right. I'm their daughter, so they'll be much more patient with *me*," Natalie warns.

Nate deflates just in time for the doorbell to ring. He freezes, Natalie frets, and they both stare at the empty entryway. So, it is the boom of Seth's boots from his office that meets the knob of the big heavy door. He, too, has a minuscule panic attack some hidden place in his spirit when he sees who is on the other side of the door. But only a hidden moment before his warm smile.

"Hello, Mr. and Mrs. Nakano! Hello, Neil. I'm glad you made it safely. Please come in. Make yourselves at home." When he steps aside for them to enter from the cold, Natalie gives Seth a little smile of gratitude before the master of the house escapes back to his office. I try to follow, but he gives me a quick head shake. I must be needed here.

I watch Eden greet her daughter with enthusiasm, but only after a look of admiration as Seth walks away. Something she experiences alone, having been the only person present not to have seen him as a man the past few years. It resonates with her enough that the first thing she says in greeting is:

"The beard really suits him." Eden was never the reason the Nakano family had moved away. That had been Ken, to whom Eden had submitted with little question. Something Natalie likely hated her for for several years. But now, before Natalie can even respond about Seth, Eden's attention is taken elsewhere.

I've seen something odd happen to a woman, regardless of her age, when she meets Nathan Holm for the first time. The response looks like a coy smile but involves her whole self. His suave, his strength, his perfect platinum hair, and charming smile on chiseled features are never lost on even the most inward introvert. He's enchanted ten-year-old bookworms with his belief that every girl is beautiful. A simple tilt of his head has earned his cheeks the lipstick of many old grandmothers. Eden's initial reaction is no different, with just a half smile from Nate.

"My goodness, Natalie. You going to introduce me to this handsome young man?"

Natalie breathes slowly, then says it. "Nate, I'd like you to meet my mom, Eden Nakano. Mom, this is my husband Nate."

But supposing Natalie herself had been just a common victim of Nate's charm is a misconception. I know surrender. It's the day a cow is better for meat than milk and hears them say it, but still surrenders to slaughter. I've tucked my tail, stopped my content napping or chewing to follow Seth. I know surrender. It's when Natalie smiles a little as she introduces Nate as her husband to a woman she swears wouldn't defend her to Jesus. The way he looks at her now, after a year of doing what he swore his whole life he'd never do. That's surrender. And if God can offend and if there is a victim at all. It is Nate, repeating Natalie's words with a fluttering heart as he shakes Eden's hand.

"I'm her husband. And you are *obviously* her mother." The spice of Natalie was swept in directly from Eden, so it is not with quiet that she accepts now the kiss to her hand, fanning herself with the other.

"Whew. I'm sold."

"*Mama*!" Natalie objects, even though she's much more aware of what her mother is currently appreciating as new.

"Says the lady in red." Then Eden's left eyebrow flicks upward in the center as she looks over Natalie head to toe, scrutinizing her. "Hmm, you cut your hair."

"Yep." Natalie's eyebrow flicks the same. An "I told you so" just for her husband.

And so it goes the remainder of the day. Before Nate heads to work, he is quietly examined in his every move. The second he leaves, it looks to me like Natalie would prefer a stab in the eye to the conversations with her parents. When alone with her family, she's on trial.

"If he loved you, he'd at least try to make it to service tonight."

"Do you realize he'd go to hell if he died today?"

Laura had saved her then with a text. Too sick to even care for Maria, she apologetically left her in Natalie's care. But the saving only lasted a moment after Natalie returned with the baby.

"You're so good with little Maria. When are you having children?"

"Why don't you want children? Marriage is pointless without children."

"Why haven't you told him about Seth? You need to be honest and then move off Seth's property."

"I wish you had let us come to the wedding."

"A temper? A man should never raise his voice to a woman."

"He's only stubborn because you are not submissive."

It is all one-sided enough for me to know exactly why Seth made me stay with Natalie. Despite her assurances that she signed a lease, that Nate loves her, that she has nightmares about hell and that the very idea of children only brings up painful memories, it seems nothing Natalie says is good enough. Then Laura comes downstairs after conquering a bad morning of nurturing unborn twins, and they suddenly change their tune.

She's nineteen and soon to be a mother of three. She's tiny and cute and naïve. But they accept her without question and schmooze endlessly about the absent Christian's enduring spirit, which Laura relishes for only a few moments before feeling the weight of Natalie's soul and awakening her servant's heart.

Laura leans over to Natalie with a smile, "I'm not supposed to say this, but Chris heard Chef talking to his wife the other day. No one but Nate ever had a chance. Chef is supposedly transferring the deed sometime this week. It's a crazy amount of responsibility, owning and running a restaurant. But Christian says Nate pretty much already does. Even the financial stuff. He's gifted—more than just as a cook."

Natalie gives a warm smile to her sister-in-law, who made sure the Nakanos were listening intently as she spoke. "Oh, I've been praying for this. Nate must be so excited. I'll pretend I don't know. He has this thing with planning surprises just right." Natalie gives a half smile.

"You're right about that." Neil, Nate's trusted confidant, speaks up, then shuts down with a smiled wince. "You'll see, *Ane*. You'll like it, I promise. Nate's awesome. I mean, Christian is awesome, too. I want to be a good husband like them someday."

Neil, the favorite and trophy son, seals the deal for Nate's acceptance in just a few words that make Laura's hormones enact as tears in her eyes. And as Natalie is thanking him and Laura is cooing, Eden smiles.

"Can we tell them?" This is directed at Ken.

"I suppose. Can you ladies keep a secret?" Ken responds.

An honest "No" from Laura and a promised "Yes" from Natalie come out at the same time. Then they giggle. And Eden speaks anyway,

"Natalie, your brother thought about hurting himself not too long ago. We didn't listen. Didn't think it was serious. By the time we did, he was able to tell us that Christian had talked him out of it directly. And both he and Nate had been helping him through some things we didn't even know were happening." Eden becomes emotional at the end. Neil hugs her a little.

"Your mother is trying to say that even though we may have some reservations about Nate, he and Christian saved Neil's life. So we bought them a very special Christmas gift. Perhaps a little elaborate and over the top, that is, if one is willing to put a price on their son's life. If Nate is going to own the restaurant they both work in, I think we made a good choice." Ken explains with determination.

"What did you buy them?" Natalie is wary, probably knowing that her parents have always had more money than even her mother's decorating and style tastes can burn through.

"We bought them each a full set of top-of-the-line professional chef's knives. Even if they have good ones, these are sure to be better and maybe last them a lifetime. That's what they told me at the shop, at least. And for six grand a set, I hope he was right." Eden lays it out.

Laura gasps but doesn't speak.

"Japanese made, of course." Ken settles.

"Are you serious? Did someone tell you?" Natalie wonders. Not thinking at all of Nate for a moment. Only of Laura and Christian and God's goodness.

"I don't follow. Tell us...?" Eden tilts her head.

"Come on, *Otouto*. Someone had to have told you." Natalie turns to Neil, almost accusingly. Laura is unable to even phonate for the state of her shock.

"What, that Christian needed knives to get a promotion he deserved but made a choice to instead buy a minivan for his wife and baby and twins on the way? Even though without that promotion, he'll never be able to afford to move his family out of Seth's house? Yes, Nate told me all that, so I told them. But only *after* they bought the knives. They said God must have been in it. Because that kind of a man deserves a lot more than he'd ever accept out of charity." Neil says enthusiastically. Laura is pacing the room in search of tissues, knowing completely the character of her husband—learning each day the character of her God. She finally exits the room for tissues.

"He's a good man. Thank you. And Nate has been complaining about his knives, too. Thank you, Mama. Papa. Neil, I'm just glad you finally have the big brothers you wanted your whole life." Natalie smiles.

No one had heard the booming boots enter the foyer. But the owner responds. "I just made him play chess when he was six and got irritated when he got bored. Is Laura okay?"

"I was a pain when I was six!" Neil's tone apologizes and invites Seth into the room, though he needs no invitation.

"You were a pain the last time you were here." Natalie realizes. Then looks at Seth. "Yeah, she's fine. Got some good news."

"Ah." Seth sits in a chair by the fireplace in the formal living room. Eden looks to Seth and begins the interrogation. "Natalie tells me you and Nate were good friends in high school? So you've known him for quite some time."

"Yes, ma'am. Best friends. The Holm family sort of took me in," Seth explains.

The sniffling and nose dabbing Laura returns. "Seriously! This guy used to get more Christmas presents than me!"

Then Eden looks between Seth and Natalie like she's seeking something out between the two old friends. Laura recognizes the look.

"I know, right? So *not* weird that it's weird. Freaks you out the second you know what happened before." Laura's perception of Seth and Natalie's relationship.

Natalie giggles. "I've told you all a hundred times. Seth and I were best friends for a decade before the stuff that would make it weird to be friends again. There's too much normal for it to be weird. What's weird is that you grew up in the same house I did. *That's* weird." She shifts the subject so that Seth need not respond.

"I grew up in Oregon!" Laura defends. "I was eleven when we moved to Colorado, so I didn't technically spend my *whole* childhood in that house. My sisters, on the other hand, grew up in your old house."

"What were they, seven when you moved in?" Natalie quickly does the math. Neil's math and smelly thirteen-year-old hormones are much stronger.

"You have sisters my age?" His ears perk.

"Yeah. Twins. Tall blondes that model for some modest Christian catalog. They're fourteen now. I honestly think Dad letting them model is outrageous, but it would kind of be a waste if they didn't. I got the music, but they got all the looks. Unfair." Laura rants for a moment before catching Natalie's eye—the one she keeps on her little brother. But Neil is already extremely intrigued.

"Shut up, you're beautiful." This is from the front door. Laura immediately lights up, squealing before she bolts for the front door and meets the waiting embrace of her beloved. His eyebrows worry.

"You been crying?"

"Hormones. Don't worry about me. It's Christmas Eve! What are you doing here? Don't you have an insane dinner service tonight?" Laura is asking in smiles.

"Three of us wanted to get out early to be with family. I pulled the wife-pregnant-with-twins card, Nate pulled some strings, and they all voted for me to get to come home," Christian explains between doting kisses.

"You didn't get fired, did you?" Laura fears the worst.

"Nate would be lost without me, m'Love. Hey, princess!" Christian smiles then joins the rest of us after Maria thunders in from her previous contentedness in the dining room stacking blocks.

The daddy's girl now in her prince's arms, Christian lights up when he sees the Nakanos. "Neil! You guys made it!"

After they put a face with Christian's legacy, he and Laura sit. Natalie smiles mischievously.

"Laura was just telling Neil about Kelli and Shelley."

Christian laughs with enormous amusement then points a finger of warning at Neil. "Dude, before you even think about looking at a Holm woman, you better be able to afford her. They are crazy fertile and Nate is crazy protective. Which you know. But they are walking up to the house right now, so a renewed warning is required."

"We brought our son to a house where teenage models live down the street," Ken tells Eden under Natalie's laughter over Christian's comments and Laura's faked offense.

Seth had heard. "Kelli and Shelley are very sweet. Neil is a great kid. They all love the Lord. Don't worry, Mr. Nakano."

"Sweet Christian girl. Good Christian boy. What could possibly go wrong?" Eden says in sarcasm, raising an eyebrow at Seth, who averts his eyes.

"Seriously, though. Shelley, the one with the glasses, is a cross country star and sassy as heck. Great to talk to, but don't try anything. And Kelli is the other one." Christian realizes he has no defense against Kelli.

"Technically, they are kind of your sisters, too. I'm married to their brother. Just ew." Natalie finally brings up.

"I'm not a pig! And girls don't always get me. But it will be nice to have someone to hang with that isn't married or old. No offense." Neil lays the issue to rest. A peacemaker. But a fiery one. The doorbell rings.

The afternoon is a mass meeting of kindred spirits. Eden and Karen almost immediately take to gossiping as if old friends. They talk about the house they both have kept and the children they raised in it. Bill and Ken are the same, but this lends them simply to periodic grunts and long periods of quiet. Neil, Kelli, and Shelley, after an awkward few moments when adults must introduce them, find themselves laughing over card games like they aren't three beautiful teens that are supposed to be falling all over one another. Maria is passed around and chased around and enjoyed by all. Seth sits back and sees what I see.

This afternoon there is no interrogation or bad blood. Only love like with Jesus. Fellowship, they call it. Pure joy and peace on Christmas Eve. They share a meal Nate had carefully prepared beforehand with instructions for Natalie to reheat, though she chose a different wine to pair it with. Then they leave for church, all dressed up for some sort of candle lighting that they say represents each of them and the way their flames all add some unique beauty of God to this world.

Thinking, at least hoping, they've all returned when the door to the garage is breached, I go to begin greetings. However, I greet a weary Nate all alone. Instead of going with the others to light a candle, he is in Seth's kitchen seeking a glass of wine after a long night of working.

He picks up and examines the recorked bottle.

"Red Bordeaux with prime rib." He makes his mouth frown funny and tilts his head back and forth. Then he reheats a testable portion, tossing me a piece of the beef. He tries the food, then the wine, and upturns his chin with sensually rolled eyes, speaking to someone who isn't in the house. "*Beautiful*, Bug."

Nate removes his chef coat, leaving behind a shirt that crinkles all wrong against the chest too broad to encompass it. All wrong for fitting, but something that I'm sure will make me worry if Natalie's heart is still alive when she sees him. He sits in the game room, examining the queen with holes, sipping wine.

"Rough night, Willow. Sometimes I think the other two sous chefs could be easily replaced by *you*. No offense to you, of course. But come

New Year's, Willow, I'm executive chef and owner of Le Cloture. You believe it? I'd be excited, except the only guy good enough to replace *me* can't afford his own set of knives. So much for their 'God' providing, right? He deserves it. But I guess nothing is ever enough."

Nate sighs. Pats my head. Sips his wine. Completely unaware that a Man is sitting on the other end of the chess board, waiting for Nate to make his move.

Chapter Twenty-Five

BASICS

This holiday makes more sense, I'll admit. But the earliness with which the people choose to begin it is disturbing. Even Seth is in his closet before the sun comes up, putting bows on boxes he leaves in his room for now. Then we both hear Laura and Christian in the window room near the massive tree they'd brought indoors and decorated.

Seth observes the little family, the two parents smiling, coaxing the child into tearing paper off packages.

"Merry Christmas, Seth!" Laura stands and hugs Seth, handing him a package wrapped in paper. "Open it!"

Seth opens the package and finds it is an engraved glass paperweight of some kind. He reads it aloud. "Seth Gowan, President and CEO."

"I was in your office about a month ago and saw that there's a wood one you made for your dad on your desk. Which is great. It's just a little outdated. So here's one with *your* name on it." Laura smiles kindly. Seth hugs her again, thanking her.

We watch as Christian and Laura end up unwrapping most of Maria's gifts themselves. Seth is enthralled at the family. Maria crawls about, playing with paper and seeming much less interested in the pile of toys and clothes she's received. Laura gives Christian a package that contains a wooden cross on a leather strap to remind him as he wears it on his neck daily, where to put his faith. I remember when Laura had asked Seth to make it. I watched him craft it even more carefully than one of his fence posts.

"Oh! Come out to the van. I want to show you something." Christian says, helping Laura to a stand as she hips Maria for a trip out to the garage. And by the time she opens her new-to-her blue minivan, her family has arrived at the front door. She finds inside two matching baby seats. Laura gasps, wiping tears.

"Merry Christmas, m'love." Christian returns to the door to the garage after opening the front door for his in-laws.

"You're so good to me." Laura returns to the doorway and kisses Christian, then goes back to examine the new seats again.

Bill joins Christian in the doorway. "Looks like someone did something right."

Christian shrugs. "Well, I'm getting closer to prepared for them to come."

Bill and Christian move aside as the rest of the blonde females pass them in the mudroom to enter the garage and coo over mere car seats. They talk across the doorway, and I sit in the van, awaiting the conclusion of the female silliness.

Bill speaks kindly to Christian. "Kids are expensive. We started with Nathan and didn't have a thing, so we bought everything in blue. Thousands of dollars' worth of stuff."

Here, Christian rolls his eyes and smiles in agreement. Bill continues.

"Then Laura came along, and we had to buy it all again in pink." Bill chuckles.

Christian pipes in. "Which is ironic because—"

"Her favorite color is blue. Yes! Believe me, I've teased Karen about that." Bill finishes. Both men laugh. "Then we were done. Had a boy and a girl. Waited a couple years until we were sure we were done and then sold all the baby stuff. Clothes and everything. Blue and pink. Not a month later, Karen tells me she's expecting again. The Holm curse, we call it. Babies come, no matter what, when you least expect them. So, I got used to it. The idea of having to buy everything again for another one. I was thinking, 'Three kids isn't so bad…'"

Christian laughs, nodding enthusiastically. "And then you see two heartbeats on the screen, and she's like, 'Oh, twins! Are they healthy?'—"

"Exactly! And we see dollar signs. Two of everything. Twice the diapers and formula and they generally require more medical attention in the first year. The girls spent four weeks in the NICU." Bill recalls.

"Don't remind me. And I'm happy. We talked about having a big family since we started dating. I love being a dad. Laura's a *great* mom. I just cannot afford them. God is definitely testing my faith here." Christian admits.

"Well. From experience? You're not doing a bad job." Bill compliments the young father, who sighs in response. "Help me get these presents inside. I apologize. Karen may have spoiled Maria a bit."

When everyone comes back inside, Nate and Seth carry some oddly shaped piece of wood furniture, with Neil holding doors and directing them along. I'd watched Seth build it but can't decide what it is for. They set it in front of the tree just as Laura makes it back in. She gasps.

"You like it?" Seth smiles. "I read that twins like to be together, so I only made one. But the dimensions for a regular bassinet seemed small for two, so I modified it. I had a mattress and a few sets of sheets specially made. And I made the mobile removable in case it gets in the way. It rocks, too."

By the end of Seth's explanation, Laura requires a tissue. "Thanks, Seth. It's beautiful. It should fit next to the bed perfectly. The sheets are blue."

Seth smiles. "Two boys. Just a guess."

But Laura is convinced, knowing Seth never guesses, nor is he ever wrong. She hands Maria to Natalie and hugs Seth fully. Christian smiles, another burden lifted. Then when he receives the knives later in the day amid wrapping paper and smiles, he must leave the room for a moment. Not to cry, but to praise God inside himself. The Provider that Nate would mock him for praising aloud.

As Christian returns to the window room with everyone else, I smell something out of place and go to the front door to investigate. But I'm nearly barreled over by two grown men on Christmas, shedding years for the sake of surprise.

"Feliz Navidad!" Derek Vargas yells, entering the room in a red hat with a white ball on one end and white fur on the other. Zeke, the more serious, seems to have been coaxed into wearing his own hat.

The two are greeted and introduced where necessary. We are told they could not resist the urge to see Nate and Natalie's families interact. The two had met for a connecting flight this morning from their separate corners of the country and family Christmases. They recognize that we are just as much family as they. When everyone settles in again, Seth clears his throat and speaks, not in the least surprised at the arrival.

"Good timing. I have a gift for all my tenants."

Seth goes to his room three times, retrieving three extremely heavy metal boxes and setting one each in front of Zeke, Vargas, and Christian. Nate and Natalie each receive an envelope. They are all confused.

"My Lawyer, Mr. Billings, told me when I was eighteen that I should rent out rooms in the house, so I didn't feel like I was wasting it. I don't like wasting things. But he told me what I should charge you for rent, and I told him that would be a waste too. Because I don't need the money. So, he suggested I do this and keep it secret. My gift to all of you today is freedom. You can all stay here as long as you want, but I'm tired of collecting rent every month, so stop giving it to me. I just thought it was time to release you from your leases."

Seth sits in his chair and watches.

"This is a fire box," Derek says with confusion. "With a bow on it."

"I needed a fire box." Zeke is the first to look at the side of his, which has a paper taped to it filled with Seth's handwriting. "I see. This is your log of the rent we gave you. I'd have kept an electronic record."

"You have a label maker? That's awesome!" Christian exclaims. Seth just smiles as they try to figure it all out. "Mine says 'Christian.' What does yours say, Zeke?"

Everyone laughs. Nate and Natalie understand because they have opened their envelopes which contain the leases they'd signed years ago—but shredded.

"Wait, why would we stop paying rent? Are you trying to kick us all out but trying to be nice?" Vargas asks.

"No." Seth keeps cool. "These two never paid me. They started out as my friends. I didn't ever charge them. Now you guys are my friends, and I don't want to charge you either. But no one ever paid 'rent.'"

Derek finally opens the lid to his fire box with the key that is taped to it. A label on the inside tells another story than the one on the outside.

"This says, 'Derek Vargas's Savings.' What does that mean?" Then he reaches in and pulls out stacks. And stacks. And stacks. Of twenty-dollar bills. He'd always cashed his checks and given Seth the second fruits of the month. Tithe first, of course.

Zeke quickly opens his and finds crisp, new $100 bills. He'd always traveled from the bank to Seth, annoyed that he wouldn't take a check or electronic transfer as payment.

Christian opens his and laughs hysterically. The more recent bills are larger, but for years, he'd scraped together smaller bills. Coins. And sometimes, where Zeke and Vargas had a clear *"February $500"* on their log, Christian's had varied from the start. He reads much of it aloud after Laura's inquiry.

"January $492.77 (will pay more next month)
February $510
March $450 (had to buy another book for school will pay me back)
Etc...."

Christian always gave everything he had, and if it wasn't enough, he made up for it later. After marrying Laura and the 'inconvenience' of Maria, he'd upped his own rent as penance.

"June $750 (Agreed that Laura will only be half since they share a room)
July $750
...
February $1000 (Added another half rent for Maria, against my wishes)
March $1000..."

Vargas sees with a rare curse word in Spanish that the total in his box is $18,000 since he'd been excluded from rent while deployed.

Zeke, a steadfast roommate, receives $32,000 he has absolutely no need for. He sees this much in a month at his job.

Christian, having underpaid, overpaid, added, and been honest, however hard, has a fire box with a total of $23,122.46.

Christian looks at Nate smugly but heart soaring at the impossibility in front of him. "This is almost the down payment the bank was looking for."

"Almost doesn't count! What, your God isn't big enough?" Nate teases. "Just kidding, Man. That's awesome."

"What are you gonna do with that chump change, Zeke? And Vargas, aren't you still trying to figure out a way to pawn off what you made while you were deployed?" Natalie asks the successful workaholic and the soldier ready to take a vow of poverty.

"I was thinking of investing mine." Vargas looks to Zeke with a wink of a lilt in his voice. "What about you, Zeke?"

"Yeah. It's nothing to me now, but in the right *place*, it could mean something." Zeke nods his head oddly in view of Vargas. Almost like a signal. Almost to Christian, who sits between them.

"You're both very wise," Bill is oblivious. "I might have some good ideas for you. Some promising options."

"Promise." Vargas, the aspiring priest, begins. "When I think of that word I always go back to Abraham, who in Romans 4, we learn, '…did not waver at the promise of God through unbelief, but was strengthened in faith, giving glory to God, and being fully convinced that what He had promised He was also able to perform. And therefore "it was accounted to him for righteousness."'"

"Well quoted, Vargas. Someday maybe I'll memorize the entire Bible like you." Zeke chuckles. "But from what you're saying, an investment with 'promise' might look like Abraham's faith in God's promises."

"But Zeke, all God promised Abraham was a bunch of descendants and a place where they'd be taken care of," Vargas says with drama as he stands. "God must have trusted Abraham was worthy enough of that promise to give him provision for it."

"Sounds familiar for some reason." Zeke rises as well. "I think I found us a promising investment, Vargas."

Christian suddenly feels small and looks up at his two standing housemates, who quickly and simultaneously nod, lift their fire boxes, and dump the entirety of their contents into (and around) Christian's fire box. Christian starts to object violently, but Zeke uses his power and stature to simply point at Christian, reducing him quickly to silence. With emotions he doesn't know how to publicly handle, he looks around for his wife.

"Laura ran upstairs," Karen reveals, with a gesture of sickness to her belly.

"Go tell wifey how big her God is." Vargas flings almost directly at Nate, who is having trouble objecting.

As Christian departs for upstairs, everyone in the room is in awe at how far God's love reaches.

"So, the lease is dissolved, including all rules?" Natalie wonders after helping Zeke neatly stack all the cash into Christian's box.

"Whew." Nate sighs dramatically. "Because I've been in violation for a year of the 'no girls in rooms' one." Nate cavorts his eyebrows at his wife, who shoves his shoulder in giggles.

"I don't know, Seth. I feel like a freeloader now." Zeke's guilt comes out.

"Apparently, you always have been." Nate chuckles. None of them can actually believe Seth's premeditated generosity.

"Wait, what about chess night?" Vargas asks suddenly.

"No longer required." Seth is saddened by this.

"But I love chess night." Natalie whines, puffing her lip.

"That's why I stick around." Zeke declares.

"Can we keep doing it? Even after Chris and Laura move out? They can still come over, right?" Natalie begs.

Seth smiles. Nods. Not having expected the loving reward until Heaven.

"What is chess night?" Neil wonders.

While all the housemates reminisce and rejoice for the guests, Natalie is in mid-laughter when Nate slips a large envelope into her hands. Mindlessly, she opens it and removes a piece of fancy cardstock with some list of words not in the language they normally read. She finally looks down, clearing her throat.

"Oh, Chef redesigned the menu?" She smiles, then gasps when she reads something in the last section, calling all to curiosity. "'Nate's "Perfect" Tiramisu. An authentic Italian classic, named and cherished by Chef Holm's muse, food writer Natalie Holm.' Nate that's so sweet, but can you put my name on the menu like that?"

Nate grabs the envelope from in front of her, tipping it upside down until a key and some small figurine fall out onto her hand. "You're the co-owner, I hope so," Nate says as though it means little to him, then references the job Natalie recently quit. "It's like the key to the choir room at that high school that didn't appreciate you. But this is your muse key. Opens every door at *Le Cloture*."

"Wait. Like, no more speculation. A done deal?" Natalie says, getting excited.

"Signed, sealed, and delivered. Well, as soon as you sign papers, too. I wanted to make sure your name was on the deed." Nate smiles dreamily.

"That's amazing, Baby. I'm so proud of you!" Natalie hugs him lovingly. Then smiles at the little figurine in her hand. A man standing in a boat, rowing it in a funny outfit. "What's this gondolier doing in here?"

"Oh, him? That's just how I wanted us to celebrate our anniversary and the restaurant. Would it be okay if I took you to the place that inspired the recipe and the whole chef thing?"

Karen gasps, knowing well whatever inspires her children. "You're kidding."

"Nate, you do realize your anniversary is in like six days, right?" Laura reminds him, returning to the room on the arm of her husband.

Both women are more informed than Natalie.

"I'm confused. What inspired your tiramisu?"

"When I was twelve, a chef took me into his kitchen when I told him his marinara was a little tangy. I guess normal twelve-year-olds don't do that. So, he taught me how to make the sauce and his tiramisu. Best in the world and close to the recipe I use now. But I bet if the best food critic in the world tasted the original, she could tell me how to make it more perfect," Nate says before a gentle kiss.

"You were living in Oregon then, right?" Natalie narrows her eyes, knowing impromptu adventures are well within the realm of her husband. She sighs. "When are we leaving?"

"Lovebug, do you really think I'd plan behind your back for two months to take you to Oregon? Come on, I have to top the surprise wedding somehow. I even had to commit fraud to update your passport." Nate and everyone else is laughing but letting her wonder.

Laura sighs. "Natalie, the restaurant is near Venice."

"Italy?" Natalie's head spins. "In six days?"

"Four, actually. I'll even let you pack your own suitcase this—" Nate tries but is cut off by Natalie's enthusiastic screeches and kisses that playfully tackle Nate to his back on the couch they occupy. Ken clears his throat.

"You are insane!" Natalie helps Nate back up to sitting.

"I hope that's enough time to do the girly shopping thing since your mom is in town. I bet my sous chef's wife will want to go, too." Nate looks up at Christian.

"Eric isn't married."

"You have better knives than slacker Eric. He's taking the job you want. You get my current job. No arguing. I need someone competent to run the place while I'm in Italy for a week." Just like that, Nate promotes his brother-in-law, setting Laura once more to tears.

While Nate is telling Natalie about a little bakery near a hotel suite, the rest are cleaning up wrapping paper and Christian is looking discouraged. Laura touches his nose lovingly in a corner of the room.

"What's the matter, Lovey? Need more prayers answered today?"

"Insane day, huh?" Christian is grateful beyond even emotion.

"Not as insane as we were to ask for it," Laura confesses, smoothing Christian's collar.

"It's funny. I go crazy for months thinking that basic things like a decent vehicle and a house and a better job were impossible. I'd never even think to consider frivolities like flying you to Venice for tiramisu. I can't really continue the perfect childhood your dad gave you like Nate does for Natalie. I hope you don't get bored of the basics. It's all I can give you, Laura." Christian won't meet her eyes.

"Basics?" Laura searches his reluctant eyes, embracing a reluctant torso. "Seth says we're having boys. When I think about you throwing a football in our own backyard with two little boys and showing Maria what a godly man looks like, Italy seems pretty superficial. I've been to Italy, Chris. Paris. Tokyo. My motherland Sweden. But poor Nate has no idea what *he's* missing."

"What, diapers and morning sickness?" Christian is smiling a little.

"Something like that." Laura bites her lip, then lights up. "And a front porch? So when we're old and pruney we can sit on a swing and watch our *grandkids* change diapers and throw a football?"

"At the same time? Gross!" Christian smirks at a flirtatious nudge from his wife. Nods. "Porch. Priority one."

Chapter Twenty-Six

One

I hear a whistle and bound toward it, nosing under the palm of Natalie's hand. She is giggling, and she and Nate allow me to lie on their front patio where they sit cross-legged. It's much better than a walk through the woods. Seth had been on a computer board meeting and couldn't have me around. Normally, these do not occur at dusk, but apparently, it is a different time somewhere Mr. Billings is vacationing.

"She's so sweet. I just love this old girl." Natalie speaks of me.

"Only dog I could ever stand. Eh, Willow?" Nate pats me, too. "Did Seth have her before you left?"

"Yeah. He got her when we were about fourteen. His psychologist recommended getting a puppy. Before that, he used to throw fits over the tiniest things and destroy his parents' house. All because he was frustrated that no one understood him. His parents loved him so much, but for a while, the way he acted was quite the strain on their marriage. Can you imagine Seth being like that? He's so calm now. Willow changed him. Well, I think God changed him. But Willow helped." Natalie takes on the joy of nostalgia.

"Ah. Reason number 562 not to become a parent. Things like Asperger's." Nate laughs.

"What are the other 561?" Natalie asks with a giggle.

"Oh no, there's an even thousand. I was just citing number 562." Nate jokes. Natalie inhales the slight gust of summer breeze, catching sight of a little white butterfly across the yard. Nate sees.

"What's the matter?"

"It's a nice evening, isn't it? Not too hot. Quiet." Natalie sighs. Suppressing a son she isn't supposed to think about.

"Reason sixty-seven. Peace and quiet. I hope Laura remembers what it was like having twins in the house. I didn't sleep for a year after the girls were born." Nate chuckles.

"So, what's reason number…17?" Natalie perpetuates.

Nate thinks a moment. But only a moment. Then growls the word.

"Venice." Then when Natalie sighs a nostalgic sigh, he elaborates.

"Romantic getaways at a moment's notice. Can't do that with kids."

"Can I ask you something?" Natalie says, getting on her knees behind Nate, rubbing his shoulders.

"Anything, Lovebug." Nate begins to scratch behind my ear. Much too hard, like always. But I enjoy the sentiment enough to enjoy the action.

"Is the 'not having kids' thing like the 'not getting married' thing?" With her question, Nate stops scratching. But Natalie keeps rubbing his shoulders.

"In what way?" He wonders.

"You went from hating the idea of marriage to becoming a willingly married man in a relatively short amount of time." She explains.

"I did that solely for the back rubs. Oooo, down. Left. Yeah, right there. Uhhhh, you're amazing." I hear Natalie's cheeks rise to a smile as Nate directs her hands.

"Alright, well, what if you got a stray hair and decided that there is some back rub equivalent with parenthood?" Natalie now bites her lip. Nate scoots away from her hands. "I don't have to stop yet. Did I rub too hard? You had a knot, sorry."

"No." Nate turns, narrowing his eyes at Natalie. "Bug, I thought we were on the same page with this. Please tell me you're not changing your mind about having kids."

"The only thing I'm having right now is a conversation, Nate. I still don't want them. I was more worried about *you* changing your mind. You swore you'd never get married, and now you're not half bad at being a husband. I don't see why this would be any different, right? I'm just doing a status check." Natalie treads lightly around Nate's temper.

"Trust me, there's a difference. I was wrong about marriage, okay? I thought we'd lose our identities. But then I realized we can still do our thing separately and then come together for backrubs and such." Nate leans and kisses the giggling Natalie quickly. "Marriage works.

Parenthood? When was the last time you heard Christian and Laura take on a piano together? They had identities when they did that. Now they just have Maria, and two boys are about to pop out. Laura used to play piano for hours and hours and hours. Now I don't even think she can reach the keys, once again. Chris got my sister to fall stupid in love with him with one song. Heck, *I* fell in love the first time I heard him sing. Now he works in a kitchen and sings lullabies at night. They are nothing but *parents*. It's gotta be devastating losing your talent and your purpose like that."

"But what if—" Natalie purses her lips. Rethinks. Rethinks again. "What if someone's purpose *is* to have kids? And all the talent is just what they did before they realized their purpose? I mean it has to be *someone's* purpose, right?"

"Well, it isn't mine. Status unchanged." Nate stands, putting hands on his hips as the breeze catches his hair and moves the gelled strands only a little. "What's your status?"

"Mostly unchanged." Natalie nods.

"Mostly? What the heck does 'mostly' mean?" Nate is smoothing his hair and turning red with frustration.

"Calm down." Natalie winces at his harshness. "I told you, I still don't want kids. But I talked to Laura the other day, and she and Christian had planned on waiting a few years to have kids, which I never would have guessed because it seems like Laura was made to be a mom. But God knew, which meant none of their plans mattered. I couldn't help but think about 'what-ifs.'"

"Christian and Laura may rely on 'God,' but you and I use more tangible methods to stay child-free, Bug. Our 'what-ifs' aren't even worth considering. So, let's be done talking about this." Nate shakes his head.

"Why are you getting so mad?" Natalie chuckles. "This is the kind of stuff husbands and wives talk about. We live our lives together, Baby. I like to know where your heart is."

"Temper can be hereditary, did you know that? Reason number one. I hate my father with a burning passion. Everyone thinks he's this loving father and great man, but he's just a sleaze. He's a liar and a cheater and a sleaze, and I *hate* him. Yet he's had this reputation for being honest since before I was born. You gotta wonder if us kids made him who he is now."

"I thought your dad was honest, too. Weird. Do you mean cheater like adultery?"

"I was referring to his gambling habit, but I'm 95 percent sure of adultery, too. Seth, the CEO, goes on half a dozen business trips a year. My dad goes on dozens. Suspicious, eh?" Nate shakes his head.

"Well, Seth doesn't do well with people—" Natalie is interrupted.

"My point is, I saw him in me. Nat, you know you're not my first. You're not even my fifteenth." Nate chuckles, like this is funny. Natalie turns her head aside. "And I'd never cheat on you. That's not my point. It's just that my dad knew what I was doing and with whom and pretended he didn't. Looked the other way. I used to steal his alcohol and have parties over here. He did nothing except insist that my dream profession was not good enough. Because money, to him, is more important than family or integrity. He raised that in me without ever trying. I would never want to subject my own flesh and blood to that." Nate is red again.

Natalie missteps, hurt. "Fifteen? I'm surprised you don't *already* have kids. Or diseases to share."

"Hey, I've been careful every single time. You know how religious I am with that. And it's probably not that many. Or maybe it's more. I didn't really keep track." Nate completely misses the hurt. Smiling.

"Wow. Your religion astonishes me." Sarcasm.

"And yours astonishes me." Truth.

"It's not a religion, it's a—"

"Relationship with Christ, blah, blah, blah." Nate finishes the familiar mantra with ridicule.

"You're a complete jerk sometimes." Natalie laughs through a tear. "Maybe you *are* like your dad."

"You just crossed the line." Nate turns to Natalie.

"Oh, I did?" More sarcasm. "I'm sorry. It's hard to *see* the line. Because making fun of the Creator and Savior of all humanity, not to mention sleeping with anywhere from ten to a hundred girls is okay. Tell me exactly where the line is." Natalie stands as well. I back up and lie in the grass.

"Come on. You know I don't do the Jesus thing," Nate accuses. "And why does my history matter suddenly? I was faithful to you before you even knew I was interested, and even when it involved complete abstinence, Nat. Did you forget that? With the rest of them, it was *just sex*. Why don't you Jesus freaks get that? You know you're the only woman I've ever loved."

"You actually expect me to believe that you've never once thought about any of those girls since you met me?" Natalie is still offended, getting vicious.

"You think I don't know I didn't marry a virgin?" Nate snaps into Natalie's ears for the first time. "If we talk history, it goes both ways, Natalie."

"I'm going inside." Natalie's voice is shaking. She tries to open the door.

"Like hell, you are." Which turns into a battle over the door. Natalie crying, and Nate screaming. But neither hurting the other physically. And I'd be amused if I didn't know how grave the situation is. Finally, Nate grabs Natalie's wrists and forces her to look him in the eyes. "Stop it! I'm talking to you!"

"*One*!" Natalie screams and sobs. "Just *one*. Your Fifteen. Five hundred. Two, whatever. Is a lot, compared to *one* who I *did* love, Nate. No, 'just sex' doesn't compute with me. My relationship with him got ruined the first time that happened. My *one* changed me forever in ways I will never be able to fix. And you *bet* I still think about him sometimes. The fact that you lost count and refuse to admit how much of yourself you *gave up* is sickening. And maybe you're okay with that. But you have a wife who feels the void. You go on and make fun of my God, but He keeps me *intact*. You fear fatherhood because you're scared you'll be just like your father? It doesn't take fatherhood to become what you hate, Nathan Holm. You are well on your way if you don't swallow your pride and find your peace with Jesus."

Nate releases Natalie's wrists. Stunned on the patio. Unable to breathe, let alone speak of the ice pick to his back he'd swear he feels. Natalie heads inside but turns once more before she slams the door.

"Next time just let me go inside."

I flinch when the door closes and watch Nate lower himself to a cross-legged slump before I return to Seth's house just in time for him to open the door for me.

"Gees," Christian says with the same sort of stun Nate just displayed. "Glad we came by, Laura. Wouldn't wanna miss *that.*"

"I give them another year, tops." Zeke's prediction.

"She really blew her top, didn't she? Doesn't seem like her." Laura worries, looking uncomfortable.

"He must have said something idiotic. He's Nate," Christian speculates.

"Not the point, Chris. Mom always taught us girls that a woman's strength is in the difference between what she *can* do or say and what she actually *chooses* to do or say." Laura winces.

"You alright, Laura?" Zeke notices the discomfort.

Laura smiles. "I'm in labor. We're headed to the hospital but dropped by to tell you guys since we left Maria with my parents."

Zeke chuckles. "This is like a walk in the park to you, isn't it?"

"Well, I could certainly scream and freak out about everything we're about to get ourselves into. *Or* I can choose to rejoice." Laura shrugs.

"How about you choose one, and I choose the other." Christian, visibly nervous, snickers a little. Winks at his wife. "You're a lot stronger than me."

Seth had been standing, arms crossed at the windows, and starts smiling a little.

"Natalie is strong as well." All eyes snap to Seth, the steel trap, who usually chooses only Sundays after never to talk about his feelings for Natalie. He must have heard—known. That Natalie, capable of tearing Nate completely apart with just the mention of Seth's name in the right context and situation, didn't do it today.

"So, Vargas is right, then. You *are* still in love with her." Zeke's wisdom is in Vargas's absence, who is now stationed in Texas near his mother, but still visits frequently.

"Irrelevant." Seth sighs and turns to the Kesslers, having wondered at something he must have heard through the glass. "Do you two still make music together at home?"

"Of course, Seth." Laura answers. "The kids just remind us how much we love it. Maria begs Chris to sing all the time, and the boys go crazy inside me whenever I try to play. You're gonna flip when you hear their names."

"Yeah, why all the secrecy?" Zeke teases as he has for months.

"Totally worth it," Christian says, high fiving his wife, who giggles before wincing at a contraction.

"Next time you feel able on chess night after the babies come, I'd like you to make music here. We miss it." Seth requests. They feel his sorrow, I think.

The Kesslers, forever grateful for all that Seth is, nod their heads. They assume Seth is just admiring the untouchable owner of his heart across the lawn. And while I'm sure it is something of the sort, that isn't what he's saying when he mentions her strength. He's seeing, even in the outburst, that there is so much she doesn't say. I've seen it before when a dark-haired infant appears on the television when they watch games and things all together. At every mention of the name "Cameron." When she's holding Maria. Or sometimes just when she's sitting all alone and staring. She's overtaken by a living child that can never leave the secluded corners of her heart.

I get to thinking that memory in Natalie must be like trying to hold back the creek from flowing. Or maybe something bigger. I wonder what kind of energy it must take to do that and still live. Still critique food. Still play piano. Still love Nate. And still pretend not to love Seth. Hold in the secrets, even knowing they all know. All except the one she'll do anything to avoid telling. All that at once. And then I wonder how long that kind of energy can be sustained.

How many rainstorms can breeze over that melting ice before that creek overflows?

Chapter Twenty-Seven

The Reaction

The Kesslers and their three children have to drive here now from a house with a porch that will fit all the children God gives them. But I think seeing them a little less makes me treasure them more. Shortly after they moved out, Vargas moved to Texas when the Army asked, which means the house is mostly empty now. Zeke could buy any house of his choosing. He chooses to stay in this one for Seth, who'd be alone with me otherwise. Nate and Natalie still occupy the guest house. The now chef de cuisine and the respected full-time food writer. The contrast running right down deep inside them. Finding success in career, but little patience for things like tenderness and courtesy with one another.

"When does he get off the oxygen?" Kelli smiles in wonder, holding the fragile survivor tethered to a tube that connects beneath his nose. Kelli had been him in all the stories of her own infancy. He is the younger twin, now three months old, and smiles right back at his doting aunt. Blue eyes and dark hair in a "faux hawk." Tempo Johnathan Kessler is his name, for Christian's lost little brother and for the persistent heartbeat suggesting strength of spirit when they'd feared for his life often in the womb.

"They're gonna test his levels again next week," Christian answers. "But I wonder if Maria will even recognize him without the tube and tank."

"Well, it's a good thing they aren't otherwise identical." Natalie proclaims. Having been a bit more reserved these days inside an increasingly rocky marriage but loving holding the strong and healthy blond-haired Opus Christian, trying to coax a smile out of the already serious little boy.

"I think Tempo looks just like Chris." Laura swoons. "I'm even gonna grow his hair long, I think."

At which Bill Holm scowls, never appreciating a boy with wild hair. Except for Christian, that is.

"It's only fair, Bill," Christian notes, smiling over at Laura, who has a toddler on her lap at the piano. "Maria looks exactly like her mom."

Shelley is sitting right next to Natalie, admiring Opus, then smiles at her sister-in-law before commenting, "We better not say who Opus looks like."

On cue, a gasped curse word comes from the kitchen as Nate apparently forgets an oven mitt again when tending to the awaited apple puffs. He's not been in his right mind either, after the fight he and Natalie had the day the twins were born. Natalie rolls her eyes, almost caught by Nate.

"They should be cool soon." Nate is nursing his slight burn. Natalie looks up at him.

"Wanna hold your little twin here, Nate?" Natalie asks what she has been since the boys were released from the hospital.

"Funny," Nate says.

"It's true, Nathan. I even looked through baby pictures of you to confirm." Karen remembers well the face of her firstborn at three months old.

Natalie stands boldly with the child, gesturing for Nate to sit in a nearby armchair. "Sit down. Just hold him a second while dessert cools, Chef."

The gentleness of her request bends him. "Are you sure I won't break him?" He heads toward the chair to sit down.

"I doubt it," Natalie says, crouching down and helping Nate place his hands on a still-fragile head and body in the chair.

Nate is tense and hates to comply with the request. He looks at his nephew and shakes his head. "Are you supposed to do something, child-with-an-unfortunate-name?"

Laura tries not to look hurt. Karen scolds him. Natalie tucks her lips and stands.

"I'm sorry," Nate tells the little boy. "I shouldn't complain. Parents like yours can name you whatever they want." He stops to react. "What? Something funny?"

Natalie looks up to see Opus smiling at Nate and even lets out a little belly laugh that makes the women in the room giggle. But as soon as the would-be joy starts, Opus spits up all over Nate's chef coat and arm.

"Take," He says simply, demanding that someone remove the child from his arms.

Shelley does so, and Natalie jumps up, retrieving from the kitchen something to clean up Nate's affliction, wiping off the white substance with apologies and haste like a servant.

"What is that, reason 89?" Natalie tries with a shaky voice as she cleans her husband's shirt.

"No, it's up there. Number six, I'd say." Nate says, sensing something amiss in his wife and trying to call it from her.

"I shouldn't have made you hold him. I'm really sorry." She tries to smile.

Nate, skilled in luring women, but still learning the art of a permanent, vulnerable relationship, tries a joke. "If this was your ploy to convince me to have kids, you kind of failed."

"Just wanted you to hold your beautiful nephew for once," Natalie says matter-of-factly, retreating to the kitchen after cleaning up her husband. She leaves him in silence with the rest of his family.

In the lull, Laura flicks her head at Christian, who is at the ready to sing after some introduction she plays at the piano. Nate stays to listen, but I follow Seth into the kitchen with his hunch.

He had caught Natalie's anxious eyes and finds her now praying silently, or maybe catching her breath, in a lean over the sink. Seth comes alongside her and grasps her shoulder. Because Seth knows something about Natalie that no one else would notice.

Natalie feels. That is all Seth will say to describe it. What he means is that whatever emotion Natalie shows, it is merely a spillover of what is on the inside. Even a grimace is actually an explosion on the inside of her. When young, Natalie had less control over the ratio of shown emotion to felt emotion. But now, though it would seem she is numbed or feels less, Seth knows that she is just stronger and *shows* less. Therefore, when she screams at her husband, she has likely murdered him a hundred times in her heart before allowing the vent. Anxiety in her eyes is not to be taken as a passing feeling. It is real, and perhaps consuming her. Enough for Seth to reach out physically to inquire, which he rarely does.

"You alright?" Seth asks with angled eyebrows beneath the hearing of the piano in the next room.

Natalie's eyes scatter as if some geyser in her has been discovered. I don't expect her to come out and tell him that she's scared to death and for whatever reason. I think inside her moment of hesitation that she will tell a half-truth about being tired. Or an irrelevant truth about her annoyance with Nate's harsh opinions. Instead, she tells a full lie like she doesn't feel at all.

"I'm fine. Why do you ask?"

To which Seth tilts his head knowingly.

Natalie smiles, her eyes glistening. Losing a little control over all that feeling. She moves Seth's hand from her shoulder lovingly. As if the loss of connection will make him less perceptive.

"You don't need to worry. God and I will figure it out." She makes the conclusion, conceding to Seth's perception.

"I'll just pray, then." Seth smiles. Natalie nods. Nate enters the kitchen to wash his hands and check on dessert.

Natalie tries to make conversation quickly, to cover any distress Nate might sense. She sees his plating process with dessert, then replicates it the best she can to help him.

"It's nice to hear them play again, isn't it?" She is gentle. Somewhat peaceful, which is the reaction Seth had been seeking by requesting the music. "They've still got it after all those kids."

Natalie is focused on creating a perfect dollop of ice cream and doesn't notice the fuming stare of Nate for a moment. She startles when she looks up.

"What is this about, Natalie?" Her full name and everything.

"What is wh—?"

"Don't even try it. Stop trying to manipulate things. I'm not having kids. Period. End of conversation." Nate takes two plates out into the dining room, smiling as if he'd been even cordial with Natalie. She breathes and looks to the still present, though often considered invisible, Seth. Clears her throat against one gigantic, burdened tear.

"I need to head home, Seth. Will you tell them I'm tired? Or dying of typhoid fever or something?" She requests of her compassionate companion.

"If that's what you want." He barely finishes before Natalie bolts out the door to bare her soul to Jesus and an empty guest house.

Months pass, and their anniversary comes, which marks two years of flirting and fighting. Public displays of affection and wrath. Accusations. Affirmations. Secrets. Soul bearing. All felt through the nerves of everyone. There is relief from it only when the potent mixture of love and hate sways in the other direction for a time. A truly erratic marriage, which the Nakanos only choose to experience for a few days this year at Christmas before returning home.

Romantic getaways are non-existent these days. Nate feels trapped, he'll tell Natalie when she finds him in the main house socializing instead of coming home to her after working one of five fourteen-hour days. It hurts her every time. Then when she enters the back door on Sunday morning to carpool with Seth and Zeke to church, her eyes are usually puffy and red. But whatever happens at church fixes that until she's fellowshipping with the Kesslers and housemates, and Nate will enter, mocking her pain, manipulating her into coming home where she doesn't want to be.

Zeke says the "honeymoon" phase is over. I think the phase is coming where Natalie needs to be honest. Secrets are killing them. Either way, we know they only hang on because they seem to love each other at least as much as they hate each other.

So tonight, they are celebrating all that pain and passion. And we are celebrating this New Year. They wait until they are all tired, and all the children are tucked away into portable cribs in other rooms. The Holms and Kesslers clink glasses with Seth and Zeke. Startling me with little sulfuric streamers from bottles with strings. They play chess for thirty minutes. Seth looks distressed when he beats Bill, but other than that, everything is the way I've known it for years.

All is well until Nate enters the front door, breathing and smelling like he does when he's run a few miles. And except for a bright red nose from the cold he only shielded with a thin button-up shirt, the rest of his face is some sick shade of ghostly green. He finds us in the game room and sits among us. Speechless. And Natalie-less. Laura rolls her eyes for all of us that suspect a typical fight.

"Happy New Year, Nate." Christian's tone is really asking why Nate is without his wife and with us on their anniversary.

Nate simply chuckles once with cruel bitterness. They all look around, wondering what that little laugh means.

"You go for a run?" Zeke ventures, never before having to coax words from Nate.

"Yep." Nate sighs, trying to stave off the heavy breathing, or maybe tears.

"At midnight? That's new." Christian scrunches his eyes, trying to tease words out of him.

"Chris, stop," Laura whispers. "They obviously had a fight. Just leave him alone."

Nate cuts off Laura's plea. His voice trembles. "She talks to you guys more than me. Especially, you know, recently since she started not talking to me at all. And I know I work a lot. But would you guys tell me if Nat was having an affair?"

The formerly hushed room explodes. Even the teenage Holm girls object to the mere idea of Natalie straying from Nate. He nods at the consensus, staring at the wall behind the chess board.

"Why would you even suspect that, Nate?" Laura worries.

"Because tonight, she finally told me what's been bothering her about us. But the last serious conversation we had, she told me that she'd been in love before and she still thinks about him sometimes. What if I didn't get the whole story? What if she's actually been running around on me with this old flame or whatever?" During which all eyes try not to land on Seth, who allays all fears with his answer.

"Natalie would never be unfaithful to you, Nate. She's devoted to you and faithful to God."

Nate nods. He'd already known the answer and her character. "Yeah." Then takes to the kind of low after pure anger is fizzled by a five-mile run.

"So, what's been bothering her?" Laura asks gently. "We're here for you, Nate. Whatever it is. We know things haven't been so great. We'll help however we can."

Nate chuckles once. Nods. "She's pregnant."

A collective gasp occurs from the twin sisters, still young enough to know the proper way to react to such news. A chorus of coos. "A baby?" "Nate, really?" "I hope it's a girl." "She'll be so pretty!" "Maybe we can babysit!"

But the rest of the room is silent, already knowing Nate's "proper" reaction is something much different. The girls, also old enough to sense this, stop their cooing after only a short time, then are shooed from the room by their mother.

"I knew it," Karen whispers to herself when the girls have exited.

Laura bites a lip. She'd known too.

"She *told* you?" Nate's temper lights up.

"No!" Laura defends. "I just have three kids. I know the signs. She stopped drinking wine and started getting upset easily."

"It broke her heart when Opus spit up on you that time," Karen adds. "That's when I started suspecting."

"What does this mean? Are you two gonna be alright?" Christian wonders.

"I have a thousand reasons why I don't want kids. She *knows* that," Nate says to himself, and the others let him continue. "But I only had *two* for not wanting to get married. And Nat *promised* me she'd make me feel at peace with them. Even when we aren't talking, or everything else is bad, she and I have always honored those two constants. Now even those are backfiring." Nate sighs, leans on his knees and buries his head.

"Constants?" Seth knows constants, and doubts he'll hear about them now.

"Yeah, one of them is that we agreed this pregnancy thing wouldn't happen. No kids. She *promised* me."

"The other?" Laura treads lightly.

"It's probably stupid." Nate gives bitter laughter. "But, I didn't want to be in the kind of relationship where a woman who demands monogamy starts withholding physical stuff because we're fighting or she was tired or whatever. I was abstinent for her, and she promised that if we got married, she wouldn't withhold anything from me." Nate smiles a little when the men give a little chuckle. "And she told me that her Bible agreed with me, so I wasn't being unreasonable by asking her to keep that promise. But I guess that constant kind of sabotaged the other, didn't it?" Nate bites his lip. "I can't help but think she did this on purpose to get my attention or something."

"Nathan." Karen begins, again reminding Nate of Natalie's character.

"I know, Mom. But what am I supposed to think? We go two years with both constants, no holding back, and no pregnancy. Then suddenly we have a conversation about what would happen if we 'accidentally' got pregnant, which ended badly enough for her to barely want to be in the same house as me for months and then bam! She's magically pregnant. She swears up and down it wasn't, but it almost seems intentional. On the other hand, I really don't think she'd do that. Because like, why now? Why when we've been fighting? It's not fair. And I should have gone for a run *before* I reacted to the news." Nate sighs. Winces deeply. Grunts at himself.

Laura turns white. "Nate. What did you say to her?"

"Just what I said here. Only less tactfully. And I may have mentioned that since she figured out a way to get pregnant, she should figure out a way to fix it." Nate sits back, readying himself for the blow.

"But it's *your baby*, you idiot!" Laura starts.

"Which I don't want," Nate finishes haughtily. "She *knows* that."

"So, you asked her to have an abortion?" Christian breathes and leans forward. "Nate, that's a serious thing."

"That Natalie would never do," Laura adds.

"Did she think that if this happened I'd just suddenly turn into a family man? It happened. Alright. Whoops. But she told me she's only twelve weeks, so it isn't legally too late. And I'm pissed, by the way. Because she says she found out at *four* weeks. Nipping this in the bud would have been much easier then." Suddenly, the family is shocked at how faint Nate's line really is. But they are reminded that his hotheadedness is only a veil for his heart. "Then on my run I remembered her Jesus thing. And remembered feeling the boys move in your belly, Laura. Seeing all your ultrasounds, so I don't even know if I'd let her go through with it, even if that's what she decided. I know it's supposed to be her choice, but she'd only be doing it for me."

"Regardless," Zeke mentions. "Your wife is currently at your house being forced to question even her most basic morality. Alone. On her wedding anniversary."

"Actually, Zeke." Nate rolls his heavy blue eyes up to the clock then over to his friend. "Our anniversary was yesterday. And she is alone because she kicked me out of the house for the evening after she didn't like my reaction to, 'Happy New Year! We're having a baby in July!' As if I was supposed to be excited. Got a couch for me, Seth?"

"Nope." Seth proclaims as he's carrying himself on knowing legs. I think he and I are breaching the guest house door before he even knows where they've taken him. But God knows he is the best candidate for comfort among us. He's done this same comforting in the past.

Natalie is practically hyperventilating, pacing the entire bottom level as if she's frantically searching for something. Sobbing. Praying aloud. Overflowing. And when Seth enters and makes his way to her, she has found what she was seeking. He catches her midstride and wraps his arms around her waist. Demands her eyes. Breathes with her as he seats her on the couch. He finds her a tissue and then she unloads the burden into the air in squeaks and sobs.

"I'm pregnant, Seth." She sobs.

"I know. Nate told us," Seth says gently. He smiles and tells her exactly what she needs to hear. "Congratulations."

Natalie first smiles through the tears as if the word is a lovely song she's never heard. "Thank you." Then she shakes her head bitterly. "Too bad my husband hates me, and our marriage, and his own unborn child."

"You know he doesn't, Natalie. He was just shocked," Seth reassures.

"He told me to have an abortion. I can't even wrap my head around that. We were sixteen and unmarried and I was more willing to rearrange my entire life than even think about—" She breathes, sobs. "And he actually thinks I did this on *purpose* or cheated on him. I can never win him. The more I try, the harder this marriage gets. I don't know if I hate that I still love him or if I just hate him."

Natalie is beyond consolable for most. But Seth tells her what she needs to hear.

"You can't hate him. She will have his blue eyes. Curls like how yours were but with a little blonde in them. Everyone that sees her will think she is the most beautiful child they've ever seen—"

"Seth, stop it." Natalie sobs.

"Nate will get worse. He will be meaner still. I hate him already for what he'll say, Natalie. But *you* love him. Just keep loving him. Pour yourself into Christ and He will pour Himself into you so you can be strong for this little girl. I *know*. I also know that Nate will want nothing to do with this baby. And then he will give her a name that will make you cry. You believe me?"

"With all my heart, Seth." She nods. And Seth embraces her again.

"This will work to God's glory. It always does."

"Okay." Natalie breathes and is calm. "Okay."

The two pray. Natalie begs Seth to stay, but Seth promises her more honorable company and reenters the house almost as quickly as we'd left.

Nate looks up at Seth. Actually, everyone does, knowing exactly his mission.

"She packed up my stuff yet?"

"No," Seth says. Not a fan of Nate these days. "Go home. She's waiting."

Chapter Twenty-Eight

Betrayed

"*Why* do I have to go? That's what I'm asking you, Natalie. Are you listening? Is that like some customary thing?" Nate is interrogating.

He is even more combative after the reluctant consensus to somehow raise a child together. Natalie is not looking at him.

"Yes, Nathan. It is customary for the father to go to prenatal appointments if he can. I made it early, so maybe you could go before work. They might do an ultrasound, and you can see the baby."

"It's not technically a baby yet." Nate sighs, breaking his wife's heart again.

"If you saw an ultrasound, you'd see it *is* a baby." Her speech is so defeated I want to lick her feet to make her giggle like always. But something tells me it wouldn't help this time.

"So, is it a boy or a girl?" Nate is annoyed that Natalie can't give him more information.

"Too early to tell. We'll find that out in a couple months."

"How do you know all this?" Nate is both impressed and suspicious.

"I read a lot." Natalie forgets the other half of the truth. "If you don't want to go, I won't make you."

"Well, I have to go in early on Tuesday. Pastry chef is off. Maybe my mom will watch Laura's kids so she can go with you. Then just tell me what they say." Nate misses the mark terribly.

The conversation is occurring where I'm laying outside Seth's office. Inside it, Seth is frustrated, shuffling the same papers over and over and over. Then he calls Zeke in to look at them. Zeke shuffles them as well, then he nods at Seth solemnly. Seth sits back in his father's old leather chair, then picks up his phone.

"Bill. Can you stop by my house on your way home today?"

Dr. William Holm does. He sits across the big desk from Seth—a man less than half his age but twice the brain and heart capacity.

"Bill. I have to fire you. I don't need you to explain. I will give you your retirement. But I want you to let me buy your house for fair market value. And I want you to give it to Nate and Natalie to raise the baby in. I will have Mr. Billings do the paperwork. You will never tell them that I orchestrated it. And I will never tell your family or the police you have been stealing from me for five years." Seth lays it out.

Bill nods, accepting all the terms. Bill becomes a hero, giving his house to his son and moving the Holm family to Florida. Laura and Christian stay. Laura misses her mother but Christian suspects the truth in it all. Zeke, unhappy with his job for years, is the new trustworthy CFO of Gowan Construction. Such is the haste of change in life. And such is the way of things when hell begins to break free.

"I'm twenty weeks. That means we're halfway there," says the desperate woman on the other end of the phone.

"Oh." Nate had come to visit after work since Vargas is in town for the week. Or to avoid Natalie, I'm not sure which.

"Tomorrow, they can tell us the gender. Then I can paint and decorate the nursery—our old room."

"Okay."

"I want you to come, Nate. To my appointment. I made it on a Thursday this time. You're off on Thursdays. I really want you to come."

"Why?"

"Because I love you. I don't want you to miss this."

"Fine." Nate hangs up and returns to the men in the window room from the seclusion of the wine cellar hallway.

"Was that wifey?" Vargas asks.

"Yeah. She thought it was a good time to guilt me into going to one of her baby doctor appointments. She said they'll be able to tell the gender, so I told her I'd go." Nate rolls his eyes. "It'll be right before chess night."

"That's great, Man!" Zeke, like everyone else, is trying to be enthusiastic enough to bring Nate to acceptance of his own child. "We'll be here. I bet Chris and Laura will want to know right away, too."

"You hoping for boy or girl?" Vargas asks.

"Neither," Nate says bitterly.

"What does Natalie want?" Seth's only care for many years.

Nate rolls his eyes. "A healthy kid. I guess that's not a bad thing to hope for."

"So hope for it," Seth suggests.

Nate sighs, taking the advice of his dearest friend. "I'll try."

All the humans tense in anticipation of a gender reveal on the Thursday night. Happiness abounds as we wait. But when Nate and Natalie come through the door to greet familiar faces, those anticipations take a terrible turn.

"I have *never* been more humiliated in all my life. You're a liar. You have this whole secret life where you were a nasty little sinner and yet you claim to be some saint. You sicken me." The friends stop Nate's cruel words as quickly as possible. Vargas's words come through clearest.

"Nate. I will punch you if you talk to your wife like that again." Vargas grits his teeth.

The damage is done. And we all presume it's been done for an entire forty-minute car ride. Natalie is stunned. Unable even, to cry. Feeling. But pouring herself into Jesus, I suppose.

"'Fat phase'?... 'I read a lot'?...'I don't ever want kids.'?... 'I've been with *one* other guy'? How about, 'Hey, Nate. Someone knocked me up when I was sixteen, and I have a living child in the world.' No. You wait for a doctor to casually mention your 'previous pregnancy' and let me correct them? And then you correct *me*? Natalie, how am I supposed to *breathe* right now? I don't even know my own wife."

Nate. The scared animal is cornered, and now forced into a chair with the strength of three men. Seth, of course, is nearly as scared as he.

"Nathan, stop saying things you'll regret in front of my children." Nate's sister warns. The tiny woman is the only one brave enough to face him.

Nate looks up at her. Never willing to lay a finger on her or any other woman. But fuming. And then with a hurt realization of a smile worthy of fear, he examines every face in the room. He shifts in the chair in the foyer as if it is a spring. Everyone waits for the volcano, standing by with caution. Laura crosses her arms defensively. Turns red. Because she knows what is coming.

"I'm the only person in the room that didn't know about this." Everyone stares blankly. Including Nate as he lays it all out. "Her parents. *My* parents. Neil. Every single person I know betrayed me."

The nods are stunned, not knowing rhetorical from interrogation—calm from storm preparation.

Christian boldly interjects while confirming the suspicions. "It wasn't our place to tell you."

"I swore them all to secrecy. That's what he means." Natalie begins with a monotone lowliness. And ends with a squeak of a sob. Then composes herself. "Nate, they didn't betray you. *I* did."

Nate clears his throat of what is likely a river of betrayed tears he's holding back. He tilts his head a little with an intense whisper. "Why would you go to such great lengths to keep this from me?"

Natalie pauses, now positioning herself at a stand in front of her husband. She whispers the pure honesty.

"I didn't think you'd take it well." The bitter irony might be amusing if the room weren't thick with awkward tension.

"Wise assumption, Natalie." Nate raises his voice again. "I'm your husband. I should have been the *first* to know about this."

"You're right." Natalie nods. All her strength gone from her. Nate continues to gnaw at Natalie's spirit. "So, was the father of the kid privileged enough to know, or did you leave him out of the loop, too? If so, I should at least be happy I know you're pregnant now. This kid is mine, right?"

"Oh, now you're accusing me of adultery again. This is really my day." Natalie finds some bitterness, at least, to deliver. "That was eight years ago, Nate. And, of *course*, he knew. He was saintly enough to let me give up his son for adoption when he hated the idea." Natalie lets out a random ironic laugh.

"Oh, this is funny?" Nate boils.

Seth has been looking out the skinny window beside that big oak front door, waiting to be involved in some way or make his escape.

"No, it's just—" Natalie tries to defend.

"Today is his eighth birthday," Seth finishes Natalie's sentence absentmindedly and to the surprise of all.

Seth and Natalie meet eyes a moment. Natalie feels some relief, knowing her burden is shared. "I didn't know you remembered that."

"I remember." Then Seth looks back out the window, deflating Natalie.

"Let me guess. Natalie let you in on her dirty little secret too." Nate is still angrily ignorant. Further proving his own plight to himself. Not knowing at all how much he will do so in the next moments.

Which is when Seth breathes. And everyone knows why. Seth has precious little mean in him but more courage than anyone understands. And decidedly enough wisdom to know the perfect way to use both.

"You're so thick, Nate." Which widens every eye because of the saintly mouth that speaks it.

"Seth, don't." Natalie begins. Still thinking she can retain the worst part of her secret.

"You too, Natalie." Seth looks at her again. Speaking firmly, though sensitive to the beatings she's received already. "You're making this worse. When are you going to be honest with him?"

"Seth, I could really do without your advice right now." Natalie gets defensive. The sign of a long-neglected battle I witnessed once before. Even Nate backs down in his confusion.

Natalie's remark sets in motion the pieces of Seth's broken heart. Introducing to all his loved ones the passion they've never seen.

"I've given you *years,* Natalie. Eight years, eight months, and thirteen days. I let you make every decision, even the really wrong ones. It's *my* turn to have a say." Seth pleads, thickening the tension until it begins to remove oxygen from the room.

"You've always had a say," Natalie speaks softly of how highly she values Seth's opinion.

Seth laughs bitterly. "A say in what actually happens, not just a worthless opinion. You of all people should take me seriously. I would have *raised* him, Natalie. It shouldn't surprise you that I remember his birthday."

"Stop it." Natalie sobs. "We were sixteen. You know that was impossible."

"Nothing is impossible." Seth nearly whispers. Nearly tears up. "It broke my heart when you left. And then I had to mourn my parents and take over a company at sixteen. All alone. How does someone survive that? Sounds impossible. There's an eight-year-old boy with half my DNA when doctors weren't even sure I'd be capable of that kind of love. *Impossible*. Nothing is impossible, Natalie. Except knowing what my son's voice sounds like, because you obeyed your dad, no matter the cost. Things are what they are. It already is. But sometimes I just wish you'd listened to *me*." Seth sniffles. "This time it isn't as impossible to be fair to the man you love. I'll do anything for you. You know that. But from now on, that doesn't include keeping secrets from your husband for you."

She concedes now, lowering her pregnant body onto the stairs in shock.

"Of course," Nate whispers. Sorting math and years of observing their odd relationship into truth.

"Nate, let me—" Natalie's words are of little interest.

Seth begins to speak too, but Nate puts up a trembling hand.

"Your Jesus. Judas betrayed Him with a kiss, right?" He frantically stands and removes car keys from his pocket as he speaks. Takes off his jacket. Hands it all to his wife of a more delicate state as a subtle loving gesture. A promise, really. Then he slams that big oak door behind him after a final blow just for Seth. "For once, I can relate to Him."

Nate takes off at a jog down the road. Blowing off well-earned steam. The silence now is far more than awkward in the fated foyer. It eats away at all present. No relief had occurred when Nathan left. Natalie paws the keys, sniffling in tears. Laura and Christian wrangle three children who don't understand the reason for the silence. Sometimes it takes a child—someone who doesn't understand—to understand.

"Baby!" Says the blonde little Maria, having been told that the modest bump on Natalie's tall frame is her cousin. She pats Natalie's belly. Repeats herself. "Hi, Baby."

Natalie clears her throat, unable to keep from smiling. "Baby *girl*. Just like you, Maria. Healthy and perfect."

Laura coos. Seth smiles outwardly. But Zeke, Christian, and Vargas's attention is on the state of his heart. Natalie looks up at Seth.

"Why did you do that?" The last word barely makes it through the first sob of many.

"After Nate runs a half marathon or so to clear his head, he'll need someone to blame. Someone to hate. Better me than you." Seth shrugs. "And better with honesty."

"How can I go home to him? He has an honest reason to *hate* me." Natalie is losing the battle with emotion. Beginning to weep.

"He loves you." Seth corrects. "Otherwise, this wouldn't hurt."

"*You* love me," Natalie argues the truth.

Seth tilts his head. "You love *him.*"

All present hearts shatter.

"Seth. If I could go back—" Finally, Natalie is overtaken by tears and no one knows what to do. No one but Seth, who bends. Breaks. And takes Natalie safely into his arms.

"It already is. No regrets, it'll make it worse." He encourages, then reveals for all what had once been natural but is now only remembered by one other person. "*Nakanai de kudasai. Subete*." Don't cry. You still have all of me.

The others look at one another, dumbfounded. Finally, Laura verbalizes as Seth releases Natalie, who is suddenly sniffling away her sobs with just a few words exchanged.

"You speak Japanese, Seth?" Laura hands Natalie a tissue.

"It's how we kept secrets as kids. Maybe we should have stuck with English." Seth watches Natalie dab her eyes. Whispers. "You gonna be okay?"

With what could be mistaken for a smile, Natalie valiantly requests something of Seth that he is reluctant to oblige. Something the others only understand a little and have never seen. "Tell me something you *know,* Seth."

"I can't, Natalie." Seth is canvassing the faces of the others. He is not at liberty to reveal future wisdom on a whim.

"Please. Anything. Even something small."

Seth clears his throat. "Okay. Zeke will offer to drive you and your car home in a minute. Then I won't see most of you for a couple months. Your husband isn't too happy with me."

"But why would that keep *us* away?" Laura asks.

"He's your brother. He'll think he's successfully caused you all to shun me by the terrible things he says about me. When in reality, you're just—" Seth snickers. Having his own revelation within theirs. "Somehow 'wisely' aware that he needs your company more than I do. Then, with his prior permission, not *without,* Natalie, you'll call me and ask me to help you with something."

"Will he ever get used to the fact that this baby is coming?" Natalie pleads.

"Nate is extremely hardheaded." Seth laughs. The others join. "He has to come to conclusions on his own, even if it means he's wrong for years before that. But when he does, Natalie. He does it all at once and with his whole heart. You know that as well as I do."

"What should I do, Seth? Things are already pretty shaky between him and me if you hadn't noticed. How do we fix this one?" Natalie's tears are gone. But her heartbreak is still fresh.

Seth shrugs, backing up, headed to his woodshop. "Step one: Go home to him."

Chapter Twenty-Nine

Gaps

Thursday nights are quiet, and chess isn't always on Thursday anymore. Today it is Saturday afternoon. Just Zeke and Seth and one game of chess after Vargas goes back home. But Zeke proves a worthy friend.

"Gowan-Young Industries. Think about it. You have six patents you use that help you make money. Exclusive to you. I went out to a site and had to ask what one of the machines was. It was genius. Your dad was a genius. Really. Those inventions are the reason you're the most successful construction company in the region. Imagine if just those magic staples were on shelves at home improvement stores." Zeke has been making the proposal for a month of Thursdays.

"Would I still do construction if I decided to manufacture more? I like having the jobs here in the states."

"No reason to outsource. You could probably employ a lot of the current go-to temps. They'd be happy to have a steady job. Seth, you could make a lot of money."

"I'm really not all that fond of money," Seth reminds Zeke. "Neither are you, Zeke."

"I live in an enormous house on twenty acres," Zeke says.

"*My* house." Seth chuckles. Then nods absentmindedly. "My parents' house."

Zeke brings him back around with a question he's only considered in recent months after Nate stopped contact with Seth as predicted.

"When did you start knowing things before they happen?"

"Time is irrelevant, really. God just gives me wisdom. But I'm sure He does that with you too, Zeke." Seth smiles.

"I suppose He does. But I went over to Nate and Natalie's last Monday and she told me you predicted her marriage to Nate a year in advance. Seth, not even *she* left for that trip knowing she'd come back married. She says you told her that the very day they went on their first date, but beforehand. That's not just wisdom, Seth." Zeke is trembling a little for the eeriness.

"I have gaps; I don't know everything. But it doesn't matter. What is *already* is. It doesn't matter who knows about it except that sometimes when we know, it affects what we do. Which is why I have gaps. I wish I had *more* gaps." Seth sighs.

"Gaps?"

"Yeah. For instance, I knew Nate would get married, even though he hated marriage. And I knew Natalie would marry an unbeliever. But I didn't know Natalie would come back, nor did I know it would be Nate and Natalie that got married. If God had told me when I met Nate that he would marry Natalie, I'd have done everything to stop it. Natalie used to be fickle, and Nate used to party. He'd get drunk and fornicate with whoever would agree to it. That's a bad combination. But by the time they met and I figured out on my own that they'd get married, I was at peace with God's will, and they had both grown into being just right for one another. Gaps are important," Seth explains.

"Explain the fence to me," Zeke asks with a chuckle, amazed by Seth's wisdom.

"I felt led to build a fence, which I continued even when I realized I would be at it for twelve years. There are gaps there too. More for you than for me. Never enough gaps," Seth says this with sorrow.

"A gift and a curse, huh?" Zeke sees the sorrow. Understands and wishes he could ease some of the burden. Seth smiles and lets him.

"You'll convince me. The Gowan-Young thing. I don't know how. But something vital to our success will only be in California. So you'll move to California."

"California?" Zeke says with disgust. "What in California is important enough for me to leave you alone in this house again?"

Seth half smiles. "Your wife."

"Man, that's creepy. More gaps, please." Zeke chuckles.

"It already is, Zeke. We just haven't seen it. Just like God already is but sometimes it takes a lot for someone to see. With your wife, all it takes is time. Much simpler." Seth smiles and snickers at Zeke's clicking mind. "Gray eyes. The rest, you'll have to see. It'll be obvious when you do."

"I've never seen a woman of color with gray eyes." Zeke accuses with attitude.

"Me neither." Seth smiles, probably thinking of Natalie's ebony eyes.

"I'll believe it when I see it." Zeke seizes the moment. "How many more kids are Chris and Laura gonna have?"

"Don't know the total. But she's expecting now and doesn't know it. A boy and a girl."

"How many kids will *I* have?"

"You'd have to be more specific with that question. But if you were, I couldn't answer it. Gaps. Checkmate."

A frustrated finger snap. "Is anyone ever going to beat you at chess?"

Seth breathes deeply. "Yes."

"Me?"

"No. Sorry. I have to go." Seth stands. His phone rings. "This is Seth." I perk my ears for the voice on the other side.

A breath. A sniffle. "Hey, Seth."

"You okay, Natalie?"

"Yeah. Nate still doesn't want to talk to you. But he wants to help me with the nursery even less. Do you know how to paint? My parents always hired painters, and I've never—I just need help, Seth."

"Can Willow come?"

"I would love for Willow to come."

When we arrive, Natalie is looking rounder than when we last saw her several weeks ago. She is sitting cross-legged, staring at a wall in a room in the house. It's the room where Nate taught Seth how to do silly childish card tricks. Laura used to stand at the door in wonder. I remember this room. Natalie's name is carved into the door frame. When I'd sit with Seth and Nate, I'd always imagined Natalie. I wondered what she looked like lying on her bed giggling on the phone with Seth late into the evenings like teenagers do in innocence.

Now Natalie is sitting in the middle of the room, remembering too. But she is sniffling at recent tears in the empty room. Empty except for paint cans and plastic bags from a home improvement store where Seth has taken me for tools and other things. Natalie is even emptier. She looks like Natalie. Smells the same. But parts of Natalie are certainly absent.

"The man at the store made sure I have everything I need. Except a ladder, which wouldn't have fit in my car." Even her voice is empty.

"I brought a ladder."

"Thank you." She begins to rise. To help. But she'd been more comfortable sitting.

"Stay there. I'll do it. It won't take me long. When does he—"

"He'll be home in a couple hours. I told him you were here, don't worry. I'm trying so hard not to keep things from him. He keeps so much from me now." Natalie begins to cry. Or resumes crying, I think. Seth crouches and looks at a paint can.

"Crushed Lavender? That seems like a flower's bad day, not a color." Seth chuckles. Natalie smiles. "I'll go get my ladder."

Paint's odor tries to take over the others, but I watch Seth cover weathered blue with crushed lavender, slowly making Natalie's face brighten as she begins not to remember, but to hope. When Seth finishes painting, she smiles.

"Done? That didn't take long. How long does it have to dry before I put up curtains and pictures and stuff?" She sounds a little more like Natalie.

"What do you need to hang up?"

Natalie rises with effort and help and moves into the next room, a guest room. She shows Seth the nursery decorations, and he spends another hour hanging pictures of purple flowers and sheer white curtains with embroidered vines—beautiful things Natalie probably thought up, chose, and bought all on her own. Zeke sometimes says she lives like a single mom-to-be these days. Nate pretends she isn't pregnant or present at all, really.

She takes comfort because he still cooks for two. For three, actually. Because he wants her healthy and well. He loves her still the way he did, he just can't fathom what it will mean to be a father.

"Do you have furniture? Clothes to put away?"

"My mom is bringing my old dresser. She's coming out here for a few weeks to be here for the birth. The clothes are in the closet. The crib is not something I can handle buying right now." Natalie smiles to cover the pain.

"Money? I can—"

"No, Seth." Natalie laughs, finally. "It's not the money. It would just make it real, you know? I spent so long thinking I'd never be a mother that I can't even decide if I'm ready for it."

"I see." Seth smiles brightly. "Be right back."

Seth walks out to his truck, meeting Nate's arrival, which I think he expected to do. Nate is civil.

"Hey, Seth. Nat told me you might drop by." He stands awkwardly.

"Help me carry something?" Seth asks after a moment.

At the back of Seth's truck, Nate is blown away. "Did you build this?"

"Building things—deciding and controlling what they become—helps me cope with things I can't control." Seth shares while climbing up to get the far end of the perfectly crafted, sturdy wooden crib.

"Seth, I—" Nate tucks his lips.

"I understand why you're mad. I do understand things, Nate. I was mad, too. Forgiveness isn't easy and healing is even harder. I know that. It might not make sense, but I care for you and Natalie more than anyone else in the world. Can I ask you to at least *try* to forgive us?" Seth pleads in his own way. The two have now lowered the crib onto the dirt path.

"I'm not even sure what to forgive you for. Sometimes I think I have no right to be angry, because what you guys did was nothing compared to all the stuff I did as a kid, right? How can I not forgive my wife for having been with one other guy when she's forgiven me for so much more? And you're my best friend, Seth. You've done nothing but encourage Nat and me in our relationship, even though you had ample opportunity to take her for yourself. It's not logical to be mad. I know that. I've already forgiven you for what happened before I met either of you, and I get why you didn't tell me." Nate's heart is broken. Torn.

"But something is still bothering you." Seth encourages.

"Yeah. It's probably stupid. But…" Nate breathes a few times before he confesses. "From what I remember, and from what she's told me, you had a lot harder time with your condition back when you were a kid. But even when we were kids, and you were awkward and hard to deal with sometimes, you were a far better man than me. I used to think, man, if only I can figure out a way to be more like Seth." Nate chuckles. "You're an even better man now."

"I don't understand." Seth already knows Nate's opinion of him.

"Then when my family met Natalie, my mom called her a 'woman of great virtue'— 'and opinion'—my dad said. They said that any man would be obscenely lucky to have her as a wife. She's not a damsel in distress. A real, classy, strong woman, but still soft on the inside." Nate is trying to sort this out. "I'm guessing she was pretty much always amazing, right?"

"Always." Seth nods, still a little confused.

Nate finally states the concern. "A man that every guy can only wish to be like, and a woman that lives her life way out of every guy's league: those two people belong *together,* right? Because the way they'd love each other would easily survive things like screwing up and having a kid at sixteen. Or years without contact, even if they hurt one another. And I'm just *me*. So, when I married Natalie, I robbed you both."

"Natalie loves you, Nate. Understandably so. Maybe your dad tries to make you think you're not good enough. But Natalie and I both see your heart." Seth tries to allay the fears.

"Fact remains, the thought of her choosing me over a saint like you is downright sickening. She deserves better than me, I know that. But it would kill me to lose her, Seth. You have no idea how much of me is invested in her." Nate's eyes overflow a little.

"I just spent the last few hours decorating your nursery." Seth smiles. "She wears it well, but it's still pretty obvious to me how much of you is invested in her."

"She's gorgeous, isn't she?" Nate laughs, and whispers to conceal tears. "Says she feels fat, but I think she makes most pregnant women jealous when they see her."

"She might like to hear that," Seth replies.

"Yeah..." Nate trails off, then smirks a little. Then frets in a sigh. "You're still in love with her."

"Yes," Seth admits in his way.

"How am I supposed to compete with that? Heck, your house is even bigger than mine." Nate is lost in his anxiety.

"I inherited it," Seth reminds. "Just like you inherited yours."

"Weird. My parents supposedly paid off this house with cash and then took out a mortgage for one-half its size in Florida." Nate shows his now acute investigative skills. "If I didn't know better, I'd think—"

"It was selfish," Seth admits. "I knew when you found out about what happened with Natalie and me that you'd get angry and move her out of my guest house. You two are my best friends. I didn't want to lose you when things got bad, so I kept you close to me when I had a chance. Pure selfishness, Nate."

"Again, how am I supposed to compete with a guy whose most selfish act involves shelling out two million dollars to buy a house for someone else?" Nate chuckles bitterly. "I pretty much just have to let her go if she goes running to you."

"A woman of great virtue wouldn't do that. And love is different than you think, Nate. I love *you*, too. I want what is best for you. I just think it would be best for everyone if you stopped making Natalie miserable." Seth's conclusion.

Nate sighs. "Agreed. Are we good, then? I hate that we aren't talking."

Seth smirks. "We're talking right now."

The reconciliation of men is swift enough to occur before even breaching the front door with the crib. They carry it up the stairs, around the corner, and into the teardrops of Natalie.

Nate explains. "He says he builds things to cope."

"It's perfect. I wasn't happy with anything I saw online. Maybe I had my heart set on this." Natalie is pawing at the natural wood sanded smooth with love and pain.

"It's to code. Standard measurements and everything. I even added fire retardant a few days ago because I had some left from something else. She'll be safe in here." Seth reassures.

"Seth, you've been coping with a lot recently." Nate wells up again.

"I've been okay recently. I don't need to build something like this to cope with a fight with a friend." Seth winces. "Don't be mad. But I built this when you were expecting Cameron."

Natalie first snaps her gaze to Nate. Nate, crouching and smoothing his hands over the crib, does not get angry. He instead sees what it took to build. Sees Seth's love for Natalie. Seth's need, his hope, his prayer, for

Natalie to be happy, no matter the cost to him. He rises with a new resolve. He embraces his wife.

"You're exquisite." Which sounds like he hasn't said it in months.

Seth then smiles and removes something from the pocket of his painted pants. "This is what I made recently."

Natalie giggles and coos over the handmade wooden rattle with a bell inside. Nate bites his lip at the gift Natalie shows him. Seth departs. I follow.

Chapter Thirty

Like Father

I startle in the night at Seth's terrible ringtone. Not the ringtone for the office, though. The ringtone for Nate, which is far more terrible. Groggy, my senses are only good enough to hear Seth's voice.

"H'lo?...Nate, stop…she…she what?...Is she okay?...I'll be there soon. Nate. You have to calm down…Call Laura too, okay?...okay…Okay, bye."

Seth dresses quickly. He stops in his office a moment and gets something out of his desk. When he reaches the hall, he sees Zeke is standing there.

"It's one in the morning. What's the matter, Man?"

"Natalie is having the baby."

"Alright. I'll get dressed."

"Thanks. I might need you. Natalie won't go to the hospital."

"What? Why?"

Seth shrugs. "She locked herself in the nursery. Her mom is in town, but Natalie won't let Nate or Eden in there. Did Vargas make it in?"

"Yeah, barely before the alarm set. I bet he's passed out now."

"Well, bring him with you. S'go Willow." I follow Seth to his truck, and we drive to Natalie's house, then go up the stairs, where Nate is yelling through the door to the room we painted a couple of months ago.

"Nat! You're in pain. They can stop the pain. Please. Just open the door, Bug." He is already exasperated. Panicked. But softens slightly at the sight of Seth and me.

"You only care about my pain! Why don't you care about the baby?!" A voice from inside the room sounds a little like Natalie but more like the tone of a screaming animal. When she stops speaking, a low moan begins. Pain. A lot of it.

"You're my wife! Of *course*, I care that you're in pain. And it's because you're having the baby. So open the door!" Nate yells. Then turns to Seth. "I just *had* to put a deadbolt and two chain bolts on there when I was a teenager."

"'*The*' baby? Why can't you ever say *our* baby? You don't even want her." At Natalie's words, Nate walks from the door breathing erratically. He's tortured for being so unable to control the situation and so far from helping his wife.

Natalie's mother stands nearby in the dark hall. Eden speaks.

"Sweetheart, you can't have this baby alone in that room."

"Why not?!" Another scream.

"It's not safe." Eden tries to remain calm.

"What do you care? You wouldn't even come in the hospital room the last time I did this."

"Natalie, Nate is very worried about you. You need to open the door."

"Nathan hates kids. He…" Another moan. More intense. I worry for Natalie and whimper, scratching at the door. After the pain, she calms a bit.

"Willow? Seth? Is Seth here?"

Seth looks first to Eden, who gives her opinion.

"Might have made the last time easier had you been there. She did the same thing. Ken had to break down the door. We're trying to avoid that this time."

Seth breathes deeply, then looks to Nate for permission.

"I don't care what you have to do, Seth. Help me get her to the hospital." He whispers.

Seth hands Eden an envelope in his hands—the one he'd gotten from his desk before we came.

"What's this?" she asks.

"Something we might need," Seth answers. Then he cautiously approaches the door. Leans his forehead on it. "Natalie?"

"Seth." She is at the region of pain when all emotion is wild. Therefore, she bursts into tears. "You came."

"I did." All eyes look to him. Including Zeke and Vargas, who reach the top of the stairs. "Why won't you open the door?"

"Because God hates me, Seth." Sobs. But less anger. She seems in grave defeat.

"How could God hate you?" Seth smiles at what is a ridiculous prospect to him.

"Oh, sweet Jesus." Eden has now looked in the envelope. She's in tears. At the same moment, another pain starts that makes Natalie have to breathe to make it go away. I whimper and scratch again.

"Willow, quit that," Nate whispers. I comply, moving to his feet. Natalie sniffles. Whimpers. "It hurts."

"They have drugs at the hospital," Nate singsongs, rocking on his heels and addressing the ceiling.

"Shut up, Nate!" Natalie cries from inside. "You wouldn't even care if we both died in here."

Nate puts his arms out in shock and re-approaches the door. "You are *all* I care about! Bug, come on. Please. Let me in."

"She doesn't even have a *name*. I asked you to come up with one. I've done this pregnancy all on my own when I'm supposedly married to someone who 'cares about' me. If you really loved me, you'd love her, too. How am I supposed to bring a child into the world whose father won't even give her a name?" Natalie rants, then whimpers and moans loudly. Nate steps back and punches a hole in the wall next to the door. He paces in the dark hallway a few times, then charges down the stairs past Vargas and Zeke, who promptly follow him.

Seth steps back to the door. "Natalie. You need to stop this and think about your baby. Don't you want her to be safe and healthy? You need to open the door. You can't do this alone."

A huff and puff of a much less pregnant woman ascends the stairs in a panic. "Where is she?"

Seth holds his hand out for Laura to quiet. He knows Natalie is thinking of opening the door. We all wait in silence. We hear sniffles.

"Seth," her voice cracks. "I don't deserve this baby."

"Natalie. It's okay if you're scared or worried. But you can be those things with the door open." It is only a few seconds before the latches unhinge and click and slide. Then Seth turns the handle. The door opens.

Quiet panic ensues from Laura and Eden, who quickly see the state of the room. A rug is soaked in a ruptured bag of waters and streaks of blood. Natalie is curled up in tears. But Seth approaches and sits on his knees in front of Natalie. She squeaks some information about pressure and timing of pains which send Laura and Eden away for towels and all other things Laura scrambles through in her mind aloud.

"Can't you make it to the hospital?" Seth asks once the other women depart.

Natalie shakes her head. "Probably not. I've been in labor five hours, I think. My water broke two hours ago, and it's a forty-minute drive. The baby could come any minute. I'd rather do this here than in a car on the way."

"Natalie, why did you wait so long?" Seth scolds gently. "I'll go get Nate. He should be here if you're that close."

"No! Wait, please—I have to—hold on." We watch this time as Natalie relaxes into the pain of the contraction. Experienced. Educated. She lets it do its work. Seth smiles.

"You're gonna be a good mom," Seth says when she comes back around.

The tears come. "Seth, I didn't even hold him. They said I could. His parents. But I didn't hold him. I just let them take him away forever. I felt cold inside for a long time because of that. That's why, Seth. That's why Nate doesn't want this baby. Because he was my own son and I didn't—" Another contraction.

Seth waits for it to finish. Laura and Eden overtake the room when it does, setting Natalie back on pillows and putting towels where they need to go.

"They didn't think you were cold, Natalie." Seth smiles to himself.

"Don't try to lie to me, Seth. They probably tell him that I was too much of a coward to keep him. And that I didn't love him. I *loved* him. I *still* love him. But he'll never know that," Natalie whimpers.

"No," Seth whispers and moves Natalie's sweaty hair out of her face. "They knew you loved him. And they saw how brave you were. And mature and selfless and loving. If you'd held him, you would have probably changed your mind about giving him up. That's the only reason you didn't."

"You're trying to make me feel better," Natalie accuses. "Stop, Seth."

Seth clears his throat. "Ron Carrington fell in love with Nancy when he was ten years old. They were good and pure and loved the Lord. They had so many dreams. Ron wanted to be a doctor for children, and Nancy wanted to be a midwife. They wanted to get married and have ten kids. They loved kids more than anything." Seth laughs a little. "Ron and Nancy went to prom together at their high school. But that night, a semi-truck driver fell asleep, and Ron was okay, but Nancy almost died after the accident. She was bleeding inside, and it took a lot to save her. Including taking her ability to ever carry a child."

"You're really bad at fairy tales, Seth." Natalie chuckles but wants Seth to continue. She begs for spiritual relief since physical pain is unavoidable. Seth waits until after the next contraction.

"But Ron and Nancy were in love, Natalie. So after high school, they got married. She became a midwife and he became a pediatrician, just like they dreamed. She would bring babies into the world, and he would keep them healthy. But they still wanted a child of their own more than anything. Even though it was physically impossible, it was something they prayed for all the time. Because…"

"Nothing is impossible," Natalie remembers and then groans at a contraction. "Except my husband magically deciding to be a father."

Natalie is only hysterical until one careful shush from Seth.

"Nothing," Seth whispers. "Not for God. The Carringtons had a lot of heartache with failed adoptions for a lot of years. So eventually, they had their whole church praying. They got another church praying, and so on and so forth. Eventually, your parents' church got word across the country the day after we told them you were expecting. Your dad didn't know how he knew. But he just *knew* that our baby wasn't meant for us to raise. He made a giant leap of faith, Natalie. I hated him for it. And everyone got worried when you asked for me your whole delivery. But the Carringtons love you for the gift you gave them, even though they saw you crying the next day when they had a picture sent to your hospital room."

"I couldn't even—I sent that picture to *you*, Seth." Natalie cries fully. "How do you know all this?"

"Because when I got the picture, I spent a lot of time and money and company resources to get past the 'closed' adoption. I found out they named him Cameron Nathaniel Carrington. Nathaniel was the closest they could get to Natalie because of the blessing you were. Which makes me smile because your husband's name is Nathan."

Natalie sobs and then complains of pressure.

"When Mr. Billings called them, they thought I was trying to take him away. But all I wanted was more pictures. So they send them twice a year. I asked them not to give a return address for the same reason you didn't hold him." Seth reaches his hand out to Eden for the envelope. Eden nods and gives it to him. He sits next to Natalie. He opens the envelope and pulls out a neat little stack of photographs. He flips through them in view of Natalie, who is now losing even more composure emotionally. Bawling, wheezing. Smiling. Coughing. As Seth thumbs through photos of a little boy with dark curly hair and his eyes. Playing the piano. Soccer. Learning chess. Smiling. Happy. Wanted. Prayed for. Loved.

"He's perfect…why did you wait until now to show me these?" Natalie finally manages.

"Because I was mad at you and your parents for leaving until the day I got the first picture. I built the crib because I was *mad*, not because I really wanted the baby. But from the time I got that picture, I have loved him more than I've ever loved anyone or anything and forgot I was ever angry. But if I'd shown you once you came back, you might have changed your mind about Nate. I couldn't allow that. I fell in love with a picture. Nate will have more than pictures. Nothing is impossible." While Seth has been talking to the trembling Natalie, Eden has been crying, thumbing through the photos again.

"What did we do?" She sobs.

"The right thing. God was in it," Seth says, standing. "And now He's here for this, too."

"Seth! Where are you going?" Natalie demands.

"To get your husband." He chuckles. I follow him down the stairs, where we encounter chaos.

I don't know if I've mentioned Nate's size. And if I haven't, I think now is a good time. Zeke is a big man. Vargas is under average height. Seth and Christian sit somewhere in-between. Nate is the tallest. He's powerful and muscular, keeping his profession off his twenties with morning runs and strength training a few times a week that Vargas instilled in him. If I were a human woman, and paired this power with the way he keeps trimmed and neat as encouraged by Zeke, I'd be seeing what Natalie has seen since long before Niagara. If a man, I'd be doing as they are—thwarting attempts at throwing armchairs at windows. Keeping him in one had obviously failed. All pictures and decorations are piled frantically in the nearby foyer. Likely an attempt to preserve them, considering one broken vase and a solid oak dining room table for twelve on its side. But since I am neither man nor woman, but a dog, I cower, taking my place with the oblivious children sleeping in the office at the front of the house.

Nate, when finally cornered by friends from things to destroy, he takes to pacing and lets out a roar of a yell, like a lion. Verbal reasoning seems like it had been futile until this point. Nate is the first to invite it through his heavy breathing.

"Well, hello, Seth. Done sweet-talking my wife? Can we go to the hospital now?"

"She isn't going to the hospital yet. Laura says she's crowning. Eden called an ambulance."

"What?" This comes from all directions and perspectives. Christian means it as an exclamation. He knows what crowning is. The others do not. Not even Nate, who asks for clarification.

"English?"

"You're gonna be a dad," Christian says, breathing heavily like from a workout. "Very soon."

"What, *here*?! Is that okay? Is she okay?" Nate nearly comes back to the root of his frustration in the panic.

"She's fine. Just waited too long to go to the hospital. You should have called me sooner. But Laura and Eden are taking care of her. I think she wants you upstairs," Seth reassures.

Nate sits on the floor and yells into his hands. Then he speaks bitterness. "Am I supposed to be excited at this point? Still not happening."

"I was." Christian brings on his sarcasm. "But hey, I was just a nineteen-year-old kid and terrified. Silly me. I even wanted to be in the room, right next to my wife when my daughter was born—my sons too. I'll probably do it again in a few months. But that's just me."

"Chris, he's going to start throwing crap again if you egg him on!" Vargas says from a place too deep not to include a thick accent. He plops onto a chair, exhausted from traveling all day and awakening to control a bear.

"Christian, why? *Why* is this so appealing to you?" Nate is rubbing his face.

"Laura and the kids are the greatest blessings in my life. By far, dude." Christian shrugs, finding it safe to take a seat on the couch.

"My dad used to say that, too." Nate starts to calm his breathing.

Zeke takes a seat on the arm of the couch.

"Pretty sure he still does." Christian chuckles, lounging, speaking to the ceiling. "Jerk."

"Glad to know I'm not alone in that," Nate says.

"How could you be? He embezzled over six million dollars from Seth's company and acted like a hero when Seth cleaned up his mess. He'd spent it all gambling and on other sinful pursuits. I'd suspected it for years but couldn't prove it. I honestly don't know how your mom stayed with him. He should be in prison." Christian tells Nate.

"He's lucky Seth is a better man than him. But I'm his son, which is what scares me. Kids tend to become their dads, no matter how much they try not to. I told Nat that was exactly why I didn't want to be a father." Nate opens up. Christian rises and begins pacing like he did years ago on the guest house porch before breaching a sacred boundary.

"That's not how it works, Man," Zeke offers. Vargas agrees. Neither one having been raised by a father at all.

"How do you know I'm not gonna turn into my sleazy dad the second this kid is born?" Nate whines his flawed logic.

Christian bursts forth with truth previously a mystery to all present. "Because I didn't start getting drunk every night and beating Laura for the heck of it the second Maria was born." Christian shakes his head through a laugh. Banishing a tear. "And I've never given the kids more than a modest spanking, let alone torching their feet or making them sleep on broken glass because they dropped a beer bottle on the way to the trash with it. If I did, I'm pretty sure Laura wouldn't defend me. I owe my father over $375,000. Did you know that? Did I steal it, you ask? No. He was a sadistic psychopath. He kept a running tab of every meal I ate. Every night

I slept in my bed or cold medicine I took. Everything. He charged me for them, and if I was lucky, he'd take off a dollar or two every time I covered for the crap he did to me. That's *my* dad. The guy they called a family man who spoiled his kids. Well, kid. I had a brother. You can guess what happened to *him*. I'm grateful he didn't have to live through what I did."

"Chris, I had no idea," Zeke speaks for the whole room.

"That's because you'll never see him in me. He may have helped my mom make me and been around for my prison of a childhood. But the fact is, he's not my Father. I took guitar lessons when I was eight and hated it, just like I hated everything then. I rode my bike home after about the third lesson and accidentally left my bike outside, like eight-year-olds do. Well, my dad locked me in a closet with my guitar still strapped to my back. I was in that closet—no food, and just a water bottle I had in my guitar case—for three days." Christian sniffles.

"Christian. Are you kidding me, Man? How did you survive that and turn out to be *you*?" Vargas, the almost priest, is both heartbroken and impressed.

"Well, most of my childhood was hell. But then there was that closet. Once I figured out I'd be in there a while, alone, just like the rest of my life, I looked around and found a musty old hymnal and opened it to the first page. Grabbed my guitar…" Then Christian sings. Transcending the bitter darkness of the room with a closed-eyed smile.

"Abide with me
Fast falls the eventide
The darkness deepens
Lord with me abide
When other helpers fail and comforts flee
Help of the helpless, Oh, abide with me.

"One verse in and God found me. Gave me peace and hope in the worst of the worst. All it took was a book of hymns. But God could have done it with less. There were times He did. My dad did a stellar job intimidating me into becoming a man. But it was the Holy Spirit, my Heavenly Father that turned me into one. That's the kind of father I strive to be." Christian is overcome with memories and emotion. Near tears still.

"Nate, there's nothing harder than being a parent. I'm not gonna lie. Laura and I didn't plan for this and certainly couldn't do it without God's strength. But there's nothing better, either. Because as a father, I get a tiny glimpse of the way God our Father loves us, and it is humbling. I'm not 'doomed' to be my father. I'm blessed to get to *try*." Christian goes and rights the wrong done to the dining table. Zeke helps him. Seth is next to join. Then Vargas.

I go to the man whose head is buried in his hands. He chuckles at the nose I give his palm and scratches my ear too hard. Natalie, who we've been hearing in whimpers and moans muffled by the distance, suddenly lets out a chilling scream like an animal. Nate is brought to his feet in fear for his wife. All eyes and bodies turn stunned to the stairs. Then another sound follows. It's a small squeak of a cry. Then a few more squeaks. Then a wail even more beautiful than Christian's singing.

Laura appears at the top of the stairs.

"Nate! Get up here, you pig! You're a dad!" She's smiling from head to toe. It is impossible to witness the miracle of birth and not smile this way.

Nate's breath grows to pain within him before he remembers to exhale. The men in the room, some of them in tears, are urging Nate to go upstairs in chorus. Then when his hands smooth over his blond hair, they are disheartened yet again.

"Don't throw anything please?" Vargas pleads.

"She hates me." Nate stands exactly where his feet don't want to let him. Talking to his sister.

"Well, the past few minutes, she's said some pretty nasty things about you." Laura giggles and sends a knowing smile to the snorting of Christian. "But now she's talking crazy saying she loves you and needs you and stuff like that. Crazy or not, you're needed. So get up here."

Finally, Nate disappears up the stairs. After a few moments of encouragement and just plain hugs for the Christian they never knew, we open the door to a team of medical personnel. It takes Natalie more than a few moments to be prepared for transport. Nate is sent down the stairs again during that time with one job. We learn this job as he practically tiptoes down the stairs.

He sits in a chair with a shimmery silver blanket that smells funny. He sets it on his lap, his skilled hands more unsure than they've ever been. He stares at it. The men who had just seen his chaos are suddenly deeply sure that it is all now peace. We all approach slowly, even though Nate's face reads only fear.

Then the thing in the blanket struggles, grunts lightly, and lets out one strong, "Neh!"

Then Nate sniffles. Smiles. Laughs. "Gah! What is going on with me?" And then he lets the tears flow as his friends chuckle.

"You're a dad," Vargas reveals.

"How is she this tiny?" Nate says in wonder. Dying inside. Melting as the thing wraps all its fingers around just one of his.

"They don't stay that way, Dude." Christian leads the sniffles and laughter.

"Well, they *should*," Nate determines, thinking he has held it together enough. Thinking he can handle the rest without tearful incident. But the baby opens her eyes to meet his stare. Nathan Holm looks down onto his lap at a too-tiny person and sees something as terrifying as it is wonderful—his very own eyes.

All the men gasp. Zeke laughs and speaks first. "Whoa, you got your work cut out for you with that one."

"*Muy bonita.*" Vargas expresses.

"Just like your mom," Nate says with wet eyes to the child. "I bet you heard how mean I was to her. I guess I didn't know you'd be this perfect. I hope you can forgive me someday for doubting."

"She already has, Dude." Christian puts a hand on Nate's shoulder. "Kids don't hold grudges. Even I forgave my dad."

"What about…" Nate sighs, shedding all his pride as he kisses little fingertips. "What about God? Do you think He forgives me?"

Every man in the room does a victory dance in his heart, even though Nate is smiling and enthralled by his baby girl, unaware.

"Are you saying you want *God* in your life now?" Vargas asks, almost condescending and to the scowls of others at the delicate heart song.

"Well, the thing is, there's no way something this perfect could have half of my DNA, unless God is *already* in my life." The men chuckle.

"There's something else at work here, you know? Maybe the same thing that was in that closet with you, Chris. Whatever that is, I want it."

The medical team is now carefully getting Natalie down the stairs on a stretcher. Nate stands after his rant sets all the men to awe of their own at God's power. A female member of the medical team tries to take the baby from Nate, who objects.

"Baby has to go in the ambulance, Dad." The medical person says gently.

"Then Dad has to go in the ambulance, too." With a wink and a smile, Nate charms the responder and the listening Natalie all at once. Then, when allowed to follow Natalie out, Nate turns to Christian.

"Will you guys come to the hospital?" Nate hadn't been finished with the conversation.

"Yeah. Do you have a car seat? And a hospital bag packed?" Christian calls after Nate. Then mumbles under his breath with a smile, "Or any idea what the heck you're doing at all?"

"Nat put all that in the car weeks ago. My keys are on the counter." Nate disappears out the front door, and Laura and Eden come down the stairs, descending from a high.

"Hey," Laura says within a sigh to the side embrace of her husband, noticing the difference in the way they all look at Christian. "Is everything okay?"

"Yeah." Christian smiles. "Did you just deliver that baby?"

"Natalie did all the hard work." Laura refuses to accept hero status today or any day she is Christian's angel.

"Psshhh." Christian rolls his eyes. "You're amazing, and you know it."

"Amazing is whatever you said to calm Nate down. He said it was you, so you're busted." Laura kisses Christian's cheek as the other men nod to Laura. She inquires. "Nate okay? I was worried when they handed him the baby."

"Nate's never been more okay." Zeke smiles. "He'll accept Christ by sunrise."

Laura chuckles. "Cute, Zeke."

Seth smiles. "Christian, I like your salvation story. *Abide With Me*. Powerful."

"They don't write 'em like that anymore." Christian smiles peacefully.

Seth nods, then causes the victory dance, holler and prayer of a family forged by God. "Nate gives his life to Christ in an ambulance with his wife while holding his newborn daughter."

"How long have you known that?" Vargas demands.

"Five years or so," Seth confesses.

"Seth, you had us all worried about him! Why wouldn't you tell us that?" Laura accuses.

Christian piggybacks. "I'm guessing you know this kid's name, too? Natalie said you told her it would make her cry, so you have to know what it is."

"Gaps are important." Seth smiles. "Let's get to the hospital."

There is nothing shameful about a blubbering man who has just seen his face in a brand-new person. There is nothing corny in nonsense words spoken to a child who cannot comprehend them. Some things in life can only be understood when under their spell. A refined woman in labor will scream. A squeamish father will caress a slimy new infant unabashedly. The human eyes are unable to resist tears at the first sound of a baby's tiny voice. These anomalies, characteristic of all, however different or hopeless they seem, unify the human race—reminding them that they all belong together as children of God.

Chapter Thirty-One

Renewed

Apparently, it is something about my hair or something about being uncivilized. But whatever it is, I'm told I'll be stuck in the truck at the hospital where we all caravan behind the white car with the flashing lights. My last memory of these took Seth's parents to a place that couldn't save them—the place they take the born and the dead and the sick. At least they get to go inside.

When we stop, Seth gets out to receive parking instructions from the man outside. I watch Nate, still with the infant in arms, carefully come out of the ambulance with Natalie in the rolling bed. They disappear into the hospital, and then Seth parks the truck in a dark building where I watch the sunrise just outside the cement half wall. Then I smell something outside the half-open window that makes me rise to see over the dashboard.

I am elevated, I find, and below is a wall of the hospital. Two brothers sit together against this wall. Nate has a funny plastic something on his wrist, and Christian has a Bible in his hand.

"You thought of a name yet?"

"Yeah." Nate chuckles.

"Well, what is it?!" Christian asks excitedly.

"Naya Lynn Holm. Naya means 'renewal.' Lynn means 'waterfall.'"

Christian guffaws. "After Niagara Falls? Wow. I know that's where you guys tied the knot, but seriously? That's cheesy."

"Says the guy with a son named Tempo," Nate teases. "What are these next twins? Sonata and Rondo?"

"Alright, touché. You still have to explain. Natalie cannot be okay with this." Christian still has lingering laughs.

"The waterfall. It's more than where we got married, Chris. It's the current that takes you where you're headed, whether you like it or not. Love led us to marriage. Marriage led us to this baby. I never wanted those things, but now I can't even think like I did before. This baby—my little Naya—helped me understand that it's not just some mindless current, you know? It has an intricate, intelligent design. Nothing is an accident. Naya shouldn't be here. I kept trying to figure out how she got here. Last night it became pretty obvious that Someone has a lot more control over my life than I do. But instead of being bitter, like I should be, I'm actually relieved. I told Natalie that I'm ready to fall. Ready to stop fighting the current. To be renewed. Nat cried for a while. I think she likes the name."

Words of Nate. I check the area to be sure I'm hearing correctly. Yes, Nate. Following God's will.

"Naya." Christian repeats. "Great name, Bro."

"Shut up." Nate punches Christian's arm with a laugh and then sniffles. His heart is someplace else.

"What's up?" Christian encourages. "Talk to me."

"Seth was here all night after the rest of you went home. We sat in the room until Nat kicked us out into the waiting room so she and Naya could sleep. It's crazy how much he knows about the Bible. But now he's just grabbing coffee before his drive home and made me read second—um—Corinthians? To give me something to do until he visits again later. Has to do his cereal thing. But since you're here and I can detain you as long as I want before work, can I ask about a verse? Something about being unequally yoked?"

Christian smirks, turning to the book in his own Bible and finding the verse without further direction.

"Second Corinthians 6:14. Here it is. '*Do not be unequally yoked together with unbelievers. For what fellowship has righteousness with lawlessness? And what communion has light with darkness?*' That the one?"

Nate chuckles. "That's it. I remember you and Laura being all excited about the 'yoke.' So, it's talking about marriage, right?"

Christian nods. "In general, yeah. Believers aren't supposed to marry unbelievers. You've been in such a marriage for a few years. I bet I don't even have to tell you why it says that."

"No. Yeah. She's been so righteous. I've been lawless, thinking I was right." Nate smiles the kind of smile that precedes, but tries to cover tears. "She's read the Bible. She gets this stuff. Why the heck did she marry me, Chris? I can't imagine the pain she's gone through. I've been—" Nate uses a thumb to wipe the first tear. "I have this amazing woman that ignored a very clear warning from God in order to give me the best parts of her. And I treat my idiot teenage dishwashers at work ten times better than I treat her. What made her think I was worth that kind of pain? No one should ever treat her the way I've treated her."

Nate pauses to put a curled hand against his mouth to sniffle tears away, then finally clears his throat and speaks.

"Chris, I want more than anything for her to not ever go home with that guy again."

"She doesn't have to," Christian reassures. "Let Christ in your marriage, and it makes a lot more sense, Man. Trust me. We were teenagers. How did you think we made that work?"

"But what Natalie gave up for me is not even the worst of it." Nate clears his throat again. "She's known me four years. And as horrible as I was, she's seen the best of me. But God was there for the rest. He saw everything terrible I've ever done. Heard every word I've spoken against Him. All that darkness and shame. Never mind an insane move like knowingly marrying all that—" Nate sniffles. Trembles. Clears his throat but still squeaks out, "He died for me. How am I worth that?"

"You're not." Christian chuckles. "That's why we call it grace."

Chapter Thirty-Two

TWELVE MINUTES

“Who is Madison Walker?” Natalie accuses, walking outside to where the men sit watching Seth emerge from the woods with his first fence panel back on the lawn.

Even though they’d been exchanging hilarious war stories of fatherhood, Nate’s face loses color when he sees that Natalie has a baby in a sling on one arm and is shaking Nate’s phone in the other.

“Uh…” Nate draws a blank, no longer willing to lie his way out of trouble.

“She called three times while I was nursing Naya, so I couldn’t answer, but she’s programmed into your contacts. Madison Walker. She sent a text, quote: *‘Nate, answer please. It’s Maddie. Peaches? I’m in town and I need to talk to you.’* Why would a woman you call ‘Peaches’ need to talk to you?”

“There is no way you are that much of an idiot,” Vargas says to the sky. Still in town. Out of the Army. Into the priesthood. And headed to a mission field far away in a few weeks.

Nate panics at the words. “No, no! I haven’t talked to her since before I met you, Bug. Maddie is an old friend.”

“Flame. He means old flame,” Zeke corrects to the betrayal of his friend.

“Isn’t she the one that left all hot and bothered that one time? Tall scrawny one with the—” Vargas gestures to his torso.

“Black lace,” Zeke enunciates. Remembering the night I’d destroyed Maddie’s shoe, and God had started a change in Nate.

“Zeke! You’re gonna get me in trouble. Bug, I have no idea why she’d be calling me.” Nate stands, taking his phone.

"There's pretty much only the one I can think of," Vargas says, laughing with Zeke.

"I missed this one," Christian mumbles, enjoying the glimpse into a Nate he never knew.

"See!" Nate points at Christian. "I haven't talked to her since the day before I met Chris. I remember, because—"

Natalie interrupts. Nowhere near as amused as the men and not interested in details of old flames. "Call her back and ask what she wants."

"Of course, Lovebug. I'll call." Nate winces.

"Now?" Natalie tilts her head.

"Yeah. Right. Okay." Nate breathes, having had few full conversations with Maddie at all, let alone one in front of his wife and God and everyone. Since he'd met the Lord, I wonder if he'd forgotten completely the man that used to talk to Maddie. But, obediently, or in fear, he dials the number.

The men around tease and chortle, but Christian is in the place of Natalie, not sure the nature of things. They all await the answer on the other end. I use my advantage to hear it clearly.

"Hi, Nate? I've been calling for an hour. Are you okay?"

"Yeah. I'm fine, Maddie. I wasn't near my phone." Then Nate makes Natalie's heart flutter when he utters the next words. "My wife just brought it to me. She was feeding the baby and couldn't really move."

"Wife? Baby? I'm sorry. This is Nathan Holm who went to Allen Prep in Colorado, right? The sous chef?" Maddie is close to hanging up for the mistake.

"Yes, Maddie. This is Nate. But I actually own that restaurant now. I've been married like two and a half years. Then we were recently *surprised* with a daughter. Blessed, I should say. God sent her at a good time." Nate winks at Natalie, who giggles, never fooled by charm.

"You are a piece of work, Nate." Natalie smiles.

Maddie cackles. "Seems like she has your number. But I totally get you. God tends to send babies right when they are needed."

Nate's knees work faster than his mind and take him to a sit on the deck. Maddie clears her throat and continues. "It's good to hear your voice. It took me a while to work up the nerve to call you."

"Yeah, I would imagine."

Natalie is afraid. She hears in Nate's tone that he has already come to some terrible resolve in his mind.

"Anyway," Maddie sighs. "Would it be alright if we got together in the next few days?"

The Holy Spirit need not even whisper for Nate to know the answer to this. "Madison, I'm *very* married and *very* in love my wife. I'm not into—"

"No! Oh gosh, Nate. I'm not interested in 'getting together' like that either. I'm so sorry. I bet that sounded terrible. No. I just need to talk to you. It's pretty important, but I'd rather not do it over the phone. I wouldn't even mind if your wife and baby came too. It would actually be better that way. Then I could bring my son." Maddie drops the bomb that Nate is mortified to have to clarify aloud.

"You have a son?"

"Yeah, Kevin is three now. Three and a half, I guess."

Nate is far less than comforted—the timing matching up with near perfection. Having nothing to lose, except everything, he trusts God and asks point-blank. "Maddie, please don't wait to tell me if you're trying to tell me your son is mine."

Natalie lets out a tear-filled sigh, thinking she'd finally won him. But even she hears the response through the phone.

"No!" Maddie stresses. "Absolutely not! My goodness, I am sucking at this phone conversation thing."

Nate, always needing to find the lowest place for relief, probably stemming from God's plea for him to bow in worship, lays flat on his back with the sigh. "Maddie, you scared the crap out of me! My wife is standing here crying."

"Oh no! Tell her I'm sorry, please. Now you see why I'd rather talk in person. Kevin's dirtbag father was originally from India. You wouldn't have even asked if you met him." She chuckles.

"I see. I'll have to ask, but Thursday is chess night over here at Seth's place. As long as you don't mind my sister's eighty million kids and my old housemates running around, you're welcome to come."

Seth has arrived in time to nod with a smile at the invitation.

"Yes. Seth says it's fine. I serve the first course at six-thirty."

"Sounds great! The more, the merrier. You'll see why. I hope, at least."

Madison Walker's recessive traits did not quite make it into her son's genetic lottery. He looks like he's walked straight from New Delhi into the foyer of Seth's house. Madison is also not what I expected to see. She is dressed in a knee-length skirt and a top that leaves far more to the imagination than what I'd last seen her in. She looks a bit heavier, but only what would make her look healthier as well. Her hair is much shorter, worn in a ponytail. She looks like a mom—like it's all she's ever been.

Nate introduces his wife lovingly. When Maddie sees her, she sees what Natalie herself rarely does. That her beauty is unsurpassable, even in the once wandering eyes of Nate. Madison, never one for verbal filters, speaks.

"You are *gorgeous*, Natalie!" Then she gasps when she catches sight of Naya in her arms. "My goodness. Look at those eyes of hers. Good job, Nate."

He laughs. "This is Naya." Then he goes around the room. "You remember Seth and my little sister, Laura. This is her husband Christian and their kids Maria, Opus, and Tempo. Two more little ones on the way. This is Vargas. And Zeke. You might remember them a little. Oh! And Willow. She's still around, too."

As Madison has been following the gesture around the room, trying to catch every name, Zeke nearly startles at his own. He's been slightly intrigued by Madison Walker's lovely gray eyes. He'd never noticed them before when she was storming out of the house in her undergarments. She speaks again.

"It's nice to meet you all. This is the love of my life Kevin. He's a little shy." Maddie rolls her eyes in sarcasm as Kevin begins giggling and scratching my belly.

"I'm not shy, Mommy. I like the doggy. The doggy is pretty. I'm hungry, Mommy. Can I have some crackers?" Kevin rambles.

Everyone falls in love.

"Crackers?" Nate crouches at the boy's side. "You kidding? I made turducken. That's way better than crackers."

"What's turducken?"

"It's turkey, duck, and chicken all cooked together. I think it was actually God's original intention for roasted bird." Nate shares with the enthralled child.

"Says the chef. I say it's an abomination. The gaminess of the duck is—" Natalie begins. Nate looks at her. "But anything you make is phenomenal, baby. You know that."

Madison giggles. "Wait, don't tell me you're *the* Natalie Holm? The food critic? Natalie, I read your reviews before I come into town. I love how you now include the family friendliness of places. I always thought the last name was a coincidence, but apparently, the world is just that small. Nate married a food critic. Seems like that would be a breeding ground for—"

"Amazing food. A cute kid. Sometimes disaster. But usually just the food." Nate shares as he seats Madison.

Nate serves all four courses, and then Seth begins board setup. The children are entering and exiting the room at will, as is becoming commonplace. Zeke finally engages Madison in conversation, though Vargas had been quietly urging him to the entire meal.

"So, where you from originally, Madison?"

"Here. I went to an all-girls Catholic school near Seth and Nate's all-boys prep school. Which kept us all perfectly out of trouble." The three high school friends snicker at the memories far enough in the past to be amusing. "I went to cosmetology school after that, which somehow landed me a glamorous job working as a receptionist for a plastic surgeon."

Zeke shows a half smile for Madison's eloquent sarcasm.

"Couldn't be too bad," he encourages.

Madison becomes serious and nods. "The job itself was great. But I was a different person back then—the kind of person who ends up spending years going back and telling other people that they don't have to live that way to be happy. I thought I was free and independent, you know? In control. Really, I was in prison. But in Christ—"

"The chains are broken," Nate boldly interjects.

Madison's face alights as her eyes meet Nate's. Tears fill her eyes. She sniffles, then giggles as Nate smiles.

"You gave your life to Christ. Nathan Holm, who knew? I saved you for last, thinking I'd get thrown out. I guess that wouldn't happen here at Seth's. Did God allow saintly Seth to finally convince you?" Madison had always been fond of him, I remember. But never of the saint part of things until today.

Nate laughs, teasing his friend. "Actually, I found out some things about Seth recently that sort of demoted him from saint status. He did a lot of reasoning with me over the years, along with everyone else in this room. Me and Natalie—things haven't always been great. This woman really took the 'better or worse' vow seriously. Wives should take lessons from her."

"Oh please, Nate. We've been together years and you didn't listen. Two minutes with *her* was what it took." Natalie takes the flattery and redirects it.

"Naya. It was your daughter, wasn't it? I can certainly relate." Madison smiles, knowing exactly who 'her' is. "God seems to use babies that way quite a bit. Like I said, I was a different person before I found Christ. The last time I left here, I was freaking out because Willow ate one of the shoes my boyfriend gave me. I was too self-absorbed to realize how spooked you were, Nate."

Nate guffaws. "I might not have been so spooked if you'd still been *wearing* the shoes when you told me you were your boss's mistress, Maddie."

"Ooo. Scandalous." Laura's eyes light up. Christian squints eyebrows at the wife who always surprises him. Natalie is shaking her head, trying to pretend she's not a little hurt.

"Lovebug." Nate takes a break from Maddie's story and charms his wife, taking her hand and kissing it. "All before you. All before Jesus."

"And for real, Natalie, Nate liked to pretend he was some kind of swinger. But even the *thought* of infidelity really bothered him. He only spent time with girls that didn't want to commit and were all wrong for him so he wouldn't fall in love. He'd go on for hours about how he'd never get married. Not because he was scared of commitment, but because he knew it was too sacred to mess around with. When you told me on the phone you were 'very married,' I knew you'd finally figured yourself out. Or accidentally fallen in love with the right woman." Maddie's insight is known, but somehow new. Natalie giggles at the desperate hand and arm kisses she's receiving before replying.

"So, how'd you go from spooking Nate to finding Christ, Maddie?" Natalie moves her arm away after a much more serious glimpse of a gaze from her doting husband.

"Well, that's why I'm here. I've since found my testimony to glorify God in miraculous ways, especially for the people that helped build it. It seems like I'm preaching to the choir here, but I'd still like to share if I could." Madison hopes visibly. Her mission is clearly of God. The others eagerly await the testimony.

She'd been young. Sinful. Weak. And she was the mistress of her boss, Ajeet Kapur, a Cosmetic Surgeon twice her age at the time. Madison was fooled into believing Dr. Kapur's promises that he'd eventually leave his wife, a wealthy heiress, and their three beautiful children.

Despite the obvious delay, and her own tendency to stray, Madison stayed in the relationship for reasons of neediness, and a soft spot for expensive shoes and other things Ajeet provided. Madison admits that her encounter with Nate got her thinking that maybe she wanted something more. And after seeing the love Ajeet had for his children, Madison got a sinful, devious, twisted, desperate idea.

Natalie sighs, seeing what is coming. Laura gasps quietly as well.

"Oh, Madison. You didn't."

Madison nods. "I did."

Madison reveals in tears that she'd been foolish and lost enough to believe Dr. Ajeet Kapur would leave his doting family for a pregnant mistress. Yet the morning she found out, Dr. Kapur fired her as his receptionist, writing her a check to cover a year's salary and an abortion.

Natalie turns to compassion. "What did you do?"

Madison smiles. "Well, hell hath no fury, right? I tore up the check, then went home and found every six-thousand-dollar suit he left there. Every pair of shoes he'd ever bought me. Even his great-grandfather's cufflinks. And put them in a biohazard container on its way to the incinerator at his office. Then I called his wife for a nice honest conversation. I was quite satisfied with myself that evening."

We are all entertained by the fury of Madison. Her smile turns. "But the next morning, I woke up with some fearsome morning sickness that reminded me I really could have used all that money."

"But you did the right thing. Kevin's a great kid." Zeke says it, and we all agree.

"Twelve minutes. God saved him with twelve minutes," She begins, engulfed in the memory.

Madison describes how she'd arrived at an abortion clinic at 8:48 a.m. only to learn that it didn't open until 9:00 a.m. She'd seen a billboard for a Christian Crisis pregnancy center and gone there in desperation. An ultrasound had turned her from a terrified ex-mistress into a mother-to-be in pursuit of God's purpose. They'd told her about grace, forgiveness, and about a Man who not only kept His promises but died to give her abundant life. They'd empowered her to raise her son for Christ, even though she still feels guilt over robbing him of a father figure. It all seemed impossible, she said, which is the very thing that made her understand it. She reveals that God has been faithful and the pregnancy center a lifesaver, so that she now seeks out people from her past and sometimes large groups, telling others her testimony on behalf of the Center.

"I'm far from being fixed, but I know it's okay," Madison says, sniffling. "God isn't done with me yet."

Laura's pregnancy hormones start the well from her eyes. Christian laughs at her. The rest of us are in just as much awe.

Zeke laughs. "Whatever this pregnancy center is just earned a million dollars."

Madison giggles. "I *wish.* Do you know what we could do with a million dollars? The ultrasound techs save the babies, so last year we had to choose between one of those and a full-time Pastor who helps save the women. Maybe we could even hire a decent finance guy."

As she's speaking, everyone else but her understands that Zeke *does* have a million dollars to throw around here and there. It would not be out of character for him in recent years to give to a charity that wins his heart. However, no one thinks Maddie is a charity case. He hasn't taken his eyes off her all evening.

Zeke chuckles, waving off the others with a hand out of Maddie's sight. "Where is it? I'd like to maybe take a look at how things operate. I'm Seth's 'finance guy.'"

Madison snorts, thinking the distance great. "I live in LA"

Zeke coughs a little. "California?"

"That's usually where Los Angeles is this time of year." Maddie flirts.

"And a far better climate for the kind of plant we need to make the tethers," Seth says randomly and out of turn to his CFO. "The Schipper Group lost another steel worker on a high rise this morning. Asked for the plans to make one of the safety tethers my dad invented since we've never lost a guy. I told him he could buy it from Gowan-Young Industries once we make the change. Zeke, I'll need you to relocate."

Everyone sees that there is some type of connection here, but assumes that clarity is lost because of the business relationship, not because Zeke is sitting next to a gray-eyed woman he'll marry—in California—soon. Zeke tests the waters, knowing that knowing is just half the battle.

"Why don't I fly out and check out Gowan-Young's preferred charity in a couple weeks. Your pregnancy center? I wasn't kidding about the million." Zeke really wasn't. "I might even throw in a few pairs of shoes to replace the ones you incinerated. I see why you did it, but man, those poor shoes."

Madison lights up. "You're the only person I've spoken with who actually saw that as a loss in this situation. And maybe it's shallow, but I mourned those things later on."

Zeke laughs. "These guys like to make fun, but as long you're right with God there's nothin' wrong with looking sharp."

"I agree." Madison coos. "But I'm redeemed, you know. I hardly even care that my last penny goes to daycare instead of a weekly mani-pedi. Kevin's teacher even told me to start *saving* my pennies because he might make it into this 'Great Young Minds' program. I'm glad his father passed down something to him. Seeing him succeed would certainly stop me cringing at my cuticles."

Zeke clears his throat, and the whole room sees it coming. He smiles sensually. "A man who appreciated you as a woman *and* a mother would make sure it *all* happened, girl. You wouldn't be underappreciated at no receptionist job, either. I know you'd rather be volunteering at that center."

Madison cackles, obviously having seen all angles of pursuit. "I'm not for sale, Zeke. Not anymore."

Nate winces at tactics he's never quite developed in Zeke.

"Naw. Couldn't put a price on you." Zeke soothes. Laura and Natalie connect eyes. Enthralled at the birth of the love story.

"Girls fall for that?" She flirts, looking around the room a little.

"Just you, so far." Zeke moves a hair from Maddie's face, and she closes her eyes.

"Is Zeke short for Ezekiel?" She asks when her eyes reopen.

"Vargas asked me the same thing a few years ago while he was off fighting a battle that isn't his. Something a guy like me didn't understand back then. I told him yeah, Ezekiel. He asked me if I'd ever read the book of Ezekiel. I laughed at him." Zeke shifts his legs and opens up with something he's never told his dearest friends, let alone a perfect stranger.

"I'm from Detroit. My mother has no clue who my father is, so it was a joke to me that she thought she could raise me to know Jesus, especially in a place where even the churches are giving up. I figured out young that hard work was the only hope for freedom and happiness. So I worked hard and became a millionaire by age twenty-four. When Vargas asked me about my name and the Bible, I was a hardened, self-serving workaholic with no values at all. That night, I called and asked my mother why she named me Ezekiel. She said she read Ezekiel when she was seventeen and scared because she knew she'd be a single mother soon and needed God's strength."

"Your Mom sounds like a good lady." Madison smiles. "What did God show her in Ezekiel?"

"I think she'd like you. She said: 'I will give you a new heart and put a new spirit within you; I will take the heart of stone out of your flesh and give you a heart of flesh. I will put My Spirit within you and cause you to walk in my statutes, and you will keep My judgments and do them.' That was Ezekiel 36:26 and 27. It's like my mother knew exactly what I'd need to hear to give my life to Christ almost three decades before I did. I had a heart of stone. But now, my heart is flesh." Apparently, that's the greatest pickup line ever. Madison wakes up somewhere inside her just before she falls. Hook, line, sinker.

"I don't leave town until Sunday. Why don't you take Kevin and me out to dinner tomorrow, and we'll talk about your travel plans to visit the center." She is straightforward. Clever. Beautiful. High Maintenance. A woman of God. Exactly what Zeke's been holding out for.

"I know a good French place downtown that my buddy owns," Zeke says, and Nate laughs a little.

Maddie smiles. "*Le Cloture*? I ate at a table for two once in their kitchen for a date. It was kinda neat seeing behind the scenes."

"What?!" Natalie accuses Nate. "You never did that for me!"

Maddie winces. Nate laughs. "Lovebug, your name is on a *deed* for two. You literally own the place. Therein lies the difference between casual dating and marriage."

"Exactly. I'm at a point in my life where I want my name on the deed. That table for two ploy is for children." Maddie laughs, then winces at Zeke. "Hope that doesn't up the ante too much for tomorrow evening."

Zeke shrugs. "Naw, tomorrow is a business meeting—for three. But I'll buy a ticket for your flight to LA on Sunday, and we'll see where things go from there. Alright with you, Boss? Can I take a few days?" Zeke's eyes are stayed on Maddie's gray ones.

"Take a month. Look at the center's finances and use a business account for the donation. Find us a site for a plant, and I'll talk to the board. We'll start the conversion process when you get back." The CEO directs.

"Yes, sir," Zeke says enthusiastically to Maddie's bitten lip of a smile.

"Okay, whoa!" Nate stands. "This is not happening."

"You met her two hours ago." Christian whines, mocking Zeke's own words from the night he met Laura.

But the night does not conclude until the sun sets, everyone heads home, and the only voices awake are Zeke's with Maddie, Kevin asleep across her lap between them until the birds start their singing at dawn. Seth is relieved to change knowing into being.

Chapter Thirty-Three

MANIPULATION

"I have Maddie in contact with a realtor. The lease on her dive is up in a month, so I'm hoping to do a cash deal on a house by then. She's hoping for oceanfront, so I guess I'm going California all the way, which I'd never have seen coming if you hadn't told me. Either way, it'll be nice to not spend every other Friday in planes." Zeke rubs at his careless brown biceps using a left hand with a gold band.

Seth builds a fence.

"And to have you in the new office permanently. The California team is a little weak when you're not there. They call me all the time."

"Most people can't just call their CEO. There's a reason your company is so successful. You run it like Jesus would, Man," Zeke compliments.

"*Our* company," Seth corrects for the recent change.

"Cold out here," Zeke says with a shiver after the flattery.

"It's January in Colorado. Should have thought to bring a coat." Seth comments on the absent-mindedness. Zeke laughs.

"I just miss me some Maddie is all. I can't even fathom the thought of her having been alone with Kev in that city for so long." Zeke is now thinking of Kevin, the still adjusting stepson.

"I can't fathom that you married her after knowing her for a month. I sent you on a business trip. You came back married." Seth reminds him.

"I'm a good multi-tasker." Zeke smiles. "We knew within hours, Man. All my work finally meant something the night I met her. The month was to get Kevin used to the idea. But technically we were married within three weeks, because I was sick of driving back to that hotel every night. And I wanted to, you know, get her name on the deed before I left, and we made the transition with the company. 'Already is,' right? Why wait?" Zeke firms his logic with a sigh and a tuck of his hands in his pockets.

"Sometimes you have to," Seth says to himself with a sigh.

"I suppose." Zeke misses the depth of Seth's tone. "I'm really gonna miss chess nights."

"You can always teach Kevin to play chess. He's really smart, and you're really good." Seth says, stashing his tools and materials in his bin. Walking toward the house.

"Not as good as you." Zeke chuckles.

"I suppose not," Seth says in truth.

Zeke laughs fully. "That's why I like you, Seth. You're honest. You never manipulate people or use them against themselves. You know? You're the best kind of friend. Trustworthy."

"I manipulate you guys all the time. All of you." More honesty.

"Manipulate? You? Nice try."

"I'll show you at Nate's."

We have reached the back door this Thursday night. Seth packs up his chess set, and the three of us pile into Seth's truck. Nate had wanted to host the dinner and chess night at his own home for once. However, when we arrive, not knocking at such a close friend's house, Nate is cursing at his stove.

"This thing is evil. It doesn't cook anything evenly. It's a wonder I did all that cooking as a teen on it."

"We could replace it, you know. I still have trouble getting it to light, and I learned to cook on it, too. I guess it's my punishment for attempting to cook when my husband is a chef." Natalie giggles.

"Exactly. *My* job. You just sit back, relax, sass me and look good doing it." We reach the kitchen just in time to catch the caress of a waist and loving little kiss. No one minds or teases or stops them when this occurs. There had been a time, not too long ago, when there had been no such tenderness. When the two had secretly thought of separating. To an outsider, Naya had been the glue at her birth. But we all know different.

"*Aishiteru.*" Natalie declares her love in Japanese, receiving another kiss from the chef.

"*J'taime.*" Nate's eyelids are heavy with enchantment. His lips with a French accent. "Sorry the soufflé was ruined by the oven."

"I'll be more lenient on the critique." Natalie bites her lip.

"I don't deserve you," he murmurs. Common now, with his recently convicted heart.

She shushes him, then turns to see us. "Hey guys!"

"Stove acting up again, Nate? You should let me buy you a new one. A chef should have the best." Seth seems adamant. Desperate even. An odd greeting.

"That's what I keep saying," Natalie says quietly to Seth. "He won't admit that he's sentimental about this old thing."

"Not sentimental. Just used to it." Nate defends.

Natalie rolls her eyes, then moves on. "Chris and Laura are running late, as usual. Something about getting five kids to cooperate long enough to get them in the van… And dinner might be a while. So just hang out for a minute, if that's okay."

That's okay, she already sees with a smile. Seth had gathered up the child that had been sitting on the blanket in the dining room. Naya smiles at him, drooling a little as she tells him some sweet nothing of a gurgle, enchanting him with her big blue eyes. Full-on flirtation at six months old. Nate approaches them.

"Naya, Baby? Seth is exactly the kind of guy you should marry, but he's a little old for you. Try again with someone your age in about forty years," Nate instructs his still cooing daughter.

"Forty might be excessive, don't you think?" Zeke laughs.

"Yeah. Thirty-five. If you can find someone good enough for your dad to not kill upon meeting. I don't think you will, Baby Girl. It's better you just stick around here and don't go outside since you're the most beautiful girl in the universe. The world doesn't deserve you." Nate talks to Naya like he's savoring a conversation with royalty.

Seth whispers to Nate their common ground. "You sound like Ken." Then winces with humor.

"I think I finally *get* Ken." Nate laughs and addresses Naya again, who grabs his nose as he speaks. "Because Naya, if you marry some deadbeat that doesn't ask me first or call me after, I will drive across the country on Valentine's Day and do everything I can to make him hate you. And there are no words for how mad I'd be if someone knocked you up at sixteen. Because you're way too perfect to be at fault in any way."

"And you were worried about becoming *your* dad?" Natalie snickers as she approaches.

"No. The problem now is that I want Naya to be just like you—which will make her an amazing woman—and cause us a lot of heartache." Nate kisses his wife's cheek as Seth chuckles the agreement.

"Don't even start. Because if we ever have a little boy and he's anything like his dad…" Natalie smiles the implication and the others snicker at the memories.

"Touché." Nate laughs.

Natalie looks to Zeke. "You and Maddie planning to have more kids?"

"We think so. Just trying to get settled a little. Get into a house. Become more of a team with Kevin and all before we bring more humans into the mix. But we're open to whatever God has in store," Zeke explains.

"You guys are so cute. I think Nate's still in shock over all of it." Natalie says.

"Who isn't?" Nate laughs jovially.

I begin my usual ritual of trying to understand how new and perfect Naya smells. Seth always makes me stop, but I enjoy this one more than all the Kessler children. Not for temperament or even her beauty. Maybe I just like her because she's a part of Natalie. And I still prefer Natalie above most.

A bound of the oldest little Kessler comes through the front door to greet me. Okay, so I like them all. Kelli and Shelley might be too old to cherish me even if they were still around to do it. All the others often pile on me, even if they've yet to crawl or walk. Even if they take two hands and pull on my fur with all their might. I don't mind the bombardment. They say I'm "mellow." Mellow enough for Christian and Laura to set near me even the children that must still remain on their backs for their age. The new boy baby has some tube that is taped to his cheek beneath his nose like Tempo had—something about his just being little. But the tube does not distract me from loving him.

"Take care of 'em, Willow." Christian commands. Tired but cheerful, as he's always been. Seth reiterates this with his eyes when he sets the excited, squealing Naya atop my side.

"What about you? Is five the magic number?" Natalie graciously brings Laura into the conversation.

"You speak as if we are in any way in control of that." Christian cackles.

"You two know how this happens, right?" Nate teases. Halfway. Part of him thinks them naïve still.

"Happened." Laura enunciates the end of the word. "The goal is to stop, and we're pretty sure tied tubes will do it this time. The last delivery was rough. I'd probably have to have a C-section if we had a third set of twins." Laura says cheerily, looking at Christian to confirms. He smiles.

"I'd probably have to have a *stroke* if we had a third set of twins." He jokes. "Five is a good number."

"What's the verdict, Nate? You want more kids?" Zeke asks of Nate. Natalie smiles and shakes her head when Nate looks at her.

"You're asking the wrong person. I'm trying to get her to have another one *now*." The stark change in Nate is still something worthy of awe.

"Naya is six months old." Natalie reasons. "All I want is a year to recover. If it happens before then, I won't complain. But ideally, I want her to be walking confidently before I do another pregnancy."

"Smart plan. I might have done the same thing if God allowed us to plan any pregnancy ever." Laura concurs, certainly knowing the other route.

"You're killin' me! I want a *son*. Even if he *is* like me. I already have a name picked out." Nate chuckles teasingly, returning to the unruly oven with a smile. Natalie, I see, loves him every moment.

"So." Zeke changes the subject. Looks to Seth to include him in the conversation he can't readily join. "Seth tells me that he regularly manipulates all of his friends. You said you'd show me? I'm curious."

"After dinner." He smiles.

Before dinner, Natalie nearly weeps when Nate leads the makeshift family in prayer. Then during dinner, all the people tease Seth about his great manipulations. How does one manipulate when he hardly ever talks and never requires anything of anyone? So it is for his character that they tease.

Then when the table and children are cleared, Seth takes out his chess set, carefully unfolds it, and sets the pieces.

"I'm going to tell you my secret." He looks up to see who will be the first to oppose him. They all listen, knowing he is about to explain.

Christian rubs his hands and takes a seat at the table across from Seth. Seth speaks as he plays.

"When I was eight, we played chess at school, and I begged my dad to get me a chess set. He got me a picture and told me to make one. Check. It took me a year to get the pieces all right. I've made dozens of sets since then, but this one is the only perfect one."

"I remember that year," Natalie recalls, rolling her eyes. "I spent most of it sitting there, watching you make this. But this is the one with the queen with the holes. Willow chewed on it the day you got her. So, it isn't technically perfect."

"It's perfect." Seth smiles. "Check. My condition doesn't allow me to understand people most of the time. Things that are natural for the rest of you like sarcasm and rhetorical questions, and social cues. I had to learn those. It was really hard. The year I finished the chess set, Natalie would play with me every day. My parents too. That's when I started to understand people. I found it easier to understand one person completely than to—check—understand general social interactions. If I learn a person by the way they play chess, it only takes me a few minutes. It takes me years otherwise. But what I learn about one person can be transferred to other people….Check. Check." A laugh. "Checkmate."

"Okay, not fair! You didn't even get to the secret before my turn. How was I supposed to beat you?" Christian's excuse.

"I did. That's the secret. Chess helps me understand a person better than they understand themselves. And that, in turn, helps me understand how they will play chess. I learn you through chess. That's why I required it from my tenants. But then I use it against you, the fact that I know you. To beat you at chess every time. That's how I manipulate you."

"That almost makes sense, Man." Zeke sits as Seth resets the pieces.

"Vargas was easy to beat, even though he was a warrior. He loves his bishops. It was so obvious with him. Once I learned that, I learned everything else about him and the way he plays chess. But the first thing I did with him was kill his bishops. He was crippled after that." Seth reveals, then smiles up at Zeke to take his first move.

"Zeke is a master strategist. He's very, very good at chess. The math of it. He likes power. Check. He uses all the power he can all at once. But he does it smart. Zeke, you are sometimes a challenge to beat at chess, so

I don't play chess with you. Check. I play *you*. Check. It was no question to me whether I would share my company with you. You're powerful and honorable. Check. Your only real flaw was your pride, but I see Maddie is softening you. Good for the company. Not so good for your chess playing." Seth falls silent for two minutes while he plays Zeke. His silence is always respected as a necessity. Then, when the battle is in his grasp, he speaks again.

"I hired Bill when I was sixteen but hadn't played chess with him until last year on New Year's—the day we found out Naya was coming. To cheat at chess, one must first believe their opponent is unintelligent and naïve. Zeke, your king. You see that, right? Check. Nate, Laura, your dad cheated. I hadn't looked into his accounts in years. Then Zeke helped me discover what he'd done. Chess is important. Now every job applicant plays chess at their interview, and I review the video before hiring them. I played all my board members personally and fired two afterward. Checkmate, Zeke." Zeke grunts in frustration and Seth resets the pieces again.

Christian squints his eyes. "You let me sign a lease before we ever played chess."

"God speaks to me too. I knew you before chess." Seth reveals. "But from chess, I learned how much I like you. How resilient you are. I like to play with you. You try to trick me, but by using the rules. But since I know you, you likely never will."

"Someday! You will see. I'm still young and spry. It will happen." Christian jokes. Laura sits down for chess, sulking.

"Laura, sometimes I worry if you'll beat me," Seth says to the shock of all.

"I'm terrible at chess." She giggles.

"Yes," Seth admits. "Which is why I beat you by playing chess. I find that when I play a good woman at chess, I'm playing a different person each time. Laura, you are a prime example of the complexity of a woman's heart. I've always known you'd be a wonderful mother. But we met when you were eleven, and I'm still getting to know you. I played chess with my mom for years and still feel like there's so much I never learned. I very much appreciate the mystery of women."

"Dude, that's my wife!" Christian jokes, accepting Seth's confession but loving how much more deeply he sees the world. The other men laugh at the remark.

This match only lasts a few minutes. Laura, terrible at chess and driven by heart, can't even concentrate when she's been read so accurately by someone who supposedly doesn't understand people.

"Checkmate." Seth smiles. Laura smiles, then rises and embraces Christian.

"I'm not playing you tonight. You're gonna get me in trouble somehow." Nate, the next opponent, jokes with Seth.

"It won't get you in trouble, I promise." Seth urges, and Nate sits down reluctantly. Seth resets the pieces.

"Nate was my best friend. It took years, but I got to know him before we ever played. I went with what I knew and beat him immediately. I've gotten to know you the most through chess, Nate. It's the evolution I like best."

"So, what's my vice? The thing you can manipulate me with?" Nate wonders as he takes a move.

"Women." Seth elicits chuckles from all around.

"Okay, you were supposed to not get me in trouble." Nate shakes his head.

"Well, I guess that's not entirely accurate. Because there's only one woman on the board. When you moved into my house, and we started playing, you hardly touched your queen." Seth pauses and smiles. "You certainly enjoyed their company, but back then, you didn't see the *value* of women like I did."

The whole room laughs. "Seth, seriously." Nate chuckles.

"I'm serious. Check. Then you met Natalie. You didn't get along with her, but in chess, you started to see the value of your queen. I knew you loved her before *you* did." Seth smiles. Natalie takes a few steps forward. Seth continues.

"Check. I knew you were planning to marry her when your queen became the center of your strategy. And the minute I took her, your whole plan would crumble. You needed her. Check. Then when you first got married, it was like playing with a five-year-old for a couple months. You men are actually all like that when you first get married. I've never beaten

Zeke as easily as I just did a few minutes ago." The room erupts in laughter. Seth smiles. "You are all good husbands. But that doesn't take the chess to see."

"Well, I wasn't always." Nate winces.

"Yes, you were. For a while, you were very bad at showing Natalie. You did something in chess that surprised me as soon as you got settled with her. You changed your strategy and started protecting your queen. Even when you two would fight and hurt each other all the time, I knew you were doing everything to hold on to her. Natalie once told me that she wishes more people saw your heart. I did. I always did. Especially since Naya has been here, you protect your queen at all costs. Check. Unfortunately, you don't protect your king. Checkmate." Nate, for a rare moment, catches Seth's eyes and sees something frightening in them when everyone else is laughing. Then Nate stands, pretending he's checking on the children. Natalie takes a seat, and the pieces are reset.

"Do we really need to do this?" Seth gives a fake smile to the extremely nervous Natalie.

"No. But you got Nate some brownie points, so I figure this can't hurt me." Natalie smiles.

"Natalie, I really don't feel comfortable with—" Seth avoids her eyes.

"Why not? You did it for the rest of us. We want to know the secret with her." Laura urges him.

"Women are complicated, remember? Really complicated," he mumbles. Nate has reentered the room.

"Seth, has she ever beaten you at chess?" Nate asks.

"No." Seth provides with a sigh.

"So, then you know how to beat her. Tell us." Nate bullies a bit.

"We don't have to if you're uncomfortable with it," Natalie says gently to her lifelong friend.

Seth sighs. "No. We can play. You have to promise not to get mad with what I say."

"Promise."

Seth makes the first move.

"I used to tell you you were smarter than me. And you'd say I was smarter. I'd say—"

"'My IQ is higher. But you're smarter, Natalie.'" Natalie recalls verbatim, distorting her voice to a man's. "I remember."

"You've played chess as long as me, with the same set. And you've never beaten me. No one has. Because I know them better than *they* know them."

"Yeah, we've been over this." Natalie chuckles, making another move. "It's remarkable."

"The problem is, Natalie, you and my parents, that's the only time I've been understood. Since they're gone, you're the only person alive that knows me. Which on its own, without understanding that's how to play chess, wouldn't help you beat me. Check."

"Right. So, you beat me at chess itself?" Natalie asks.

"No. You're too smart for that. You knew how to handle my fits better than my own mother as a kid. Because you learn behavior. Catch on easy. Check. You adapt. Find ways when you're told you can't. You're competitive and strong-willed. You're brilliant, Natalie. You also see people's hearts like I do with chess, only you don't need chess. That's why you married Nate. Your instincts are flawless. That makes you an excellent chess player. You have strategy and you see someone else's. I bet you could even beat Zeke. I can't beat you at chess. And you have me completely figured out. And you're complex like any good woman. You could certainly use what Mom called 'fickle' against me. Trick me. Seduce me, even. *Subete*, Natalie." Seth breathes. Natalie has just been reprimanded in the gentle tone of Seth. But that isn't what Nate heard.

"Okay, I'm freaked out right now. What the heck does '*subete*' mean? I trust you, Seth. I respect you. You know that. But you can't just sit here and talk about my wife seducing you."

"Um…" Natalie is torn between keeping old secrets with Seth and being transparent with her husband. Only a moment before realizing the proper choice. "*Subete* means 'all.' It's how he used to tell me how he felt about me when we were kids."

The room gets tense. But before Nate can react, Seth explains. "But Nate, all it means in this context is that there are a hundred ways that Natalie could beat me at chess." Seth sighs. Hoping to conclude and end the tension.

Natalie fights back. "That's sort of irrelevant, Seth. I've never come close to beating you at chess."

Seth stops a moment. Makes a move. Calms himself. "Which is impossible. *Impossible*, Natalie."

"Nothing is impossible, remember? Obviously. You always win." Natalie reasons, somewhat offended.

"Only because you don't want to. You lose on *purpose* every time." Seth concludes. "Checkmate."

"Seth, how dare you?" Natalie accuses. "Are you saying I'm a liar?"

"Yes. But since I know, you're really only fooling yourself."

"About what, exactly, Seth? I'm lying because I lose? That makes no sense." She attacks as Seth stands and gathers his chess set. The others are stunned by the awkwardness. Seth and Natalie rarely brawl like this.

"I've never cared about winning or losing with you, Natalie. I just wish you'd play." He defends.

"I play. Just like everybody else. And I lose like everybody else." Natalie is highly agitated. Now standing too.

"But you're *not* everybody else." Seth takes the moment she tries to come up with a rebuttal to make his exit. "Thanks for dinner, Nate. S'go, Willow."

I follow Seth out into the dark. Zeke runs after to catch his ride. He knows better than to interrogate Seth. Natalie, being a woman, does not. But her phone calls go unanswered all night long.

Chapter Thirty-Four

All Costs

It is an unspoken understanding that Seth and Natalie do not engage in chess matches. Zeke is gone to California. The other three find it amusing that even though they know his "strategy," Seth still wins every time. But mostly, the girls talk about babies. The men talk about babies. And Seth sits and admires them, watching them grow in stature and in spirit.

Naya is devious, sassy, and charming—even at just over a year old. Seth adores her. But to Nate, Naya is the greatest feat in God's creation. His heart is hers completely. He begins to let her "help" in the kitchen the moment she can stand. They steal endless kisses and cuddles from each other. Naya calls Nate "Dadda." Nate, never wanting to be a father at all, now lives only as his snug and joyful wrap around Naya's finger allows. Singing to her. Teaching her to pray and trust in God. Knowing it is never too early.

Nate distances himself from who he was more every day. He's still Nate, wild and passionate, but with eyes that see the meaning in it. One chess night, he wanders around our house as if it is an art gallery. He looks at paintings of Stacy Gowan's he has seen thousands of times like they are new, smiling at the way the house is depicted through her eyes. Squinting when he looks at a painting in darker hues. A view of the night over a city that he'd always enjoyed from the rooftop as a teenager.

"She was good," Natalie says, wrapping arms around his back and waist as he's mentally placing the painted rose bushes at the guest house where they still thrive today.

"Yeah," Nate agrees in his new calm sort of wild. "There's just something about these paintings. I can't put my finger on it."

"I always felt the same way about them." Natalie coos, kissing the back of his shoulder.

"There's so many. I bet it makes Seth feel like his parents are still sort of here. If you look at them just right, they almost seem…. I'm not sure." He sighs. "I thought of going in her art studio to see if there were any more. But I don't even think Seth's been in there. Some things are just sacred, I guess."

"So, now you're an art lover?" Natalie discovers.

"Definite possibility." From the unchanged but transformed voice of Nate.

They all depart for church on Sundays and even sit around and talk about Jesus for hours afterward. The friends have dwindled some. Seth only sees Zeke on weekly video calls for work. Derek Vargas has left the Army and teaches people about Jesus in a country that he can't

identify to us for safety's sake. His letters come through many hands and weeks before we see them. Dwindled indeed. But counting the five Kessler children and one little Holm, I'd say we've increased in number. But that's only math, I suppose. And when everyone is at their own home, there are only two of us at this one.

So, it's odd today that Nathan and Naya are entering the backyard while Seth works on his fence in late October. When he carries her before putting her down, she seems so tiny in his powerful arms.

"Hey, Nate. You off today?" Seth inquires of the oddity but seems to have expected Nate's intrusion.

"Yeah, Nat's working on a review, so we decided to take a walk. It's still insane that my little princess is walking now. I'm pretty sure there's nothing cuter than her little penguin walk, though, so we decided to come up here to show you." Nate chuckles. He's nervous for some reason.

"She's getting big fast." Seth continues the conversation. He's waiting for something.

Nate clears his throat. "Nat tells me twelve years. That's how long this will take in total. Where are you now?"

"Ten years, four months." Seth doesn't need to dig for this knowledge.

Nate instinctively keeps an eye on Naya, who is sitting in the grass examining a fallen leaf. "The fence. I get it. Nat's told me about how you know things you shouldn't know. How you knew what Naya would look like and even her name. Specific things. Ever since the last time you played chess with Natalie several months ago, I've been thinking. And I figured it out, Seth. Your fence." This had been what Nate came to talk about. I know from his confident tone.

"Oh?" Seth is curious.

"Yeah," Nate says with surety. Pointing as he speaks. "You started back there. Near the shed, that makes sense. Started out shaky, trying to figure things out. Then you got a system. I remember you talking about needing to build a big cart for all your supplies. For convenience, I guess. That was back in high school. Then I remember you going through the woods and chopping trees. That took a lot of work. I remember. Now you're coming back into the open. Back around. Relatively soon now, you'll be done. But if I'd paid more attention—to a lot of things—well, there's a lot more I would have picked up on. You need chess. I know you from this snow fence."

Seth just nods. Smiles a little that he's known.

"You're methodical. I guess you have to be. But you're also *productive*, Seth. You're a multimillionaire because you know how to use your limited time to get things done right."

"Yeah?" Seth turns and scrunches his eyebrows.

"Which means you're not building a fence that will take twelve years. You're taking twelve years to build this fence. On purpose." Nate concludes.

Seth frets a little. Only a little. "Yeah."

"Which makes me wonder: Why twelve years? What happens after twelve years? Has to be something bigger than the fence, right? But with how much time you're taking with this, that thing would have to be *way* bigger." Nate asks what has never been asked of Seth.

Seth nearly falters. "If you didn't know what it was, you wouldn't have asked." Odd words. But words Nate seems to understand. Fear washes through and over him and then dissipates, replaced by peace.

"I finally convinced Nat to try for another baby. I wasn't supposed to tell anyone just so that there wasn't any pressure. Still, I think under the circumstances—" Nate sighs to shift his reasoning. "Anyway, I wanted a second chance to be a good dad from the beginning."

"You've always been a good dad, Nate," Seth encourages.

"You should know that if I ever had a son, I'd name him Seth." Nate nods, almost in tears.

"Don't do that." Seth teases, honored at the gesture. "None of the kids can say my name right."

Nate chuckles. "Yeah, I heard Opus calling you 'Def' the other day. One syllable, you think it'd be easy." Then Nate sighs heavily. "But they'll learn. I wouldn't worry."

The fits start sometime around Thanksgiving. But it is only I that see them at first. In his woodshop, Seth is no longer satisfied with the first—or fifth—of the fence posts he makes for the week. The ones that do not please him are pitched in anger across the shop. It'd be a waste, if not for the abundance of wood in the shop. I'd also be scared, if not for staying close to his feet.

And then chess suffers. He begins yelling at Nate for not protecting his king. Nate stops playing after a while—unable to win, but unwilling to lose again. Then Seth first starts wincing when Natalie and Nate show their affection for one another. Or when Nate tosses Naya into the air. Or when Nate does anything at all, really. Wincing first and then leaving the room. I begin to wonder how Seth came to hate his best friend so.

Hate wrapped in love and love in hate. Otherwise, it isn't honest. That's what Nate always says. That's not how their God teaches it, many might say. Love is love, right? So many miss so much when they see God's love that way. Love is Naya's smile. Then it is easy. No one misses it then.

But it is still love when she cries, and it isn't so easy, but they still calm her in love. Love when someone is unlovable? That's Jesus. But then there are the times when love is too big for just love. When Naya reaches up to touch a propane flame at the Holm house's unruly stove, Nate looks at her in anger and raises his voice to scold her—enough anger to scare her into crying.

But Nate loves Naya more than that flame or any cuisine that has ever touched it. That's how I know Nate is right, and God is often misunderstood. Nate would not be angry over Naya's near hurt if he didn't love her. So, it brings me to pain when Seth is so hateful to his friend. Because I can see now that it isn't hate at all.

The biggest of the fits comes on Christmas Day at the Holm house over turducken with Natalie's family. Natalie does not like turducken, and I often reap the benefits of this. Today, Nate catches her in the act.

"So you're comparing my cooking to *dog* food?" Nate teases.

"No, it's just Christmas. Willow should get some too." Natalie winks.

"Nat, you are so picky sometimes. It is almost impossible to please you!"

"*Me*? How about the time—" Natalie says with a smile. They have a past now, with nasty fights and fears, near misses, and bullseyes.

But this time when she tries to bring up some innocence of the past at the dinner table on Christmas, Seth breaks the rules. Not just of a couple fighting. But of him and who he is. Every rule.

"JUST. STOP. FIGHTING! It hurts you. Both of you. Don't do it. You just don't know how blessed you are. Don't spend every minute fighting. *Trust* me!" And then Seth departs Christmas dinner.

"Were we fighting?" Natalie whispers to her husband, bewildered at Seth's departure into the other room.

"No, Bug. I was teasing." Nate promises, glancing at the also stunned Neil and Ken.

"Is he okay?" Laura worries, bouncing the ever-bubbly Sonata or "Sonny" on her lap.

"He's been acting a little funny." Christian breaks pieces of bread up for the ever-hungry Rondo. "Ronny," they call him.

"He's handicapped. Aren't these outbursts to be expected?" Ken speculates.

"Ken!" Eden scolds quietly.

"I wish I was 'handicapped' like Seth." Nate chuckles bitterly at his father-in-law and enters the next room to implement whatever he is to Seth that makes a brother seem trifling. I stay under the gentle hands of Maria, wishing I'd followed.

Back home, it is after midnight, so no longer Christmas. Seth doesn't seem to have been asleep. But I am awakened by the smell that catches my nose across distance and through walls.

It's something like the branding of wood, and something else like the cooking of food. Seth sees me searching.

"What is it, Willow? You smell something?"

He releases me from his room while buttoning his second shirt. He looks out windows in every wing on the level when he begins to smell it too. And when he finally sees, I worry. His heart seizes longer than is possible to live. Then, his phone rings and shocks it again.

"This is Seth."

But what comes from the other end is just as startling and not even a bit comprehensible. Seth scurries into the garage. We climb into his truck, and head right to the place most would drive from. The smoke overtakes us when we arrive. And we only find our way when we hear the desperate screams of Natalie. The wind finally shifts to show us that the deafening roar is no animal. But the entire Holm house is engulfed in flames.

Seth grabs Natalie's face to find reason. "Where are Nate and the baby?"

Natalie's coughing and wheezing and sobbing only allow her to point right at the house. Seth looks up in terror, hand over his mouth. He looks, analyzes, and sees no clearing from the fire. Finally, Seth straps a leash on me, which he never does, and looks me in the eyes.

I know what he's saying. I see what he's asking. They always portray the animal as selfless and brave when it runs into a burning building to remove a trapped person. But the last thing I'd ever do is die in a fire for a person when persons are the reason for fire in the first place. But it takes little convincing for Seth to turn all my fear into a fire inside me.

"I need you to find Naya. S'go Willow."

But for Naya Lynn. The renewal and the waterfall. I'd do all the dying available to do. I recall it, but all the smoke makes it hard to even remember her pure, perfect smell. So, I panic. Until I hear *Him.*

"Follow Me, Willow."

It is like a flame, but brighter, and like a Man I've seen. I know the Voice. Except I don't know how. Then I remember as I go after the Flame that it was the Voice that kept me at peace when I was leaving the farm. That told me just how and when and why to take care of Seth when his parents were gone and I was all he had. I trust it, even into the impassable house of fire.

I don't see or smell or comprehend the openings or worry if they are big enough for Seth on the other end of the leash. I only follow the Flame through them. Under them, over them. Until It stops at a doorknob to something I think was a bathroom. Then It disappears. So I scratch at the door, though it singes my paws. Seth removes his outer shirt and uses it to open the door to not burn his hand. Inside, we hear coughing. Nate.

Nate is inside a bathtub holding a soaked blanket filled with something very still. He yells over the roar of the fire.

"Seth! Where is Natalie?"

"She's outside. She's safe." Seth yells.

I don't think I've seen before a more relieved face from a human than I do in Nate now.

"Can you get back out?" A cough. Nate hands Seth the blanket but doesn't rise from the bathtub.

"Willow knows the way! But we have to be quick." Seth takes the blanket over his shoulder. Then the little bunny stuffed animal that contains a piece of Naya's soul.

But then Seth frowns when he realizes the same thing as me. There was no bathtub in this bathroom. I'd seen. This is the bathtub from upstairs. The evidence of the fall is in the tilt of the bathtub. Pieces of floor and ceiling are pinning Nate into the tub at his waist. There is blood at his torso. He's so pale.

"It already is, Seth. Take care of them. Please. Whatever it takes. You have to go. Now!" Nate yells.

At this request, I try to lift the debris off him. I dig at it, whimper, and fight until my will simply changes at the sound of my name.

"Follow Me, Willow."

Seth and Nate are meeting penitent eyes—exchanging something without speaking that all the words they wish they had time to say still could never mention. But I am pulling Seth and the blanket and the bunny behind me, following that Flame. As we are leaving, I hear things sickening and bending and breaking. When we reach the outside, we hear Natalie's hysterics again, and another voice.

"Ma'am. I understand. But at this point, the structure is well involved—"

"The *structure*?! That's my house! My husband and my—" Natalie takes to sobbing alone.

"I think they may have gained access around back. We're doing all we can." And then the man in the funny hat and ugly dirty clothes with bright strips sees us emerge.

Seth hands the blanket to Natalie and then nearly falls over. The other man catches him. Seth is coughing uncontrollably. Natalie sets the blanket on the grass and pulls the blanket part off. It is Naya. She'd been wrapped in a wet blanket to keep the fire from her. Natalie is panicked because Naya is sleeping. But she awakens.

Coughs. "Dadda?"

Natalie embraces her in a multitude of tears, then looks to Seth, who looks to me. I assess the house once again, seeking out the Flame. I see It standing where the garage was. Then through It walks another man in a funny hat carrying some smelly charred something with light hair and setting it on the ground. He looks to the other man.

And shakes his head.

One of those ambulance things arrives, and people rush over just in time for Natalie to notice the head shaking. They take Naya from her, and Naya's age demands that one ambulance depart immediately. I'm reminded now of the day Seth asked me to smell my way to his parents. I remember the way he collapsed when he'd seen they were gone from him forever. He'd had nothing to do but cry. Cry. Cry. But Seth had known. God had told him where they'd be and that they were gone. I know that now. Natalie hadn't known about Nate. She had only loved him. Hated him. Until moments before he was gone forever.

So, Natalie must first scream and run in her singed nightgown to her husband on the path where moving trucks had parked, and cribs of penance had been carried. His face is cruelly preserved in perfection, but no breath emits. He is warm, just sleeping. Or so Natalie screams at anyone who comes near her and the face she thumbs and paws. Coughing. Crying. And screaming in turn that she loves him. And hates him. Both. In two or three languages. No one can keep Natalie from him even to check if she's alright. They put a mask on Seth as someone takes me and flashes lights and things in my eyes and ears and such. But after a moment, Seth calmly removes the mask and moves a hand of a medical person away when she tries to restrain him.

"Please contact Christian Kessler. Also, Ken Nakano is staying at the hotel at the end of Plaid Row. Tell them all the hospital you are taking us to." He talks like a CEO. Therefore, the person gets on a radio and obeys.

Seth approaches the hysterics with calm, as he's done for many years. He merely crouches to the level of the ground where Natalie is. First, she fights him off. And then she wraps herself within and around him like a child might. So, he lifts her and carries her to the ambulance in the depth of her tears as a father might. He hands her over to the medical people.

"Natalie. Go with them, okay? They already took Naya. I have to take care of Willow. I will stay here with Nate as long as I can."

Natalie obeys as the mask is put on her and the doors are closed. Seth and I approach Nate. I lick him a few times on his face, but he won't even yell at me for doing so. We sit near him as the firemen begin to subdue the flames completely with their water. A firefighting person approaches.

"We have another ambulance on the way for you and the four-legged hero here. There's a vet waiting at the hospital to check her over. Someone will be here for him soon too. Was he a friend of yours, or are you just a neighbor?"

Was. Sometimes the simplest of words spoken into a stranger's life can change a moment from the calm of grim to the anguish of grief. That one "was" changes Seth into the teenager that grasped me and cried before those emergency people could ever see it. Seth is new today. More than authentic. He's believable. When those tears are seen by many.

Chapter Thirty-Five

The Hero

At last. Inside that hospital. They call me a hero and give me free rein to wander the floor where they admit Naya. Don't they know all I did was follow that Flame? Will they ever?

Seth and Natalie had both been released after some brief treatment for what the smoke did in their lungs. But Naya was nearly killed by that smoke, and we are all gathered now in her room and silent. On the hospital bed, Naya clutches her toy bunny. Natalie holds onto Naya, stroking her hair. Eden holds onto Natalie. Silent tears stream across their noses and into the pillow under their heads. All that beauty assembled. All that sadness.

Laura is in that same sad, stunned place in her heart, but occupies a chair all curled up like a child. Her husband and children are at home. I think she's thinking about what to say to them. Seth sits on the floor of the room in a corner. The silence is sadder than the people. A woman knocks on the door.

"Y'all need anything?" She asks gently. Laura shakes her head kindly. At least the silence was broken. The woman exits.

"Two minutes. That was the difference between both of them and just one," Natalie says from some hollow place. "They said the ceiling fell again right where he had Naya. The whole downstairs was on fire. He made me get out. He had Naya but wanted to wrap her in a wet blanket. The stairs collapsed right behind me. They wouldn't have made it if they weren't in the bathroom. Oh, and if Neil had decided to stay with us instead of the hotel. I've never felt God's mercy like that. I just wish—" And then she bursts into tears again like she has on and off for many hours.

"I should have tried harder. I can't believe I just left him there to die," Seth grumbles from a smoke-hoarse voice. "I'm sorry, Natalie. I should have tried."

Laura sniffles. "What, with a leash in one hand and a toddler in the other? I can't believe they are calling *Willow* a hero. I mean, you did great, Willow. But *you're* the hero, Seth. Naya would have died if—"

"She wasn't going to die." Seth sighs.

Natalie composes herself again. "Did you know, Seth?"

"Natalie, this is not a good time," Seth rasps.

"Did you *know*!?" She sits up. Still beautiful with tears and hair a mess and smudged face. She looks at Seth with fiery eyes.

"Yes," Seth admits. "So did Nate."

"Why didn't you tell me?" She sobs, laying back down at her mother's urging. "I could have said goodbye. The last thing I said to him was *all* sass. 'Yes! I have my phone.' The last thing. Ever. I'm so mad at him. I hate that I'm mad."

Another knock taps at the door as Eden shushes her daughter. It's a social worker and a nurse. One leans by the bed, speaking low to Natalie.

"Mrs. Holm? A lot of concerned citizens saw the smoke all over town, and the press would like to make a statement. Have you gotten in touch with your in-laws yet?"

"No." Laura sniffles the monotone response, glancing at her phone yet again. "I've been trying for hours."

"We could just release the address and his age and gender—" The social worker suggests.

"No!" Natalie says firmly. "He spent the last part of his childhood in that house. My mother-in-law knows it well. Don't release a thing until we approve it." Then she sighs again. "I mean, is she still my mother-in-law if Nate is gone?"

"Yes, Natalie. You were my sister way before you married him. Don't do that, okay?" Laura encourages. A tear escapes, darkening a path all the way down the front of her blue shirt.

The nurse speaks. "We can release Naya in the morning unless you don't have a place to stay. Then we can keep her a couple days, for your sake. Do you have any family or neighbors? No other houses were affected, but I'm afraid there may be little to recover from yours."

"I don't even have *anything* of his." Natalie sobs, the professional losing her for reason.

Eden speaks kindly. "Natalie, she's right there, baby. You have Naya. What more do you need of his?"

"She can stay with me." Seth offers with determination to the woman by the bed.

"No." Natalie reasons. "The guest house is too dangerous for Naya with the loft and the ladder. And she might try to get out the door and wander in the woods if we stay downstairs. I can't lose her too."

"No, no." Seth clarifies the depth of his generosity in tears. "You can stay in the main house. Whatever rooms you want. I'm not using them. I can build her all new furniture and a gate for the stairs. I still have my Mom's clothes that fit you, and I'll make sure Naya has clothes too. All the toys she had. I'll replace everything. Nate asked me to take care of you and Naya. That's the last thing he ever said, Natalie. So don't worry about anything, okay? I'm doing what Nate asked."

"Thank you, Seth," Eden speaks gently. "But you've already done enough. Ken and I already decided that Natalie would benefit from a move back home to South Carolina. We'll take care of her."

"Alright," Seth concedes, devastated. "Just tell me how I can help."

Laura's tears begin again. She's losing the rest of her family in one night. Then her phone rings. She stares at it a moment. "It's Mom. She's calling me back. What do I say, Seth? How do I—Seth, I can't imagine losing one of my boys. She only *has* one. This isn't fair." She looks to Seth.

"God will give you the words," Seth encourages. Laura answers the phone.

It is Karen Holm, in frantic realization that her phone had been called and texted dozens and dozens of times but was buried under wrapping paper an entire floor away.

"Is everything alright, sweetheart?" She asks at the end of the rant.

"No. Something happened, Mom." Laura sniffles then leaves the hospital room. I see before the door closes that God has sent the arms of two Nakano men from which she must deliver it. But I'm glad to be subjected now to Natalie's grieved rambling, and not Karen Holm's reception of news.

"I don't even have a toothbrush. Gosh, I barely grabbed my purse. I can't believe this. My whole life is just gone." Natalie stares past the nurse with a hand at her forehead. "Oh, The restaurant! Nate's gone. I don't even know where to start. Nate. Oh, Nathan. Things were finally so wonderful." She sniffles and shatters all hearts in the room.

"God is in control even now, Natalie." Seth sniffles as well. Wisdom, even in devastation. "Nathan is with Him. He's at peace."

"We can stay to help with whatever you need us to. Then we'll take you home, okay? God can help us through this together."

Eden tries to keep her daughter's mind on less troubling things, unsuccessfully.

"Mama?" Natalie squeaks, trembling in fear.

"Yes, Baby?"

"This is my home. And Naya's home. I'm not going with you and Papa. I'm staying with Seth."

"Baby, Seth lives right up the street from—we raised you in that house. Nate's family lived there. It's gone now. Nate is gone. Now there's too much pain on Plaid Row. That's why we left the first time."

Eden almost slaps Seth in the face with the words. Natalie sniffles. And if she weren't in so much grief, I'd think she's smiling a little when she whispers.

"That's not how *I* remember things."

They are meant to meet at Seth's house. But after a mysteriously delayed arrival of some family, days before the funeral, Seth's phone rings. A common occurrence. But not from this caller.

"This is Seth."

"Seth, this is Neil. My parents want you to come down to Natalie's house. The foundation, I mean. Whatever this is." Probably the most even-keeled voice to call, all changed like a man's now.

We drive up in Seth's truck to the devastation of ash and foundation that is a landmark I've never been without on this road. We see that the Nakano family is standing outside of the taped-off ruin, along with Laura and Christian. The delay is explained. No children are present. They are likely at the park with the recently arrived Holms. Karen has not been able, in her heart, to drive up the road just yet, but finds some peace in the chaos of her six grandchildren.

They are all staring silently at the pain of Plaid Row, which simply looks like a woman sitting cross-legged, back to the rest of us, in a cold, barren nothing where she was raised. The last place her love put his arms around her. It is the first she's seen of it in the few days since the fire, having been urged to stay at the hotel with her family until they needed to leave. That makes today New Year's Eve—Natalie and Nate's fourth anniversary.

Seth approaches the family. "What's wrong?"

Ken speaks sadly. "I understand you are a bit of an expert at convincing Natalie to do things she absolutely does not wish to do."

All eyes rest with hope and desperation on Seth.

"She is easily swayed if he knows she isn't doing the best thing," Seth suggests. Still grieving and scared to help Natalie travel the road he's far too fond of.

Laura sniffles. "Ken's been trying but hasn't gotten an inspector out here yet to see how safe it is. So she shouldn't be over there. But she's just pretending she doesn't hear us when we tell her that."

"We've tried everything besides dragging her out of there." Neil supplies. "She just keeps sitting there."

"It's cold. I'm worried about her." Eden speaks gently.

"She doesn't seem compelled to do the 'best thing,'" Christian explains.

"She's probably already doing it." Seth nods, then reaches back into his truck and pulls out a blanket and a flashlight, though it is not yet dark. He carefully crosses a tape line, stepping on wood and cement, determining the area's safety. He allows me to follow where he walks. So different from our last entrance into the house. The murmurs behind him don't stop him, and when he reaches Natalie, he doesn't even utter a word, despite the effort it takes to get to her.

Her face is expressionless. Her eyes stare into the distance. And instead of wondering the pain or intent of the grieving woman, Seth opens the blanket and wraps it around shoulders that may not feel the cold otherwise. He places the flashlight by her side, then makes his way back across the tape, stopping suddenly just where the front room of angrily tossed furniture once was. Seth reaches down and picks up something black with one flat side.

"What's that?" Christian wonders as Seth returns to the group, some of them scowling, and hands Christian the strange object.

When Christian receives it, he inhales quickly, exhaling only with tears, trying to stop sobs in which Laura can only join as she embraces him. A chef's knife. Identical to one of Christian's except the slight melt and char. That sets Eden and Neil to audible grief as well. Seth turns his offended attention to Ken.

"My father, who passed down his company to me, took me out on my first construction site when I was six months old. I know structures and building materials and paperwork and regulations and inspectors better than most. You need only ask, Ken. I will not hesitate to use my resources when it comes to Natalie. Why does no one ever call me soon enough? Regardless, my house is warm and waiting to welcome you all. Let Natalie be." Seth gets in his truck and heads home. Reluctantly, the others follow.

It is hours into the darkness, and all family has gathered at Seth's house to begin remembering Nate. The doorbell rings a few times as the day darkens. First to arrive are Zeke and Madison, who has a bump on her belly no one knew about. Kevin strokes my hair, awaiting the playmates he'd met before. Next to arrive is Derek Vargas, in rags and riches of his missionary's soul, glad he'd been contacted just in time to make it home. Next, Bill, Shelley, and Kelli scramble to bring in the five Kessler children and little Naya.

Laura notes the void after greeting her children. "Where's Mom?"

Bill sighs and points outside into the darkness. "With Natalie."

The people all try to combat the terrible silence. The Holm twins walk in even greater beauty these days, but as usual, Neil only notices as is appropriate for light conversation and a game of cards with Kelli. Shelley is enthralled by stories of a forbidden mission field through the telling of Vargas. Bill and Ken grunt about this and that, and the children play. Seth sits with Zeke and Christian, and their wives, in view of the path out the front window. All as if there isn't a heavy sadness about them all. I travel among them.

"So, are you gonna be a dad, Zeke, or are we pretending Maddie is smuggling watermelons?" Christian wonders with a smile.

Zeke sighs. "We didn't want to take the focus away from the family. But yes, we are expecting a little boy."

"Nathan Ezekiel. We'd been having trouble thinking of a name and decided on the plane. I hope your mom and Natalie don't get too mad. We just thought someone like him should be a namesake, you know?" Maddie says before a sniffle.

"They won't be mad," Laura says quickly. "That's wonderful, guys. Congrats. We certainly need news like that about now."

"I'm thinking I want to get a nursing degree and then get into some missions stuff. Life is too short not to make a difference somehow." Shelley tells the priest as I move to their conversation.

"Absolutely. I'll keep in touch. We could use a nurse where I am. Ours is thinking of retiring soon." Vargas offers.

"I text non-stop. Drives Shelley crazy. So that's actually a perfect way to contact me." Kelli tells Neil over the forsaken card game.

"Great!" Neil says, transferring numbers between his and Kelli's phones. "Nate and I used to text all day long. My phone's been way too quiet. It'll be nice to not have to go through all this alone."

I walk next to where Bill sits with Ken.

"I really messed up with Nate. But despite that, he led a good life. I wonder if he had any idea," Bill says in a rare show of emotion. "How proud I am of him."

"He was a good man, Bill," Ken tells him. "I only wish I'd looked him in the eye and told him that when I had the chance."

Seth crosses the rooms to stand by the front door and monitor the flashlight making its way up the street. Bill joins him, something on his heart. Ken looks away, suppressing all wishes involving Seth.

"I'm sure that 'thank you' does not suffice."

"For what, Bill?" Seth shakes his hand in generous civility.

"For that." Bill nods, eyes becoming wet. Grateful beyond measure for all the humble, Christlike ways of Seth Gowan. A heart where all transgressions are barely a memory.

Natalie and Karen arrive at the door hand in hand. Karen is received by all, in tears that may never dry for her only son. Natalie leaves the room, requesting an audience with Seth as she passes. When Seth turns from closing his office door to speak with Natalie, she slaps him across the face.

"I—" Seth is stunned. Confused.

"Fire retardant. On the crib. It survived, Seth. Karen and I found it. You knew the house would burn down, and you still bought it for us. Why would you do that?" Natalie says sternly.

"I didn't know where or how it would happen, Natalie. I only knew Naya would be fine. I wanted to be sure." He explains himself while rubbing his cheek. The next words involve sniffles. "I've done lots of things to try to prevent it. You know I'd have given anything…. Natalie I can't express how hard it was for me to leave him in that bathroom."

Natalie begins to cry. "I just slapped you. I'm so out of control, Seth. I'm sorry."

"Natalie, I won't hold you responsible for anything you do in the next few months," Seth tells her. "But today, you have lots of people that want to comfort you. While they are here, let them do it, even if you feel like being alone or screaming at them or me. You have work to do, Natalie. Let them help you say goodbye to Nate. When they leave, you can be out of control again, okay? I won't stop you."

"Okay." Natalie understands. I'm not sure I do. But thus is the way of these two humans' condition.

Nate's memorial service in the chapel is one of a sinner with a passion for life. And when that sinner had found Christ, the whole of the memorial service was reminded how much more passionately Nathan Holm lived. He is remembered well. Christian and Laura take on a piano, barely holding it together with a song that touched Nate in life.

Hold thou thy cross before my closing eyes
Shine through the gloom and point me to the skies
Heaven's morning breaks and Earth's vain shadows flee
In life, in death, oh Lord,
Abide with me.

And then Natalie leaves Naya with her parents to travel to Niagara Falls alone and scatter ashes where Nathan could fall. But this time into the arms of Jesus.

Chapter Thirty-Six

Just Breathe

Natalie has always been even stronger than she looks, though she already intimidates with her beauty and grace. While she does spend a fair amount of time alone in her room—the room where Seth's crib had once been—she refuses to let the well-being of her child suffer just for the sake of grief. Seth says God was smart to give her Naya.

There is a deep and hushed cruelty in humanity after a celebration. A new baby is well celebrated but is then a daunting and permanent task for the parents. A high school graduate is congratulated but then must live the life that follows graduation. But grief after a memorial is far crueler.

The countless days left to heal after the floral arrangements begin to wilt are much more trying than even the night Nate lay lifeless beneath that glowing fire. Now the world rotates on as if Natalie isn't left with a void that filled with grief the moment her heart first beat without him. It isn't fair. And Natalie is strong. But she feels so weak when the whole world is cruelly unaware of all the pain that remains.

She's still Natalie, but amplified. She's fickle and spicy and wild. Part of me likes her better this way. She doesn't simply feel. She's honest. She will go from sleepily at peace to the screaming of an animal like the night Naya was born. And when she is quiet, it is between the storms. Because there isn't really peace at all in her. She hates and curses whenever Naya is sleeping. Seth keeps his distance. She cries alone when I'm the only one to hear. After the exodus from the funeral, Seth and Natalie do not speak more than a few necessary words at a time for weeks, even when they cross paths in the vast empty house.

"I gave Naya an apple while you were napping. I cut it up like you do. I hope that's okay."

"That's fine. Thank you, Seth."

Then after those weeks, in the quiet Seth and I have enjoyed for years: his leather Book and glass of wine and a fire crackling in the sitting area of his bedroom, we are interrupted by a knock at the bedroom door.

"H'lo?" He asks.

Sniffles. Common now. And Natalie enters, stretching sleeves over wrists like a child might.

"I'm not pregnant." She shares first.

Seth is beyond confused. "Um, is that good or bad? I don't understand."

"We were trying to have a baby, Seth. And I thought maybe God would have left a piece of him with me. But the one time I want more than anything to be pregnant, I'm not. I have Naya. I know that. But I just want Nate." Then Natalie bursts into tears a millisecond before Seth surrenders Bible and wine glass to the end table and rises, leading her to the loveseat in the room, where she finds what she needs with her head on a pillow on his lap. He's grasping her upper arm like a memory from their teen years. Natalie finally opens up.

"It just *hurts*. And that word is such a stupid way of explaining it. It's like—" She sniffles, words not coming easily.

"Like an elephant sitting on your chest. Like crying feels more natural because you feel your whole body ache otherwise. Like you'll die if you have to feel the pain one more second, but the only thing that could fix it is impossible. Because nothing can make him come back." Seth breathes out, eyes glistening a little.

"Nail on the head, Seth. You've done this before with your parents. Can you really feel this way and survive?" Natalie asks.

"I'll let you know if I survive it this time," Seth responds. Natalie's eyes are opened. Of course. Nate was his best friend too. Not the father of his child and the sharer of his life. No. But something like a brother.

"I have this memory in my head, Seth. Of coming back after all those years and seeing your parents' grave and wondering how in the world you got through it. Then suddenly, you were standing there. And you *smiled* at me. But maybe I'm wrong because that's impossible. You lost the people closest to you in the universe. How do you feel *joy*? I don't see how this pain will ever stop. People tell me that one day I'll just wake up and be okay. But no one wants to talk about the meantime. I was thinking. I know everything you do has a method, Seth. If you figured out a way to thrive after losing your parents, maybe you can tell me what you did? I know I can't have him back. I just want to be able to *breathe* again without him." Natalie succumbs to her tears.

"Meet me in the kitchen at six in the morning," Seth says after a moment. "I know that's eight hours away, and I know how long eight hours can be. But if you hold out until then, I think I can help."

With something just short of a smile, Seth hears her come down the stairs at 5:55 a.m. We join her at the breakfast bar, where she is sitting, head on the counter, in pajamas, next to what is widely known to be Seth's spot. He sets his Bible in that spot, like always. And today, Seth grabs two bowls. Two spoons. And pours a food critic a bowl of cold cereal as she looks on with anticipation. He takes a couple of bites. She stares at the bowl, waiting for Seth's miracle cure for grief that happened before my eyes over a decade ago. As expected, Seth begins at that same spot of that tattered old Book, reading aloud.

"Psalms one. 'Blessed is the man who walks not in the counsel of the ungodly, Nor stands in the path of sinners, Nor sits in the seat of the scornful; But his delight is in the law of the Lord, and in His law he meditates day and night.'" Seth takes another bite as Natalie waits.

"'He shall be like a tree planted by the rivers of water, That brings forth its fruit in its season, Whose leaf also shall wither; and Whatever he does shall prosper. The ungodly are not so, but are like the chaff which the wind drives away. Therefore the ungodly shall not stand in the congregation of the righteous. For the Lord knows the way of the righteous, But the way of the ungodly shall perish.'"

By now, Natalie is crying. But these tears are like the way pus is drawn from a wound. Such is the power of God's Word. She sniffles.

"Read it again?" Then she closes her eyes as Seth reads, letting the words seep into her like ointment. She cries a little. "Now what?"

"Go back to bed. When you wake up later, just survive today. One minute at a time. Don't try to be strong for more than *one* minute each time, Natalie. It's too long. Then meet me back here tomorrow."

"Okay." Natalie whispers, then nods before slinking and sniffling back up the stairs in her pajamas without having touched her cereal.

When Seth hears doors shut upstairs, he looks at the clock on the wall, and watches the hand that ticks circle around once. He whispers with quiet triumph, "One."

The same happens the following day. Seth pours cereal and begins. "'Psalm Two. Why do the nations rage, And the people plot a vain thing?...'" And he reads that whole Psalm. Natalie makes him read it again, beginning to cry at the end. "'Kiss the Son, lest He be angry, and you perish in the way, When His wrath is kindled but a little. Blessed are those who put their trust in Him.'"

"Can God really heal this? I mean, I'm willing, He's all I have, Seth. My only constant. Everything else dies. But can He really—" Natalie is both faithful and skeptical.

"Nothing is impossible. Trust Him and pray. And take today two minutes at a time. Go get some sleep." Seth says gently.

I'm told there are 150 Psalms. And I suppose I remember that. By day five, Natalie decides to take a few bites of cereal in five minutes of strength. By day ten, she sighs heavily after she hears the Psalm and finishes her cereal. On day 45, Natalie doesn't go back to bed after Seth reads the Psalm. She showers and prepares Naya's breakfast a little early in her minutes of strength. Then the Psalms are routine and begin the day. More important than breakfast. On day 64, Seth and Natalie have a conversation about Nate after they empty their cereal bowls. On day 71, a similar conversation leads them both to laughter, then tears. By day 100, Natalie begins to read the Psalms. On day 119, they take turns reading, and both cry without speaking when they are done. And on day 150, Seth smiles a little when Natalie's footsteps sound a little different. A little more like Natalie.

It is Seth that finishes the final Psalm, "'Let everything that has breath praise the Lord. Praise the Lord!'"

Natalie's tears are streaming. She's smiling. Laughing a little. "Seth, I woke up this morning. *Breathing*. I figured I can either decide to grieve today every 150 minutes. Or I can use the breath I have to praise the God who gave it to me. I have no idea what to do, or even who I am without Nate. Heck, I even eat cereal now. My palate is destroyed," (Seth chuckles here) "But Seth, God is *constant*."

"Yeah." Seth smiles. "Yeah, He is."

"I'm so glad I decided to stay with you." Then Natalie smiles. "Can we start Proverbs tomorrow?"

"Of course." Seth delights, for the first time in a long time, in the hopeful smile of his best friend.

Chapter Thirty-Seven

The Beauty of Solitude

It is by chance after putting Naya down for her midday nap that Natalie uses the correct staircase to take her past Seth's office on the rare occasion that he chooses to work with the door open. It is a typical Wednesday with nibbles of lunch between filing papers, checking productivity, and quick swallows before he answers an annoyingly familiar piano concerto on his phone with,

"This is Seth."

Natalie stands in the doorway as he explains to someone obviously far below his intelligence the proper procedure for submitting a workman's comp claim and warmly reciting the name and phone number of the human resources representative that handles them. After hanging up, Seth emails that rep himself, telling him to expect a call. Then Natalie listens as Seth calls and orders flowers for that hurt employee and then calls his family, telling a worried wife to call if she needs anything. After the call, he smiles at listening Natalie a split second as he continues his routine chaos.

"You're a good boss," Natalie compliments.

"I have good people that work for me. I never understood corporations who mistreated employees to try and make money. Happy, valued employees stick around and work hard, consequently making us and themselves money." Seth explains this as he's typing something else on his computer and then taking a folder from a massive stack of things to be filed, carrying it to a file cabinet as tall and wide as he.

"Nate believed the same thing. People loved working for him. I'm glad I can trust Christian to carry that on." Natalie speaks of the restaurant she's recently signed over to Christian and Laura, the best possible hands for Nate's legacy. Then looks back to Seth. "So this is what you do all day?"

"Essentially," Seth says with a permanent marker in his mouth.

"Doesn't a millionaire President and CEO usually attend board meetings and approve ideas and order people to do his bidding?" Natalie asks, making her way across the wood floor to take the current folder from his hand.

"I have a board meeting in twenty minutes. I'm already checked in online. I just have some filing to do before it starts."

"Doesn't Zeke have a secretary?" Natalie is concerned and begins examining the folder and the files in the drawers, seeing how they correspond.

"Only because he's sleeping with her," Seth says, marking something in another folder on his desk before turning back to the stunned Natalie. He chuckles. "It's something Zeke says all the time. Maddie got fed up with Zeke's workaholic thing and hired a nanny to watch little Nathan in Zeke's office suite. That way she can help Zeke out with things and spend more time with him. He'd never had an assistant before her."

"Well, he also has an entire team of accountants and other various people in that building. You have you. And all of *them* answer to you. Have you ever thought of hiring someone to help with silly stuff like filing and answering the phone?"

"No, Natalie. We have an open communication policy. Every employee has my personal cell phone number. I only get a couple of calls a day, but it has to be me that answers." Seth checks the clock on his laptop screen and sighs in frustration. Running behind.

"That's really cool." Natalie sits on Seth's desk after easily filing the papers he was fretting over. She crosses her legs and clears her throat.

"How long can we stay?" Able to ask for the first time, now nine months after Nate took his flight.

The rubble has been removed from the house's foundation. The foundation was sold, and a new house is being erected for a stranger. Natalie had found few things intact, including Naya's crib and a few knives Christian displays as a memorial in *Le Cloture*. Natalie's work with picking up pieces is concluding. Now she's looking ahead at how to reassemble them.

"As long as you need to, Natalie. You know that." Seth reminds his long-term house guest. Confused why she'd even ask.

"I can't write anymore. They gave me time off, but food just tastes different, so I quit my job. And no one is looking for an accompanist. But I can't just crash at your house my whole life, Seth. I need to figure out what the heck I'm doing because eventually I'm going to wear out my welcome. But you'd never tell me when that happened." Seth watches Natalie lean back onto her hands atop the desk and toss her hair aside as she stares up at Seth's bookshelves. A could-be supermodel or rocket scientist without a purpose.

Seth shakes his head. "You would never wear out your welcome. If you raise Naya here, it won't be too long for you to stay." Seth smiles and sits back in his gigantic leather chair with a squeak and a rock.

Natalie bites her lip. "Nate and I were hoping to *add* to our family. The fact that I'm a single mom now is a little hard to swallow. But I guess I have to." Natalie sighs, then turns the pain inward and smiles up at the filing cabinets. "Your filing system is illogical. Doesn't seem like you."

"I just took over where my dad had it. I think a lot differently than he did, but I'm used to it now."

"Why don't you let me fix it? Give me something to do. It'll give you time to do CEO-type stuff. Let me be your assistant while I'm figuring things out."

"The filing system is fine. I've been doing this eleven years, Natalie. I can handle it."

"Seth, I'm not arguing. You get attached to stuff like ovens and file systems, and being alone, and it can backfire. Sometimes literally. Go on and be sentimental. But don't sacrifice vast improvement for something that will ruin your life in the long run." Natalie insists from a place of pain.

Seth laughs. "What do you want me to pay you?"

"I'd say the roof over mine and my child's head will suffice."

"And I get to pay for groceries." Seth negotiates.

"Only if I get to go to board meetings."

"You can be in the room. Not on the screen. Most of the board has known me most of my life. If they see you, they'll tease." Seth rolls his eyes.

"Okay. I'll try to be good. But why would they tease?"

"Mrs. Patterson, the Director of Human Resources, asks me at every meeting if I'm seeing anyone because they assume that being single equates with being miserable. You're a beautiful woman. They know you're staying with me, but God only knows what they'll assume if they see you. They're like another family. My dad put in his will that Mr. Billings check up on m, so they schedule ninety-minute board meetings—sixty for business, thirty to ask about me. Just be invisible? I don't even usually let Willow in the room."

Natalie has a terrible smile on her face. "This just got a hundred times more interesting. But I have a theory."

"About?"

"If they ever determine that you're *not* miserable, I bet your board meetings will be shorter." Natalie tosses that jet-black hair again.

"I'm not miserable," Seth argues.

Natalie narrows her eyes. "How are you not miserable? I've been alone nine months, and I'm miserable. You've been alone what, ten years?"

"That depends on the definition of 'alone.' I have been without *romantic* attachment for eleven years, three months," Seth says, sounding like he's been counting the hours, when in reality, he counts everything. "But I've never been alone. Even when I haven't had other people living with me, I've always had Willow, and of course, the presence of the Holy Spirit."

"You know what I mean, Seth. It's not even about romantic attachment." Natalie remembers. "You spend a great deal of time in complete solitude, do you not realize that? Some time alone with God is important. But you've spent most of the last 'eleven years, three months' in your woodshop, or in this office, or building that fence. Even when you had a house full of tenants, you chose to be alone most of the time. You chose misery."

"There can be beauty in solitude," Seth smirks and checks the clock and types something on his computer.

"Beauty?" Natalie seems to be more curious than mocking. "Seth, if there's a method you have to deal with loneliness, and you aren't telling me, we're gonna have to change this. Right now, nine months feels a lot more like eleven years. You got me through the worst of the grief. Get me through this."

"You know I'm going to point you in that same direction, right?" Seth promises. "God had the answers, not me."

"That's what I'm hoping." Natalie smiles, hopping down from his desk.

"I'll be out at my fence tomorrow at about one." Seth offers. "After you put Naya down for her nap, you should come out there."

"It's a date." Natalie nods, seeking out a pencil and paper and a wingback chair to listen to the meeting.

After a moment, Seth's face lights up. "Hey, Zeke. Do you have sound today?"

"Sure do!" Zeke's voice from the machine.

Natalie smiles at the familiar voice. Giddy over something routine to Seth.

"Hi, Zeke!" She can't contain it and runs to the other side of the desk where Maddie has heard her speak inside Zeke's office far away. The two women chat a moment while the co-presidents await the other board members.

Natalie misses Seth's cue to leave the screen and hears a gasp from an older woman.

"Seth, who is this young lady?"

"I'm Natalie. I'm Seth's new assistant slash freeloading widow. You must be Mrs. Patterson," Natalie says with friendly ease. After the short conversation, the rest of the board has arrived, and Natalie sits across the room and sticks out her tongue.

"Seth, she's gorgeous. Are you sleeping with her yet?" Mrs. Patterson's voice. Zeke's laughter.

"That would be inappropriate for a number of reasons. And she's still in the room, Mrs. Patterson." Seth is embarrassed, even having warned the amused Natalie.

Chapter Thirty-Eight

NIGHTMARES

"Wow. You're getting pretty close to being done." Natalie joins us at the fence after putting Naya down for a nap, as instructed.

"Nine months left," Seth confirms.

Natalie fits the light jacket around her a little tighter for the chilling air.

"The infamous fence that not one of us understands. You finally going to tell me why you built it?" Natalie hopes.

"Nope," Seth confesses, dusting off his next fence post.

"Okay…" Natalie sits in the browning grass, confused. "I thought you were going to share some wisdom about the 'beauty of solitude.'"

"Wisdom is something you have to seek." Seth reminds, not even looking at her.

"And I'm sitting here seeking." She laughs a little.

"Well, you're asking the wrong person," Seth says, as his father might have. "I'm just a guy building a fence."

"But you asked me to come out here." She tilts her head.

"I know." Seth smiles to himself.

"Alright." Natalie gives up the fight against the eccentric for the day and just watches him build the fence. The section takes him thirty minutes of just the sound of stapling and such. Then he stashes his tools and we head back to the house.

"I'll be back out here on Monday," Seth says, leaving Natalie scratching her head.

"Want help?" She asks on Monday.

"Nope," Seth replies.

"So why am I here?"

"I think you walked," Seth teases.

"You're driving me crazy. Explain the fence, Seth."

"Nope." He reiterates.

She begins to go crazy considering it in her mind. If she is quiet while watching him work, it is only because she's angry he won't talk or thinking about why he keeps asking her to come out.

In November, she starts the twenty-questions approach.

"I get it. It keeps your mind focused on something so your thoughts don't stray from God." A reasonable assumption, I think.

"You volunteered to be my assistant because I was doing too much." Seth has plenty to think about. That's right.

"So, is there a certain number of posts and pickets that mean something? You like numbers. You love my new, logical, numerical filing system," Natalie suggests.

"I do like numbers."

"Aha!"

"But no. The number of pickets can vary, which is hard for me, but of no significance."

December is peaceful. Natalie stops asking and assumes she is supposed to notice something tangible, and thus remains silent. I think Seth likes December the best, when she simply watches the skill and strength, and focus of his movements. Admires him, though she doesn't understand.

Christmas is difficult for Natalie with the absence of Nate. The Kesslers come, of course. But no one else. They all feel him gone as much as they felt him here before. All except Naya, who is beginning to not notice the void, or even recognize Nate as a memory when looking at a picture. Only a picture. And when night falls on Christmas, after Seth and Christian rearrange his office furniture for the desk he built for Natalie, her giddy gratitude is still not enough to cover the memory.

Seth is deeply asleep next to me on his bed. His bedroom door opens to the once familiar sniffling sounds of Natalie's tears. Seth tries to wake up quickly as Natalie shuts the door, walks past his sitting room, then through the French doors into his actual bedroom.

"What's wrong, Natalie?"

"It's Christmas again. I'm terrified, Seth. I smell smoke every time I start to fall asleep." Natalie closes the French doors behind her.

"I'm sorry, Natalie. It's really late, though." Seth is still groggy. Then Natalie breaches more boundaries. I feel her gently slip under the covers and move me aside as she takes up a little portion of Seth's king-size bed.

"Natalie! What are you doing? I can't let you—"

"I just don't want to be alone right now. Will you please, *please* hold me for a minute?"

"I don't know how I feel about this, Natalie."

"About holding me? You used to hold me all the time when the kids at church would make fun of us. Please, Seth? I feel safe with you." Natalie sniffles more, and her voice sounds funny.

Seth sighs. And I hear a swish of persons travel into the middle under the covers. I move to the side. Natalie speaks.

"How long has Willow slept with you?"

"Her whole life. Mom bought her a bed when she was a puppy, but she never uses it."

"See? She feels safe with you too." Natalie sniffles again, but I hear her smile. "I bet it was nice to have her when your parents passed, huh?"

"It was." Seth yawns.

"Sorry. I know you have a busy day tomorrow. I'll go back upstairs if you want me to." Natalie stirs.

"Stay." Seth hums his sleepiness and lets down his guard a little.

"Promise you won't try anything?" Natalie jokes.

"I'm too tired." Seth chuckles.

"When Nate and I first got married, it was really weird sleeping with a man next to me. I got used to it, but it took a while. I'd never even shared a room." Natalie remembers, giggling.

"Did he still snore? He'd stay over a lot when we were kids, and I'd hear him snoring even from another room. Zeke and Vargas and Christian used to say the same thing when they all lived upstairs." Seth captures the giggle and tries to perpetuate it.

"Yes!" Natalie laughs. "Gah, that snoring! I used to hate it. But when I finally realized I couldn't stop him, I just let it lull me to sleep. Now I can't sleep. It's too quiet."

Seth waits a moment and then fake snores loudly. Natalie laughs, fully comforted by her friend's silliness. My wakefulness fades long before their conversation.

Then Natalie awakens me with her gasp after not too long. The gasp is followed by sobs and frantic nonsense in the moments she is sitting up, but between asleep and awake.

"Smoke! Nate, I can't see anything! Naya! Where's Naya?" I hear Seth sit up, and his hand gently connects with Natalie's back. Another gasp.

"Seth." The tone is not disappointment, like I'd expect when she had just been seeking Nate. But relief.

"We must have fallen asleep. You were dreaming," Seth tells her, eyes seeking eyes in pitch darkness until he taps on a touch lamp on the bedside. He gives her a groggy hug to calm her trembling shoulders.

"I'm sorry. My counselor says the nightmares can last years. Sometimes it takes me a minute to remember I'm safe." Natalie confesses, still trembling and a little bewildered. "Thanks for waking me up."

"You're always safe here." Seth reiterates. Then something in Natalie shifts. Something that scares her.

"I better go check on Naya. Her room is like half a mile from here." She smiles to sugarcoat the fact that she's leaving Seth and me alone again. "Thanks Seth. See you tomorrow."

The morning comes, and I watch Seth awaken. I smile at the smell of Natalie she'd inadvertently left behind. Sweet, tangy, soothing. Maybe just a combination of shampoo and sleepy mocha skin. But whatever it is, it has power over at least one.

"*Subete.*" He whispers to himself as he takes in what his soul recognizes, even if his feeble nose had failed him. As he rises and sits at the edge of his bed, his soul sickens a little at the sight of a soft purple robe draped across a chair by the bedroom door. Natalie came to live with him with nothing, so this is the same robe she'd worn in the guest house at age sixteen. The shower is not nearly as steamy as usual, and I hear intermittent words of silent prayers over cereal he eats alone. He wants what lingers at his nose as a memory he can never touch.

Natalie zips a designer winter coat to guard her against the frigid December air. "This coat is beautiful. Remind me to thank your mom for leaving clothes in my size when we get to Heaven. I've still barely started to replace everything the fire took. I haven't had time to shop with all you have me do for you every day. I don't know how you ever did it alone."

Seth smiles. "Glad I held onto them."

Natalie clears her throat. She's being fickle. "Did you see the Christmas picture of little Nathan? Looks just like Maddie, I think."

"Yeah. Zeke's nose, though." Seth's lifelong love for children shines a moment.

"I'm sorry." Natalie offers. "You forgive me?"

"For what?" Seth asks.

"For freaking you out last night and then ditching you this morning like a bad date." Natalie sniffles for the cold. "I was thinking maybe I should have a separate quiet time from you? Not that I don't love our morning cereal, I'm just—"

"Healing?" Seth turns and smiles.

"Something like that." Natalie nods. "So, you're not upset?"

"No. I spend a lot of time with you during the day."

"And I'm still coming out here twice a week to bug you about this fence." Natalie points at Seth, soothing him.

"Deal." Seth smiles out of her view.

I hear the driveway crackle and raise my head in the direction, smelling the chilly wind. But when I barely catch a whiff, five beautiful children come running around the side of the house.

"Look who came for 'Boxing Day' as promised. I think it really bothered Laura that we didn't take down the decorations for months after the funeral last year. Guess we have work to do." Natalie smiles, rising, waiting for Seth.

"Go ahead. I'll be up in a minute." He gives her permission and watches her join the Kessler children and Laura up at the house.

Christian joins Seth and me at the fence. Old friends cut to the chase, I notice.

"I know that look," Christian says with an incriminating smile. "Haven't seen it in you, though. That's weird. About time. But still weird."

Seth never holds back honesty when asked. "I can't figure out what's wrong with me. I've been in love with her most of my life and most of the time from quite a distance. Why is it suddenly…?"

Christian gasps at the counsel Seth is seeking. Knowing exactly what words he hadn't said. "Seth Gowan is a human! I knew it all along." Christian punches a shoulder.

Seth laughs in response.

"But to answer your question, you didn't feel like this before because she was off-limits. Not to like, turn your world upside down, but the woman you love is sort of *available* now," Christian explains.

"Natalie is my best friend's widow. That doesn't make her available," Seth defends Nate, even still.

Christian laughs. "She's not your best friend's *widow,* Seth. *She* is your best friend. That was the case even before we lost Nate. Don't ignore that. Natalie and Laura are close, but you know you're the first person Natalie runs to most of the time. It was a little different when Nate got saved, but all of us know that what you and she have had very little to do with Nate."

"That may very well be the case." Seth nods. "But she's still in love with Nate, even if he's gone. She's told me she misses him and wants *him.* So, I need to remain only her friend."

"But you'd rather not." Christian caught the tone.

"What I want doesn't matter. I want to do what is best for her. She's been through a lot. The only thing is she has nightmares." Seth sighs. I hadn't realized a simple truth could make a man so distraught and helpless.

"I see." Christian does. He knows what the simple words mean. It had been the knowledge of nightmares that had helped God transform a seventeen-year-old girl into his wife. Therefore, Christian is suddenly aware of Seth's tumultuous dilemma. "So, what's the plan?"

"I'm still seeking God's plan. I'll let you know." Seth reveals to us both.

"Alright. You know I'm here for you. Whatever you need. But in the meantime? Natalie was on the phone with Laura at 6:00 a.m., freaking out about something involving your bedroom. I'd say avoid that situation at all costs, considering past events and recent feelings and what not." Christian tells Seth as he helps him stow materials, and the two walk toward the house.

"Understood." Seth nods. The wise man is always open to counsel. "Thank you."

Chapter Thirty-Nine

Fenced In

Twice a week, Natalie takes the journey with Seth out to the fence after mornings of secretarial duties and Naya coloring and chatting in Seth's office. After putting Naya down for a nap, Natalie sits on the frozen grass, or snow, or mud.

In January, she ups her game. She convinces herself that it isn't driving her insane that she doesn't understand the fence. And she starts learning the intricacies, even though Seth won't let her help.

"So, eleven and a half years ago, you used staples. Just staples for a fence. Aren't you worried that the ones at the beginning of the fence will start rusting away?"

"No. Dad invented these staples. They use them on electrical work in high rises that will last a hundred years." Seth explains.

Natalie would marvel if her heart wasn't half spice. "How would he know? He didn't exactly live to be a hundred. And that's indoors."

"When we were kids, Nate used to get drunk and climb out what was later Vargas's window to sit on the roof." Seth smiles and Natalie gasps. "So I stapled it shut from outside. That window gets direct sunlight and rain and wind. Vargas has never been able to open it. My fence is fine."

Natalie laughs. "I never knew that! Magic staples. Who knew? No wonder you're rich."

In February, I watch Natalie pace the remaining line to fence a few times.

"Your math is off. You say June is your deadline. You won't get it done in time unless you do three sections a week." She determines with much thought and a calculator app.

Seth shrugs. “Three sections it is.” One more time with Natalie watching him is what he’s thinking.

In March, the sun is shining one day when Natalie closes her eyes and breathes in the spring breeze. She changes her tune completely, just enjoying her time with Seth.

“Do you remember chess under the willow?” Natalie nostalgizes.

“You remember *making out* under the willow?” Seth teases, also in truthful nostalgia.

“I cannot believe you just asked me that!” Natalie smiles as a handful of wet spring snow flings at Seth’s back.

“Ow!” Seth responds with a laugh. “I can’t believe you asked if I remember the willow.”

In April, Natalie makes Seth drop his stapler like she doesn’t even care about the fence.

“Why’d you let me marry your best friend—?”

“Natalie!” He scolds before she completes the familiar grief-laden question Seth banned several months ago.

“No, Seth. I mean why’d you let me marry your best friend when you knew full well I was still in love with you?”

“You were good for each other.” Seth smiles at the slowly fading memories and at a fact that is new to him.

“Is it possible to be in love with two people at once?”

“I wouldn’t know.” Seth chuckles. “Why?”

“That guy at church. Aaron? The GI Joe replica that Nate used to threaten for staring at me? Well, every time you’re out of town, he asks me out,” Natalie confesses.

“You going to go out with him?” Seth wonders, trying to stop his heart from screaming something else.

“No! You kidding? I’m finally able to function after losing my husband. I have a little girl. Why in the world would I get involved with a guy that could go fight and die for his country and at the very least be gone for long periods of time? Being a military wife takes a special person, and I am not her.” Natalie thought it through, it seems.

“He seems like a nice enough guy, though.” Seth smiles.

"Yeah." Natalie doesn't accept the reasoning. "But I'm a widow. I get to be picky. Oh! We liked your breakfast casserole last night. You should teach me to make it. Meant to ask you for the recipe this morning."

"You were married to a master chef, and you like my casserole? My Mom got that recipe from a magazine just before they left. It's just food. Nothing special." Seth chuckles.

"You should still teach me. Naya loved it."

"No." Seth's answer startles Natalie.

"No?" She laughs.

"If I teach you, you'll move out," Seth admits his reasoning.

"Or make you eat more than just cereal in the morning." Natalie bites her lip. "You always start to crash and ask for coffee at 10:30 or so. A better breakfast might prevent that."

"I like cereal." Seth is almost offended. "And you make good coffee."

In May, on a Wednesday, in a lull between lunch and the weekly board meeting, Natalie returns with a sigh from her routine of putting Naya down. She smiles, leaning back in her chair in Seth's office a moment.

"She was too funny this morning. Trying so hard to say 'clip.' It's like she can tell she's not saying the 'L' right but doesn't know how to make her mouth do it." Natalie giggles over her little treasure. Seth, with perfect intentions, missteps.

"I just love that little girl. You two are really a blessing."

"I miss him. But so much good has come from him being gone, you know? It causes some heart conflict. I just try to take it at face value, I guess." Natalie stands, cleaning up Seth's work area of clips and clamps. Not liking when it is a mess for his meetings—especially if Naya caused the mess.

Seth sees his misstep. "I'd have *joyfully* watched you grow old with him."

Seth glances up at the beauty now hopping up on his desk. He stands to throw something away, then stops in front of her as she reaches out to fix his sometimes-disorderly hair. He rests his hands on his desk, on either side of her legs. The sight occurs often. Natalie wants Seth to look his best for meetings.

"I know you would have," Natalie replies with depth, then looks up into his eyes.

It happens quickly. I'm not sure who thought what when. My best guess is that they both had the same thought at the same time—a stray thought attached to stray ember of a fire thought to be long burned out. The only truth I know is that their lips join in passionate breathlessness until Seth removes his abruptly, extremely angry with himself.

"I'm so sorry. I don't know how that happened." Seth frets, accidentally mussing his hair again.

"It doesn't have to *stop* happening." Natalie allows a seductive tone, pecking him once more with a smile.

"Natalie, stop. This is not okay," Seth says, barely fighting something desperate in him.

"How is it not okay? We're both single, remember?" She whispers.

"You're a widow. That's not the same as single." Seth is almost scolding.

"It's not a sin to kiss a widow, Seth." Natalie is hurt.

"You just said you miss him. That isn't a good reason to kiss *me*. I'm not him." Seth is hurt, too.

"Of course, I miss him. We *all* miss him. But kissing you has nothing to do with him." Natalie's whisper trembles. Her eyes glisten. Her emotions now under control again, I know that the show of them is a spillover of something powerful. "I kissed you because I don't ever want to kiss anyone else again."

"Natalie, just because it's convenient—" Seth's heart, trained otherwise, is unable to accept even blatant truth.

"What, for me to fall in love with the guy that selflessly took me and my daughter in and replaced our wardrobes and belongings like it was nothing? And helped me figure out everything from paperwork to how to get up in the morning after my husband died? And he happens to be handsome and single and wonderful? Yeah, I guess that's convenient. But looking back at all the years I knew how you felt but gave everything to your best friend instead and then realized I never stopped loving *you*? That's the farthest thing from convenient. It's *excruciating*. But even with that and the grief and trying to start all over without even a winter coat to my name, I have so much peace in my life right now. I thought maybe I was just getting used to being alone. But it's not the solitude that's peaceful. It's being with *you*." Natalie releases a tear. "I love you, Seth. If you don't want us to kiss, that's okay. But I'm still going to love you."

"But—" Seth is trying so hard to both believe her and protect his heart. He uses his right hand to bring her left into his view. "When did you stop wearing your ring?"

"I'm not married, Seth. I took it off months ago." She slides her hand away from his.

"Didn't that make you sad?" Seth, caring only for Natalie. Wanting what she wants.

"I was avoiding it because I thought it might. Then I got scared and cuddled up with you and told you about how weird it was to sleep next to Nate at first. Then I realized that night that sleeping next to *you* was the most natural thing I'd ever done." Natalie kisses Seth again, almost accidentally. "I couldn't wear his ring after that."

He stops her yet again. "Stop, Natalie. We need to do this right this time. Please." He takes her promises and moves on to his concern.

"I wish I had your patience, Seth." Natalie seems far more desperate than Seth.

"*Subete*." He assures her. All. Not just patience, but his heart and soul, too. Then he embraces her lovingly. Clears his throat as he backs up, smiling a little. "I have a board meeting."

"Right. Yeah." Natalie fixes Seth's hair again and removes the shimmer of Chapstick from his face. "I'll leave you alone today. Probably best."

"It's never best to be alone." Seth rebuts with wisdom new to him. "Stay where I can see you. Did you email them the agenda and print me one?"

"Of course." Natalie smiles, handing him a piece of paper as he takes a seat in his chair, trying to recover from kisses he'd been denied for far too many years.

I hear the sound that means someone is joining the conference online, allowed these days for the first time in years to be present when this occurs.

Zeke's laughter. "I know *that* look."

"Why does everyone keep saying that?" Seth rolls his eyes at his friend.

"Only people that ended up husbands keep saying that, Man." Zeke warns. Natalie giggles. As does Maddie on the other end.

"Did Madison make all the arrangements for next week?" Seth cuts through the uncomfortable.

"Yes, sir. Three adults and six children from Colorado to California and back. You just need to get them to the airport. I'll have Maddie email the flight times. Kevin is pretty excited to see everyone." Zeke reveals.

Natalie, quick and clever and far too observant, cocks her head sideways in the silence the men allow for her to think.

"You know, Maddie isn't the only assistant that knows how to make travel arrangements," Natalie says defensively.

"No, but it would have ruined the surprise if I asked you to do it." Seth begins. Then explains while Natalie's mind clicks. "I need to take a trip. I want to drive, so I can take Willow. But then you'd be alone without Willow for about ten days. I feel better about my trips when I know she's here with you. So I had Madison plan a trip for you and Naya and Christian and Laura and the kids to go to Disneyland in California next week. Zeke and Maddie will meet you there. Hope that's okay."

Natalie bursts into appreciative laughter. "Are you serious?"

"Yes." Seth smiles. "Maria has school, so I had to wait until she was done for the year."

"But your fence—if you take a ten-day trip, you'll get behind." Natalie seems concerned, and not just for the appeasement of her curiosity.

Seth tilts his head. "Your math was off. I got ahead."

"Oh. That's what you get for trusting my far inferior IQ." Natalie shakes her head. Then hops down from the desk and plants a little kiss on Seth's forehead just in time for Mrs. Patterson to see it. "You're so good to me."

Zeke chuckles. "Do we need to sign off so she can thank you properly?"

"Won't be necessary. We have a lot of things to discuss since Zeke and I won't be present for the meeting next week. Mr. Billings, will you lead us in prayer, please?" Before bowing his head, Seth scowls playfully at Natalie, who takes her usual spot in the chair across the room to take notes.

He'd arranged for us to leave directly from the airport. He bought a new truck with a backseat just so that Naya could ride in it. She pets me and tells me sweet nothings all the way to the airport and Natalie giggles the whole way, excited for the trip. After we arrive at the drop-off and someone parks the Kessler minivan that had been tailing us, Laura and Christian are making a plan of action for successfully getting five children and their car seats and bags checked in and onto a plane.

Naya kisses me on the mouth as she hops down from her newly loosed car seat. "I wuv you Wiyyow! I gotta go see Mickey!"

Then she meets Seth next to the funny-smelling truck and wraps her very soul around his leg.

"I wuv you Sef, bye bye!" Then she kisses his thigh, humorous for all involved.

"Love you too, Naya. You have fun and take care of Mommy."

"Okay!" Naya is already bouncing over into the care of the Kesslers.

Natalie steps in front of Seth. "Are you sure you can't come with us?"

"My trip is important." Seth smiles.

"I wish you'd tell me where you're going, you know, so that if there's a natural disaster, I can know whether or not to worry." She is concerned about something else, I can tell.

"East," Seth replies. "But don't worry either way. I have Willow and God. Not in that order, of course."

Natalie strokes the hair she's allowed to grow for years now. I like her with long hair. "Normally, your business trips involve conference rooms and job sites and manufacturing plants. There's nothing on the master schedule, and I—"

"It's not a business trip," He confesses.

"Oh." Natalie's heart sinks. She laughs a little. "You got a woman on the East Coast?"

"No. She's headed to the West Coast." Seth tilts his head as Natalie beams a smile.

"So where—?"

"Can you trust that I'd never stay away from you if it wasn't in your best interest?" Seth asks a great deal; he knows.

"Seth, if I come back and you've bought me a house or some craziness, I will not be happy. I'm not ready to move away from you yet. I really think you do better with me around and I certainly do better with you. If this is about what happened in your office last week, I've apologized to you a hundred times. But if you want me to leave, just tell me. Don't—" Natalie's quivering speech is stopped suddenly by something peculiar. Something that if I didn't know the self-control of my master, I'd think was a quick, tender kiss on her lips as a promise. Then an embrace as deep as it is loving. And a whisper,

"I'll come pick you up in ten days and take you back home with me." Seth looks into the enchantment of Natalie's eyes for her understanding.

"Call me when you stop for the night?" Natalie requests.

"Send me pictures of Naya having a blast?" Seth requests.

Both nod. Seth nods at the Kesslers, Laura nearly as enchanted as Natalie. And we depart.

I can't say I have a memory of more peace than driving for hours on end each day with my dearest companion. He doesn't speak or listen to music. He just drives. When he gets tired, we stop and he pays whatever they ask to let me stay in a hotel room with him. I dine on kibble and morsels of whatever he is having, like always. It is hard for me to remember that there was a time when life was only the two of us and a truck. But even though the peace reminds me how we got through, I miss Natalie and all the others, aching for them. Wondering why Seth would send them one place and drive to another. They had never been a bother to him before.

Finally, following directions on Seth's phone, we come to a house with heartwarming charm and elegant landscaping and size. With one whiff of wet air, I know where we are. Jacksonville, Florida, I've been told in the past. Seth takes me to the door with him. We are greeted in happy tears by Karen and Bill Holm. Shelley even brushes me while I sleep, and Seth says things to Karen and Bill that make them cry and hug him and feed us and pretend like no years or people or wrongs had passed since we first met the extension of the family.

After a time, Seth asks, "Where is Kelli?"

Karen sighs. "She's up in Savannah. It's about two hours up the coast. She has some friends up there."

Shelley is forcing a quiet that Seth sees. She winks, which Seth understands to be a secret that will later be told. Seth then gets a picture on his phone of Natalie and Naya with funny hats with ears. Everyone coos. Karen sees Nate's eyes in Naya and misses him again.

"I'll take care of them. I know I'm not him, but I'll do the best I can." Seth promises. Odd. He is already taking care of Natalie and Naya.

"You'll do better, sweetheart." Karen says through blurry eyes. "You're *you*."

Karen insists we stay the night in the guest room, then come morning, we say goodbye and drive half a day to arrive at a house with much of the same charm as the last. But Seth says a prayer in his heart before even considering exiting his smoldering truck. I give him a whimper for it.

"I know, Willow. This one won't be near as easy." Finally, he sighs and I follow him out the open door of the truck.

He approaches the house slowly, his heart pounding. Then he rings the bell, and an overwhelmingly confused Eden Nakano answers the door.

"Seth?" She wonders against the midday light.

"Hello, Eden. Is it alright if we come in? Willow got brushed last night, she shouldn't shed too much." Seth gestures to me.

"Of course, Baby." Eden nods, and Seth's heart sets to racing again when we all join an already seated Ken Nakano in the front sitting room. But to my surprise, he stands.

"A little far from home, aren't you?" Ken wonders, smiling as he shakes Seth's hand.

"I suppose. Is this the house you moved to from Plaid Row?" Seth wonders, looking around. Probably feeling Natalie there.

Eden answers with a gesture to the front window. "Natalie used to sit and stare out that window during the pregnancy. You want to see her old room?"

"Eden!" Ken tries to scold. Eden sets her eyes aflame and leads the way around a corner in a lovely labyrinth of a ranch-style house.

Seth knows the door immediately, running fingers along the door frame. Seeing that it is in a state of awful attempted repair. The rest of the house is so well kept.

Ken explains. "I had to break that down when she was in labor. Never could fix it properly. Wood is not my forte."

"This is my fault. Let me fix it." Seth offers. The mystery of the random tools he'd thrown in the back of the truck was solved.

As Seth returns with the materials, we stand in a wide hallway with mirrors and a table with fake flowers. Natalie has always said how her mother could find ways to make every little space as beautiful as possible. Seth starts to work, easily cutting and sanding and staining what he'd broken using only hand tools. He's glad he can occupy his hands while he speaks to Natalie's parents. Not meeting their eyes, or he'd know they are smiling the whole time.

"Where is Neil? I was hoping he'd be here." Seth realizes the void.

Eden sighs, taking a seat in the chair beside Natalie's bedroom door. "Neil has a class down in Savannah on Saturdays. He's also looking for work down there."

Seth smiles as he makes a connection he doesn't quite understand. Then looks up, knowing they don't share the same déjà vu of an explanation as he. He shakes away the smile and begins talking.

"I sent Natalie and Naya to Disneyland this week, so I don't want you to be worried that she's alone. Not that she's helpless or anything. I just usually leave Willow for an extra set of ears at night when I travel. I sent Chris and Laura too. Naya would be upset if her cousins missed out." Seth starts to explain.

"Just how rich are you?" Ken chuckles.

Seth gives a familiar excuse for his lavish generosity. "Can't take it with me."

"You want to marry Natalie, don't you?" Eden receives a scolding stare from her husband for cutting to the chase accidentally. But she'd done it with a smile. Seth is somewhat relieved.

"I do." Seth smiles, clears his throat, and then explains. "Marriage would be the most honorable way I could take care of her at this point. She lives with me, and I want her to feel comfortable staying. She also takes pretty good care of *me*, and I don't want her to worry that I don't appreciate her."

"That's wise, Seth." Ken nods. "Generous of you."

But Eden's heart sinks. "And that's all there is to it. Just an arrangement? So that she's 'taken care of'?"

Seth laughs at himself. "It sounded that way, didn't it?"

"But Ken is right. It does make sense. I'm thankful that you're so willing to take her in," Eden concedes, not wanting to step on toes.

Seth smiles and sniffs away the pungent scent of the stain. "Some of my reasons to marry her are purely practical. For instance, there's a clawfoot tub in my bathroom she's been eyeing for decades. But you should know from this broken door that there's a *lot* more to it."

Eden is nearly in tears with relief. Or maybe it's the stain. I know that's my issue.

"And do you think she's ready for that kind of a relationship?" Ken plays devil's advocate. Probably having hoped for the "arrangement."

"Ken!" Eden accuses.

"He has a valid concern, Eden. Nate was my friend, and losing him was difficult for me. And he was Natalie's husband. So, I certainly don't take her need for healing lightly. But recently, she's made it abundantly clear where she stands." Seth chuckles and quotes an old friend. "A woman of great virtue—and opinion."

"You know her well." Ken laughs, then opens up like I don't know if I've seen. "I did everything in my power all those years ago—and even more recently—to keep you two apart. You know that. Why would you come to me now and ask permission? She's living in your house. She chose to grieve with you, not us. You *won*, Seth. Why would you consider our thoughts? You are a powerful man. You could have married her without our knowledge or consent, and no one would have questioned it. Even Nathan got away with that."

"It isn't a contest, sir." Seth shrugs. "Coming to you was the right thing to do. You should know from the past that even when it is extremely difficult and painful and ruins my life, that I will come to you when it is the right thing to do. But mostly, I want what Natalie wants. And according to my memory of her childhood dreams, she wants you walking her down the aisle, Ken."

"In your chapel." Ken smiles, remembering dreams of his baby girl.

"And she wanted Stacy to paint her out by your willow tree—" Eden remembers, looking to Ken.

"In a big white fluffy princess dress." Seth laughs.

"Next to *you*." Ken clears his throat. Nods. "Dreams we chose to crush when we thought a child might change them, or worse—make them come true. Perhaps the biggest regret of my life."

"Regret is pointless when you consider God's grace. I can still give her everything she wanted as soon as you say the word. *Almost* everything." Seth sighs a nervous sigh. Trying not to think of his mother and her paintings.

"Nate was meant to love Natalie for a season. A season that took great strength of character for you to allow. Nate needed Natalie to end his life a good man. But she's always been yours. And you've *always* been a good man. We see that now." Ken gives his permission in his own way. He concedes after years of refusing to see it. Eden, I think from her tears of excitement, had seen it all along.

Finally. June. The day he'd started the fence but twelve years later. It is a Thursday afternoon before the chess night that started up again recently at Natalie's request. It is part of her healing process, though she still refuses to play.

"Holy—!" Natalie's intentionally shortened, but completely shocked sentence.

"Holy what?" Seth starts, having been quietly and contently looking over details of some paperwork before signing.

"Hody what?" Naya imitates.

"The bill pay portion of your bank's website is down for maintenance, which I figured out when I tried to pay your utility bill just now, and it got rejected. I'd never actually *looked* at your personal checking account. I just use it when you ask me to." Natalie must clear her throat, still staring at the screen, to recover from shock.

"Why? I got you a debit card months ago." Seth is confused.

"Which I've used about twice at the grocery store when you forced me to. I've never had a need to log in to the account. You balance your checkbook. Not sure why you'd bother." She laughs a little.

"I like numbers, remember?" Seth reasons.

"Well, that's a *lot* of numbers to like. Suddenly the fancy hotel in Disneyland is no longer a blemish on my conscience." Natalie comments, typing something. Making herself a note to pay the bill tomorrow.

"Dineywand! Mickey!" Naya contributes a memory.

Seth chuckles. "It's not just for groceries, you know. You can use the card for whatever you want. Buy clothes, toys for Naya, change some of the decorations you've been complaining about—"

"Purchase small islands." Natalie shakes her head smiling. "I don't need your money, Seth."

"Neither do I. Use it. I'm serious. Use Nate's life insurance for Naya to go to private school or college or something. Let me take care of the rest."

"No way. I don't ever want to be accused of owing you something. People already talk, Seth." Natalie sighs. "Hey!" She suddenly lights up. "Don't you finish the fence today?"

Seth laughs. "You're more excited than I am."

Then Natalie bites her lip. "Because I figured it out finally. Took me long enough. But I guess that's the point, right?"

This afternoon, Natalie bounds to the fence like a little girl after barely getting her own to sleep. She reminds me of the day I met her and I didn't have a name yet.

"Final fence date," says Natalie. "Bittersweet."

"Well, we should probably come up with a new way to 'date' now," Seth suggests. "Maybe you could start playing chess again?"

"Maybe." Natalie comes down from her high a little, sitting behind Seth like always and starting cryptically, heavily. "This fence isn't a destination. It's a journey. You took twelve years on purpose. Like a hiatus."

"So discovered Nate a couple months before he died." Seth reveals with a nod.

"Did he know from what?" Natalie is surprised.

"Yeah." Seth nods. "He had peace about it. When did you figure out the fence?"

"In California. One night I sat there with my Bible, scared to death you were about to kick me out, even though you said you weren't. I stumbled upon the parable about the lost sheep. And the shepherd that left the ninety-nine faithful sheep to go out in search of the one who strayed. Which, if you're a faithful sheep, sucks!" Seth chuckles. Natalie continues. "Because here you are, being faithful, doing what you're supposed to do. And suddenly, your shepherd leaves. I would imagine that for a sheep, life would be difficult—scary at times. But God knows that even if He has to rearrange the entire lives of the faithful and test them to their absolute limit of patience and trust in Him, that they will rejoice with

Him when He returns with that one lost sheep. That sheep would have died in his wandering, all alone, if not for whatever it took for God to go after him. Even if it was the discomfort of the faithful." Natalie's eyes are tearing up. Seth listens with all his heart, though his back is turned.

"I had so many choices along the way. But I see now that it already was. That God needed me to make sure Nate got home safely. And I loved him. *God,* I loved him. But I was always yours, heart and soul. I never stopped loving you and didn't know why until I realized the fence was your way of staying patiently connected to me while we waited for God to bring Nate home. It was your way of remembering that God kept us all together while Nate was lost. Patience. The fence is patience. And proof that God is sovereign. Because you started it twelve years ago before you even met that lost sheep. Your faith is so powerful, Seth. But it's inside such a quiet, humble package, no one would ever know it." Natalie is sniffing at tears, admiring Seth completely.

"*You* know it," Seth says plainly. Stretches out barbed wire. Staples. Smiles a little when he cuts the end.

Natalie watches him work. Staple his very last pickets. Looking down into the woods, back up to the other side of the house at God's great work over his past twelve years. He laughs once. Unable to believe the timing. The sovereignty of God. Then Natalie looks confused when she sees that Seth is standing not against a completed fence, but in a four-foot gap before the fence is joined with the first post Seth set a dozen years ago to mark the end.

"Oh. I thought you'd be done today. You still have one section left." She laughs a little. Feeling silly.

"I'm finished," Seth assures her.

"Seth, there's a huge gap there. It's like, blaringly not done." Natalie points to the void in the fence. The chasm separating twelve years of work from the satisfaction of completion.

"It isn't done," Seth says. "But *I* am finished."

"What does that mean?" Natalie asks. "Won't the sheep get out?"

"I don't know. I started not done, and I'm finishing, not done just like everyone. We don't always get to see the end of our own work." Seth shrugs. Nods. "God is still faithful to complete it."

Natalie falls silent, never hoping to fully understand Seth. But appreciating him regardless.

"I have another date idea for us," Seth says, satisfied. Or maybe not.

"And what's that? You want to start painting the fence from the beginning?" She teases.

"Painted wood is an abomination." Seth laughs at his well-known opinion.

"So what's your idea?" Natalie seems wary, but smiles when I place my head on her lap.

"You should move downstairs into my room with me. To give you easy access to the clothes you wear and the bathtub you like, my mom's best wines—and to *me*." Seth seeks a rise. And a rise he gets.

"Seth! Handsome as you are, and as long as it's been, I don't think sin is a good date ever. I'm sorry if kissing you made you think otherwise, but I'm a righteous woman now. Teen pregnancy pretty much forces that on a God-fearing girl." Natalie begins to rant. "I have to raise Naya right, Seth. It's bad enough she tells people at church that we live with you."

Seth's peace stops her fretting. "I'll take care of you the rest of your life whether or not you marry me." Seth smiles at Natalie's stunned face. Sits in front of her and takes a little velvet pouch from his pocket. He places it in her hands, then puts his worn and weathered hands around hers.

"That was a proposal?" Natalie clarifies. Concealing fifty or so contradicting emotions behind her slight smile.

"Yes." Seth sighs. Removing his hands from around hers.

"Well, why aren't you on one knee?" Natalie demands.

"I don't want you to feel pressured to give me an answer right away. There is a lot to consider. So I want you to consider it all before you decide." Natalie smiles the understanding.

"What's in here?" She touches the pouch but doesn't open it yet.

"When we were kids, you always used to say how much you loved my mom's engagement ring. She loved you. I bet she'd be honored for you to wear it now that she's gone. If that's what you decide." Seth looks to the ground and misses Natalie's smitten smile. But she doesn't answer or open the pouch at all. Seth clears his throat.

"My dad once told me that marriage is like a fence." Seth smiles. "A fence keeps—"

"Good things in and bad things out." Natalie smiles, remembering what he told her twelve years ago. Then gasps. "You originally brought me out here to show me how you deal with the whole singleness thing."

"Natalie, everything can be dealt with when you know God has a plan."

"I'll have to talk to my parents. And probably Bill and Karen, too. So I do need a little time, is that okay?" Natalie smiles with a glistening eye, returning to that question in loom.

Seth half smiles into Natalie's eyes.

"You didn't!" She lights up completely. "*East.* That's where you went! Did you ask my dad's permission?"

"Of course, I did. But please take your time deciding." Seth is truthful. Pained. But as always, he wants what Natalie wants. "The choice has always been yours."

"Okay," Natalie whispers, in tears. Before Seth stands, he leans forward and kisses Natalie on the forehead, which I think travels for miles through her bloodstream before fizzling out. Seth smiles, taking his fence supplies to the shed forever.

I stay with Natalie a moment after Seth walks away. And I watch her open that pouch. It contains a ring I remember used to be on Mom's hand. Natalie falls madly in love with it immediately but dares not turn so Seth can see. Then she feels that there is something else in the pouch. Something bigger. She shakes it into her hand. Tears stream when she sees it is that chess queen with the holes.

She had always been the fastest remedy for his fits. She had always encouraged him. And she'd always been the only person alive who understood him. Seth's mind is for perfection. But he'd always kept that queen. Incomplete and imperfect. In the open all these years. To remind him why he built the fence.

Pizza. That is the chosen meal for chess night. Natalie says it is difficult to pair with wine, so she doesn't drink wine anymore. But tonight, Natalie is absent during dinner. And afterward, Christian has Maria on his lap, teaching her to play chess. Seth patiently lets her choose her moves and goes easy on her. Only checkmating her after she's learned enough from each of the five games they play.

"A little woman," Seth says after Maria hops down to go start a movie for all her siblings and her cousin. He is resetting the pieces for his game with Christian.

Christian chuckles, kissing the hand of his nearby wife. "What's with the new chess set? I thought your other one was 'perfect.'"

"Not anymore." Seth smiles in severe nervousness.

Halfway through the men's match, Natalie finally appears in the doorway of the game room, eating a slice of pizza.

"Hey, Natalie! Where you been?" Laura lights up.

"Just needed an extended quiet time today. Lost track of time, sorry."

"No apology needed." Laura agrees.

"Checkmate." Seth smiles as Christian grumbles. He catches Natalie's eyes before she retreats back across to the kitchen for a drink. She returns with a bottle of water after Seth and Laura begin their game.

"I play winner." Natalie declares to the shock of all.

"You haven't played in years." Seth reminds her with a snicker.

"Technically, I've *never* played, according to you, Seth." Natalie goes as far as to wink at him.

Laura, far more interested in whatever that wink meant, tilts her king onto his side, forfeiting the match.

"I was two moves away. Don't give up next time." Seth shakes his head, resetting the pieces. He stirs a little as Natalie sits down.

Natalie breathes deeply and examines the board. Looks up at Seth and examines him. Then makes her first move cautiously. Seth takes his move with ease. Natalie clears her throat, then looks to Laura and Christian.

"Remember the night Seth ripped us all apart and told us how he uses us against ourselves to beat us at this game?" Natalie remembers.

"When he accused you of losing of purpose?" Christian knows no one has ever forgotten that night.

"And told Nate he was going to die?" Laura had taken even more from the night.

"I suppose he did." Natalie smiles. Then looks with cruel but smiling eyes at her opponent. "But something you'd never notice about Seth is that even if it just seems like he puts up with people, and he has a condition that sometimes separates him from others, he actually *lives* for other people. The biggest to the smallest of us. He loves all of us. He needs us, more than you'd ever guess. Even if he's just an observer, he loves watching us love each other, and fight and feel joy and pain, just as much as if he was experiencing it himself." Natalie tells the secret against Seth's squinted eyebrows. "It shows in his chess playing, but you guys can't read him the way he reads us. See, he uses all of his pieces like power pieces. They *all* matter. He's a chess expert; we all kind of are after enough years with him. But even on a bad day, none of you will ever beat him. He knows you too well and loves you too much."

"We love Seth, too!" Laura defends.

"Not like he loves you," Natalie reveals. "See, with most of you, when Seth plays chess with you, it's like a really deep conversation. But if you ever got close enough, you'd realize you've never loved anyone the way Seth loves everyone. And he was right about me. I'm the only person who has ever been that close to him."

"So, you really did lose on purpose? Can you beat him, Natalie? Why would you lose on purpose? You're pretty competitive." Laura asks in pure wonder.

"She doesn't want to win." Seth shrugs.

"I would have loved to win and have that title for everyone to see." Natalie smiles. "But it would have required a near intimate level of getting into your head to accomplish. When we were kids, that scared me because your intelligence was intimidating for me. I know I could have seen the limit of it if I beat you. So back then, I let you win out of respect. I guess I liked the mystery."

"No way. You've been letting him win that long?" Christian marvels.

"Yeah, then we started dating our whole relationship was different. We even played the game differently. So, I'd have had to use some pretty manipulative tactics to get you to lose if I still wanted to respect your mysterious intellect. I didn't think that was right." Natalie sniffles, concentrating fully on her next move.

"It would have worked." Seth shrugs.

"Again. It wasn't about winning. Then I moved away. And I came back, and you had grown so much that I basically had to relearn how to play chess with you. You'd gotten ten times better, and I hadn't played in years. Eventually, I got back into the swing of things. But by that time, I was with Nate. At which time, the only tactics that would have worked would have also been adultery." Natalie winces. She watches Seth complete a move, then takes her next one with ease, commenting on it. "But now I know you all over again, and I totally saw that one coming, even though we haven't played in years. You cannot have my bishop, Mr. Gowan. How presumptuous!"

Laura gasps. Seth chuckles. Christian moves on.

"What's your excuse today?"

"As I was saying, Seth loves people in a way that is the closest thing I've seen to Christlike here on Earth. If I play too hard and still lose, it'll make everyone aware of the fact that my heart is extremely inferior to his. Selfish, even."

"Inferior?" Seth shakes his head at his next move. "That's ridiculous, Natalie. Just play me. See? You just lost that pawn on purpose! Move your rook. You know he's next if you don't."

"Why would you think you're selfish?" Laura accuses, beginning to cry. "You were married to my brother before he knew Christ. We used to talk about how amazing you were. Any judge would have spent five minutes in a room with you two and *begged* you to get a divorce. But you didn't give up on him. Seth said you cussed out all the paramedics the night he died until you were absolutely sure. God is never going to forget the way you loved him, Natalie. There's nothing selfish about you."

"Which is why you've been letting me win for twenty years, even though you're competitive. But now that we know will you at least play?" Seth concludes lovingly.

"As long as you don't just let me win." Natalie insists.

"I don't even know how to do that." Seth laughs.

"So honest, my Seth." Natalie coos. Christian and Laura are a little intrigued at her terminology. *My* Seth.

Christian pleads. "Play dirty, Natalie. Do what you gotta do. I *have* to see him lose."

Natalie winces. Seth smiles an invitation. Natalie obliges. "Seth, I was just trying to work through some logistics. With our conversation at the fence earlier?"

"Okay?" Seth chuckles a little, not having lost focus.

Natalie continues. "Could you have an intercom installed in the security system? Naya would be pretty far from me at night, and I'd want to be able to talk back to her if she gets scared or something."

"I'll have my assistant make a call tomorrow. She has full access to my accounts. Make sure it's state of the art." Seth demands.

"At night?" Laura wonders, suddenly realizing she's in the dark.

"Do you want other children?" Natalie asks. Christian and Laura snicker into awkward laughter, nearly covering the next word. "Check."

"Do we have to decide that now?" I can smell Seth's adrenaline. And other smells I haven't smelled since he was a teenager. He's now struggling to keep up with Natalie in chess. This would be distressing if he wasn't perfectly aware of what she is doing.

"I suppose not." Natalie sighs. Putting Seth in check again. "I want all the kids involved, including Kevin and little Nathan. So obviously, I want Zeke and Maddie here. My parents. And Bill and Karen if that's not weird. Obviously, Vargas needs to officiate. So, we need to make travel arrangements soon. I want to do this before the end of the summer so that I can get into that clawfoot tub before the evenings get too cold."

Seth chuckles as he looks wide-eyed at the board when he makes a move. "You still haven't told me your decision."

Natalie puts a graceful finger on a rustic queen, and smirks triumphantly as she moves it. "Checkmate."

"Is that a yes?" Seth asks.

"I've been wearing this the whole time." Natalie upturns her hand, showing Seth the ring. Laura and Christian are amused to the point of hysterical laughter and sending texts to all parts of the country.

Seth, always even-keeled and calm, now releases an almost childlike breathlessness of laughter at his failure to notice the ring, and the joy of her decision.

"I haven't heard you laugh like that in years." Natalie joins in, warmed to her spirit by the laughter.

"Do you like it? The ring? You don't have to wear that one. I can afford any ring in the universe." Seth unintentionally boasts as Natalie clasps her hand with his as if she'd never been a dozen years removed from doing so.

"Which is exactly why I want this one." Natalie bats her eyes.

"Thanks for finally playing me. We should do this more often." Seth sighs.

"It's a date." Natalie giggles, answering the question completely.

And when he merely kisses her hand across a table of little wooden figures, both of their eyes overflow. Because they are pouring years of separation and fence building. Family building. Pain, love, hate. All into that kiss with sobs of relief. Like this always already was.

Chapter Forty

Church Family

"Ah!" Laura screams. "My sissies!"

Three blonde women embrace in the foyer, touching faces, sharing travel stories, and causing Christian to nearly become sick with the girliness he'd left work early to pick up from the local airport. Natalie enters and joins the embrace.

"Thank you, girls, for coming a few days early to help me out. Laura's been great, but with all these kiddos running around, we could use a few extra hands." She, too, is examining each of them for wellness like a mother. Still very much like their big sister, with no hope for a mere loss of the common relative or marriage to another to change it.

"I heard Naya got you in trouble last night!" Shelley tattles. "When she told Seth you bought some simple green dress to marry him in."

"Yes." Natalie admits. "He wants me to be a princess for a day, so now I have four days to find a dress in the right size that doesn't cost too much. And that has a separate skirt so I can change into my jeans when I get tired of being a princess."

"That's a lot of parameters. But it's a good thing you're shaped like the women that model the dresses." Kelli says, absentmindedly looking about the room.

Natalie notices and teases. "Who you looking for?"

"No one." Kelli reddens. "Where's Seth?"

Natalie tosses her hair back in all her poise and smiles. "He's headed back from Denver with my brother. I just got off the phone with Neil, and he said they were ten minutes out."

Kelli accidentally smiles. Christian returns to the house with luggage, having exited to escape the abundant estrogen.

"Kelli, how long did you think a sweet little daddy's girl and a mama's boy could keep a secret like that?" He lounges in a chair in the front room.

Kelli sighs, cradles herself with nervous arms. "How long have you known?"

Natalie giggles. "Kelli, my mom has been having coffee with yours every other week in Savannah since Nate passed. It's a good halfway point between their houses. You and Neil were busted after two months of doing the same thing. You only *thought* it took them six months to figure it out. You've been dating what, a year now?"

"Mom and Dad promised not to tell you guys." Kelli panics. "We knew you'd think it was weird, just like they did. And it wasn't our intention. We were just touching base and talking. Then after we started meeting and took a class together, we just sort of—"

"Fell in love?" Natalie tilts her head. "Same thing happened to me recently. It's not weird. The only thing that would make it mildly weird is that your siblings were married. But Nate is gone and I'm marrying Seth. It's not weird at all, Kelli. When Seth told me a couple months ago, I was pretty excited."

"Good." Kelli is near tears with relief. "So, um, wedding dress. We modeled them last spring, so we can probably help. Do you have a designer in mind?"

"No! I had a *dress* until last night. We'll just have to go shopping as soon as Seth gives me a budget. He's being really stubborn about it." Natalie rolls her eyes, and Seth sneaks in the front door and whispers in her ear.

"*Subete*. That's your budget. You ladies need to find her a proper gown."

"'All' is not a budget, Seth!" Natalie argues as Seth hugs the women after setting down some luggage.

"All I have is yours. Go shopping. I'll look after Naya." Seth kisses Natalie's cheek as Neil walks in the front door and has to avert his eyes immediately when he sees Kelli, not knowing they all know.

"Hey, Neil." Kelli bites her lip in some type of anticipation, thereby capturing the undivided attention of the handsome young man.

"Hey, beautiful," He manages with eerie eloquence. And all attention spans are cut short and redirected to the exchange. "How was the flight?"

“Good,” she says, shrugging nervously. Then whispers, “They know.”

Neil sighs heavily, dropping the bags he’s holding, and advances toward the giggling Kelli. He lifts her off the ground with strength and kisses, muffling his voice in her shoulder. “I missed you.”

But when the two young loves have completed their greeting, there is a heaviness present that everyone can feel. Neil and Kelli seem to be deciding something between them. But how could there be another secret?

“We promised to tell them the minute we were all together, you can’t back out on me.” Neil finally says aloud.

“Oh no.” Natalie assumes the worst, looking to Kelli. “You’re knocked up.”

“No!” Kelli turns red. “We don’t—”

“*Gees*, Ane! You see a ring on her finger? I’m not that dumb.” Neil defends. Then remembers. “No offense to anyone that may have been at some point.”

Natalie and Laura sigh in relief, hands on their pounding hearts.

“Then what’s wrong, guys?” Christian wonders, leading everyone to take a seat.

Neil and Kelli, a perfect couple under somewhat odd circumstances, sit together holding hands. Then Neil sighs and starts.

“So, Kelli and I are really serious. And we’ve even been talking to our parents about maybe—” Neil sighs.

Laura gasps. “Getting *married*?!”

Kelli smiles coyly. Neil clears his throat. “Yeah. And when we told my dad a couple months ago, he seemed pretty supportive. I think you must have primed him for us, Seth. And I’m still sorry I missed you. I was down in Savannah with Kelli.”

“What about Bill and Karen?” Natalie wonders.

“They were excited!” Shelley exclaims, then rolls her eyes. “You know Mom and Eden love sharing kids and grandkids.”

“Yeah.” Neil nods. “And the four of them came to a wise suggestion that we find a church in Savannah, since that’s where we’ll likely live later on. They said we should worship together.”

Kelli smiles. “So now instead of meeting on Saturdays, we started going to church together on Sundays. Neil’s parents had this network of churches they’d used once before and helped us find this amazing little church with wonderful people. I don't know if our parents were trying to deter us from getting married, but our church family made *us* want to be a family. We hope to get married there at some point."

A conclusion, one might think. But there is still noticeable tension; the young couple avoiding the eyes of Seth and Natalie.

"That's great, guys. I don't understand." Natalie shifts in her seat.

"The church. They uh—" Neil breathes slow. "They assigned us a mentor couple for premarital counseling, to make sure it's what we want to do. I think they are biased, though, because they got married young and she's a midwife and he's a pediatrician. They are already waiting for us to pop out some kids, I think. We're really close to them, you know? It just seemed like God drew us to them. Then it all made sense when we met their son."

Kelli piggy backs. "He and Neil get along so well. We thought it was so funny that they had the same hair. Neil noticed right away the resemblance. Ron and Nancy's son is adopted. His name is Cameron. Carrington is their last name. And he looks almost exactly like you, Seth."

Natalie stands and begins pacing. Hyperventilating almost, and definitely fighting the feeling. Trying to retain control. Then she glares at Seth. "Did you know?"

"No," he says with determination, standing with her, trying to meet her eyes. "Natalie, I promise you. I had no idea. The pictures don't come with a return address, so I always assumed they were in South Carolina."

Natalie nods, losing her inner battle over the one thing her heart cannot cover with control. "I just—I can't—I'll be—" Then she escapes into Seth's office. Seth sighs and rubs hands on pants for a moment.

"You're sure?" Seth asks Neil.

"Positive, Seth." Neil sighs. "They haven't told Cameron, but Ron and Nancy confirmed everything. They figured it out before we did because of my last name."

"Cameron. What are the odds?" Christian has caught on.

"Is Natalie going to be okay? Are *you* going to be okay?" Laura's servant's heart.

"Just um…" Seth tries to keep his head. "Be ready to take her shopping when she comes out. I think if she's focused, she might be okay. Willow, stay. Excuse me." Then he clears the tears from his throat as he leaves for his office.

"Stuff like this doesn't just happen." Laura reminds them all. "I know if I gave up a child, I'd spend every day wondering what he was like, even if I knew I couldn't have him back. How is Cameron?"

Neil laughs. "Kid's spoiled rotten. Great parents."

"He really loves the Lord. Plays piano beautifully. He's handsome, charming." Kelli says.

"Stubborn pain in the butt, which drives Nancy and Ron crazy, because he didn't get it from them." Neil chuckles and everyone smiles, knowing Natalie. "But he's a great kid."

Seth and Natalie return. Natalie sniffling a little, but the two are focused elsewhere. Seth gives instructions. "Big, white, fluffy, princess. Like you always wanted."

"I'm a widow. White is totally dishonest," Natalie whines.

"It was dishonest at your *first* wedding." Seth's eyes flicker once like the spark of a match. Everyone enjoys this.

As the women depart, chatting and planning, the men simply breathe once in their absence. Then Seth hands Neil an envelope of pictures. Neil looks through them, chuckling.

"That's Cameron. Small world, eh?"

"Big God." Seth's wisdom.

"You two okay?" Christian wonders.

"We'll be fine." Seth nods. "You'll look after him, Neil?"

"I know an instruction from God when I hear it, Seth. We have it covered." Neil hands him back the envelope and reaches for the backpack he'd brought in not too long ago. "And I figure it'll make a lot of things easier once I can move into the apartment I leased with money from the job I took in Savannah. Closer to Cameron. More time with Kelli once she lives there."

Both Christian and Seth become silently defensive over a little sister they sort of share, about to interrogate a sort of brother.

Then Neil smiles, glances out the door one more time, and pulls out a treasure in a velvet box to show the men.

"I knew it! The families will be in town and everything. Genius, Man." Christian alights.

"When are you asking her?"
Neil winks.

Chapter Forty-One

Constant

Natalie descends the stairs with a sigh after tucking in a tuckered out little girl. A day of attention and dancing and joy in a princess gown will cause such fatigue. Natalie and Naya are therefore in the same boat.

Vargas had been happy for the contrast to joy from the solemnity of his last visit. Zeke had been appalled at hearing of Seth's defeat at chess, demanding to witness a rematch in the coming days. Laura had played on an expensive, rare, antique piano, since Seth had needed to buy one for the chapel, unable to move the other again. A gift for Natalie.

Moments ago, Seth had slipped out of the game room where Vargas and Shelley sit with Neil, Kelli, a recently placed engagement ring, and a fast-paced game of cards. The four are still wired from helping tirelessly with the wedding for a few days straight, and gathering from previous nights, will be at the card game for hours still. The twins are staying in the guest house, and the boys upstairs. Natalie looks around, then inquires.

"Where did my husband run off to?" Natalie smiles at the ability to ask.

"Said he'd be back in a minute." Vargas growls at something about the card game and Shelley cackles.

"Is Naya asleep?" Kelli wonders.

"Yeah." Natalie sighs, sitting down in jeans and a strapless, shimmering top she'd worn to marry Seth twelve hours ago when the house was bustling with people.

"She'll be fine, Nat." Shelley is the only Holm, or person at all, to retain the nickname.

"Me and Neil got the kid if she wakes up. You two do the married thing," Vargas reiterates with an exaggerated wince.

"'Married thing'?" Neil is amused by the terminology.

"You'll figure it out pretty soon, Neil." Shelley winks at Neil and nudges her sister.

Natalie is still distracted. "Promise if she's really upset that you'll let me know, *Otouto*. I don't want her thinking I've abandoned her now that I married Seth. We aren't even taking a honeymoon I was so concerned about it." Natalie frets over her baby. Something human parents do even when their children outgrow them. But since Naya is three, Natalie has special rights to worry, I guess.

"*Ane*! Seth would never allow Naya to think she'd been replaced. He loves that kid like his own. And she's my niece, I'll take care of her." Neil promises.

Then we hear familiar leather boots attached to a familiar bearer of handsome warmth. Seth leans in the doorway with his jeans and plaid—what everyone had insisted he wear under the suit jacket to marry Natalie. It fits him, just like Natalie fits him. The way she smiles when she sees him in the doorway is something all eyes turn to meet. Seth immediately stirs at the attention on him.

"Everything okay?" He inquires gently. Natalie's smile deepens, and Neil shakes his head. Vargas speaks for the current thought of all in the next moment.

"Do people ever ask if you're the handyman when you answer the door to your mansion?" Everyone snorts laughter at Seth's humble:

"Well, I *am* the handyman." Proving their point.

Natalie groans. "Oh my gosh! I just realized that I can't tell people I'm your 'assistant' anymore. I mean, I still am, but now I can't say it." Seth tilts his head and feeds his eyes on Natalie's class and beauty.

"I think 'lady of the house' suits you much better."

"Talk about a promotion." Shelley remarks under her breath. Her twin reacts in giggles.

Then they all bite their tongues when Seth walks over to the seated Natalie and puts his hand out for her to take.

"I have something for you." He speaks gently, softly. Natalie's heart flutters, her nerves calming a bit.

"What is it?" Natalie asks, rising with the hand she takes.

"Probably another antique piano," Shelley jokes.

"Or a private jet." Vargas suggests in the dull laughter.

I follow the recent bride and groom to discover Seth's request. When Natalie arrives in the kitchen, Seth hands her a long skinny gift bag with a smile.

"What's this?" She wonders timidly.

"Just a little wedding present." Seth explains as she takes it.

"Someday, you need to stop spoiling me." Natalie flirts.

"Why?" Seth snickers. A valid point.

Natalie is confused by the gift, but opens the bag, pulling out a bottle of wine she begins to examine immediately. It has a note attached, but not from Seth. When Natalie reads the note I'd been read many years ago, she begins to cry. The wine had been intended for a private twentieth anniversary celebration that had instead been enjoyed in Heaven. The note is from Seth's dad to his mom. The wine now twelve years older than it was. Seth explains quietly in the dim kitchen.

"I found that in their room collecting dust when I moved in two years after they died. It was bottled the year they got married, and he bought it the summer we—"

"Screwed up royally?" Natalie smiles.

"Yeah." Seth smiles as well. "I thought it was only appropriate that we share this the night we set things right."

"Seth, this wine is thirty-two years old. It looks like it was expensive to begin with. I bet this would be worth something if you kept it even longer." The foodie in Natalie reawakens as she carefully paws the bottle, wanting nothing more than to taste it.

"It's worth something *tonight*," Seth whispers, enough to make Natalie nervous.

She covers the nerves by turning and reaching into the cabinet for Seth's fine stemware.

He puts a gentle hand on her arm. A rumble in her ear. "We have wine glasses in our room."

Natalie smiles. Comments on Seth's angle as she turns to him. "Oh, you're *good*."

Seth snickers. Then steps forward and claims her lips with his, leaving all angles and pretenses behind. Giving her the honesty she cherishes in him. And calling out of her a level of careless intoxication of spirit that not even wine need aid. A part of her that only Seth has ever had. She's always been the free spirit, stubbornly in control of her fickleness. But when Seth finishes these few kisses, he's brought her to a place that not even her incessant argument or bull's head can enter. A place where a man deemed lesser than others gains more control than anyone taller or physically stronger or blonder for that matter. Natalie loved him when he was just a child by many standards. But now he is a man by any rite. Seth worries a little when he sees in her eyes how much more than all of her he receives twelve years later. Because tears are flowing.

"Did I do something wrong?" He wonders, though he's obviously found no flaw in Natalie.

She laughs a little. Sniffles. Whispers. "You're funny."

"So then—" Seth wonders sweetly, but Natalie interrupts.

"I know it's not true, but now that we're married, it feels like I had a long-term, public affair when I chose not to be with you." Natalie admits a multitude of guilt and confusion in only a few words.

"So, you regret *Nate*?" Seth seems hurt.

"No." Natalie answers quickly. "I just suddenly realize how much I missed you."

Seth pulls his new wife against him with some kind of hunger and a snicker. "So why are we in the *kitchen*?"

Natalie giggles agreement. Then Seth takes an old bottle of wine in one hand, and his new wife's hand in the other. "Stay, Willow."

They depart into their hallway, and I return to the others with a little whine as I plop beneath the card table, when it hits me that I'm no longer the lady of the house. They all laugh.

"I'm sure Seth will let you in a little later, Willow." Shelley reassures.

They all laugh. I think they know I'm happier tonight than for twelve years. Happy that Seth is finally happy for him. Not that the happiness he shares for others isn't good enough. Maybe it's just that I like Natalie and the way his happiness works best when her happiness is wrapped in his.

"All I know is…" Then Vargas smiles as he recites his familiar mantra. "Vow of chastity."

At six in the morning, I curl beneath Seth's feet to the gentle crunching and the turn of Bible pages. Cereal at six, even after an exhausting few days. Derek Vargas enters the kitchen stretching limbs to prepare for a run. He laughs at the anomaly.

"Six a.m. cereal, eh?" The fond memories return.

"Yep." Seth smiles. "I do well with a constant."

Seth finishes his Psalm of the day and looks up at Vargas.

"That's a pretty stubborn constant." Vargas chuckles.

"The true definition of a constant." Seth smiles.

"I guess that makes sense. I know you read a psalm usually, right? I bet that got you through all those rough patches you've been through. Wait, have you had a *not* rough patch in the past twelve years?" Vargas realizes the constant plight of Seth.

"Not really," Seth admits with a laugh.

"So that makes sense. The constant of God through the hard stuff. Six a.m. cereal." Vargas lowers his voice. "But didn't you leave a beautiful woman in your room to come out here? I'm sure God would understand."

"I think this might be the best bowl of cereal I've ever had. Tastes different." Seth lifts his spoon and examines it like some wonder of the universe, smiling at a level of peacefulness even he has only attained today.

"You *too*?!" Vargas throws his hands in the air. "I'm all out of friends that understand my position."

Seth recites, not actually needing his Bible for most of the Psalms anymore. "'Every day I will bless You, And I will praise Your name forever and ever. Great is the Lord and greatly to be praised; And His greatness is unsearchable.' I understand your position. Even though I'm married, we still have the same constant, Vargas."

Vargas shakes his head, abandoning the notion of ever changing or challenging Seth. "Go back to bed, you raging fool!"

Seth chuckles as he puts his bowl in the dishwasher and then gives his friend a fist bump before Derek Vargas sets off on a morning run all alone. Seth is nearly startled as he begins to cross the family room.

"Sef?" A sweet little voice on the verge of tears.

"Hey, Naya. You're up a little early." Seth soothes as he drops to her level.

"I can't find my mommy."

Seth smiles deeply before he says the next words. "Well, Mommy is sleeping in my room now, remember?"

"In your room?" The sleepy little girl repeats.

"Yeah. I'll show you." Seth lifts the girl and her bunny and carries her into a true master suite.

I follow them into what upon first glance is a sitting room with a mini bar. But Seth's cautious feet gently plod to the French doors that lead to his bedroom. I've always thought it eerie that one man should occupy such a room—such a house—all alone. But today when the massive bed inside the massive room sighs and swishes gently beneath the covers, I realize that it had only been eerie because she had never been here to stay.

Seth sets the child on the edge of the bed, then surrenders the robe over his t-shirt and plaid pants to a nearby hook. I watch as every part of him sighs and emotes silently when the weary voice speaks just one word to his back.

"Hey." Natalie, with mussed hair and morning breath. Something more beautiful to Seth than the way she looked yesterday, dolled up in white wedding glory.

"Hey." He turns to see that Naya is finding her way beneath the covers with her mother. "Looks like we have a stowaway."

"I stow-way." Naya imitates.

Seth and Natalie coo as Seth climbs back under the covers, mirroring Natalie's lean on one elbow. I use the stairs Seth has built for the comfort of my hips to find a spot against his legs. The two adults find one another with their arms under the covers but atop the child between them.

Then Naya smiles brightly when she realizes what is happening. She speaks, tapping noses as she goes.

"Sef and Mommy and Wiyyow and Naya and Bunny." Over and over. Memorizing the family that swells her heart until she wearies with a yawn. "I seepy."

"Mmm, I agree with her." Natalie says, but instead of immediately settling back in, she first helps herself to a tender morning kiss that makes Seth's heart race and his breath to sigh. I wonder if he thinks he's dreaming the same dream he's likely had now for a dozen years.

Natalie worries at Seth's silence. "I hope this is okay. She won't do this all the time."

"Natalie." Seth laughs and shakes his head as he glances at the three females he shelters atop barely half his bed. "This is *perfect.*"

"Shhh!" Naya demands. "I seepy."

Seth chuckles at his giggling wife and daughter in an ecstasy only a dozen years would recognize.

"What if we expand and then business slows down? I don't want to lay anyone off. I've actually never done that, neither did my dad. Most of our guys have families." Seth and Zeke sit in the breakfast nook, hiding from their wives for an impromptu conference.

"As it stands, a lot of them are working overtime to cover the workload. Think about that. Excessive overtime gained me a hot assistant, but not before a lot of grief for not being there for my f*amily*." Zeke reasons. "We need to open another plant."

"I'll think about it." He groans.

Natalie enters the kitchen with a gasp.

"You said we were off today, Mr. Gowan! I will not have you talking shop in my kitchen. That counts as work!" She accuses, loving being his wife, even if it's brand-new.

"Off. See?" Seth stands, opening his arms for his wife. "And I'll pretend I didn't see you having an extensive conversation with Mrs. Patterson at the wedding yesterday."

"That had very little to do with work, trust me. But since we are both in violation of our time off, I might as well mention that it would be ludicrous not to build another plant. It would create jobs, reduce overtime premiums and relieve the workload. No one loses." Natalie melds into his embrace, giving him a swaying kiss as she runs her fingers endearingly along his shirt buttons.

Seth smiles the way he smiles when he's been divinely notified of a certain direction. His business partner and old friend recognizes the look and laughs.

"So, all I had to do was snuggle up and kiss on you a little? Natalie, while you're at it, I have a few more things I've been thinking of a way to mention." Zeke jokes.

"No, I'm off today, and so is my assistant." Seth kisses her once more after the gentle admonishment.

"Good!" Shelley pokes her head in the kitchen door, Vargas at her side, both with smiles of anticipation. "Because we were promised a chess rematch from the newlyweds."

"My money's on you, Seth. But not everyone has as much faith as me." Vargas looks to Shelley with disdain.

"Don't let me down, Nat," Shelley encourages.

Natalie captures her husband's eyes. "Shall we?"

Chapter Forty-Two

A Mother Knows

Summer lingers. So, the best place for a girl of my age is the stone tile floor that supports my worst hip. I listen to the flip of thin, shiny pages with the intermittent giggles of my second favorite person and the lap of water whenever she moves in the clawfoot tub. I look up to see she is biting her lip with some kind of affection, even alone in the bathroom with me. It's something Seth enjoys when he enters and quietly takes a seat in a chair after swiping a towel from the chair's twin by the tub.

He puts up a finger to his lips at me to remain quiet, though I hadn't intended to move or make a sound. Natalie is focused on her magazine, curled up in the tub that contrasts her chocolate skin exquisitely enough for Seth to give away his presence with a beholden sigh.

"Hey, you." Natalie smiles contently when she sees him. He's far too calm a presence for her to have startled.

"What are you reading?"

"Some magazine that came in the mail. It's about Christian businesses and money and stuff. Most of it is boring except the article about some multi-million dollar construction company turned manufacturing giant. The CEO is quite dashing. Have you read it?" Natalie giggles again, biting her lip.

"Not yet." Seth now knows exactly what she's reading.

"Well, most of it is about how you overcame Asperger's, took over your dad's company at sixteen and other reasons you're completely remarkable. He mentioned how you gave his whole crew a chess set and wouldn't even talk to them until you creamed them all at chess. Millionaire without a college degree, blah, blah, blah. All the employees have your cell phone number, even though you work from home. They must have interviewed Zeke, because it mentions how you run the company how God might, and then you said God *does* run the company. There's a part about Willow and about how you married your secretary last year and you're raising her daughter. But the end is my favorite, I think." Natalie sits back and smiles, wetting the page a bit with pruned fingers and clearing her throat.

"'In speaking with this humble, generous millionaire, I am directed to wise words from the book of Micah: "He has shown you, O man, what is good; And what does the Lord require of you But to do justly, To love mercy, And to walk humbly with your God?" Well done, Seth Gowan. It was a blessing to meet you.' Rich *and* famous. I'm keeping you!" Natalie giggles and lowers the magazine to my level to show me the picture. Seth is leaning against the desk in his office, arm around Natalie who is holding Naya, looking down at me as I look up at Seth.

"People will only be looking at you," Seth suggests with sincerity as always.

"I don't know, Willow was looking pretty cute that day, too." Natalie chuckles and sets the magazine aside then searches for the towel she'd put on the chair next to the tub. "Did you see a towel here?"

"Did it look like this one?" Seth unfolds the towel across the room.

Natalie giggles. "How did I not notice that? Must be getting old. Can you bring it over here, though? I'm freezing."

"The water was warm two hours ago." Seth's joke reminds Natalie only of the doting nature of her husband. She's beyond spoiled in every way, and reciprocates with the ease that is submitting to and serving Seth. The perfect marriage, I'd say, despite occasional conflict. An appreciation and righteousness born of the years they spent apart yet so close in proximity. Seth stands and helps his wife from the tub, pretending not to watch her wrap her towel around herself. He clears his throat.

"I went over the first proposed budget. I only needed to make a few changes, so I think we're done for the day. I didn't mean to disturb your bath. I just came to ask if you wanted to take a walk with me while Naya sleeps."

"Like old times?" Natalie is amused, quickening their pulses with a few crafty kisses. "I'm not dressed for a walk."

"Don't tempt me." Seth smiles. "We may have a visitor coming within the next hour."

"Oh." Natalie winces. "Who's coming by? Christian?"

"Don't know." Seth releases Natalie and leads the way into their closet. He takes a seat on one of the upholstered benches inside it, loving every moment he's permitted in the private presence of Natalie.

"How should I dress?" Natalie flirts, disappearing around the corner to her area of the closet.

"In clothes." Seth chuckles as Natalie intentionally stands out of sight and throws her towel into sight.

"How do you know we'll have a visitor?" Drawers and hangers clack and slide out of our sight.

"Just a feeling. I don't have feelings as much anymore, but when I do I can still rely on them. I had another one recently, too." Seth smiles, having only suddenly remembered it.

"Bout what?" We hear the soft commotion of Natalie dressing.

"Aria Joy Kessler." Seth laughs once. "She'll be born next spring. Red hair."

"You're kidding! I bet Laura is livid. Red hair, are you sure? From where?" Natalie is ecstatic.

"Genes are funny like that." Seth narrows his eyes when Natalie emerges with a sigh, retrieving her towel, reading him deeply for a moment. "You alright? You *look* beautiful."

Natalie smiles. A flowing and fancy blue top and jeans do well to define the earthy finesse of the lady of this house. She tosses the towel in the basket, then takes a seat at her vanity in the dressing room, looking with narrowed eyes and accusation at the brush that takes some effort to get through her hair.

"What's wrong? Did I do something? It's hard for me to just know what I did. I prefer you tell me." Seth notices every change in expression. Every shift of mannerism or slip of character in his love. Something he's thought incapable of.

"I've known that about you most of my life, Seth. There's nothing wrong." Natalie smiles a quick smile to soothe him, then sweeps her hair up into a ponytail before standing and approaching Seth's bench. "I don't really feel up to walking, is that okay?"

Seth nods. "I'll make you some tea and we can sit out front. How does that sound?"

"Like we're getting old." Natalie giggles. "One sugar, please."

Natalie sips tea and Seth caresses bare brown feet and bright blue nails atop his lap on the bench out front.

"What does our mystery visitor drive?" Natalie wonders at Seth's nervous eyes fixed on the quiet road.

"He'd probably come by taxi or something."

"You said before you didn't know who. You just said 'he.'"

"I know now."

"So tell me."

"You'd run away and lock yourself inside if I told you." Seth turns his head toward Natalie with a smile. "I didn't bring my keys out."

Before Natalie can respond to her projected response, the crackle of gravel reveals a dark sedan—a car service—the two had watched drive up Plaid Row with caution. A boy of twelve is released from the back seat and tips the driver, who he tells to leave him. The boy's eyes are fixed on the enormity of the house.

"Whoa." The unchanged wonder of a child. But since he is alone, both of my closest companions fear the rebellion of teenhood. Especially since something in his gait, and some glimmer of a memory causes Natalie the need to set her tea on the table at her side for the tremble in her hands. Standing and backing up with incomprehensible gasps of tears until the corner of the porch forces her to cease. Seth, the master of the house, must leave her in distress, descending the steps to greet the guest with a hand shake.

"Are you Seth? I read an article about you in a magazine." The boy asks. Sounding like he'd prefer a lightning strike to any answer at all.

"I am." Seth sighs. "Hello, Cameron."

"You know my name." Cameron is taken aback.

"Would you come inside please?"

The two must pass the stunned Natalie on the porch. Cameron enters the foyer, hunched for the fullness of his backpack. Seth procures Natalie's hand.

"Seth, I can't," She whispers. "I *can't*."

"Neither can *I*, alone." Seth squeezes her hand. Natalie nods. Sniffles, and follows us all into the window room, where the fascinated preteen sets down his bag and takes a seat.

"Where are your parents?" Seth begins. Natalie is unable to speak or take a seat.

The flippant way of a young boy comes out. "They are *not* my parents."

"They need to know you are safe. Did you run away?"

"Whatever. I called them from the bus on the way here. They yelled at me. Can you believe that? As if that would make me go home." The boy shakes his head, then looks at Natalie and nods up at her. "Are you Natalie?"

"Yes. This is my wife. She's usually more talkative." Seth pats the couch next to him, waking up Natalie enough to join him.

"You look a lot like Neil." Cameron says to the floor. Bitter. Hurt.

"Actually he looks like *me*." Natalie's spirit returns a little, with some tears in her voice.

"Why did you come here, Cameron? I bet your mom is frantic."

"Do y'all know who I am?" Cameron asks. Obviously seeking the fantasy of an adoptive child.

Natalie's tears start to flow. Seth squeezes her hand and answers. "Yeah. We know who you are."

Seth and Natalie are patient, answering hows, whys and what-ifs about their life, and listening to typical laments of a preteen boy. Frustrations over just learning that his good friend Neil is actually his uncle, and his biological parents are millionaires. They show compassion for his rebellion, but foster trust in the parents God gave him. Mostly, I think Seth is fascinated by a voice he thought it impossible to ever hear.

"I think," Natalie offers, "All parents are appointed by God. He puts parents with kids the way they are supposed to be up in Heaven. Sometimes they are our biological parents. But sometimes God's plan is much greater for one person than just two people can accomplish in raising them. Maybe sometimes God needs the genes from two and then the parenting expertise of one or two more. Like Willow. She's not our child by blood, but we certainly needed her. And Seth, for whatever reason, needed to be on his own at sixteen. And Seth isn't Naya's father, because—" She has to stop. Concludes. "But God meant it all for good."

Seth puts an arm around Natalie for the welling tears she tries to sniffle and smile away.

Cameron nods, receiving a large dose of perspective. But Seth gives him another that seems to stitch his gaping need to understand his lot.

"Can you imagine how Jesus felt?" Seth's thoughts seem to scatter. "The Lord of all creation had to come be born in a stable, live like a pauper and be raised by humans. I bet Heaven missed Him. But instead, He wanted to adopt us. Die for us so that we could all be connected by His blood. Natalie tells me she still remembers the first time she felt you move. The only way we get through a day is knowing that even though you'll never die for the sins of the world, you're almost that much of a treasure to your parents. So much that even a house big enough for ten of you wouldn't have been as good as how precious you are to them."

"I mean I know they 'treasure' me. I just wish they understood me a little better. At least Mary and Joseph knew Jesus's purpose." Cameron pats my head gently, impressing his birth parents with his wisdom and a deep Georgia accent.

"They didn't always. But they always tried to do what was best. And trust me, parents always know and understand about ten, or maybe a thousand times more than we think they do." Natalie seems to disappear in her brain for a moment, avoiding a glance at Seth.

"But I don't want to deliver babies or treat kids' sniffles like they do. I mean, it's great what they do. They just automatically think I want to do the same thing. They're talking about sending me to a prep school to get me ready for medical school. That is the farthest thing from what I want and they won't even listen to me!"

"Well what *do* you want to do?" Seth asks.

"My dad thinks it's beneath me. I just like to build things. With wood. Like a carpenter. And trust me, I've tried the 'Jesus was a carpenter' bit. Doesn't work. He says Jesus was poor. Like money is all that matters. Of course, I'm telling this to a couple of millionaires." Cameron, young and wise and wild, smiles almost as big and with the same smile as Seth.

"If you tell Natalie your parents' phone number, I'd like to show you something you'll appreciate." Seth stands. Cameron hands Natalie his phone. I follow them—the same carefree walk—to the wing of the house few enter.

"Whoa!" Is Cameron's reaction when Seth illuminates the warehouse-sized space at the end of the north hall. "This used to be a chapel. I was probably four years old when I wandered in here and saw that great big wooden cross on the wall. My mom really liked the stained glass. But I asked my dad about that cross every five minutes until he taught me how to make one. Woodshop. Sanctuary. It's all the same to me." Seth sighs at his place of greatest peace.

"This is amazing, Seth! Would you teach me? All I do is little stuff like—" Then Cameron smiles as he takes a portable chess set off a shelf. Marveling at the perfection.

"Why don't you take that home with you? I've made probably a hundred of those. Chess is a fixation that I just have never gotten over."

"I *love* chess." Cameron says, moving to a pile of reject fence posts. "What are these?"

And then my hip is tested as they walk the snow fence together.

"So she really just follows you around everywhere you go?" Cameron asks as Seth waits for me to arrive at the fence.

"Sometimes she follows Natalie around." Seth is truthful. "She's always liked Natalie."

"She's real pretty. Natalie. Is that weird to say about my birth mother?" Cameron asks.

"No, I agree." Seth chuckles.

"What's your stepdaughter's name?...Are you having other kids?...Do you hate peas as much as me?...How long did this fence take?" And a hundred other similar questions as they slowly walk the fence. Cameron asking, and Seth answering honestly and patiently. Natalie meets them as they make it back up to the house, Naya following groggily.

"Wow! Look at those eyes!" Cameron joins the fascination of all that have ever met the child.

"This is Naya." Natalie introduces.

"Sef. Are you anoder Sef?" Naya is confused at the resemblance of Cameron to her stepfather.

"No, Baby. Cameron. This is Cameron."

"Camewa? Say cheese and take a picher!"

Everyone laughs.

"Cameron, your parents made arrangements to fly here as soon as you called them from that bus, even though you didn't tell them where you were going. They seem to know you pretty well. They're at a hotel right now. Tonight is Thursday and we always have family over. Your parents said they'd love to come."

"They're mad at me?"

"They're glad you're safe."

After the scrambled parade of Kessler children finds Naya in the toy room (Zeke's old office), Laura and Christian find Natalie in the kitchen, ordering pizza on her tablet.

"Hey, Sis!" Laura exclaims.

"Hey guys. I have kind of an awkward surprise for you."

"And what's that?" Christian asks after causing Laura to jump when he passes behind her.

But Laura doesn't wait for the answer. She instead squints her eyes at the top of Natalie's head and touches it.

"Natalie, your roots are like wavy. Is that your awkward surprise?"

"No, that was a surprise to me, too." Natalie smiles. "My hair was actually really curly like Neil's when I was a kid. All the way up until I went through my first pregnancy. Something in the hormones or Seth's DNA literally changed the way my hair grew. That's why it was straight so long. Weird, huh?"

"So why is it suddenly changing back?" Laura squints her eyes.

There is a beat of silence. Then Laura gasps, eyes wide. Natalie shushes her.

"No, I'm not shushing!" Laura's voice is low. "Are you expecting? I have to know. Because I am too!"

"I know." Natalie winces. "Seth told me this morning. I thought you two were done!"

"So did we." Christian chuckles through his nose.

"But it's just one baby this time, thank God. Easier pregnancy and delivery." Laura says in the direction of the once again shell-shocked Christian. "So if Seth knows I'm expecting, did he know at like the moment of conception with you?"

"Oddly, no. I haven't told him. I thought maybe he knew but was just waiting for me to tell him. But Laura, he told me your baby's *name*. And

I could tell he had no clue that his own child is going to be born. Amazed me." Natalie laughs once. "Which leads us to the awkward surprise."

"So there's something besides that?" Christian chuckles.

"There are some people in Seth's office with him. Nancy and Ron Carrington. Their brilliant but rebellious twelve-year-old found his way across the country to meet his biological parents." Natalie sighs, fighting tears.

"Holy cow. You mean Cameron?" Laura lowers her voice.

"Yeah." Natalie allows a tear. "He's beautiful. Has this precious little accent."

"Well, you were right about the awkward part." Christian laughs.

We all hear Seth's office open across the house. The four people emerge, and Laura and Christian are introduced to a couple in their early forties with hair likely grayed by the good-looking twelve-year-old Laura can't believe could look so much like Seth.

"These two are married? You look to be in high school, young lady." Nancy catches in Laura what many do. The youth refuses to leave her face, and she is barely over five-foot-one. The youth also allowed her nearly to return to wedding weight even after delivering five children.

Laura tucks a shy hair behind her ear. "I just turned twenty-four."

"Oh, I apologize. Newlyweds?" Nancy tries to clarify.

"Seven years. Five kids." Christian chuckles. Winks at his wife, then points to her belly. "Number six just started brewing."

Nancy gasps. "Oh! You're Kelli's sister! I'm her midwife and she just kept talking about what a good mom you are and how well you did with your labors. Kelli says you also delivered Natalie's little girl when you were pregnant with twins yourself? She certainly admires you."

"For good reason." Christian earns a brownie point or two before Laura can even speak.

"Oh, shush." Then Laura giggles at her husband's flattery. "If Kelli looks up to me too much, she'll end up needing your services quite a bit."

"But Savannah's so beautiful, I don't see why they should stop now! All that dark hair and dark eyes. Of course, the next could be a blonde like Kelli." Nancy comments.

"True. I still haven't met little Savannah. They got married and had her so fast, we missed all of it. I can't wait to bombard that sweetheart with her cousins at Christmas." Laura's heart quickens, missing the little sister most like herself.

On cue, a child cries out in pain.

"Rondo. Gosh, Tempo and his biting phase." Christian rolls his eyes, identifying the situation. Puts his fist on a flatted hand in front of Laura. They play a game of rock paper scissors and Laura grunts when she loses, exiting the kitchen.

"That was number four crying. The older of the second set of twins. Tempo is the younger of the first set." Natalie laughs at the shock of Ron and Nancy. "These two are some of the best parents I know."

"All glory be to God." Christian chuckles, exiting after Laura when another child erupts.

"So Laura is your sister-in-law two ways?" Nancy tries to understand the family.

"We're an interesting brood." Natalie laughs the nod.

"Natalie, I saw your Steinway in Seth's woodshop. Do you still play?" Cameron shifts the subject.

"Took lessons my whole childhood. So I suppose I play the best I can compared to Laura." Natalie is smiling.

"Mystery solved, Nanc! I had no idea where the music came from." Ron causes his wife a smile.

"I'd love to hear you play if it's not a lot to ask." Natalie's request brings Cameron to a bright smile, and Seth leads them all into the formal living room where one piano sits.

Cameron sits down and smiles as he delivers something already on the level of Laura. Laura is drawn out from the toy room with a dropped jaw. The evening progresses, Cameron nearly beating his birth father at chess. Childhood stories are told. Children are enjoyed, Cameron falling in love with his half sister. And then, as soon as he'd appeared, Cameron must fly from our lives with his parents. Natalie cries as she hugs him on the porch. Then she turns to Nancy and hugs her deeply.

"Thank you. He's wonderful. I'm so thankful he has you guys. God is so good." She requires a tissue to fix the tears of relief.

"We don't mind if y'all stay in touch." Nancy offers. "So long as Cameron brings us if he wants to come visit again. Is that okay Cam?"

"Yeah! Seth said he'd teach me how to be a carpenter." Cameron tells his mom.

"Cameron, listen to your mom and dad, okay? And walk with Jesus. Read your Bible. There's nothing more important." Seth starts.

"Absolutely." Natalie agrees. "And call us if you ever need anything. But chances are, you won't."

Ron's phone rings. He smiles before answering. "Hello Neil!... Yes...Found him at your sister's house, safe and sound."

We watch the three walk and then drive away in a rental car. Except Natalie. Natalie watches Seth's shoulder up close while hers bounce up and down in sobs. She cries from so many places in herself that I'm not sure even she understands just why she's crying. But Seth holds her all the same until the sobs die down enough for them to join Christian, Laura and the children. I think that's what husbands are for.

We re-enter the foyer and listen to the children a moment.

"Daddy! I was a monster and the other monster came to get me! Raaarrrr." Opus proclaims.

"Oh! Is that right? Who is the other monster?" Christian wonders.

"Waaaaawwwrrrrrr." Little Sonata growls to the delight of us all.

"N' Daddy. M'ria is the monster mommy and Tempo is the monster daddy." Rondo's high-pitched voice carries into our hearts.

Tempo immediately objects.

"I don't wanna be the daddy! Opus, you be the daddy." Tempo whines.

"Fine! But next time you be the daddy. I want to be the monster Willow dog." Opus concedes.

"That's pretty awkward, guys." Christian says in an excited tone.

Maria giggles. "It's just for pretend, Daddy. You're all of our daddy. 'Cept Naya. Her daddy is in Heaven."

"Seth?" Natalie sighs, looking up at him even amid the chaos of the room. Her voice seems peaceful and sorrowful all at once. Maybe mixed with some hesitation.

"Yes?" He wonders, catching her tone.

"I think I want to show you something. Is that okay?" Natalie says this also for Laura to hear. Asking if the two, and myself, of course, can escape for a moment. Laura smiles coyly, thinking she knows the exact need for the aloneness. There's something Natalie needs to tell Seth.

Seth nods, a little confused, but follows Natalie up the stairs as she talks to him. Like she's making a confession of some kind. Which in Natalie, sounds a lot like rambling.

"So the day you asked me to marry you, I had a lot of trouble trying to make that kind of decision right away. I was crazy about you, but I wanted to consider everything. My guilt over you being alone twelve years, and over Cameron. Wondering if I was ever supposed to be with Nate or have Naya at all. So many questions with impossible answers, right? That day, I decided I needed a change of scenery to clear my head, but since Naya was sleeping, I couldn't really go for a drive or anything. So don't get mad, but I went into the forbidden room. The art room." Natalie seems extremely nervous.

"Is it haunted?" Seth does his best to joke with his distraught wife.

Natalie winces. "I'd really like to say it isn't. But I think I know why your Mom used to say that."

By now, even me and my bum hips have reached that forbidden door. But Seth, I see, does not want to open it.

"I've never been in here." He admits.

"I know." Natalie smiles a little as she opens the door.

The room is filled with dust that illuminates once Natalie makes her way to the window to let in the last of the daylight, a room full of canvases leaning against walls and covered by sheets. Not for the dust, Stacy Gowan never allowed such things to accumulate in life. But like she was hiding something. I see that many are even stacked in the closet. In fact, not one painting is readily visible. Even the one on the easel is covered by a sheet.

The house is decorated with landscapes and impressionistic faces and forms. Beautiful paintings Stacy always found a tasteful way to display, and Dad would make sure guests admired them. She liked it when he did that. I'm wondering, therefore, why all of these are hiding.

Natalie clears her throat, then coughs a little from the dust, then speaks. "The day you proposed last year, I came in here to think, but I got curious. I thought maybe these were all just blank canvases. I know she always had a supply because you used to make them. You'd staple the fabric on frames you built, I remember. Anyway, I decided I'd just uncover *one*."

Then Natalie bites her lip and grabs the canvas closest to the door, turning it with a huge smile so Seth can see. Seth laughs appreciatively.

It is a painting of two children playing chess under a willow tree. One peach little boy with dark hair and one brown little girl with wild black curls. A dog—me—accompanying them. A memory of which we are all fond, signed at the bottom by *Stacy G*. The year painted beneath. Some year they likely shouted on some midnight I hid under a table somewhere.

"This was all it took for me to have my final decision to marry you. Remembering when I first fell in love with you. Your mom was very gifted, Seth." Natalie's eyes soften.

"She always used to talk about your curls. I had no idea she painted this. Seems like she'd have hung it in the house somewhere." Seth opens up and speaks fondly of his mother.

"That's what I thought! I sat here for twenty minutes just staring at this one painting. Then something hit me that almost made me sick, Seth. I bet you'll catch it before I did." Natalie says, the painting trembling in her arms a little.

"No." Seth's eyes narrow, and he points to the year. "That can't be right. That was the year I made the first chess set. But Willow wouldn't have been born yet. They hadn't even thought to get me a puppy."

"I knew you would," Natalie compliments. "Took me a while. I thought it was a mistake, so I grabbed another painting from over here." Natalie crosses the room to another wall and grabs another painting, turning it around. "This one gave me chills."

I like this one, very much, sad as it is. A view of the front of a house that I recognize is no more. In the painting there are boxes and furniture all scattered. And a young couple embraces a goodbye. The detail is precise for the day Natalie left. It is a devastating image.

An image Stacy Gowan never saw.

"But—" Seth hiccups. "Mom went missing right after you left. She couldn't have painted this. She never set foot in this room again." He is arguing. "Are you sure you didn't paint these?"

"You know I can't paint!" Natalie reminds Seth of the still-beloved attempt at a painting in the chapel. She is as dumbfounded as us. Grabbing another painting. "This one is dated a year before I left. We weren't even dating yet. It's downright surreal."

Natalie's childhood dream of a painting. Seth and Natalie in their wedding clothes, including Stacy's former wedding ring, in front of their beloved willow. Dated far too many years in advance. Seth seems a bit angry. Crosses to yet another wall and takes a random painting from a stack to examine. He nearly passes out when he picks out the very painting that will cause it best. A man with a beard, dark hair, boots, and plaid. Seth. Holding a little girl in the air at arm's length. A girl with light brown curls and blue eyes. Naya, whose genetics were always meant to be Nate's. He nearly drops the painting when he hears something heart-stopping occur behind him.

"Daddy." Naya's tiny little voice. "Sef, you're my daddy." Naya paws her favorite of the paintings.

Seth clears his throat. "This is impossible. Naya, I'm your stepdaddy. You know that. Your daddy is in Heaven."

Naya puts her hands on her hips and looks up at Seth. A familiar and terrifying confrontation from the little girl. A bone to pick. Just as Stacy Gowan herself may have said it, Naya declares, "The picher says! You are my *daddy*!"

Seth chuckles. Natalie coos.

"That's right, Baby. Seth is your daddy." Then addresses Seth with a wince. "Just like I told Cameron, God designs these things. I do apologize that your daughter is part Nathan Holm."

"Cameron." We had all missed more footsteps. The voice is Laura's. "How…"

She's holding a painting of a preteen boy shaking hands with Seth. The content should put the paint still wet from today, which Laura tests with a fingertip, only to receive dust. Seth sits in the middle of the room, his thoughts too heavy a burden for his legs to handle.

"She was really worried. I remember. She told Dad. She knew exactly what we'd do and how we'd handle it. She never worried but she did when they left. It was—She saw him—" Seth is all but babbling to himself. He laughs once. "I got the idea for my fence from a painting in the hall."

"Maria? Opus, Tempo, Ronny, and Sonny, and…red hair?!" Christian exclaims at what a decade ago would have been a painting of six random children playing in the creek outside. Today, Christian recognizes each of them clearly. Accepting truth over the impossible. This sort of exclamation occurs over and over, and paintings are revealed of people Mom never met, and a time she didn't live to see.

Vargas in uniform. Nate in a chef coat. Zeke, hand in hand with Maddie. Niagara Falls. Two grieving women sitting in a charred ruin of a home at dusk. All dated years or decades in advance. Perhaps she saw them as could-be's and fantasies. But we see a history. And now that I remember the way she locked this room and banned all humans and dogs from it, I realize exactly why she told us it was haunted. Not with dark ghosts or entities, which she'd never had near her. But of knowings, long before she could have known.

"She didn't miss *anything*, Seth." Natalie says after a time. "She even left these so you'd know that once she was gone. I can't believe we never knew this about her."

"In hindsight…" Is all Seth can manage before he looks up at the easel. Knowing it is the newest painting. Likely thirteen years old, which means nothing at all. Except that this is the last piece of beauty she left behind.

"Seth, don't." Natalie has already seen this painting. "I mean, before you do, just—"

"Natalie, for twelve years, I saw the worst parts of my life *twice*. I can handle a painting." Seth soothes his wife, reminding her of his own gift.

He slowly lets the dusty sheet displace the dust on the ground. The entire room gasps.

It is a painting of a makeshift wooden cross made of old rejected fence posts. The cross is beneath the willow tree. In the background is a distant view of a fence. In the foreground, a child of about three is curled up in sorrow in front of the cross. Dark hair. A little boy. On the cross is carved one word I need not be read by a person to have learned in fifteen years. "Willow."

"It's still years away, Seth. I know that'll be a hard day, but—" Natalie comforts in advance, whispering a little so that I don't hear. But I already know.

Seth smiles instead of mourning. He's used to this kind of thing and refuses to miss me before he has to miss me. His focus is on the young child that makes no sense according to the ages and looks of the Kessler children. Then he laughs. Points.

"Who is *that*?" Then his pointing hand is redirected by his wife, his palms placed on Natalie's belly as she speaks softly.

"I was thinking we could call him Randall." Natalie's bit lip is met with snickers and cackles from Laura and Christian. And confusion from Seth.

"Wait." Seth blinks. "Right now? You're—I mean we're—"

"Due in April." Natalie clarifies with a nod.

Seth holds his breath. Then releases it with a sigh and a tear. And embraces his wife warmly. Then Seth kisses her quick and looks her in the eyes.

"I don't care what your dad says. We are keeping him," He insists unnecessarily.

"It already is." Natalie nods at the painting.

"There's no way you didn't see this coming," Christian decides, punching the new father-to-be in the arm.

"I didn't," Seth confesses. Much more relieved than shocked. Embracing his love as long-foretold children storm the haunted room. "But I can live with gaps."

Notes

Text from the following public domain works was quoted or referenced.

Chapters Twelve and Fourteen

Schubert, Franz. *Ave Maria*. 1923.

Chapter Twenty-three

Martin, Civilla D. *His Eye Is on the Sparrow*. 1905.

Neale, John M, trans. *O Come, O Come, Emmanuel*. 1851.

Chapters Thirty and Thirty-five

Lyte, Henry F. *Abide With Me.*1847.

Acknowledgements

First Edition

To my dog Sugar. I'll start there, because no one ever reads this page anyway, but maybe now, you might. The most annoying puppy I'd ever had was napping at my feet as I outlined this novel. When I finished, she had chosen mine as the feet she'd follow anywhere. Oh, to understand surrender and servitude the way you do. You're my hero, Sugar. I often wonder what I look like through your eyes…

To anyone who is reading this book. You are the holding a piece of my heart in your hands. Thank you for reading.

To Outskirts Press. Thanks for the chance to take this further than I ever would have alone.

To Aunt Ann and Uncle Greg, Brian "Dan" and Jennifer, Kathleen and Jason, and "Papa," who believed in me enough to make this become a reality. Thanks for the donations, but especially for your belief that I had been given something to say.

Thank you to the row of young men at church who all wore plaid shirts Sunday after Sunday during the season of inspiration for this book. With your brotherly bond and the look on your faces when one of you brought (gasp) a girl, I wanted to know your story. But since I didn't, I hope this one will suffice.

To my parents. Because basically, I couldn't complete this page of "Thank you's" without mentioning you. You created this monster, and constantly enable it. Like it or not, you are partially responsible. Thanks.

To Melanie. I was sure that when your literarily trained eyes saw my fiction, you'd give me a kind wince and stop reading. Your encouragement, as well as your red pen and almost willing paintbrush have truly helped bring this to fruition. Thank you.

To my children. My hardheaded, wild, perfect babies – so little when I wrote this. Thanks for being patient with Mommy while she "types," keeping me responsible, and for being born at your perfectly appointed time. I love you more than you will ever understand…I want to specifically thank the part of my son that we eventually realized was Autism. You have taken me places I never saw my life going. You've brought me to tears. To my knees. Challenged me to

my breaking point. And eventually, you ended up in this book. For that. All of that. Thanks.

R.J., I dedicated this book to you, did you see? Without you taking over for me, devoid of complaint, all the times I've locked myself in a room with a laptop, I couldn't have written a word. Thanks for staying partially awake while I bounced ideas across our bedroom walls and for working way too hard. You'll forever inspire any love story that passes through my fingertips. I got the best one.

Last and greatest of all: To a God big enough to know the number of my days, but warm enough that I can call You Father. You are everything, I am nothing. Thank You for these words.

Other Works by

Rebekah Tyne McKamie

The Foolish Things
April 2020

If Self Doubt could speak, how would it tell your story?

To My Beloved Richie
May 2017

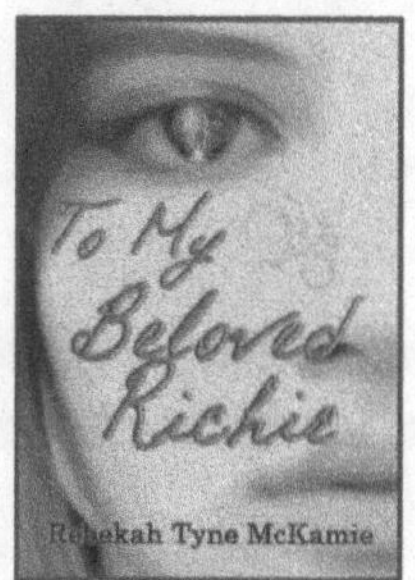

How could he be beloved?

Edited and published by

SETTINGS CHRISTIAN PUBLISHING, LLC

A word fitly spoken is like apples of gold

in **settings** *of silver.*

Proverbs 25:11 NKJV

Settings Christian Publishing

LLC

In case you feel led to reach out...

Website

www.rebekahtynemckamie.com

Instagram

@rebekahspelledlikethebible

Facebook

www.facebook.com/rebekahtyne

Photo by R.J. McKamie

www.ingramcontent.com/pod-product-compliance
Lightning Source LLC
Chambersburg PA
CBHW010142030826
48979CB00028B/2165/J

* 9 7 8 1 7 3 4 8 0 4 0 3 4 *